"I'LL NEVER CONSENT TO MARRY YOU!" LILY EXCLAIMED. "I'LL ENTER A CONVENT FIRST!"

"I think not, little one," Matt said with quiet determination. "I'm making the decision for you. After today you'll have no choice but to marry me."

"What are you going to do?"

His answer was to reach out and pull her roughly against his hard body. Twisting in his arms, she fought desperately to free herself, but his strong arms were locked securely around her. She felt her soft curves mold to the contours of his lean body and his hot breath against her ear as he whispered, "Relax, little one. I'll make this as pleasant as possible."

PROMISE ME FOREVER

CONNIE MASON

LOVE SPELL BOOKS   ◆   NEW YORK CITY

LOVE SPELL®

January 1998

Published by

Dorchester Publishing Co., Inc.
276 Fifth Avenue
New York, NY 10001

ISBN 0-505-52246-2

To the Councilman family in Pingree, ND
and
To my readers in Raleigh, NC, whose letters bring me
great pleasure.

Part 1

1811–1813

Her plan was daring, her actions brave,
Until they were foiled by an arrogant knave.

Chapter 1

Her red-gold curls tossing in wild disarray, Lily Montague flounced across the room to stare into the tall pier glass. Her fury was boundless when she reflected on how she would be put on display tonight at the ball given in her honor by her father. She had glimpsed the guest list and every eligible bachelor in England, regardless of age, was invited. That alone was enough to instill rebellion in her young heart. It was no secret her father was actively seeking a husband for her.

It wasn't fair, Lily fumed in impotent rage. She was only seventeen, had just returned from finishing school in France and looked forward to spending several years with her father before facing the prospect of matrimony. But Leonie, her father's wife-to-be, had put conditions on becoming Lord Stuart Montague's wife. Leonie had her own twelve-year-old daughter to consider and wanted no reminders of Stuart Montague's happy first marriage.

Lily did not doubt that her father loved her, but it had become increasingly evident since her return from France that he loved Leonie more. Since Leonie had burst into Stuart Montague's life he seemed a different man. When Lily's mother died four years ago Stuart was bereft, certain his life had run its course. Unable to cope with a thirteen-year-old daughter, he sent Lily to a fashionable boarding school in France where she remained for four boring years, years in which Lily constantly pined for England and her remaining parent. Their joyous reunion only two months before had been short-lived. In her absence Leonie had come into her father's life and nothing was the same.

With cold dispassion Lily scrutinized her reflection in the pier glass. She knew she was attractive but did not consider herself beautiful. Her large, almond-shaped eyes, a soft, glowing amber, were too unconventional for real beauty; her mouth a shade too full, her cheekbones too high and prominent. How many truly beautiful women could boast of red-gold hair that rioted in haphazard disarray over such narrow shoulders? Most women of the day were luscious blondes, plump and dimpled, with rosebud mouths.

In Lily's opinion her own willowy figure, though curved in all the right places, compared unfavorably with the more womanly curves of most girls her age. Her breasts, firm and high, were a shade too large, while her slender hips appeared too boyish in comparison. Only her legs pleased her and they were one part of her body that would remain completely out of sight. Long, lithe thighs, slender ankles and perfectly turned calves were destined for her eyes alone, until she married. And then the right to view her in her entirety would belong only to her husband.

She didn't look forward to it.

Lily shuddered, turning her striking features away from the glass. She didn't realize the full impact all of her combined parts had upon the opposite sex. No milk-white maiden, her skin was like peach-tinted satin, a legacy from her French mother. Her wrists were delicate, her neck long and regal. There was a melting softness to her young body that Lily failed to consider in evaluating her appeal. Had she done so she would have been pleasantly shocked. But her physical appeal was clearly recognized by both her father and Leonie, who could not abide her stepdaughter-to-be.

"Aren't you dressed yet?"

Lily's thoughts scattered as she wheeled to face Leonie, who had entered the room without knocking. It galled Lily to think that Leonie already acted like the mistress of the house. "I didn't hear you knock, Leonie." She was not so young and innocent as to be frightened by her future stepmother, no matter how imposing the woman might be, Lily fumed, fixing Leonie with a quelling look.

"Don't get sassy with me, missy," Leonie retorted testily. "I may not be old enough to be your mother but I am going to marry your father and the sooner you reconcile yourself to that fact the better we'll get along. But I doubt you'll be here long enough for us to get in each other's hair," she added slyly.

"What kind of statement is that?" demanded Lily.

"You're smart enough to know what I'm talking about. Why do you think your father is giving this ball? And has invited mostly eligible men of good family? It's time you thought of marriage, young lady." Lily was well aware of her father's intentions concerning her future but it hurt to have Leonie put them into words.

"I've only been home a short time," Lily shot back defensively. "Father will—"

"Your father wants what is best for you, naturally," interrupted Leonie. "We both want the same thing. It isn't as if you are destitute and being foisted off on just anyone. You are an heiress in your own right, thanks to your mother and the lack of a male heir. Your dowry is extremely generous. Generous enough to attract the best possible match."

"Father loves me," Lily declared bravely, her small chin thrust forward at a rebellious angle. "He won't force me into marriage if I am unwilling." Her heart beat like a trip-hammer at the thought of marrying a man she didn't know and could never love.

"Silly chit," chided Leonie. "Stuart deserves some happiness. He's been a lonely man for far too long and I intend to change all that. It's time you found your own place in society. Let someone else assume responsibility for you and your inheritance."

"Leonie, why can't we all live here in harmony? Why must I leave? I—I promise not to interfere in your lives."

"Look at yourself, Lily. Go on, take a good look," Leonie insisted when Lily gave her image in the mirror only a cursory glance. "Do you fail to see what both your father and I clearly recognize?"

"What—what do you see?" Lily asked haltingly, gazing at herself uncertainly.

"I see a woman full grown. A woman ripe for marriage. Tonight every man at the ball will recognize what you are either too stupid or unwilling to see. Your body speaks eloquently of your readiness to be bedded whether you want to admit it or not."

"How dare you!" Lily sputtered, shocked at Leonie's crude suggestion. "How dare you speak to me of such things. I know nothing of what you are talking about. Not everyone is like you. Any fool can see Father is besotted with you. Why, he can hardly keep his hands off you. I think you're—you're disgusting!"

Leonie laughed, her generous mouth curving upward as she recalled her own life's experience. Married at fifteen, a mother at sixteen and widowed at twenty. At age twenty-eight, Leonie was a stunning blonde of medium height with fine blue eyes and milk-white skin that Lily secretly admired. Her figure, a bit plump in comparison to Lily's lissome form, was considered perfect for the day and age. Her well-padded breasts, tiny waist and flaring hips had enthralled Stuart Montague until the generously endowed widow became an obsession with him. He had pursued her relentlessly until she'd consented to become his.

"Disgusting I may be, Lily, but you'd do well to heed my words, for your father and I will wed in two months despite your disapproval. Before that day arrives I expect you to be gone from this house to a home and husband of your own. Once we are wed Stuart will have no time for you as he will not only have me but my Amy on which to lavish his love and affection."

"Two months!" Lily gasped. "Do you expect me to decide my future in just two months? How can I choose when I know so little about men?"

"That's the reason for the ball tonight, my dear. Astute of your father, wasn't it, to lay the cream of London society at your feet? Look your best," Leonie advised, "for it is entirely possible—no," she amended, "highly likely, that you will meet your future husband tonight."

Soon afterward Leonie left to allow Lily to finish dressing for the ball. Furious and distraught, Lily could do little more than pace back and forth. How dare they parade her before scores of prospective suitors like a piece of goods on display, dangling her abundant dowry as bait! No matter what her father decreed, Lily was determined to prove she was not a puppet to be led about on a string. She had a mind of her own and ideas about the kind of future she wanted. And that future certainly didn't include acting as a meek wife and doormat for some man while he spent her fortune at his leisure!

Suddenly a devious smile curved her generous mouth as an idea came to her. It was daring. It was reckless. It was utterly outrageous. But desperation often drove one to act totally at odds with one's character. Her father wanted her to be popular and popular she would be. In fact, she would become the talk of London! She would flirt disgracefully. She would tease scandalously and wickedly tempt each man in turn, until she had them all panting after her. She wouldn't cease until her reputation lay in shreds and no man would want her. Before the evening ended, she vowed, no respectable man would dare ask for her hand in marriage for fear of being cuckolded before the ink on the marriage papers was dry. She knew word of her audacious behavior would spread quickly, until not even her generous dowry could secure her a husband.

Unfortunately, Lily did not fully consider the consequences of her impulsive plan. Not only would it enrage and alienate her father, it would give Leonie one more reason to be rid of her stepdaughter. But Lily did not dwell on the repercussions from her ill-advised scheme that went against her true nature and everything she had been taught. The important thing was that it would buy her time. Time to look around and select a man of her own choosing. A man she could love.

Determined that nothing or no one would interfere with her plan, Lily grimly set out to make herself as irresistible as possible. By some miracle her maid had tamed her unruly mass of flaming hair into a riot of curls and loops, held securely in place by a diamond-and-emerald tiara that had once belonged to her mother. Tiny ringlets were purposely allowed to escape, creating a perfect frame for Lily's exquisite features.

Her gown, a dazzling confection in leaf-green satin, left her neck and shoulders enticingly bare. A decorative, gauzy material demurely filled in the decolletage of the fitted bodice that dipped to a deep vee in front. Huge puffed sleeves clung to her upper arms and the full skirt was pulled up at intervals, allowing enticing glimpses of the gold tissue petticoat underneath. Gold slippers and gloves completed the fetching ensemble.

When Lily pirouetted before the mirror she encountered a woman as beautiful as any she had ever seen. A knock at the door interrupted her fascination with her own image. At Lily's bidding, Lord Montague entered the room. His breath caught in his throat when he spied his beautiful daughter, and he came to an abrupt halt. Never had he seen such an enchanting vision. How could this glorious creature be his little girl?, he wondered in amazement. It seemed only yesterday that he'd sent a chubby, pigtailed child off to France to be turned into a young lady of charm and culture. Little had he realized she would return a ravishing beauty. She would set all of London on its ear, just as Leonie had predicted.

"My dear," Lord Montague said proudly, "I can't begin to tell you how lovely you look or how much you resemble your beloved mother."

"Thank you, Father." Lily flushed, pleased despite her resolve to foil her sire's plans for her future.

"All the men attending the ball will be wild about you," he continued blithely. "You will have the cream of London's young men to choose from. And if you prefer someone more mature there will be several older men in attendance who are looking for a wife. Few women are luckly enough to be offered so wide a selection of suitors."

Lily's lips turned down in a scowl and she deliberately turned away from her father's fond scrutiny. Didn't he realize she didn't want to be put on display like a prize mare? Didn't he understand she longed to spend time with him in their own home without Leonie's interference? Why was it necessary to wed in haste when her heart yearned for his love?

"I'm not looking for a husband, Father," she said with quiet dignity. "I won't marry without love and it's highly unlikely I'll find it tonight at the ball.

Don't get me wrong, I want to marry. I want a home and children, but I'm still young. I've been away four years and I want to enjoy my home before going off with a husband."

Stuart Montague's eyes softened, but only for a moment. Two women under the same roof just wouldn't work and Leonie had already given him an ultimatum. Either his daughter went or no marriage. And he couldn't let Leonie go. He was obsessed with the young widow who had wisely refused to bed him until she was his wife. It wasn't as if he was a young man with years yet in which to find happiness. Time was passing him by and Leonie offered him his youth back. He could no more let Leonie go than he could give up eating or drinking. He needed Leonie, wanted her with a lust that was reminiscent of his youth, and he wanted to hold on to that feeling for as long as life allowed. If it meant finding a husband for his lovely daughter, so be it.

"Father, did you hear me? I've no wish to marry now."

Hardening his heart, Stuart replied, "You're ripe for marriage, Lily. Your mother and I talked often of making an advantageous match for you so it isn't something I've just dreamed up. Leonie and I are marrying soon and she sees you as a threat to our happiness."

"No, I'd never interfere, Father, believe me."

"Leonie will be my wife, I must abide by her wishes if we are to have a serene marriage. I want Leonie, Lily dear, don't defy me on this. Choose wisely tonight and your life will be as happy as I intend mine to be with my new wife and daughter."

Lily's mouth tightened into a thin white line. Rather than raise her alone, her father had sent her away to France to be taught by strangers. And now he was enthusiastically accepting the responsibility of raising a young girl the same age as she had been when he'd sent her away. Amy would now know the comfort of a father Lily had never truly had. Amy would have the love Lily craved but never got.

Amy and Leonie.

A new wife and a new daughter.

I won't be foisted off so easily. Lily bristled in silent indignation.

"I'll leave you now, daughter, the guests are starting to arrive. I'm certain every eye will be on you tonight when you walk down those stairs."

I'll make certain they are, Lily vowed. *After tonight all of London will be talking about Lily Montague.*

The moment Lord Montague left the room Lily set to work with grim determination. When she began her slow descent down the stairs some time later, she was radiant, a creature of seductive beauty and mysterious allure. The jewellike brilliance of her gown was not nearly as dazzling as the woman who wore it. Her scissors and her ingenuity had turned her demure gown, which had been quite suitable for a young lady just out of the schoolroom, into a creation meant to tease and tantalize. The moment her father had left her room she had quickly and ruthlessly made dramatic changes to her ball gown. First she had painstakingly snipped the offending piece of gauze from her dress, baring her breasts nearly to their dusky tips. Next she had discarded some of her voluminous petticoats so that the gown hugged her curves more closely, outlining her long supple legs.

Swallowing past the lump of terror rising in her throat, Lily pasted a brilliant smile on her face and gracefully floated down the stairs. She wasn't out to impress people, she was out to shock them. Ruining her reputation was going to take all the courage and daring she could muster. It wasn't going to be easy but her father and Leonie had driven her to venture things she would never dare if left in peace. Glancing down one last time at the twin mounds of glorious

womanhood so blatantly displayed at her neckline,
Lily raised her chin at a defiant angle and blithely
sailed into the den of lions. In the press of people she
could see neither her father nor Leonie, which suited
her just fine.

Dozens of pairs of eyes followed Lily's progress as
she gracefully descended the staircase in the palatial
Montague mansion situated prominently in fashionable Saint George Park. But none were more intent
than the dark, penetrating eyes of a tall, imposing
figure lounging carelessly against a huge white col-
umn across the room. His fathomless eyes missed
nothing as they raked Lily's lithe form outrageously
displayed in the revealing green gown.

Somehow Matthew Hawke hadn't expected such
an ostentatious display by a young girl—seventeen,
he believed, and barely out of the schoolroom. Her
disgraceful decolletage left little to the imagination.
What must her father be thinking? Matt wondered
idly as he watched with a jaundiced eye the crush of
suitors rallying to her side. Perhaps she learned more
in that school in France than her father bargained for,
he thought wryly. He continued his perusal of the
delectable redhead for some minutes before ambling
over to join her circle of admirers. Deftly he snatched
her dance card from a smooth-cheeked swain and
scrawled his name in the space reserved for the last
dance. That done, he moved unerringly back to the
position he had just vacated on the sidelines. His
dark eyes thoughtful, he spent the rest of the evening
in watchful speculation.

"Well, what do you think, Matt?" his companion
asked. "Does the lady suit your purposes?"

"Oh, the lady suits well enough." Matt grinned
wolfishly, leaving little doubt to his meaning. "The
lady is wealthy enough to suit no matter how she
looks or the lack of her morals. Hell's fire, Chris, that

young lady creating such a sensation with the men is the reason I am in England instead of home preparing for a war between our two countries."

Christopher Hawke had always idolized his cousin Matt. Though Matt's origins were English, Chris never doubted for a moment where Matt's loyalties lay. Matthew Hawke was a loyal American and a fervent believer in American freedom. He now made his home in Boston in the grand house built by his father. Hawkeshaven was a product of Carlton Hawke's success as a Boston lawyer and became home to his family, which consisted of Matt and Matt's sister, Sarah, born a year after their arrival in America. Matt had been ten at the time. Carlton Hawke had had great hopes of his son's following in his footsteps and becoming a barrister, but Matt's yearnings did not lean toward the law. The sea had intrigued him since he was a small child.

"Do you really think war is inevitable?" Chris asked, well aware of his cousin's views on the subject. "Your father should have kept his title and remained in England."

"Father never wanted the title," Matt said quietly, still watching Lily and the way her gown revealed parts of her marvelous body when she moved. "It fits your father far better than it ever fit mine. And yes, war will come, sooner than we expect. It is inevitable when your government is providing arms and ammunition to the Indians settled along the Canadian frontier. Do you think it just that those arms are directed against Americans?"

Chris flushed, abashed by Matt's fervor on the subject. Like most Englishmen, he knew little of what was taking place on those far frontiers and suspected what his cousin said was true, although he hated to admit to his ignorance. "Let's not dwell on politics tonight," he urged to cover his lack of knowledge.

"This is a party, remember. It took a lot of doing on my part to get you an invitation."

Matt nodded, turning his attention back to the lively girl in shimmering green flirting outrageously with her latest partner. His midnight eyes widened, then narrowed when he spied the couple slipping through the door that led to the dark gardens beyond.

"Lily Montague is behaving more like an experienced demimonde than a young lady recently returned from boarding school," Chris commented dryly, following the direction of Matt's gaze. "If I'm not mistaken that's the third fellow she has lured out into the garden. Have you noticed the way she flirts with each of her partners? Disgraceful! Had I known what she was like I wouldn't have invited you here tonight."

"Fourth," corrected Matt, hardly amused. "The little tease. Doesn't she realize she's playing a dangerous game?"

"Whatever the game, she appears well versed in the moves," quipped Chris, grinning.

"My sentiments exactly," agreed Matt with a hint of sarcasm. "She makes Clarissa appear almost innocent. Even the dowagers sitting on the sidelines are whispering about her behind their fans."

"Ah, yes, your mistress. What does Clarissa think about all this? Surely she isn't happy with your decision to marry. What do you think little Miss Montague will say if by some remote possibility your offer for her is accepted and she discovers you have a mistress tucked away?"

"If fortune should shine on me and I return to Boston with an extremely wealthy bride, I will be a model husband—by long distance. Look here, Chris, I'm not the monster you think me. My wife will be well treated and want for nothing. All of Hawkeshaven will be at her complete disposal. But I do not intend to reside there with her. My life will continue as it always has, wife or no. I have no time for sentimental love or flowery speeches."

"Does Clarissa agree with this?"

"It's none of Clarissa's business whether or not I marry. She knows it's necessary and inevitable. Clarissa has been with me for many years but I don't think she's pining for me while I'm in London. She's a beautiful woman, life will never pass her by."

"Good luck, old chap. Lily Montague doesn't look the type to stand for your dallying. She might retaliate with a dalliance or two of her own. For her sake as well as yours, I hope your offer is turned down." It was amazing how astute Chris could be at times.

Matt laughed, his grin a white slash in his deeply tanned face. "Is that any way to talk? I wouldn't be here today if not for you. Your letters telling me about the wealthy heiress months before she returned from school in France are what brought me to London in the first place."

"But I never expected you'd be so determined to marry money that you would select a wife on those merits alone," Chris complained. "When my sister Diane told me about Lily and I in turn mentioned her to you, I had no idea you'd hie yourself here so quickly. I was merely filling space in an otherwise dull letter."

"You were wise to do so, Chris. You were correct in assuming Lily Montague would be on the marriage mart the moment she returned to England. I'm glad I arrived in time. I need money, lots of it. Your navy has beggared me by stealing my cargoes and pirating sailors off my ships."

"So you intend to go ahead with your scheme."

"I must, Chris. I've sunk every cent I own into those three ships. I've already received permission from President Madison to convert them to privateers and I desperately need cash—and soon. Until war is declared I aim to harass the English just as they harassed me."

"Aren't there any heiresses in America?" asked Chris.

"Not with the kind of fortune at Miss Montague's command. And if there are I've no time to look for them."

"It sounds so—so—ruthless. What about Sarah's dowry? Wouldn't it be better to borrow that for your venture?"

"That money belongs to Sarah. I'd never take it from her." Matt's voice sounded so serious Chris wisely did not pursue the subject.

"Is there no—"

"Look!" whispered Matt, cutting Chris off in mid-sentence. "Lily has just returned from the garden with her latest conquest and he looks quite frazzled. Wonder what went on out there?"

Matt was not the only person present to mark Lily's return from the garden with the young man she had left with a short time ago. His face was flushed and it was not difficult to assume that he had been granted forbidden liberties by the beautiful young woman at his side. In fact, the entire room was abuzz, scandalized by Lily's wanton behavior. Everyone was aware of not only how often Lily had disappeared into the dark night but also how long she had dallied with each man. She was shameless, declared some. Brazen, ventured others. Lily's father was livid when he found out what she was up to. Leonie was scowling furiously. Lily would have been immensely pleased to know how well her plan to discredit herself was succeeding.

Her current partner, Homer Fenton, a brash youth given to exaggeration, which suited Lily's purposes admirably, left her to be claimed for the next dance and made unerringly for the knot of young men clustered together near the sidelines not far from where

Matt stood chatting with Christopher. All talk stopped as Homer swaggered up to the group, grinning from ear to ear.

"Did you enjoy your dance with the belle of the ball?" snickered one of the young blades.

"I enjoyed more than just a dance," boasted Homer.

"We noticed," spoke up another fellow.

"I think the lady has a certain fondness for me," Homer confided, preening excessively. "She—she allowed me to kiss her and—and—" Suddenly he halted, shrugging his thin shoulders eloquently. "Gentlemen don't brag about their conquests."

Laughter met his words as he looked from one to another, perplexed by their hilarity. "You've been treated no better than the rest of us, old chap," guffawed a nattily dressed young man. "The 'lady'—and I use the term lightly—appears to like all men equally. Lily generously showered her favors upon all of us."

Homer blanched. "You mean I wasn't the only man who kissed her tonight? She was teasing me? Leading me on? What kind of woman would toy with a man's affections?" Homer was not one to take an affront, imagined or real, lightly. "I pity the man who offers for her, should anyone be so foolish."

"After her shameless behavior tonight I doubt even her dowry will be sufficient to gain her a respectable marriage," sniffed the nattily dressed man. "Why, any man here could lift her skirts and have at her. I, for one, have no intention of being cuckolded by a faithless wife."

Matt smiled smugly, having heard all of the exchange between the young men. He glanced at Chris. "Young Lily is a bold little piece, but all the better for my purposes. The field is rapidly diminishing and she has brought it all about herself. It will be interesting to challenge her at her own game."

Chris did not care for the devious smile curving his cousin's lips.

Chris and Matt had become fast friends several years before when Matt was sent to England for formal schooling. Determined that Matt should become the best barrister in America, Carlton Hawke had insisted on the best schools. Though Matt's grades were good, his passion was prowling the waterfront and learning his way around ships. He studied law to please his father but he never intended to use that knowledge. He was merely biding his time, learning to fend for himself, gaining strength and knowledge for the day he would command his own ship.

During those formative years Christopher Hawke became Matt's shadow and willing accomplice. Matt grew to maturity in England, his six-foot-three-inch frame honed and hardened into superb condition. Though his lessons did not suffer, much of his time was given to women, brawling and drinking. If at times Chris thought him a shade too ruthless, he tended to forgive him, for Matt was always unfailingly kind and generous toward his younger cousin. When Matt was summoned back to America at the age of twenty-one by his ailing father, Chris missed him dreadfully. This was the first time the cousins had seen one another in seven years. During that time Matt had become harder, more cynical, having learned to trust no one but himself and depend solely on his own judgment. It was a lesson gentle-natured Chris had failed to grasp.

And he wasn't certain he liked what Matt had become.

Chapter 2

Lily knew he was watching her. She felt his dark, brooding eyes on her, sensed his disapproval. Though she had never seen him before her eyes strayed time and again to his arresting face: high cheekbones, strong nose, full lips and penetrating dark eyes. He was dark, too dark to be an English gentleman accustomed to spending long hours indoors gaming and wenching. And his brawny physique and healthy tan suggested hard physical labor performed in the outdoors. Yet there was a compelling sensuality about him that both repelled and attracted her. Whenever she chanced to glance in his direction his heavy-lidded gaze was upon her, assessingly.

Lily shivered. Something about him disturbed her. Perhaps it was his pensive, moody expression. Or the way his lips curved in amusement when her outrageous behavior set off another round of gossip. Then again it might be his critical appraisal whenever she returned from the garden with one of her partners. Whatever the attraction, it made Lily uncomfortable. Deliberately she turned away from the handsome stranger's mesmerizing gaze to concentrate on her current partner. When he whispered into her ear, she nodded eagerly and led the way through the open

French doors, aware of the buzz of gossip following in her wake.

After watching Lily's provocative behavior, Stuart Montague was ready to explode. Gossip in the crowded room ran rampant. The very air was alive with speculation and condemnation for his naughty, teasing daughter. What had gotten into her? He fumed in impotent rage. With a few well-placed snips she had transformed an elegant, demure gown into a tawdry, cheap creation worthy of the most expensive whore. Her full breasts were all but bared and the shape of her legs was clearly visible beneath the single petticoat she wore. Where had he gone wrong? As the evening progressed it became increasingly evident that Lily was engaged in the most blatant seduction he had ever witnessed. What could Lily be thinking of? he wondered in silent condemnation as he saw her reenter the ballroom from one of her many excursions in the garden accompanied by yet another young man.

Stuart had hoped his daughter's entrance into society tonight would take London by storm. And so it has, he thought wryly. Only not in the way he wished. Without a doubt Lily's name was on the tip of every tongue, and the topic of conversation shamed him. The snickers, the snide remarks, the derogatory asides were not lost on him. When Leonie found him she was vicious in her attack upon Lily.

"You must stop her, Stuart," she urged when she nudged him into a deserted alcove so they might speak alone. "If Lily continues to flaunt herself in such a brazen manner she will make you the laughingstock of London. After tonight's fiasco there isn't a single man in England foolish enough to offer for her, fortune or no, and like it or not she will be on our hands for years to come. How can you stand idly by while she brazenly ruins her reputation and your good name?"

Goaded by Leonie's taunts, Stuart vowed to put a stop to Lily's antics once and for all. When he noticed that Lily stood alone waiting for her next partner to appear, he resolutely made his way toward her, intending to banish her to her room before she could shred what was left of her reputation. But his good intentions were thwarted when Lily was claimed by her current partner and whisked onto the dance floor. Twice more Stuart attempted to intervene without making a scene, but each time his efforts were foiled.

Lily hated what she was doing but that didn't prevent her from continuing with her audacious plan. She was well aware of the gossip circulating in the room and expected her father to confront her momentarily and banish her from the party. She was not happy with her performance tonight, nor with the image she projected to her father's friends. It suited her purpose to be labeled a tease and a lady of loose morals but not her conscience. Though it was too late now to consider the consequences, she fervently hoped they didn't ruin her life forever. Londoners were a fickle lot. She would remain the main topic of gossip only until another came along to displace her. She prayed it wouldn't be too long until something more newsworthy replaced her.

Despite her misgivings, Lily was pleased with her performance and the stir she was creating. It wasn't until the last dance of the evening, shortly before a midnight supper was to be served, that her composure was severely damaged.

He showed up to claim his dance. The mysterious, brooding man who had been staring at her all night.

Thus far only Homer Fenton had succeeded in jolting her equilibrium. When she offered cool lips to the smitten young man, expecting a chaste peck, she found herself crushed in a bruising embrace and literally devoured by his burst of passion. It took considerable dexterity to prevent his hands from straying to her breasts and she wasn't totally successful. Inexperience had made her incautious, but after that unpleasant encounter Lily quickly learned to recognize the signs and took steps to dampen the ardor of the other young men who came after Homer, allowing them no more than a brief kiss on the lips.

Lily watched warily as her last dance partner's long, muscular legs swiftly closed the distance between them. She had learned much about men and women tonight, but from deep inside came the forbidden thought that this man could teach her things no chaste young lady should know. He moved smoothly and the sight of his narrow hips encased in tight black trousers brought a blush to her cheeks. He was nearly upon her before her naughty gaze traveled upward to sweep the broad expanse of his chest and finally settle on his lips. The bottom lip was slightly fuller than the upper, providing him with a brooding expression and an air of mystery. His face was deeply tanned and his eyes were blacker than the blackest midnight. They stared at her with such intensity she felt her insides heat and her mouth go dry.

"I believe this is my dance, Miss Montague." His voice, deep and sensual, sent a ripple of awareness through Lily, and she made a great show of studying her dance card to allow her heart time to slow down to a normal beat.

"Captain Matthew Hawke?" she asked, recovering her composure.

Matt nodded, at the same time sweeping her onto the dance floor with amazing ease. He was pleasantly surprised by the sound of her voice. It was wonderfully low, yet soft and musical. The slightly breathless quality lent it a sensuality that made it difficult for him to concentrate. With a will of their own, his arms closed possessively around her, holding her closer than society deemed proper.

Lily thought Captain Hawke was holding her much too closely, but because it fit her mood and circumstances, she did not rebuke him. Instead she studied him surreptitiously from beneath long feathery lashes the color of old gold. She thought him rather handsome, in a rugged sort of way, and definitely more virile than any man she had seen thus far tonight. The clean lithe look of him and air of authority surrounding him pleased her, though she was relieved to know she'd never be subjected to his masterful domination.

Even his manner of dress marked him as out of the ordinary. Instead of being decked out like a strutting peacock in brilliant velvets and satins like most of the men present, he was plainly yet elegantly clad in black broadcloth trousers, hugging him tightly at hips and thighs and thrust into shiny black knee-length boots. A superbly fitted buff jacket stretched across massive shoulders and immaculate white lace all but concealed large, long-fingered hands. Lily gave an involuntary shudder, secretly envisioning the power of those broad tanned hands. His brooding, penetrating gaze so utterly discomposed Lily that she was oblivious to the fact that Matt was slowly but steadily edging her toward the open door. Only when she smelled the overpowering scent of roses and felt a cooling breeze touch her burning skin did she realize she was outside. The thought struck her that he moved with agile grace, unusual in a man his size.

"Captain Hawke, you assume too much," Lily said haughtily as she turned back toward the house. For some unexplained reason Matthew Hawke exuded a danger she'd felt with none of the other men she had taunted and teased.

Lily sensed a difference in him that set him apart

from the callow youths she had shamelessly goaded and tormented all evening. His air of authority and commanding presence demanded caution, and Lily instinctively knew the subtle seduction she had employed this night would be lost on Matthew Hawke.

"Come now, Miss Montague, are you going to withhold me from that which you willingly bestowed on nearly every male present tonight?"

Lily blanched. She knew exactly what everyone thought of her for she had worked diligently to that effect all evening, but it somehow sounded much worse coming from Matthew Hawke. Her golden eyes narrowed, then opened wide as sudden anger gripped her. "How dare you, sir! How despicable of you to damage a lady's reputation by repeating malicious gossip."

"Is it gossip, Miss Montague?" Matt asked with cool disdain. His expression held a note of censure, serving only to fuel Lily's anger. "I've watched you from the moment you began your little dalliances and finally lost count of the various men you've entertained out here in the garden. Is there something you dislike about me that makes me unworthy of your . . . attention?"

"For one thing you are rude and impertinent," Lily claimed with a toss of her strawberry curls. "And conceited," she added, finally finding an appropriate word to describe his behavior. "Now if you'll excuse me—"

"I don't know what game you're playing, Miss Montague, but you'll find I am a master at any game you choose. And I make my own rules, which you'll discover in time."

Lily had no time to form a reply or even to react as Matt pulled her deep into the shadows, covering her mouth with his when she began to protest wildly. His kiss was no gentle pressing of lips; it was like nothing Lily had ever known. It was teasing, taunting, searching. Soul-shattering. She was **startled** when she felt him nudge her lips apart with **the tip** of his tongue and probe inside with ungentlemanly thoroughness. Overpowered and totally consumed by his male magnetism, Lily was indeed convinced that Matthew Hawke made his own rules and lived by them.

Gasping in outrage, Lily finally managed to pull away. Never had she been treated in such an outrageous manner, not even by that brash Homer Fenton. "What do you think you're doing, Captain?" she sputtered indignantly, swishing her skirts in a show of anger.

"Collecting my reward," Matt said smoothly. "Just as your other partners collected theirs," His arrogant smile infuriated her.

"You're—you're—disgusting!"

"I've been called many things by ladies, but never disgusting."

"Then you haven't known many ladies!" retorted Lily hotly.

"Oh! And I suppose you consider yourself one?"

"Certainly!"

"There are many here tonight who would dispute that statement. Your father, for one." Matt paused, watching the play of emotion upon Lily's expressive face. Damnation, she was beautiful. "I wonder what you're up to, young lady?"

"If I am 'up to' something it certainly is no concern of yours," Lily retaliated.

"You're wrong, little one, because everything concerning you is my business."

He allowed Lily no time to ponder his profound statement as he drew her back into his embrace, her body so close to his she could feel the buttons on his coat pressing indentations on the soft skin of her partially exposed breasts.

Lily's screech of protest never left her lips as the

force of his kiss sucked the breath from her lungs. When he deepened the kiss, sending his tongue past the barrier of her lips, her anger turned to scalding rage. Summoning every ounce of strength she possessed, she dragged her lips from his, staring at him as if he were the spawn of the devil.

Breathless, shaking and angry over his sensual onslaught, Lily suddenly became aware of Matt's hands roving over her body, from the small of her back to her trim little buttocks, before finally coming to rest on the rounded tops of her breasts where they overflowed the confines of her bodice.

"Stop! You have no right to treat me like this!"

"I thought you enjoyed this kind of treatment," Matt said blandly.

Lily cried out in dismay when the neckline of her gown was pushed down even further and her breasts popped free like ripe fruits ready for plucking. Doubling her fists, she pounded his chest with relentless fury. A low mirthless chuckle rumbled from Matt's chest as he dragged Lily even closer against the rigid length of his body. She drew a shuddering breath, renewing her efforts to free herself. Something—something hard and unyielding was pressing against her stomach and a bud of panic flared in her breast. Completely out of her element, Lily began to struggle almost frantically.

"How dare you accuse me of wanting this!" Lily cried, nearly incoherent now with rage.

It was neither his conscience nor Lily's tears that dampened Matt's ardor as he pushed her away and yanked her bodice up to cover her quivering breasts. It was the inexplicable knowledge that Lily Montague was an innocent playing a dangerous game. And he fully intended to discover her reason for deliberately setting out to destroy her reputation.

"Just as I thought," he said with a hint of disgust. "You are merely a child playing at seduction. Next time you'll know not to trifle with a man unless you mean business. Stick to untried boys."

"But—but—I didn't tri—trifle—with you," Lily stuttered, tugging frantically at her bodice.

"Maybe not," Matt conceded grudgingly, "but your wanton behavior tonight led me to believe you'd be receptive to my advances. Surely you don't expect to snare a husband by boldly flaunting your charms before every man in sight, do you? No respectable man wants a wife who will cuckold him at the first opportunity."

Lily's tears dried instantly. Hot indignation surged through her as she retorted, "That's the whole point! I don't want a husband! I don't want to be offered on the marriage mart like a piece of goods." No sooner were the words unintentionally blurted out than she wanted to gulp them back.

"So that's your game, little one." Matt whistled softly as comprehension gave him insight into Lily's little plot. "You had no intention of attracting a potential husband tonight, did you? Your purpose was to discourage all prospective bridegrooms paraded before you by your father. Why are you so anxious to remain a spinster?" Matthew Hawke was an astute man and it wasn't difficult for him to put all the pieces together.

"Hardly a spinster, Captain Hawke," Lily replied caustically. "I am only seventeen and not yet ready to marry a man I do not love no matter what Father and Leonie want."

Matt contemplated Lily in silent appraisal. Chris had told him Lord Montague planned to marry an attractive young widow soon and from what Lily had just said the man simply wanted his daughter out of the way. The extravagant ball tonight was to introduce her to the cream of London society and hopefully secure her a wealthy, titled husband. From the disparaging way in which Lily had uttered

Leonie's name, Matt assumed the woman cared little for her future husband's daughter. Obviously Leonie did not want a flesh-and-blood reminder of Lord Montague's first marriage.

Lily's outrageous behavior tonight led Matt to believe that she resented being foisted off in such a manner and was clearly out to sabotage her father's plans for her. This piece of valuable information reassured Matt that his own plan for the feisty young miss would succeed. If Lily's antics had discouraged all other suitors, and Lord Montague was still anxious to marry off his daughter, then Matt felt certain his quest for the lady's hand would yield him the fortune he so desperately needed.

Though Matt's loins still ached with the need to possess the lovely young woman, he no longer felt seduction was the right course to take. He would have Lily Montague—and her fortune—whether she liked it or not. But if he was to marry the chit, propriety demanded that he return her promptly to the house. She had already provoked enough gossip for one night.

"I admire your spirit, Miss Montague," Matt said, helping her to her feet. "But I fear all your endeavors have been in vain. Due to your wealth and generous dowry, nothing you do will ultimately matter."

"We'll see about that, Captain Hawke," Lily retorted, hastily putting her gown and hair to rights. "I thank God you aren't interested in either. If you were after my fortune you wouldn't have insulted me with your despicable behavior. What you did to me is inexcusable."

"Since when is it an insult to want to make love to a desirable woman? Besides, it would be stupid of me to turn down a fortune."

"Oh, you're—you're . . ."

"Despicable? Disgusting," supplied Matt with a wry chuckle.

"Exactly," Lily agreed, anxious to escape from his intimidating presence. He made her feel things she didn't understand.

"Take my arm, I'll escort you back inside," he offered gallantly, ignoring the glacial glow in her amber eyes.

A hush fell over the crowd and every eye was upon them when they returned to the ballroom a few minutes later. Malicious gossip raged around them like wildfire. Their sojourn in the garden had lasted far too long to be innocent. Despite her anger at Matt she was grateful for his stalwart presence beside her during supper. Not only did it prevent her father from making a scene but it discouraged outright rudeness from the guests. All too soon she would be forced to face her father's rage and suffer the punishment she had incurred. Her one consolation was that she had never known her father to be overly harsh with her. But then she had never angered him to such an extent before.

Lily blinked repeatedly in an effort to escape the sunlight stabbing against her closed eyelids. Finally she turned on her stomach, jamming the pillow down over her tousled curls. She knew it must be very late but it had been nearly dawn when she finally collapsed in bed, having successfully avoided both her father and Leonie all evening.

Her head cushioned by a mound of feathers, Lily did not hear the knock on her door so was startled by the entrance of her father into her room. Leonie was close on his heels.

"You won't evade me this time, Lily," Lord Montague declared as he stormed into the room. His great, angry strides led him directly to her bed. He was nattily dressed in a riding habit and carried in one hand a riding crop, which he slapped repeatedly against his thigh in quick, angry jerks.

"Oh!" Startled, Lily raised up on her elbows. The sheet fell away, revealing a delicately curved back and trim little buttocks enticingly displayed in a clinging silk nightgown.

But Stuart Montague noticed none of this. What he did see was a willful girl on the verge of womanhood who had deliberately and recklessly destroyed her chances for an advantageous marriage by wantonly displaying her body and making herself available to one and all. Her shameless conduct with Captain Hawke, young Christopher Hawke's cousin and an upstart American at that, was the final indignation. Unfortunately Lily and the American had been seen by a pair of guests who had left the ballroom for some air. The guests had returned to the house agog with the news that they had seen Lily and the American in a compromising position in the garden. A position that left little to the imagination.

"Well, young lady, have you nothing to say about your sluttish behavior last night?" Lord Montague demanded. "Is that what they taught you in that fancy school in France? Had I known I would have brought you home before you were corrupted."

"Father, you don't understand," Lily tried unsuccessfully to explain.

"I want to, Lily, truly I do, but nothing you can say will change my opinion. You force me to do something I have never done before. Leonie has pleaded with me to deal harshly with you and my own conscience tells me that I must."

"Father, please!" Glancing at Leonie's smirking features, Lily knew a moment of fear.

Until now Leonie had stood silently by, a gloating smile turning her features almost ugly. "How dare you flaunt yourself like a brazen hussy, flagrantly disregarding manners and morals! she lashed out. "Thank God your father has finally come to his senses where you are concerned. Something must be done immediately for I will not marry Stuart and bring my innocent Amy into this household until you are gone."

Sadly, Montague nodded in agreement. "I resisted the notion that you were a disrupting influence, Lily, but last night proved Leonie was correct in assessing your true nature. I love Leonie and we *will* wed on schedule. And one way or another you must be gone from here before then."

Lily was devastated. She could not allow her father to go on thinking of her as a woman of loose morals. It pained her to realize that Leonie had been poisoning his mind against her all along. She had no recourse but to explain the reason for her outrageous behavior last night.

"Father, I am not what you think. I acted as I did because—"

"Are you going to get on with it, Stuart?" cut in Leonie, bristling with impatience. "You promised to take me riding and I am growing impatient."

"You're right, darling, I'm wasting time," Montague agreed, sighing regretfully.

Then, before Lily knew what he intended, he raised his riding crop high in the air and brought it whistling down on her tender back. Lily cried out, and the sound of her voice, so filled with pain and shock, crumbled Montague's resolve. He loved his daughter too much to give her more pain, no matter what she had done. With a cry of dismay, he threw the riding crop to the floor and turned away. "Confine yourself to your room, daughter, until I send for you," he said. Then he strode angrily out the door. Lily dragged in a shuddering breath but her relief was short-lived.

"Tenderhearted fool," Leonie spat disgustedly. Suddenly a sly smile split her features and she bent to retrieve the riding crop. For what seemed like an eternity she stood motionless over Lily, eyeing her tender flesh with loathing. "Stuart may be too squea-mish and weak-willed to inflict punishment but I am not."

"Leonie, no!" Leonie swung back her arm and Lily reacted instinctively, knocking the crop aside and leaping from the bed. No one but her father had the right to whip her.

Leonie's face grew mottled with rage as she raised the crop again and advanced toward Lily.

"Touch me with that crop and you'll be sorry," Lily promised ominously as she brazenly stood her ground. The intensity and quiet menace of Lily's de-fiant words stopped Leonie in her tracks.

Leonie decided that retreat was the better part of valor. "Heed my words, Lily, find someone to marry. I won't allow you to remain here and corrupt my Amy. She is at an impressionablé age. If you don't settle on someone soon your father will be forced to choose for you. And you can be certain his choice won't be to your liking for I have great influence over his decisions."

Then she was gone, leaving Lily distraught over the upheaval she had caused by her reckless behav-ior. So much for taking charge of her own destiny, she thought ruefully. The plan she had deemed so simple and foolproof had succeeded so well it alien-ated her father and deprived her of his love and respect.

Lily would have felt no urgency to leave the con-fines of her room the remainder of that day even if her father hadn't forbid it. She experienced a certain amount of soreness and stiffness where the riding crop had lacerated her skin but the pain wasn't un-bearable. Thank God Leonie hadn't had her way or she'd be in even sorrier straights than she was now. She was provided with a meal at noon but for some reason her supper was withheld. Leonie's doings?

When morning arrived she was no closer to solving the dilemma of her rather uncertain future in her father's home than she had been the day before. She wondered what would become of her once Leonie and her father married and if indeed she would be forced to wed someone she loathed. Isolated from the rest of the household, Lily was unaware that her future was being decided without her knowledge or approval by two men ensconced at that moment in Lord Montague's study.

Captain Matthew Hawke had come calling. Upon asking for Miss Montague he was promptly ushered into Lord Montague's study where he was kept cooling his heels until the older man was ready to acknowledge him. Matt cleared his throat loudly and was rewarded with a black scowl.

"What is your business with my daughter, Captain Hawke?" Montague asked bluntly.

Taken aback by Montague's abrupt manner, Matt's reply was equally concise. "What does any man want with a beautiful woman, sir? I'd like to court her. Perhaps take her riding this afternoon. If you have no objections, that is."

"Do you realize that my daughter's reputation has suffered because of you?" Montague contended, eyeing Matt narrowly.

"Sir, I hardly think walking out in the garden sufficient grounds for such an accusation. Your daughter walked out with several men that night, if I remember correctly."

"Indeed," snapped Montague with asperity. "But you, Captain, were the only one seen compromising her." Matt had the good sense to look startled. "Don't try to deny it, you and Lily were seen cavorting in a flagrant disregard for propriety."

Matt flushed, surprised that he had been seen compromising Lily's virtue but not entirely sorry it had happened. He was astute enough to realize it could work to his advantage by speeding along their marriage. True, he'd assumed the delectable Lily had bestowed the same favors on other suitors that night, until he discovered that she was merely playing a dangerous game. Lord Montague mistook Matt's flushed countenance for an admission of guilt and he sputtered in rage.

"Did my foolish daughter gift you with her virginity, Captain? Tell me, did you or did you not relieve her of her maidenhead that night in my garden?"

Matt's enigmatic smile sent Lord Montague's temper soaring. "I'd be a fool to admit to such a thing, wouldn't I? Besides, I'd be doing your lovely daughter a grave injustice by kissing and telling, so to speak."

"You bounder! I sincerely hope Lily had the good sense to refuse you."

Matt shifted uncomfortably, unaccustomed to being placed in such an embarrassing position. "That, Lord Montague, is between Lily and me."

"I hope you're prepared to do what society expects of you, young man."

Chapter 3

Matt couldn't believe his incredible luck. Everything was working wonderfully in his favor.

"Are you hinting that I offer for your daughter?" Matt asked, unable to disguise his enthusiasm for the match.

"You could do worse. It's no secret Lily is an heiress. She is also a lovely young woman and probably too good for a Colonial, but since you are from good English stock I won't object."

Matt hung on to his temper with amazing fortitude. "How gracious of you."

"You're not married, are you?" Montague asked sharply.

"There is no wife in America waiting for me," Matt replied curtly. "Nor is there a fiancée."

His answer seemed to satisfy Montague. "You are aware, of course, that Lily's conduct the other night all but destroyed her chances for an advantageous marriage. A good share of the blame lies with you."

"I assume then that you would favor my request for your daughter's hand," Matt said politely. Though vastly amused by the turn of events he tried not to show it. Wait until Chris learned how things were falling neatly into place for him, he thought gleefully. And it was happening with greater speed than he dared hope.

"I don't presume to tell you anything, Captain Hawke, you are old enough to know where your duty lies," Montague replied with asperity.

Matt was silent a long time, pretending to mull over the older man's words while inwardly rejoicing. "I don't wish to seem crass but am I to assume that the man your daughter marries will have complete control over her inheritance?"

"That's the law," Montague said tightly.

"Any wife of mine will naturally accompany me to my home in Boston."

Stuart nodded agreeably. "That's as it should be. Removing Lily from London's gossipmongers would be quite the right thing to do under the circumstances. Without her presence to feed the gossip mill this whole deplorable episode will die a natural death."

"Love would not be a deciding factor," Matt said with brutal honesty. "Lily and I barely know one another."

"I respect your candor, Captain, but few young couples are in love when they marry."

Astutely Matt exhibited the correct amount of misgiving before giving the impression that Montague's subtle persuasion had swayed him into offering for Lily. "If Lily and I are to marry perhaps we should become better acquainted," he suggested blandly. "I've a carriage waiting outside, a ride and a word in private would give us the opportunity to know one another better and to test the ground, so to speak, about a match between us."

Slowly Montague nodded. "I'll have Lily summoned immediately."

When informed by her maid that her father wanted to see her, Lily dressed quickly, hoping he had changed his mind about forgiving her for her behavior at her party. Her back was still sore and except for being hungry—she hadn't been served breakfast yet—she felt fully prepared to face his anger. She was stunned to find Matt Hawke in intimate conversation with her parent.

Lily's subdued manner surprised Matt when she walked into the room. He wondered what Montague had done to dampen the spirits of his feisty daughter, recalling her grit and determination to avoid a forced marriage.

"There you are, Lily," Montague said, motioning her into the room. He dismissed her somber mood as remorse over her outrageous behavior at the party. "Captain Hawke has announced his intentions to court you. He suggested a ride in his carriage and I have given my permission."

Lily gave Matt a quelling glance. "I don't wish to go anywhere with Captain Hawke, Father."

"You'd be wise to accept," Montague returned harshly.

Unwilling to incur her father's condemnation again, Lily acquiesced with a marked lack of enthusiasm. When Matt offered his arm, she allowed him to guide her from the house and into a neat little open carriage waiting outside at the curb. She spoke little as Matt took up the reins, answering his questions by nodding or shaking her head. She was in no mood to talk, especially to Captain Matthew Hawke. He was an arrogant, overbearing Colonial and he wasn't helping her situation any by taking her out in public today. They drove in complete silence for a long time. Lily stared straight ahead while Matt, having given up all attempts at conversation, cast surreptitious glances in her direction from time to time.

They were driving in the country now, the sun-dappled roads nearly devoid of traffic, when Matt suddenly spit out an oath and drove off the road into a copse of trees beside a narrow meandering stream.

"Why are we stopping?" Lily asked, finally breaking her long silence. "I haven't forgotten the despicable way in which you treated me in the garden. You're doing everything in your power to ruin my reputation, aren't you?"

Matt ground his teeth in vexation. "You've already done that to yourself, Lily. What in bloody hell is wrong with you? Can't you see I'm trying to help?"

He could tell by Lily's mutinous expression that nothing he could say would placate her. Still, he had to try. Grasping her slim shoulders in his large hands, he gave her a little shake. "Did you hear me, Lily, let's talk about this."

Lily winced and her face paled. "Please, you're hurting me."

Matt's glowering features grew even darker. "I'm barely touching you so how can I be hurting you?"

Lily bit her lower lip, enduring the pressure of his hands on her back but unable to prevent the look of pain that glazed her eyes.

Immediately Matt released his hold on Lily's shoulders. Perhaps he didn't know his own strength, he mused in rueful reflection. Suddenly his eyes narrowed, realizing something was definitely amiss, something not of his doing. "Lily, what is it? Are you ill?"

"It's nothing, Captain Hawke, nothing at all. I—I'm fine."

"You don't look fine. Are you in pain?"

Shame and embarrassment warred inside Lily. She didn't want Matt to know how she had been punished for defying convention. "I told you, nothing is wrong."

Matt slanted her a skeptical glance. Suddenly he reached out and clasped her shoulders again, and this time Lily couldn't stifle her cry as his fingers bit cruelly into the welt her father's single blow with the riding crop had raised on her back. "Something is wrong. Turn around."

When Lily refused to budge, he turned her himself,

staring in disbelief at the back of her dress where drops of blood had seeped through the cloth.

"Sweet Jesus! Did your father do this to you? How could he abuse his own flesh and blood in such a vile manner?" As he spoke he unfastened the hooks at the back of her dress and flung the edges aside.

"It isn't so bad," Lily declared defiantly. "He only struck me once then couldn't continue. But if it was left to Leonie my entire back would be crisscrossed with bloody stripes."

"Vindictive bitch," Matt muttered beneath his breath.

"I told her she'd be sorry if she struck me," Lily said softly. "I think she believed me."

With gentle fingers Matt hooked her dress back up again, then turned her to face him. "Did you know we were seen in a compromising position in the garden the other night?"

"Oh, God, no wonder Father was so angry," Lily said, abashed. "If you hadn't tried to assault me this would never have happened."

"It's too late for regrets, Lily," Matt said slowly. "As a consequence your father suggested that I do my duty by you."

"Both Father and Leonie want me out of their lives," Lily revealed, sick with fury and shame. "I assume he mentioned the fortune that I will inherit upon my marriage."

"I believe he mentioned it," Matt said dryly.

"No matter what Father expects, there is no need for you to offer for me, Captain. I refuse to be bartered. When I marry it will be for love and not because Father used my fortune as bait to gain me a husband."

"Love," Matt scoffed derisively. "Too much is made of love. There are more important things in life than silly love words and promises that few keep once the honeymoon is over."

"Money, for instance?" Lily said with a hint of sarcasm.

"Exactly. I'll be brutally honest with you, little one, because you deserve it. I fully intend to marry you. Not only do I find you a pleasant diversion but I have great need of your fortune. Obviously you need a husband and I'm the only one unconcerned with gossip and interested enough to offer for you right now. If you choose to remain at home after your father and Leonie marry your life will become unbearable."

"Do you care for me?" Lily asked naively.

The smile he gave her was subtly taunting. Matt recognized a strange fragile quality about her, almost like fine crystal that could be shattered with one careless word. Still, he didn't want to disillusion her. "You are lovely, little one, it wouldn't be difficult to learn to care for you."

"I assume then that you are only interested in my fortune. Are you so cynical that you don't believe in love?"

"If love exists I have yet to see proof of it. My parents were well matched but I can't truthfully say they displayed a great abiding love for one another. People marry for convenience and what the alliance will bring them. If you marry me you'll be well treated and have complete jurisdiction over Hawkeshaven, my home in Boston. And I'm experienced enough to know I don't repulse you."

A tingle of excitement shook her when Matt reached out and placed a protective arm carefully around her shoulders. With one hand he pushed a loose tendril of flaming hair away from her face, his fingers gently brushing a flushed cheek. Then he kissed her, tenderly pressing his lips against hers before gently covering her mouth. Parting her lips, she raised herself to meet his kiss, shocked at her eager response to his touch.

Matt would have been pleasantly surprised if he had had insight into Lily's thoughts. Never had she encountered a man who radiated such virile power and sexual magnetism. The very air vibrated around him. No, she thought wryly, Matt certainly didn't repulse her. Then her thoughts scattered as she immersed herself in his kiss, a kiss that was disturbing to her in every way possible. He brought her untried senses to life and challenged her emotions with mysterious stirrings. Obviously she would have no difficulty responding to Matthew Hawke physically, but Lily was astute enough to know few marriages survived on physical attraction alone. She wanted more, much more from a marriage.

Matt's fingertips danced along the pulse at the base of her throat as his lips slid down to nibble at a pretty pink earlobe. Lily gasped as Matt led her expertly to the edge of seduction, where she tottered dizzily. Only when she felt his fingers press hotly against the thrusting peak of one breast did she realize he was dragging her much too fast into his world of sensual pleasure. Abruptly she pulled away, her sherry eyes soft and luminous with her first taste of physical arousal. It was warm and heady and something she could easily grow to like, but not now. Not without love. And certainly not with Matthew Hawke, who admittedly coveted her fortune.

"Matt, stop," she cried, realizing that she was completely out of her element. "Please, take me home."

Matt looked at her sharply, noting that her eyes were overbright and her skin had taken on a waxy pallor. She looked utterly dazed and Matt chided himself for moving too fast. He roundly cursed Leonie and Stuart Montague beneath his breath for making Lily's life an undeserved hell.

"You look pale, Lily," he said, not unkindly. "Did you have breakfast this morning?"

Lily laughed ruefully. "Breakfast was a bit late. I

suppose Leonie saw to it that the servants neglected to bring me breakfast. She'll be their mistress soon and they fear her."

"My God!" Matt exclaimed angrily. "Is there no end to what that woman will stoop to where you are concerned? I'm going to buy you the best meal in town."

Replete, Lily sat back and sighed. The dinner Matt had ordered for her dispelled the lingering weakness she had suffered earlier. Her natural exuberance and youthful spirit reasserted themselves and only a slight stinging remained where her father had struck her.

Lily was about to suggest they leave when she became suddenly aware that Matt was staring across the room at a striking brunette. His dark eyes flashed angrily. Lily thought the woman one of the most magnificent creatures she had ever seen. She couldn't blame Matt for staring at her. She was in her late twenties, with jet-black hair, her voluptuous figure stunning in a blatant sort of way. With exaggerated slowness she turned dark, velvet eyes on Lily and Matt, her full red lips curved upward into an enigmatic smile.

"Christ!" Matt spat as he tore his eyes from the brunette. His glowering features were dark and brooding, his midnight eyes narrowed dangerously. "Let's get out of here." He threw down his napkin, slanted a chilling glance at the brunette and literally dragged Lily from the restaurant.

"Matt, do you know that woman?" Lily asked curiously. "She's very beautiful."

"Damnation," Matt mumbled beneath his breath. What in the hell was Clarissa Hartley doing in London? He had left her weeks ago in Boston. Her acting troupe was to perform there for the season. What was she trying to do, ruin all his plans? "No, I've never seen the woman before," Matt lied blandly. He couldn't wait until he got his hands on the little vixen.

"I wonder why she was staring at us so strangely?" Lily mused curiously.

"Forget the woman, little one," Matt urged, "she's unimportant. I'll take you home now, I just recalled something I must do today.

"Come in, Matt," Clarissa called through the door. "I've been waiting."

Grinding his teeth in frustration, Matt flung open the door, walked into the room and slammed it shut behind him with a loud bang that shook the walls. He looked furious and anyone but Clarissa would have had the good sense to be frightened. Clarissa had been dining at the hotel where he had taken Lily to eat so Matt knew exactly where to find her. The obliging desk clerk had provided him with the room number and he took the stairs two at a time.

"You little bitch! How dare you follow me to England."

"I missed you," Clarissa pouted prettily. She was reclining in bed when Matt entered but now she sat up, and the sheet fell away, exposing two firm, upthrust breasts with protruding dusky nipples surrounded by large dark areolas. Matt was too angry to notice.

"After what you did this afternoon I ought to beat you."

His words brought a provocative smile to Clarissa's lips. "What did I do that was so terrible?" she asked innocently. "I was merely having dinner. How did I know you would show up in the same place at the same time? Was that the woman you intend to marry? I'm ashamed of you, darling, she's little more than a child. How unlike you to rob the cradle."

"Dammit, Clarrie, don't change the subject. What are you doing in London?"

"I've been offered a position with a prestigious London acting company," Clarissa explained, "but I haven't decided to accept yet."

"You followed me here, don't deny it!"

"Think what you like. Why don't you take your clothes off, darling? We can talk after we've greeted one another properly."

"I'm waiting for an explanation," Matt bit out, unwilling to be drawn into her web of seduction.

"Very well." Clarissa sighed. "I wanted a look at my competition. I've been pleasing you for five years with no complaints and hope to continue to do so for many years to come. You belong to me, Matthew Hawke, and no little girl is going to steal you from me. She may be an aristocrat but she can never satisfy you like I do. Go ahead, marry the child if you must. Deflower her, get her with child, but in the end you'll come back to me. It's inevitable."

"The only thing that's inevitable is this damnable war that's brewing between England and America. I need to get back home in time to convert my ships, Clarrie, and I need Lily Montague's money to do it. Don't ruin my chances for this marriage. Stay away from me and Lily."

"I won't interfere, Matt, now that I've seen the blushing little bride. She's no competition. Now come to bed, let me show you how much I missed you." She held out her arms, her dark eyes promising hours of delightful games at which she was a master.

The blood drummed in Matt's head as he stared at Clarrie's magnificent breasts, recalling the countless times she had given him exquisite pleasure. She was one of the most experienced lovers he had ever known, that's why he had kept her for five years. She suited him so well and made no demands that he marry her, though he knew she would jump at the chance to become Mrs. Matthew Hawke. He had always performed magnificently with Clarissa, usually becoming aroused and marble hard by merely touching her. Sometimes lust drove him to take her two or three times a night. But tonight he felt no urgent need to make love to Clarrie.

For some obscure reason his mind was obsessed with Lily and her provoking innocence. It had been years since he'd had a woman young enough to be a virgin. Though the thoughts of making love to Lily titillated his senses, he seriously doubted an untried girl would satisfy him for long. Clarissa had a strong hold upon his emotions; he seemed to crave excessively her experienced hands and practiced mouth. Her knowledge of sexual matters was phenomenal. Yet amazingly, Clarissa's ample charms did not tempt him tonight.

Clarissa's sloe eyes narrowed as she watched Matt, suddenly realizing she was about to be rejected. Nothing like this had ever occurred before in their long illustrious relationship. She and Matt were bound together by the silken cord of passion and she had but to shorten the cord to draw him once again into her arms. A mere child was no competition, she silently scoffed as she rolled her eyes beguilingly at Matt. She would have been astounded had she known that at that very moment she was being compared unfavorably with Lily's youthful beauty and guileless innocence.

"Come, Matt," Clarissa urged, licking her lush lips with the tip of her tongue like a hungry cat.

"Sorry, Clarrie," Matt replied, baffled by his lack of desire for his longtime mistress. "I'm not in the mood. Nor will I be seeing you again while I'm in London. If the Montagues get wind of our association there will be hell to pay. I fully intend to marry Lily Montague and will countenance no interference from you. I suggest you go back to America before hostilities break out." He turned to leave.

"Matt, no! Don't leave me like this, I need you!"

"If you need a man, Clarrie, I suggest you get dressed and go find one."

"Wait! Will I see you in Boston?"

"I don't know, Clarrie, I truly don't know."

Matt's courtship of Lily was accomplished with the enthusiasm and determination of a man driven by desperation. Time was running out, talk of war grew ominous and the impending thunder of cannon haunted his dreams. In the same manner with which he'd conquered every problem he'd ever encountered, Matt was a veritable whirlwind of persistence and fortitude. Yet whenever Matt and Lily were together the tension stretched between them like a tightly strung wire.

During the following weeks Matt called on Lily nearly every day. When weather permitted they rode in his rented carriage, and when Lily's back healed and she was no longer in pain, they rode blooded stock from the Montague stables. When at first Lily had sought to refuse his company, her father had insisted she accompany Matt. Since Matt had thus far remained a perfect gentleman on their outings, Lily made no further protests, though deep in her heart she secretly vowed never to allow herself to forget Matthew Hawke's motives for courting her. What she didn't understand was the dark, hungry way he would gaze at her when he thought she wasn't looking.

One particularly warm fall day Matt arrived with a suggestion for a picnic. He brought with him a picnic basket loaded with food and against Lily's better judgment they rode out to a picturesque spot beside a stream to enjoy their repast. Little by little Matt's good behavior laid Lily's misgivings to rest and after the food was consumed and the picnic things put away, she leaned back against a tree, lazily contemplating the play of dancing sunbeams through the broad-leafed branches overhead. The meal and warmth combined to make her drowsy and she found it increasingly difficult to stay awake.

"Lily, I think it's time we told your father that we're going to marry."

Like a dash of cold water, Matt's words brought Lily abruptly awake. "What! Are you insane? I have no intention of marrying you." Her tone was emphatic and final. "You don't love me and I certainly am not in love with you. I expect more from marriage than companionship. And even that wouldn't apply in your case for you'd be gone most of the time."

"Life with me wouldn't be so bad." Matt scowled, clearly piqued by Lily's words. "We don't repel one another." If he was totally honest he'd admit he was wildly attracted to her. "I'd not treat you harshly and you'd have a beautiful home to run as you see fit. I would welcome any children that come of our union. And since I'd be at sea for long periods of time I'd not be around to interfere in your life."

"The type of marriage you just described doesn't appeal to me," Lily refuted sourly.

"How do you know, you're still a child," Matt shot back, annoyed. Rejection did not sit well with him. Clarissa had waited years for just such a declaration.

"I'm old enough to know what I want," Lily retaliated. "And it certainly isn't an arrogant, coldhearted man who would marry a sow if she had enough money. Why is money so important to you?"

Keeping a tight rein on his temper, Matt said, "I need the money for a just cause. The sea is my profession and once my ships are properly armed my days and nights will be spent pursuing the enemy."

"The enemy? A just cause?" puzzled Lily.

"War between England and America is inevitable. I've lost a fortune to the English who have stopped my ships on the high seas, stolen my cargoes and impressed my men into their navy. Once my ships are armed as privateers I intend to relentlessly pursue the enemy and make them pay for depriving me of my livelihood."

"My God!" Lily gasped. "You want to use my fortune against the country of my birth? Never! Not a farthing of my money will be spent for such vile purposes. I'll never consent to marry you. I'll enter a convent first."

"I think not, little one," Matt said with quiet determination. "I'm making the decision for you. After today you'll have no choice but to marry me."

A hard knot of fear formed in Lily's breast. "Wha—what are you going to do?"

His answer was to reach out and pull her roughly against his hard body. Twisting in his arms and arching her back, Lily fought desperately to free herself, but his strong arms were locked securely around her spine. She felt her soft curves mold to the contours of his lean body and his hot breath against her ear whispering, "Relax, little one, I'll make this as pleasant as possible."

Suddenly Matt's intentions were clear. He meant to rape her in order to force her compliance. She didn't know exactly what all that entailed but the girls at school had talked often enough about it, and some were more experienced than others so she had some inkling what to expect. "No, don't do this, Matt, please!"

"I hoped this wouldn't be necessary, Lily."

Suddenly Lily felt the heady sensation of his mouth against her neck. Then his warm tongue was tracing the soft fullness of her lips. Now his lips parted hers while his tongue explored the inner recesses of her mouth. With his arms still locked around her, he eased her down onto the soft grass, his fingers fumbling with the fastenings on the front of her dress.

Pushing frantically against the hard wall of his chest, Lily cried, "Stop! This isn't right!"

Matt's hot palms brushed against the silken flesh of her breasts and suddenly his breath was rasping from his throat in great gulps and his heart was pounding furiously in his chest. "Smooth, so smooth. You feel so bloody wonderful," he murmured, ignoring her protests. His touch was light and painfully teasing, completely at odds with what one would expect from a man bent on rape.

Lily shuddered as Matt's tan hands slid the dress off her shoulders to her waist, crying out in dismay as his tongue found her nipples. With tantalizing strokes of his hot, wet tongue he teased the tight little buds until they puckered and grew hard as pebbles. He paused to shove her dress over her hips, one hand searing a path down her abdomen and onto her thigh. Then he found her lips again, scorching her with his kiss, whispering words she didn't understand. When he spread her legs and settled his weight between them, Lily despaired, knowing she would never leave this place in the same condition in which she arrived.

Matt was on fire. When he realized he had to do something drastic to persuade Lily to marry him, he thought deflowering her would be a simple solution. The moral code of the day being what it was, he realized she was expected to bring her virginity to her marriage bed. A condition Matt sought to remedy immediately. Once Lily was relieved of her virginity she would have no choice but to marry him. Then something happened. Something so unexpected it caught Matt totally off guard. The moment he began to make love to Lily his passion grew wings and soared until he wanted her as he had never wanted another woman. She ignited his rather jaded appetite and excited him in ways he never thought possible. Her firm, silken body, untouched and untried, drove him wild to possess her. But he didn't want to hurt her, and he certainly didn't want her to hate him.

Just when Lily gave up all hope of retaining her virtue, she felt Matt's great weight shift off of her. With an anguished groan he sat down beside her, burying his head in his hands as he struggled to control his rampaging passion. How could an inexperienced girl like Lily have such a devastating effect on him? he wondered dully. For the second time in his memory he had deliberately practiced restraint with a woman. What amazed him even more was that both those times he had been with Lily. He could have taken her so easily in her garden the night of her party if he had pressed her. He was certain Chris would laud him for his restraint but that did little to alleviate his situation or gain him what he needed most. Was he growing soft in his old age? What was there about Lily Montague that made him want to protect her? He had always hated men who vacillated. He despised weak men who didn't know their own minds and refused to go after what they wanted no matter who they had to hurt in the process.

Bloody hell! Had he become a softhearted fool? Had he lost everything because he was too faint-hearted to take a woman without her consent?

Unaware of Matt's provocative thoughts, Lily stared at him in horror and fear. Leaping to her feet, she turned her back and hastily put her clothes in order. She was just slipping her arms into the sleeves when she realized she and Matt weren't alone. A lone rider had invaded their secluded spot beside the lazy stream to water her horse and was staring at them through narrowed lids, a shocked expression upon her face.

"Leonie!"

With heavy heart Lily realized that nothing would save her from marriage now.

Chapter 4

Married. The world didn't look any different yet Lily knew nothing would ever be the same again. Whether she liked it or not she was Mrs. Matthew Hawke for the rest of her life. Matters had moved swiftly after Leonie had inadvertently—or was it deliberately?—intruded on their picnic. One look at Lily, disheveled and struggling into her dress, had sent Leonie rushing headlong back to Stuart Montague hellbent on destroying what was left of Lily's reputation with the tale of what she had seen with her own eyes. Stuart was waiting for them when Lily and Matt returned. Lily wished she could have blocked from her memory forever the scene that followed.

Stuart Montague was livid while Leonie acted strangely calm and complacent. Leonie's wish was about to be granted. Stuart was finally convinced his daughter was a wanton creature who needed a stern husband to deal harshly with her bold behavior. And since she had chosen the upstart American to dally with he should be the one to pay with his freedom. Stuart would accept nothing less than marriage and Lily saw no way to circumvent his wishes. An ultimatum was given, accepted by Matt, and within two weeks they were wed. And despite the fact that win-

52

ter was nearly upon them they were to board a ship for America that very same day.

Lily seethed with impotent rage when she recalled how Matt had tried to force himself on her that afternoon in the glade. If there had been a shred of love involved she could have found it in her heart to forgive him, especially since he hadn't completed the act. Both Leonie and her father thought otherwise, so in the end it didn't matter whether or not Matt had stopped just short of ravaging her. But obviously Matt had gotten what he wanted. At this very minute Matt was closeted with her father and his lawyer signing the papers necessary to transfer her inheritance to Matt. Lily wondered what her father would say if he knew her money would be used to arm ships destined to wreak destruction on the British navy. It probably wouldn't make any difference, she told herself bleakly. As long as Leonie was happy, her father was content.

If not for Leonie, Lily reflected ruefully, she and her father could have had a normal, loving relationship. Instead she was forced into marriage to an arrogant, ruthless man who didn't love her, a man who had set out with calculating efficiency to acquire her fortune. He had painstakingly masterminded this entire debacle from start to finish, but he hadn't won yet. He might have her money but that's all he would ever get from her. She had left school a naive girl but the intervening weeks had taught her much about life. She had been a victim once but never again. She had a surprise up her sleeve for Captain Matthew Hawke.

How strange it seemed, Lily thought wistfully, to be watching the city of her birth fade away in the distance knowing she might never see it again. She leaned against the rail of the *Proud Lady*, shivering in the cold November air, straining her eyes toward the diminishing shoreline while Matt stood with one arm casually draped around her shoulders. She hardened her heart and vowed that this man would never come to mean anything to her. His high-handed methods had earned him her everlasting disrespect—and worse.

There were about a dozen passengers aboard the American sloop *Proud Lady*, but she and Matt had been given the best accommodations owing to the fact that they were newlyweds. The cabin was not overly large but comfortable and roomy enough to hold two people and their luggage. A bed large enough to accommodate Matt's great size brought a blush to Lily's cheeks. She had hoped for separate cabins but realized Matt was not the kind of man to deny himself. However, that did not stop Lily from making her own plans. Her body was her own to give or withhold as she saw fit. In her estimation the money her marriage brought Matt had earned her the right to dictate terms to Matt and that's exactly what she intended to do.

"Would you like me to order supper in our cabin?" Matt asked when he turned her from the rail to lead her down the passageway to their accommodations. His voice was low, his dark eyes glowing with anticipation.

"No," Lily said quickly. "I'd like to meet some of the other passengers tonight."

The pulse in Matt's throat jumped erratically but he tried to contain his disappointment. Since the day he had tried and failed to seduce Lily he had thought of nothing but possessing her body. His fingers itched to explore every inch of her virgin flesh, to bring her slowly to climax with his hands and mouth before fitting himself into her tight sheath. He wanted to touch her everywhere, to watch her face when he roused her to passion, to teach her how to give him pleasure. He wanted— Damnation! He had grown so hard just thinking about Lily and what he wanted to do to her he had to rearrange his trousers in order to accommodate his hardening body.

Hanging on to the frayed threads of restraint, Matt said, "I'd rather we took supper alone. This is our honeymoon."

Lily gave him an austere look, deliberately turned her back on him and joined the other passengers who were gathering in the dining salon for dinner. Glowering darkly, Matt had no recourse but to follow. Lily blithely ignored his brooding during supper, secretly pleased that he was finding her not quite as malleable as he originally thought.

Suddenly Lily heard Matt utter a strangled curse deep in his throat and she turned from her conversation with an elderly woman passenger to look at him. His eyes were vibrant with such repressed fury she was momentarily stunned, thinking his anger was directed at her. But when she saw that he was staring at someone across the room and she followed his gaze. Lily saw an exotic, dark-haired woman sitting at a small table with another couple. She was dressed in red and looked magnificent. Lily was certain she had seen the woman before and that Matt had reacted in the exact same way to her as he was reacting now.

"Matt," Lily said in a low voice. "Who is that woman? I'm positive I've seen her before."

Matt's scowl grew even darker. "It's unlikely you've seen her before." He shrugged in a vague manner that set Lily's teeth on edge. It was all Matt could do to drag his eyes away from the laughing woman. He was so enraged at Clarissa he wanted to leap across the room and strangle her with his bare hands. What in bloody hell made her take this particular ship to America?

Clarissa smirked knowingly as she glanced sidelong at Matt and Lily. Three days ago she had been

on her way to book passage home when she saw
Matt on the docks. She followed him and when she
learned he had booked passage for two on the *Proud
Lady* for three days hence, she had gleefully secured
a cabin for herself on the same ship. She knew Matt
would be furious but it rankled to think that he
would be sharing a bed with his young wife for the
length of the voyage. Clarissa's perverse nature
couldn't pass up the opportunity to disrupt her lover's honeymoon. Clarissa worried that without her
interference Matt might learn to enjoy making love to
the little chit he had married. Astutely Clarissa realized she could never allow that to happen.

After the meal Captain Brad Archer, a friend and
fellow Bostonian, engaged Matt in a lengthy conversation having to do with impending war. Lily took
the opportunity to slip away unnoticed. She quickly
washed, undressed, slipped a pristine white nightgown over her head and slid into bed, falling almost
immediately asleep.

Matt had the devil's own time getting away from
Captain Archer. When war and politics were discussed time had no meaning. But for Matt each minute was an agony devised for the express purpose of
torturing him. Tonight his mind wasn't on war, it
was on Lily and their first night together. It seemed
like hours before he was finally able to make a graceful exit, and when he entered the cabin he was disappointed to find Lily sound asleep. A soft curse left
his lips. He wanted her awake and aware of all he
was doing to her. He wanted her to feel him make
love to her as he aroused her body slowly to passion.

A low flame burned in the lamp swinging from the
bulkhead and Matt could easily make out the riot of
red-gold curls spread across the pillow and the soft
curve of an apricot-hued cheek silhouetted against
the white sheet. With a minimum of effort he quickly
peeled off his clothes and slid naked into bed.

With shaking hands Matt pulled the sheet away from Lily's sleeping form, wrinkling his nose in distaste when he saw the voluminous high-necked nightgown she had chosen for her wedding night. He'd much prefer her naked in his arms. Just then Lily shifted to her back, her high, firm breasts clearly outlined beneath the fine lawn, their pointed nipples prominent beneath the thin material. Matt's body reacted instantly. He hardened and swelled as unerringly his hands untied the strings holding together the edges of her nightgown, laying bare to his hungry gaze the perfect twin mounds of soft alabaster flesh. His tongue, moist and warm, curled around one tempting nipple as he shoved the hem of her gown to her waist.

Then his fingers found her, that soft sweet place between her thighs. Lost in a delicious dream, Lily moaned and shifted again, allowing his fingers free access to her secret treasure. Matt's answering response was to insert a large tan finger inside her tight moistness, pushing inside as far as it would go then retreating, only to begin the whole procedure again, moving increasingly faster each time. Abruptly Lily jerked awake, her body on fire, the intimate folds of her flesh swollen beneath Matt's teasing fingers. She writhed and moaned softly as she moved sinuously against his demanding hand. It took several minutes for her to realize what was taking place and when she did she fought desperately to quell her rising ardor. Inexperienced as she was, she knew Matt had the advantage over her and would surely get what he wanted unless she put a stop to it immediately.

"Stop! Stop right now!"

Stunned, Matt went still as he stared down at Lily. Her face was flushed with sexual excitement and he could have sworn she was enjoying what he was doing to her.

"You don't really mean that," he murmured huskily.

"I do. I hoped for separate cabins so we might avoid all this," Lily declared. She lowered her gaze, unwilling to face the fury in Matt's dark eyes.

"Exactly what do you mean by 'all this'?" The chill in his voice brought an involuntary shiver to Lily. "We're married, remember? Married people usually share a bed."

"You have everything you're going to get from me," Lily declared. The determined tilt to her chin told Matt she was dead serious. "Marriage to you wasn't my choice. You have my fortune, leave my body alone."

"I don't want to hurt you, little one, but I do want to make love to you," Matt said in a low, coaxing tone. "I've looked forward to this since the night we met and you acted like a wanton little vixen."

"You've looked forward to controlling my money," Lily shot back defiantly.

"You really are serious, aren't you?" Matt bit out tightly. He was so aroused he wanted to tear off her prim, sexless nightgown and ravish her whether she wanted it or not.

"How astute of you to guess," Lily mocked sarcastically as she slapped his hands away from her body. "If I'm forced to share this bed with you there will be nothing going on except sleeping."

"Dammit, Lily," Matt cursed, thwarted passion setting him on edge. "You're not the only woman aboard this ship. All women are blessed with the same equipment and most are willing to use it. Of what good is an immature child like you when there are real women available and willing to bed with me? You needed a husband and I needed your money. Just remember, I never promised to be faithful."

"You made it perfectly clear from the beginning

that you were only interested in me for my money," Lily contended, stung by his words. Wasn't faithfulness a part of marriage? "While I, Matthew Hawke, didn't want you for any reason. All I have left is my pride and my body and you'll not rob me of either."

Spurts of hot anger raged through Matt as he flung himself from the bunk and stared down at Lily. "Keep your bloody virginity, I don't need it," he tossed out cruelly. "But I want you to look at me, Lily, take a good look."

Lily refused, keeping her eyes deliberately averted from his nakedness. But Matt would have none of it. Grasping her cheeks between his strong fingers, he turned her head to look at him. She tried desperately to concentrate on his face but he forced her head down his long torso until it was level with his male appendage, which thrust boldly upward. Lily wanted to shut her eyes but something perverse and dark inside her kept her staring at the awesome sight of a fully aroused male. It was frightening, it was beautiful; a marvelous, wondrous creation of inflexible steel sheathed in soft, velvety flesh. She gasped and swallowed convulsively, trying to dislodge the lump forming in her throat.

Her reaction pleased Matt but he wasn't quite finished with her. Grasping her hand, he forced her to touch him, wrapping her fingers around his pulsating erection. "This is what a man feels like when he wants a woman," he said, deliberately goading her with his crude taunts.

"Matt, don't!" She licked her lips, unable to tear her eyes from that place where her hand barely fit around him.

"Don't worry, Lily, I won't force you, but one day you'll beg me for this. You're not a cold woman and some day you'll crave a man's touch, yearn to be made love to. But I'm giving you fair warning, don't cuckold me. You're mine and whether or not we share a bed no one will share your body but me."

"Why is it all right for men to be unfaithful but not women?" Lily baited in a fit of rage. No matter what Matt did she would never defile her marriage vows but she'd never admit that to him. "If you take a lover,-so will I."

Matt froze, his eyes so dark and forbidding Lily cringed. "Try it, Lily, and I promise you won't like the consequences."

Flinging her hand away from his body, Matt threw on his clothes and stormed from the cabin, leaving Lily bewildered and frightened. What had she done? Had she unleashed a monster in Matthew Hawke by refusing to allow him is marital rights? Were all men demanding, egotistical creatures who bullied their wives and forced them to serve their needs whether they wanted to or not? Maybe she was too young and naive to know better but Matt was going to get nothing from her she wasn't willing to give.

In two days she would be eighteen and no longer a child who fantasized about marrying her prince and riding off happily into the sunset. She was a woman full grown whose dreams had been shattered by the reality of an unwanted marriage to a husband who thought he owned her body and soul.

Lily hoped Matt wouldn't be back tonight and tried to relax enough to fall asleep. But just when her eyes drooped shut, her memory of Matt's hard body rose up to taunt her. He was magnificent, she reflected, shocked at the direction of her thoughts. Solid bone and muscle, he hadn't an ounce of spare flesh anywhere on his lean body. She knew a man had an appendage but not in her wildest dreams had she imagined it so huge. Were all men so generously endowed? she wondered naughtily. Somehow she doubted it. Matt wasn't like most men. He was bigger than life and twice as impressive. When her hand

held him she could barely reach around him. It was
fortunate she had denied him, she thought with a
flash of insight, for surely he would rent her in two.
Her mental musings kept her awake far longer than
she would have liked, for most of them involved
Matt and how his naked body had looked and felt.

Matt paced the deck in a towering rage, too angry
to go back to the cabin he shared with Lily. There
was no way in God's earth he could lie beside her
and not ravish her. She was his wife, for God's sake,
it was her duty to accommodate him! When she held
him in her hand it was only the helpless look in her
eyes that kept him from tossing her gown over her
head and thrusting inside her until she begged for
mercy. Lily was so damn young and innocent, and
completely inexperienced where men and women
were concerned. She knew nothing of the pleasure to
be gained from a passionate relationship. He might
be a coldhearted bastard but he drew the line at
forcing his own wife and souring her forever on the
physical side of marriage. But one way or another
he'd have her, and on his own terms, he promised
himself.

Leaning against the rail, Matt groaned in real pain.
He was still aroused, still obsessed with making love
to Lily.

"What's the matter, darling, are you in pain?"

Matt whirled, glaring fiercely at Clarissa, who had
approached on silent feet and now stood beside him.
"You! Why have you deliberately defied me?"
Though he wasn't pleased to see Clarissa he was relieved to find someone else to focus his anger on besides Lily.

"I'm going back to Boston just as you advised,"
Clarissa said, her eyes wide with feigned innocence.
"Isn't it amazing that we have both chosen the same
ship to travel on?"

"It's more than amazing, Clarrie, it's downright

contentious. You'll never convince me it was a coincidence. What did you hope to gain by it?"

"Why nothing, darling, except perhaps to prove to myself that that little girl you married isn't woman enough for you. I'm right, aren't I, darling? You do need a woman tonight, don't you? A real woman, not a child with no knowledge of what a man likes. I know you were married today and that tonight is your honeymoon. Have you already tired of her childish ways and inexperience?"

Clarissa stood so close to Matt her plump, tantalizing breasts stabbed into his chest with relentless eagerness. When Matt groaned beneath his breath, Clarissa reached out and stroked between his legs, pleased to find he was already hard. She had always affected him violently and tonight was no different, she gloated smugly. "You want me, Matt. Even if you've already bedded your little virgin, you still want me."

Matt did need a woman—desperately. But not Clarissa. He wanted his wife and her sweet, untouched body, not Clarrie's overblown charms.

If Lily refuses to have anything to do with you why not take what Clarissa so generously offers? a voice inside him prodded.

Because nothing less than Lily would satisfy you, that same voice replied.

"Not this time, Clarrie," Matt said regretfully. Never had he thought he'd live to see the day he would reject Clarissa's sexual favors. Or for that matter those of any other attractive woman.

Clarissa's dark eyes gleamed dangerously up at Matt. "What has Lily done to you, Matt?" she hissed through clenched teeth. "I've never known you to turn me down. You know what I can do for you, how I make you feel. What about your promise that things wouldn't change between us after your marriage? Before you left Boston you vowed we'd go on like we were before."

"Don't press, Clarrie," Matt bit out angrily. "I'm still furious with you for booking passage on the *Proud Lady* knowing Lily and I would be aboard. Keep out of our way during this voyage. We'll discuss this when we dock in Boston." Deliberately he turned his back and walked away. If Clarissa's outraged looks were daggers Matt would be dead.

Lily was up and dressed the following morning when Matt appeared in their cabin. She had no inkling where he spent the night and was too proud to ask. Nor did he offer an explanation. He greeted Lily sourly and immediately began stripping off his wrinkled clothing. When Lily realized he intended to perform his morning ablutions in front of her she excused herself and quit the cabin. His mocking laughter and dark, brooding eyes followed her out the door. She paced the deck, shivering in the cold wind until Matt joined her and they went together to the dining saloon for breakfast.

Lily was pleased to note that the dark, mysterious woman was absent this morning. With growing conviction she felt that the woman and Matt were somehow connected, but since no proof existed she could accuse him of nothing. Perhaps it was all in her mind, she rationalized, turning her attention to the food on her plate, which was surprisingly well prepared for ship's fare. Suddenly his angry retort last night came back to haunt her. "Don't expect me to be faithful." She had gone into this marriage with few expectations and now had one more item to add to her growing list of things not to expect from her husband. Faithfulness. Had denying him her bed relieved her of the right to judge him or demand his fidelity? Lily wondered bleakly.

As one dull day followed another, Matt showed no

inclination or desire to share Lily's bed. After that first confrontation he used their cabin only to change clothes and bathe. For the sake of propriety, they treated one another with respect and courtesy in their dealings with other passengers, but privately they were like strangers passing each other in the daily course of their lives. Lily thought often of the heady sensations Matt had aroused in her when he touched her, but reasoned that if he truly wanted her he wouldn't have given up so easily when she resisted.

To Matt the voyage was becoming a nightmare. Having been denied his wife's bed, he found his unwillingness to avail himself of Clarrie's charms strangely disturbing, especially when her inviting glances made it abundantly obvious that she was ready and eager to oblige. It was not only mystifying but so disrupting to his libido that he began to doubt his own virility. Amazingly it was his own wife he desired; fresh, young Lily whose sweet, lithe body lured him like the forbidden fruit of Eden. Did he want her so desperately because she had denied him? he wondered curiously. Matt never thought the day would come when he would reject Clarissa's overblown charms. After five years perhaps their affair had run its course, he reasoned with a curious lack of regret.

Not that he was ready to settle down to marriage, Matt was quick to acknowledge. He had a war to fight, battles to win, and becoming a full-time husband to the child/woman he had taken to wife had little to commend it at this particular time in his life. As for love, Matt doubted it existed in the full sense of the word. He loved to make love, he loved the sea, he loved the feeling power gave him, but he had never told a woman he loved her and he seriously doubted he ever would. Words like *desire, need, sexual excitement* and *lust* came to mind. To Matt those simple phrases better described what was in his heart.

Until he had proof that love existed he refused to falsely utter so misleading a word to any woman.

The storm stuck suddenly. It seemed to Lily that the fluffy white clouds scudding across the gray-tinged sky changed within minutes to angry dark mounds boiling dangerously above a darkening horizon that was set ablaze with brilliant streaks of flashing light. Lashed by the bone-chilling wind, Lily watched in fascination as the sea rose and fell, spewing foam and debris onto the slippery deck. Matt was lending a hand with the sails and she knew she should be in her cabin but was unable to tear her eyes from the awesome sight of a sea churned white with turbulent fury. The blatant display of raw, unleashed power fascinated her, reminding her of the dark, explosive forces behind Matt's brooding facade.

"Get below! It's too dangerous for you out here." Matt was only a step behind her and Lily whirled to face him, clinging to the rail for support.

"I'll go below when the mood strikes me," Lily shot back defiantly. They had barely spoken in days and she wasn't about to let him dictate to her now, despite the fact that freezing sleet was turning the deck into an icy blanket. It surprised her that he seemed concerned about her safety. If she was swept overboard her fortune would still be his. "You're staying on deck, why can't I?"

His face was like a thundercloud as he swept her off her feet and carried her to the passageway. "The sea is my profession, my life. I can take care of myself, but not if I have to worry about you." Suddenly, through the wild concerto of the rising storm came the sound of a voice demanding Matt's immediate attention. "I'm needed," he said, setting Lily on her feet at the top of the stairs leading down to the passenger cabins. "Get below, Lily, I mean it." Then he disappeared into the swirling, freezing rain washing across the deck in numbing torrents.

Cautiously Lily slid one foot forward, searching for the first rung, but encroaching darkness all but obscured the narrow passageway. When the ship heaved she fell against the handrail, wishing she hadn't been so stubborn and had returned to her cabin before the storm became violent. Righting herself, she began a slow descent, but once again the ship shuddered, then lurched to the starboard. Lily clung tenaciously to the handrail but something or someone shoved her, sending her flying through the blackness, tumbling, clawing the air, her cries lost in the wail of the screeching wind. She hit the bottom and knew nothing more.

Chapter 5

Lily slowly opened her eyes two days later and found Matt sitting beside her, looking anxious and concerned. The breath shuddered through him as he said, "Thank God! You had me worried sick. How do you feel, Lily?"

Lily's answer was a muted groan. Matt bent toward her solicitously. "Where do you hurt? The ship doctor assured me there were no broken bones. You were bloody lucky, little one."

Lily's hands touched her head gingerly, as if wanting to make certain it was still attached to her shoulders. "My head," she complained, "it hurts. What happened?"

"I was hoping you could tell me."

"I—I don't remember. My last recollection was returning to my cabin just like you instructed."

"You probably lost your footing at the top of the ladder when the ship lurched and went tumbling to the bottom," Matt surmised. "Evidently you lay there for hours before you were found by one of the crewmen on his way to check on the passengers after the storm abated."

"How long have I been out?" Lily asked. It seemed like only minutes but could have been hours.

"Two days."

"Two days! That's not possible," Lily insisted. "Who took care of me?"

"I did."

Lily gasped and turned away. Her cheeks were so red they burned. She imagined all sorts of personal chores he must have had to deal with. Did he touch her intimately? Fondle her when she was unable to defend herself properly? Take liberties with her body she intended to withhold from him? She peeked at herself beneath the covers and saw she was primly clad in her white nightgown. Had Matt undressed her?

"I didn't mind," Matt said with a wolfish grin. His voice was hoarse and gravelly and Lily flinched at the look of raw hunger in his eyes.

Matt had raged like a madman when Lily had been discovered lying unconscious at the foot of the ladder. Once the doctor had treated her and pronounced her suffering from a slight concussion, Matt would trust no one with her but himself. Many of the well-meaning passengers had volunteered their services but Matt turned them away with thanks, staunchly declaring he would care for Lily himself. During the two days she had lain in a stupor Matt had slept little, performing all the mundane chores associated with caring for an invalid without complaint.

He had bathed her as tenderly as one did an infant.

He had touched her.

Her skin was soft as velvet and he was so wild to do more than merely soothe the silken surface of her flesh.

He wanted to caress her from the inside out. He wanted to bury himself deep inside her and thrust until she cried out.

He wanted to love her.

"Will I be all right?" Lily asked, startling Matt from

his sensual journey. It took considerable restraint to bring his wayward thoughts back along normal lines. He could feel himself expand and pulse and he ruefully thought it was a condition he had grown accustomed to these past weeks.

It was a condition utterly foreign to him and he hated it.

"The doctor said you have a concussion," Matt said at length. "A day or two in bed and you should be right as rain."

The doctor's prognosis proved correct. Two days later Lily was feeling much like her old self and ready to face the world again. It puzzled her how solicitous Matt had been since her fall and she was more leery of him than ever during the following days. She was grateful for his care of her but she felt certain he was leading up to something. When he wasn't looking she caught him watching her with the lean, hungry look of a starving wolf. Whatever it meant, Lily didn't like it. He had even insisted on sharing the bed with her, although to his credit he made no overt move to seduce her. Not only was having Matt in the same bed disturbing, it made Lily nervous. She didn't trust him.

The day Lily took a turn on deck, Matt was at her side. After a half hour Matt decided she had had enough exercise for her first day out and turned her toward their cabin.

"I'm not ready yet to go in, Matt," Lily protested. "It's beautiful out here and the sun will do me good."

"Sunshine will make no difference for what I have in mind." His voice was low and harsh, his face tense with some inner conflict he could no longer control.

"Matt, no!" Lily knew exactly what he intended and she wasn't going to let him have his way. But his determination and confidence seemed to suggest otherwise as he easily propelled her down the passageway and inside their cabin. He closed the door and turned to face her. His voice was hoarse with desire, his eyes dark with anticipation.

"This has gone on long enough, Lily."

"I don't know what you're talking about," Lily retorted, presenting her back.

"I've tended you for days. Each time I touched you or performed an intimate task gave me more pain than consigning me to the darkest hell. I suffered more agony than I can ever recall and had to turn away lest I turn to ash. You're my wife, for Christ's sake! It's time you acted like one."

"This isn't a normal marriage," Lily observed, refusing to face him and his implacable anger.

"In case you haven't noticed, I'm a normal man!" Matt shouted, by now beyond mere anger. "And I hope to God you're a normal woman." He grasped her arm and swung her to face him, frightening her with his predatory smile. "Unless a marriage is consummated there are grounds for annulment. It's the law."

"An annulment would suit me just fine," Lily declared defiantly. For some unexplained reason Matt's smile frightened her more than his rage.

"It doesn't suit me, Lily," Matt said, dragging her against the hard wall of his chest. "This marriage is real. I'm no monk and certainly don't intend to become one just because I married a child who is too immature to honor her marriage vows."

"Im—immature," sputtered Lily. "If our vows meant anything to you you wouldn't have taunted me by insisting you never intended to remain faithful. Is there no one aboard ship to assuage your lust? Has the dearth of eligible females driven you to your own wife?"

Matt grit his teeth in frustration. What was it about Lily that made him want to strangle her and make love to her all in the same breath? Why was she being so damn obstinate? He could see now why Stuart Montague had been so anxious to rid himself of his feisty daughter. But if he let her get the upper hand now he'd never be able to control her.

"There are plenty of females aboard who would happily accommodate me," he ground out from between clenched teeth.

"Good! You have my permission to bed them as often as you please."

"I don't need your permission. If I wanted another woman I'd bloody well have her! For some reason completely beyond my comprehension, I want *you*. Call me a fool, but don't try to change my mind. I want *you*, Lily Hawke."

He lowered his head and found her mouth.

Lily struggled, but he held her head forcibly with his hands, allowing her no escape as his mouth searched hers, gently at first, then fiercely, demanding. He teased the moist corners with his tongue, brushing their sweet fullness with slow relish. Murmurs of protest gurgled from her throat, but he ignored them, deepening the kiss, thrusting his tongue into her sweet mouth until he felt his tenuous control slip. He nearly lost it completely when Lily swayed against him and moaned.

His chest was heaving, his breath rasping in great shudders when he broke off the kiss, afraid if he continued he'd throw her on her back and ravish her. It wasn't what he wanted for his wife but he was so aroused he would take her any way he could get her. He drew back and looked at her. Her eyes, like warm sherry, were wide and frightened, her mouth full and red from the pressure of his kiss. His eyes strayed to her breasts, heaving beneath the green silk covering her bosom. He continued to stare, mesmerized, then, with exaggerated slowness, he removed his shirt.

The sight of his bare chest brought a blush to Lily's cheeks. With gut-wrenching realization she knew that nothing would stop Matt from making her his wife in more than name only tonight. She could fight; she could protest; she could scream her head off. Matt wanted her and nothing short of a miracle would save her.

Unless—

"Matt, don't, I—I can't. Not tonight. It's the wrong time of the month." Her cheeks, already red, grew fiery. Never in her wildest dreams had she thought she'd say something of so intimate a nature to a man. Even if that man was her husband. But it was the only thing she could think of.

Matt went still, his black eyes narrowed in disbelief. "When did this happen?"

"To—today," she stammered, praying he'd be gentleman enough not to ask for proof.

"How long, Lily? How long will you be indisposed?"

Lily hesitated, trying to calculate how long she could drag out her lie. If she could make her reprieve last a week perhaps by then she'd be able to think of something else.

"Don't lie to me, little one, I'm well acquainted with a woman's anatomy and bodily functions."

"One week," Lily blurted out, praying he'd take her word and not question her.

Wrong!

"I'll give you three days, Lily. But no longer. Do you think me a fool? Meantime," he said with sly innuendo, "perhaps I'll find someone who isn't afraid to act like a woman." Abruptly he turned and stormed from the cabin.

Lily's legs were shaking. It was a close call but she had won. How long could she hold him off? she wondered bleakly. Matt might be many things but like he said, he was no fool. Why did he even bother when obviously he could have any woman he wanted? She was willing to bet that exotic brunette would be more than willing to take care of his needs. Perhaps she already was. It was unnerving the way the woman followed them with her dark glowing eyes; always watching, always waiting, always curious. Though the brunette had never spoken to her and Matt, Lily felt there were things the woman could tell her that would probably shock her.

Matt turned his face into the cold bite of the wind. He was a bloody fool to allow Lily to dupe him like she did. Never had he hurt so bad from wanting. In all his adult years he had never been without a woman for more than a few days except for those times when he was at sea. He could feel his erection stretching taut the material of his trousers and was stunned by how quickly Lily was becoming an obsession with him. His own wife, for Christ's sake! Wouldn't his friends laugh if they discovered he desired his own wife with so fierce a need it nearly unmanned him? He'd never live it down.

"How is your wife, darling? I heard she took a nasty fall."

Matt recognized her voice immediately. Why in bloody hell did Clarissa have to show up now when Lily had stoked his need for a woman into a blazing inferno? "Lily is fine," Matt said with amazing control for a man in his condition.

"Why aren't you with her? Is your honeymoon so dull you've abandoned your bride so soon? I could have sworn I saw you curled up on a couch in the saloon one night when I couldn't sleep and strolled the deck. Are you ready now to admit you need a real woman?"

"Damn you, Clarissa," Matt hissed from between clenched teeth. "Don't you ever give up?"

"Not where you're concerned, darling." She leaned close, so close he could smell the intoxicating scent of aroused female. It drove him mad.

Grasping her by the elbows, he dragged her be-

•

hind some barrels stacked on the deserted deck. It was dinner time and the passengers had already assembled in the saloon to enjoy their meal. The sky had turned to deep violet and darkness was only moments away. No one but the watch was about and the barrels concealed them from passersby.

Clarissa was jubilant. This was the moment she had waited for. The moment when Matt admitted he needed her, that his young wife meant nothing to him, and she savored it. She lifted her face to his, recognizing his need and answering it with a need of her own. She swayed, leaning into his muscular chest, eager for his kiss and the feel of his big hands on her flesh. She could feel his great erection through the material of her skirts and took his hand, placing it on her right breast.

Lily left the cabin and made her way to the dining saloon. When she saw Matt hadn't yet arrived she took a seat and enjoyed a delicious meal without his glowering looks and the tense silence that was so much a part of his character. She hoped he would stay away all night, and every night after that. But she knew she was whistling in the wind. In three days he expected to bed her and if she didn't think of something by then it was likely to happen. She didn't linger with the other passengers after the meal to socialize as they were wont to do but climbed the ladder to the deck for a breath of air. The decks were deserted and she walked to the rail, surprised at how cool and windy it had grown since that afternoon.

She didn't want to go back to her cabin yet but neither did she wish to buck the chilling breeze, so she chose another course. She spied several barrels stacked up against the quarterdeck and thought they would provide adequate shelter from the wind without hampering her enjoyment of the night air. Unerringly she made her way toward the barrels, spying one that would provide a comfortable seat on which to perch. She was surprised when she heard voices coming from behind one of the barrels. Peeking around the corner, she nearly swooned when she saw Matt with the same striking brunette whose interest in them was unnerving. She was leaning against his chest and staring into his eyes in a most provocative manner, and Matt had his hand—dear God!—he had his hand on her breast!

Fortunately neither of them heard Lily's strangled gasp as she turned to flee. Once safe in her cabin she threw herself on the bunk and pounded the pillow with her fists, wishing it was Matt—that faithless swine who had obviously lied to her about knowing the woman. What else should she expect from a man who had boldly announced that he never intended to be faithful? Why did she even care? Why did finding him with another woman hurt so badly?

Matt's hand tightened on Clarissa's breast, her moan of pleasure bringing back memories of how it was between them. He tried to picture her soft white breasts overflowing his hands, the more than generous curve of her hips, the yielding flesh of her buttocks. But all he could think of was large firm breasts with their ripe pink tips. Hips slim yet unmistakably all woman. A waist so narrow he could span it with his hands. And the twin mounds of buttocks perfect and unyielding against the pressure of his hands.

Lily.

Lily, with the downy bloom of youth on her velvety cheeks.

His body made its choice in the most basic way as his manhood instantly withered and grew flaccid. It was a condition Matt had never experienced before in his life. If Lily had done this to him, prevented him from enjoying other women, she must surely be a witch and he rued the day he met her.

"Matt, darling," Clarissa said, panting jerkily.

"Come to my cabin, it's not private enough here for what we intend." She was so aroused she was unaware that desire had left him, that she no longer held any interest for him.

Thrusting her away, Matt said, "Sorry, Clarrie, I fear that's impossible tonight." His voice had an edge to it that puzzled her.

"Of course it's possible, darling, anything is possible with you. Who would know better than I?"

Matt laughed harshly. Deliberately he grasped her hand, bringing it to his groin. "Now do you believe me?"

"Oh . . ." Dismay stole the words from her mouth.

"Good night, Clarrie."

"Matt, wait. I know what to do to make you want me. You've always loved my mouth. Please, Matt, don't give up so easily."

"Good night, Clarrie," he repeated, too plagued by doubts to discuss his distressing lack of desire. Damn Lily to hell and back!

When Matt didn't return to the cabin that night Lily wasn't certain if she was relieved or just plain enraged. Obviously he was spending the night with the brunette and that should have pleased her, but instead it shocked and hurt her, hurt her more deeply than she was willing to admit. Pain clutched at her heart and squeezed until nothing was left but an empty shell. Was it her fault Matt was a randy goat who needed a woman every night? she asked herself. No, but it was her fault he went looking for another woman in the first place, her conscience answered. Fine, she tossed back. Who needed him? At least she didn't have to worry about him showing up in three days to consummate their marriage.

Except for meals Lily saw little of Matt during the following two days. She passed the time pleasantly, visiting with the other passengers and strolling the deck. It truly surprised her that each time she saw Matt he was either alone or in the company of Captain Archer. Knowing he was the kind of man who wouldn't be without female companionship for any length of time, she had expected to see the brunette hanging on his arm. Did he fear ridicule if he was seen openly flaunting his mistress? Had the brunette become his mistress? Lily had nearly forgotten Matt's ultimatum when he approached her after supper on the third night and held out his arm.

"Allow me to escort you to our cabin, Lily." His expression betrayed not the slightest hint of his intention, unless one could call the nerve twitching along the hard line of his jaw an indication of what was to follow. But Lily was astute enough to know immediately what he wanted. His languorous movements, the sensuous curve to his full lips, each spoke eloquently of the desire raging inside him.

"Matt," she began shakily, "this is a mistake."

"The mistake was allowing you to have your own way in this," Matt returned shortly. "Unless you wish to cause a scene I suggest you come along quietly."

Lily glanced at the other passengers gathered nearby and saw that they were indeed looking at them curiously. Particularly the brunette, who had just finished her dinner and was walking toward them. Lily never learned if she intended to stop and talk to them for Matt was already propelling her out of the saloon and down the passageway toward their cabin. Once inside he slammed the door and shot the bolt. After lighting the lamp he turned to confront her. The muscle in his jaw jumped and Lily felt a thrill of danger shoot through her. He took a step closer and when she tried to back away, the bunk came in hard contact with the back of her knees.

He reached out and caressed the smooth curve of her cheek. Though his touch was tender, Lily could feel the awesome force of unleashed power behind the innocent gesture.

"Don't touch me," Lily warned. The breath hissed through her teeth in a wild shudder.

"You're my wife. I want you, little one. Yield to me and I won't hurt you. I want to bring you pleasure."

"I don't need your kind of pleasure."

"How do you know when you've never experienced it before?" His eyes were dark and enigmatic, glowing with the devil's own fire.

Lily squealed in real terror when he reached out and pulled her against the swollen firmness of his body. It seemed that he was in a perpetual state of arousal since he'd married the little vixen. He was more excited at this moment than he could ever remember. Then he lowered his head and his lips found hers as he kissed her over and over. Lily opened her mouth to protest and his tongue slipped inside. He moaned in pure bliss as he tasted her sweetness. Lily was panting for lack of breath when he broke off the kiss and slid his mouth to the pulse beating furiously at the base of her throat.

"Matt, please, I don't want this," Lily said, trying to keep her fragile control. "You have my money, must you force yourself on me to prove your masculinity?"

A swift shadow of anger swept across his face but was quickly gone as another emotion took its place. "I don't need to prove my masculinity, Lily. What I need is my wife. Nor do I intend to use force."

Then he kissed her again and despite her struggles he slid her dress from her shoulders, kicking it aside with his booted foot. Her petticoats followed.

Matt stepped back, a strange light in his eyes as he looked his fill. After several unbearable minutes in which Lily seemed rooted to the spot, he slid her backward onto the soft surface of the bunk. Then, with measured thoroughness he finished undressing her. When she was naked he began removing his own clothes.

Lily tried not to look but it was impossible. So powerful, so wonderfully male, muscles rippling beneath bronze skin. His manhood was thick, pulsing with a life of its own, eager. Frightening. He came down on her and she gasped.

Matt's blood was pounding in his brain, his body aflame with the taste and essence of the woman beneath him. He wanted her. God, he wanted her. "I want to make you happy, little one," he breathed against her mouth. "I'll try not to hurt you. Open your legs, sweetheart."

The fierce need Matt felt for his innocent wife was unexpected. He'd always wanted her, but not with this driving compulsion of a madman. His face was rigid with desire, his eyes glazed with lust. It was difficult to think let alone pace himself until he had prepared her to accept him without unnecessary pain.

"Why do you want me when you've been bedding that brunette?" Matt looked puzzled and Lily added, "You know, the one who enjoys ogling you." The moment they were out of her mouth Lily wished she could have called the words back.

Matt stiffened with anger. "Damnation, Lily, can't you tell I've not had another woman in longer than I care to remember? Can't you feel how much I want you?" He pressed his erection against her.

Lily bit her lip. Truth to tell she had no idea what Matt was talking about. Unless he was referring to that part of him that had grown so large and formidable she knew it would kill her if he put it inside her. Then she felt his hand slipping between her legs, seeking and finding the tiny hidden button nestled below her belly. Lily jerked in response when he began a gentle massage with the soft pads of his fingertips. She squirmed and writhed but could not escape his arousing fingers. She tried to rise but he forced her back on the bed.

He kissed her mouth, hard, then moved to her throat, her neck, the cleavage between her breasts. With his tongue and teeth he teased the tips of her breasts, alternately sucking and biting until Lily cried out. Waves of scorching heat coursed through Lily's veins, and she was shocked by the intensity of her response to something she had hoped to avoid. She tried desperately to hate every minute she was forced to endure the arousing things Matt was doing to her but failed miserably.

A piece of paper bound them together but she'd never intended to submit to his lust. How could she ever forget Matt had married her for her fortune? How could she even consider being used as a convenience and a vessel for his lust when not one word of love was ever exchanged between them? How could she think when her body burned from his outrageous caresses and her lips tingled from his drugging kisses?

"Please stop! I don't want this. I don't want you," Lily cried, fearing he would steal her sanity if she allowed him to continue.

"I can't stop now, little one." Matt panted raggedly. "Open wider."

For a brief, wild moment, Lily resisted with a renewed surge of vigor, but quickly realized the futility of her actions. Matt was bigger, stronger, and obviously set on consummating their marriage. Her legs parted.

"Good girl. You're not ready yet but soon— soon ..."

His fingers grew bolder, slipping along her moist crevice to slide full and deep inside her. He felt the taut barrier of her maidenhead and retreated slightly, wetting his dry lips with the tip of his tongue as incredible excitement spurred him on. With slow deliberation he worked in another finger, stretching her, pleased to find her growing moist beneath his gentle probing. While his fingers moved inside her in a most provocative manner, Lily moaned, tossing her head from side to side.

"That's it, sweetheart, you're doing everything just perfect. You're almost ready. Someday you'll beg me to do this to you."

"Never!" Lily denied hotly.

Then her thoughts scattered as Matt withdrew his hand and settled between her parted thighs. "The first time will hurt but I'll try to make it as painless as possible."

"Just get it over with," Lily grit out from between clenched teeth.

He positioned the smooth tip of his shaft against her. Lily held her breath, waiting. But instead of shoving himself inside her like she expected, causing a painful rending, he paused just beyond the opening, teasing her with gentle, upward strokes. But still he restrained himself as he continued to arouse her, licking her nipples, fondling her hips, stomach and buttocks with long tan fingers. His sensual assault left Lily breathless, and Matt was fully aware of the subtle change in her. When his hand drifted between them again and located that tender bud he had discovered earlier, Lily stiffened, her body drawn taut as a bowstring.

Forgetting her anger, her sense of betrayal, she moved against his fingers. She was panting now, seeking to alleviate the terrible need building inside her. Her passion both surprised and pleased Matt. With a start he realized she was on the verge of climax and he reacted with infallible instinct.

Lily felt him pressing inside her and waited for the pain. He was so big, so hard, so damn infuriatingly virile! She felt herself widen to accommodate him. Unconsciously Lily shifted her hips in order to make herself more easily accessible, and Matt chose that moment to lunge sharply forward. The thin membrane guarding her virginity held for a moment then tore beneath the force of his thrust. A scream ripped from Lily's throat.

"Don't move!" It was an order Matt tried to obey himself as he drew in great shuddering breaths.

"Stop! You're hurting me," Lily sobbed.

"Try to relax, the pain won't last long."

He drew back, nearly withdrawing, then thrust his full length into her. "I'm all the way in!" he exulted. "I've never felt anything so incredibly wonderful." His big hands tilted her hips and he slid deeper . . . deeper still.

Lily felt herself stretching, felt the pain and rawness, and wondered if it would ever stop hurting. Matt rocked gently, teaching her the rhythm, clutching her buttocks to move her back and forth to meet his thrusts. The subtle pressure of his hands and gentle words of encouragement brought her body to a pitch of response Lily would have never thought possible.

"Lock your legs around my hips," he instructed. Unconsciously she obeyed and he embedded himself even deeper. "Oh God!" It was a moan. It was a plea. It was sublime ecstasy.

Suddenly Lily felt his fingers coming between their bodies to find her and caress her. She pressed against him. He was filling her, thrusting, his fingers moving against her in a circular motion, and then reality ceased. Release shot through her in long shuddering spurts of molten fire.

Lily screamed.

Then his hands were gripping her hips and he thrust again and again inside her, spilling hot liquid in her womb. He grew motionless and rigid for long, breath-stopping moments.

Gradually the earth stopped spinning and Lily

glared up at Matt. He was grinning down at her with such an outrageous expression, Lily's temper exploded.

"What are you grinning at?'

"You, little one. I never expected such passion in that beautiful body. I might even enjoy being married to you."

"I'm going to hate it."

Chapter 6

Even at the edge of sleep Lily could sense Matt staring at her. He had peeled the sheet away from her sleeping form and rose on his elbows looking down on her, raking her lush curves with dark, glowing eyes. Lily flushed, realizing it was morning and she had slept in Matt's arms all night. She grasped the sheet, sliding it up to her chin.

"Must you stare at me? It—it's not decent."

Matt chuckled. The sound gave her little comfort. "I enjoy looking at you. I've been waiting for you to awaken." One large tanned hand moved possessively to her breast, one finger stroking her nipple which was clearly defined beneath the sheet.

Lily groaned. "Oh no, not again! Wasn't last night enough?"

Matt threw back his head and roared with laughter. "Your innocence never ceases to amaze me, little one. I could have taken you three times last night and still be ready to make love to you again this morning." Deliberately he tore the sheet from her fingers and flung it aside. Then he slowly slid his hand down over her stomach and between her legs, stroking gently. "Do you hurt?"

Lily blushed. Did all husbands and wives talk so openly about intimate things? she wondered curiously. Somehow she doubted it. "Of course I hurt,"

84

Lily said frankly. "You're much too big for me. I don't ever want to go through that again."

"I promise it will be better next time," Matt said in a soothing voice.

"There's not going to be a next time," Lily declared defiantly. "The marriage is consummated, there is no further need to keep up pretenses. Please take your hands off me."

Matt's face was like a thundercloud, dark and stormy. He had hoped that once he made love to Lily the terrible craving that gnawed at him would abate, but all it did was whet his appetite for more. Her passion had surprised and delighted him. Her money was still important to him but somehow during the past weeks Lily had gotten under his skin and refused to be dislodged. She had reduced him to someone he didn't recognize; a man whose manhood had failed him for the very first time since he had taken his first woman at the tender age of twelve. He didn't like it. And if he allowed Lily to dictate to him, there was no telling how far she would go.

"Of course there will be a next time, Lily. It arrived the moment I awoke. I'm not through with you yet. I hope you don't think I'm some young dolt so besotted with his bride that I'd let you make a fool of me. I want you. Now."

Lily's expression grew mutinous and her mouth clamped shut tightly. "I don't want you. I hate you. I hate what you did to me."

"You could have fooled me." Matt grinned wolfishly.

Lily thought his dark features reminded her of the devil luring souls to Hell. If she allowed him to make love to her again that's exactly where she would end up. In Hell.

"I could teach you many things about making love," Matt continued blithely as he moved his hand in a suggestive manner between her legs.

Lily's amber eyes brightened with a devilish gleam. "Perhaps," she mused thoughtfully. "I'm certain my future lovers would appreciate your lessons." Some perverse imp inside goaded her, knowing she was deliberately courting danger by provoking Matt.

Matt glared at her through narrowed eyes. "If you're trying to make me angry enough to leave your bed it won't work. And if you ever cuckold me you'll live to regret it. Now, my beautiful little witch, I'm going to love you again."

His hand rose higher between her legs as he stroked her with his fingers, inside and out. Lily gasped as her blood slowly heated and her body flushed with a pleasure she tried desperately to deny.

"Leave me alone, Matt, I don't want this."

"Your body tells me otherwise."

His fingers were thrusting deeper and Lily rotated her pelvis against his hand. The motion was barely perceptible but Matt, attuned to every nuance of lovemaking, perceived it and bit back a smile. His thumb found the tiny button nestled between her legs and rubbed it gently as his fingers thrust and withdrew. Lily groaned, no longer able to contain the jolts of raw fire surging through her veins. Adding to her woes, Matt took a nipple deep into his mouth and sucked greedily.

"You—you bastard!" Lily panted, using the word for the first time in her life. She had never felt the need before.

"So I've been told," Matt agreed blandly.

"Oh . . ."

"Ah, sweetheart, you do have a way of expressing yourself."

His voice was strangled, his erection throbbing as he saw Lily's face contort with the beginning of her climax. She looked so beautiful it nearly took his breath away. Abruptly he removed his hand and rubbed the tip of his thick sex against her swollen flesh. He thrust inside her and Lily exploded. He rode her fast, furious, his face contorted with the intensity of his own need. He arched his back, shooting his seed into her again and again. Then he dropped to lie drained and spent on top of her.

When he opened his eyes Lily was staring at him with an expression of pure loathing. Her face was pale, her eyes hostile yet curiously puzzled. As if she couldn't understand what had just taken place between them. Lifting himself off her, he fell to her side. He was exhausted yet more exhilarated than he had ever been in his life. Clarissa was good but she never made him feel like this.

Instantly Lily rolled away, presenting her back. She hated the way Matt's touch sensitized her body to every nuance of physical love. She loathed the way he made her blood sing and her flesh tingle. She despised his total disregard for her feelings. And he had done it without one single word of love!

Her voice was utterly devoid of warmth when she said, "This will never happen again. The next time you want your marital rights you'll have to force me." She meant every word.

"Are you suggesting I find my pleasure elsewhere?"

Lily bit her tongue to keep from screaming that he had already taken his pleasure. "Men like you have little difficulty finding their own pleasure."

"You're right," Matt said tightly. "I have little use for spoiled children. Give me a woman any day. You will have to beg me next time you want me in your bed."

It was a bitter cold day in January when the *Proud Lady* slipped into Boston Harbor. True to his word, Matt had taken special care never to be in their cabin at the same time as Lily. She had no idea where he slept but as long as it wasn't with her she didn't care. Or so she tried to tell herself. She tried not to think of all those wonderfully erotic things he did to her with his hands and mouth. Or the way his body rose so proudly and felt so splendid inside hers. If she hadn't experienced it herself she would have never thought it possible for his huge sex to fit so perfectly inside her. Nothing her schoolmates had told her in furtive whispers had prepared her for the real thing.

If only Matt loved her.

Young as she was Lily realized that lovemaking would be a thousand times more rewarding if love was involved. It wouldn't be difficult to love Matt, she reflected in a moment of rare insight. He was an overbearing, egotistical, arrogant swine, but Lily sensed redeeming qualities in him that would make it all worthwhile if he'd only learn to give and accept love. Not that she wanted to offer love, she snorted in disgust. Far be it from her to change the incorrigible devil. He wasn't worth the effort.

Lily was on deck to watch the docking. She joined the other passengers braving the weather to hug the rail as the ship slipped into the harbor. Though the cold was bone-chilling, the sun shone brightly on her first sighting of America.

"I suspect Sarah will be here to meet us."

Lily started, unaware that Matt had come up to join her. He looked terrible, as if he hadn't slept in several nights. Lily would have been shocked at how close to the truth she had come. Since Lily had banished him from her bed he had made do with the sofa in the saloon, seeking out its meager comfort long after all the passengers had sought their cabins and leaving before the crew arrived to prepare breakfast. Not only was the sofa uncomfortable but angry thoughts of Lily asleep in the comfortable bunk in their cabin kept him tossing and turning most of the night. Then the moment he did fall into an uneasy sleep the dreams began.

Her flesh was soft and fragrant beneath his hands and mouth. Her moans of pleasure drove him nearly wild to thrust into her. She fit him so tightly just thinking about her taut woman's flesh closing around him cost him his hard-won control. If not for his damnable pride he would have demanded his marital rights and the hell with Lily. But begging was not his style. Neither was rape. One day, he thought with grim satisfaction, Lily would beg him to make love to her.

"Sarah is your sister," Lily replied, suddenly alert. She had nearly forgotten that Matt had a sister the same age as herself. Suddenly she panicked at the thought of meeting a member of his family. "Do—do you think Sarah will like me?"

Something melted in Matt when he gazed at Lily's upturned face. He was aware of her fear and apprehension and tried to ease her worries, remembering that she had been uprooted from the land of her birth and brought to a strange country where she knew no one but him. "Sarah will love you."

Lily nodded solemnly and turned once more to the teeming city and busy docks stretching out before her. From her vantage point high above the street she saw the city of Boston rising on ground connected to the mainland by a narrow neck. The houses were constructed mostly of wood but there were some built of brick and stone. Lily noted that the town was surrounded by several hills.

"It's not London, but Boston is growing in leaps and bounds," Matt said with a hint of pride. "At last count the city had swelled to over twenty thousand souls. Not an inconsiderable number in this new country." Lily nodded, fascinated. "Over there," Matt pointed out eagerly, "is Beacon's Hill. That's where the State House is located. There's Cotton Hill." He gestured, sweeping his hand onward. "And there's Cobb's Hill. If you look closely you can just make out Hawkeshaven rising from its crest."

Hawkeshaven! Her new home. Straining her eyes, Lily could make out nothing but the indistinct outline of the imposing brick mansion. Then the gangplank was run out and conversation came to a halt as Matt guided her down the ramp onto the dock.

"There's Sarah!" Matt whooped, taking Lily's hand and pulling her toward an elegant black coach parked at the edge of the quay.

Lily hung back as a tall, slim girl with deep mahogany hair flying in the wind jumped from the coach and rushed into Matt's outstretched arms.

"Oh, Matt, how I missed you!" Sarah squealed, hugging her brother with the exuberance of a young puppy.

Matt's black eyes overflowed with love and absently Lily wondered what it would feel like to have Matt look at her like that. The thought was so ludicrous it didn't bear thinking about.

"Don't tell me your fiancé hasn't kept you busy in my absence?" teased Matt fondly. "Truth to tell, you little imp, I missed you too."

Lily felt like an intruder as brother and sister continued their tender greeting. She glanced away for a moment, not wishing to invade their privacy. That's when she saw the beautiful brunette whom she had seen in Matt's arms aboard ship. She was standing a few feet away, her narrowed eyes taking in the scene with unfeigned interest. For a brief moment Lily thought the woman was going to approach them, but at the last minute she turned away, walking briskly in the opposite direction. But not before spearing Lily with a look of such utter malice Lily recoiled as if from a blow.

Suddenly Sarah noticed Lily standing alone, looking forlorn and lost. She pulled out of Matt's embrace, slanted him an exasperated look and said, "Don't be rude, Matt, introduce me to your ... friend."

Not until Sarah turned and smiled at Lily did Lily get her first good look at Matt's sister. Sarah shared the same bold handsomeness with her brother, softened by feminine traits and characteristics. Though her hair was a deep burnished mahogany, her eyes were the same blue-black velvet fringed by incredibly long lashes. Even though she was several inches taller than Lily, Sarah's head came only to her brother's broad shoulders. Her figure was outstanding, gently curved with generous bust and long slim legs.

Sarah looked curiously from Matt to Lily, bewildered by what she saw. Had Matt found a new mistress? she wondered. Sarah found it difficult to believe that a woman so young and apparently innocent would attract her roguish brother. Matt's taste usually ran to older, more experienced women, like that dreadful Clarissa Hartley. Sarah had known about Clarissa and the almost possessive hold she had on Matt these past five years and silently applauded any woman who could take Matt away from his manipulative mistress.

Matt grinned, genuinely amused at Sarah's assumption. So attuned was he to his sister's inner thoughts he could read her mind. "I'm sorry I had no time to write, Sarah, and I know this will come as a shock, but I married while in England. This is my wife, Lily. Lily, greet my sister, Sarah. Sarah is my only living relative in America."

Sarah gasped. She'd had no idea that Matt's hasty trip to England would yield him a wife. She was not aware of Matt's search for a wealthy wife for he had deliberately kept her in the dark, unwilling to show his beloved sister a side of him she didn't know existed. Sarah knew he was a rogue but he couldn't bear for her to think of him as a mercenary bastard.

And that's exactly what she would think if she knew he had married Lily for her fortune.

"Your wife! That is shocking news! I thought you went to England to find backing for your shipping venture."

Lily shrank inwardly, thinking Sarah resented her. She had so wanted to be friends with Matt's sister. She had no one in America and desperately longed for someone to confide in. Immediately Sarah noted Lily's withdrawal and hastened to make amends.

"Oh, Lily, do forgive me. I meant no offense. It's just that my oaf of a brother takes such delight in surprising me. There is nothing I'd like better than to see my unprincipled brother happily married and settled. But you're so young . . . I had thought . . . but never mind." She smiled affectionately. "I can see now you are perfect for Matt. Welcome to Boston."

Lily accepted Sarah's exuberant hug with a shy smile. "Thank you, Sarah, I will enjoy having you for a sister. I'm certain I won't be lonely with you at Hawkeshaven."

"Lonely?" Sarah scoffed with an impish twinkle. "How could a lovely new bride like you suffer from loneliness—unless . . ." She gave Matt an austere glance. "Unless my brother has been neglecting you. Perhaps I should have a long talk with him. If he is remiss in his duty it is because marriage is so foreign to him. I'm certain he will improve with time."

Crimson stained Lily's cheeks and she was saved from replying when Matt conveniently chose that moment to intervene. "Come along, ladies, you can continue this conversation inside the coach where it is warmer. You're both shivering, and I am most anxious to show Lily her new home." Lily looked at him gratefully.

Enthralled, Lily watched out the window as the carriage wended its way through the sprawling city and up Cobb's Hill to Hawkeshaven. Sarah kept up a lively chatter the whole time, pointing out places of interest along the way. When the full grandeur of Hawkeshaven came into view Lily crowed with delight.

"It's magnificent," she breathed, immediately falling in love with Matt's home. "You never said it was so grand."

"Not as grand as your London town house," returned Matt dryly, "but quite adequate."

"More than adequate," insisted Lily. Her eyes glinted with excitement as the coach rolled up to a stop before the imposing mansion.

Hawkeshaven sat atop Cobb's Hill like a stately queen perched on a throne. Constructed entirely of brick, it rose tall and majestic into the sky. All three stories. The double front doors were nearly six feet wide, ornately carved and very tall. There seemed to be an overabundance of long, narrow windows.

The front doors swung open immediately and a servant stepped forward. He was tall and gaunt, dressed in austere black as befitted a proper butler, and his bald head was fringed in dark hair liberally sprinkled with white. Lily thought his twinkling blue eyes relieved the haughty decorum he projected and lent him a more human quality.

"Welcome home, sir," he intoned as the trio passed beneath the portals.

"Joseph," Matt said, greeting him affectionately. "By God, it's good to be home!"

Just inside the enormous entry a number of servants had lined up to welcome their employer. Lily hung back as Matt greeted each by name. Obviously the man wasn't all bad, Lily reflected grudgingly, for the servants seemed to fawn over him. Suddenly she felt herself being pushed forward.

"I'm glad you are all assembled here today," Matt said, smiling at Lily in a way that made her nervous. "I have an announcement to make. I brought a wife home from England. I want you all to greet your new mistress and make her welcome. Henceforth she will make all the decisions concerning household matters. Obey her in all things." Matt's words brought a flush to Lily's cheeks. Since they were not the normal married couple she had expected him to more or less set her adrift in his household with nothing to occupy her time.

Lily was greeted by everyone, from Mrs. Geary, the housekeeper, to the maids, the cook and the lesser servants who served as kitchen helpers. When the introductions were completed, Matt said, "Mary is Sarah's personal maid but you may have Jenny if you like."

Jenny was a pert young Irish lass with brash red hair stuffed demurely beneath a white mop cap and brilliant blue eyes. Lily liked her immediately. "Jenny will suit me fine," she told Matt.

"Come along, Lily, I'll show you our rooms." Grasping her arm in a possessive manner, Matt led her toward a wide, curved stairway rising from the right of the entrance.

Lily had little time in which to admire the gleaming wood of the highly polished stairs and banister, the crystal chandeliers, or the rich Aubusson carpet underfoot as Matt propelled her up the stairs and down an incredibly long hallway.

"These are Sarah's rooms," he said, pointing off to the right. "She has a bedroom and sitting room. The suite at the end of the hall contains our chambers. They consist of adjoining bedrooms with dressing rooms and separate sitting rooms. I think you'll find them quite adequate."

Adequate was hardly the word Lily would use to describe her rooms. *Elegant, enormous, beautiful,* would be more fitting. Decorated in shades of blue and gold, the furniture was of dainty French design. The walls were papered with a blue floral material repeated in the chairs and lounge. Gold brocade drapes hung at the two long windows. The roomy dressing room featured a large brass tub for bathing. Each room boasted a fireplace, even the dressing-bathing room. Matt threw open a door leading from the dressing room to reveal another bedroom similar to hers but definitely more masculine, decorated in earth tones.

"My bedroom," he said, slanting her an eloquent glance. "There is no key so don't bother to ask for one."

Flustered, Lily turned away. Did Matt intend to make use of the door? she wondered. "My rooms are lovely, Matt," she said, choosing to ignore his words as she turned her back on his mocking smile. "I hadn't expected such grandeur."

"Did you think we lived like savages in America?" he asked, vastly amused. "My father built Hawkeshaven with his inheritance, modeling it after the Hawke estate in England. I'm not quite as destitute as you thought. The problem is that most of my available funds are invested in my ships. And the English have taken a heavy toll on shipping recently. There is always Sarah's dowry but I'd not have her go to her husband a pauper."

A short time later Matt left Lily to her unpacking. Jenny arrived to help put her clothes away in the huge wardrobes lining the wall and when the maid shyly suggested a bath, Lily eagerly agreed. A bath and short nap before dinner sounded wonderful.

Lily sank gratefully into the steaming tub of water. She spent several blissful minutes just soaking before taking up soap and cloth and scrubbing her skin until it glowed a healthy pink. Casting a fearful glance at the connecting door, she wondered if she had time to wash her hair, fearing that Matt might walk in on her if she lingered overlong. Throwing caution to the wind, she ducked her head beneath the water then worked up a rich lather. When soap dripped into her eyes, she squeezed them tightly shut then continued to lather and rinse her hair.

Matt stood poised in the doorway, his hand on the knob of the door connecting their chambers. He had forgotten to tell Lily what time to come down to dinner and had entered her rooms to correct the oversight. He wasn't prepared for the sight of Lily enticingly displayed in her bath. His body reacted violently. She was even lovelier than he remembered.

Long coppery tresses swirled in wild disarray about delicate pink shoulders and lay limp and wet against the most perfect breasts Matt had ever had the privilege of viewing. Her eyes were closed as she rinsed the last vestiges of soap from her hair. Her arms were raised, offering her breasts to his hungry gaze. The rapidly chilling water brought her nipples to full, flowering erection. His eyes slid lower, below the waterline, where thick down the color of rust concealed the pink folds of her womanhood. His gaze traveled downward along slim tapered legs then swept upward again to focus on that spot that had given him so much pleasure. Matt's rampant manhood leaped in remembrance.

His sanity skidded out of control when he recalled how wonderful it felt to slide full and deep inside her, how magnificently she closed around him, so tight, so hot ... so damn good. How surprised and pleased he had been with her response to his touch. His sensual musings jolted his sex to full arousal and a low moan rumbled from his throat.

Lily froze, fearing to open her eyes, hoping she was mistaken. But there was no mistaking that sound. Her worst fears had come to pass. Every sensitive pore in her body felt his magnetic presence. It was just like Matt to boldly walk into her room at a time when she was most vulnerable. She knew if she opened her eyes she'd find him staring at her, his eyes dark with hunger.

Lily's temper flared, ready to vent her spleen at Matt for his appalling lack of manners. With amazing fortitude she opened her eyes and glared at him balefully. He was leaning against the doorjamb, arms crossed, legs spread apart. His eyes were hooded and lazy, his face unreadable as he raked her nude body from head to toe. Lily's hands flew to her breasts in a purely reflexive gesture. When his eyes slid downward, her hands followed the direction of his gaze, protecting her woman's mound from his penetrating perusal.

"Get out of here, Matthew Hawke!"

"This is my house, Lily Hawke, and you are my wife. I go where I please, do what I please."

"Not with me," she denied defiantly.

His eyes flickered in amusement. "I've seen you naked before, sweetheart. Don't mind me, continue with your bath."

"I—I'm finished," Lily contended. "Please leave so I can dress."

"Modesty doesn't become you. I've seen you flushed with passion and writhing with pleasure."

Lily's cheeks burned. Her wanton behavior was simply too embarrassing to think about, but it was all too true. Matt was an expert lover who could make her body react in ways totally foreign to her. She hated what he did to her and detested the way he made her feel, she tried to tell herself. His dark, penetrating gaze sent her on a giddy ride to oblivion and she refused to allow a repeat of her humiliating performance aboard ship on the night he made her his wife.

"Get out of the tub, Lily." He strode into the room and handed her the towel.

Lily's eyes blazed. "Not until you leave." Dear

God, when he looked at her like that she felt herself go all hot and liquid inside. She hated the feeling.

When he reached out for her, Lily jumped from the tub of her own volition, afraid to have him touch her, knowing full well where it would lead. She stood poised on the balls of her feet, panting, wondering what he would do next. Glistening drops of water slid down her slick body, swept over her breasts and hips. Matt's rough command disabused her of any notion she might have of escaping his attention.

"Get into bed."

"Like hell I will!"

She turned to flee into the bedroom, intending to slam the door in his face. But Matt was too fast for her. She was swept off her feet and into his arms before she had taken two steps. Then she was carried into the bedroom and slammed down on the bed with such force the air left her lungs.

"Why are you tormenting me?" Lily gasped once she found her breath.

"You don't know what torment is, sweetheart," Matt said dryly, "but if I have my way you'll soon find out." Then he lay on top of her.

"Matt, you promised you wouldn't do this again," cried Lily, grasping at straws. If she gave into him again her pride would suffer irreparable damage. Sex without love was like selling her body. And Matt didn't know the difference between lust and love. "You said I'd—I'd have to beg you if I wanted you to bed me. I definitely am not begging you."

"I lied." Matt panted, desperate to love Lily again. They had been married for weeks and one night with her had only whetted his appetite for his young wife.

Before Lily could upbraid him his mouth bore down on hers, his kiss fierce, hungry, demanding. She began to beat his back and shoulders in vigorous protest, but Matt felt nothing except the fire raging in his blood and the clamor of his heart pounding in furious rhythm against the hard wall of his chest. He wanted Lily so fiercely he felt that he must have her or die.

"God, I'd forgotten how soft you are." Matt sighed against her mouth.

His fingers stroked the curve of one breast, taking the nipple and rolling it gently between thumb and forefinger. Somehow it no longer mattered that Lily had not begged him to make love to her, or that his resolve had crumbled and he was doing exactly what he said he'd never do. All that seemed to matter was that Lily was spread naked beneath him and he needed her with a desperate, gnawing desire that transcended his deepest yearning.

He shifted slightly and slid his pants over his hips, kicking them off with a minimum of effort. His shirt went next. He was already barefoot since he had been in his bedroom dressing before he entered Lily's room. Lily gasped when his manhood prodded her stomach. It was glistening and throbbing, so huge she cringed in fright. How had she ever endured being impaled by so fearful a monster?

Then he was kissing her again, her mouth, her throat, nibbling on her breasts, taking a nipple into his mouth and tonguing it into erection. She felt her insides contract when he slid downward, his moist tongue leaving a trail of raw fire in its wake. He dipped his head into the soft furry triangle between her thighs. Lily stiffened, her face suffused with liquid heat as his tongue probed gently into the swollen flesh of her secret place.

"Matt! No! For God's sake, what are you doing?" She tried to shove him away but he was implacable.

"I'm going to love you, Lily." Matt panted raggedly. "There are many ways to love a woman and this is but one of them."

Intrigued, Lily asked, "How is that possible?"

"Open your legs, sweetheart, and I'll show you."

Chapter 7

Lily was sorely tempted to spread her legs and let him have his way, but to do so would relinquish her very soul. "No, Matt, I don't want your lessons." She squeezed her thighs tightly together.

"Relax, sweetheart, you're going to enjoy this." His face was fierce as he pried her legs apart and lowered his head.

"Oh God, Matt, no, you wouldn't! You can't!"

He could and he did.

Lily felt the moist warmth of his mouth close around her, his tongue probing relentlessly, and she stiffened, the feeling so wonderfully arousing it angered her to think he could make her body respond to his touch despite her resolve to resist.

She hated it.

She loved it.

She wanted to die.

Lily writhed, all her senses concentrating on that tender place where his mouth teased and his tongue probed. The feeling was sublime agony. She wanted Matt to stop. Now. "Please, Matt, don't do this to me!"

Matt raised his head, a wicked smile curving his full lips. "Do you want me to stop, sweetheart?" As he spoke his fingers replaced his mouth, sliding inside her to continue his torment. "Tell me what you want."

"I want . . ." His thumb found the tiny bud of her womanhood, rubbing it gently.

"What? What do you want?"

"I want . . . oh God! I can't think!"

"You'll have to tell me what you want." Then his mouth returned to his succulent feast, sending her deep—deeper into the throes of sexual excitement so profound it drove her to desperation.

Matt held on to his control with admirable restraint. Lily never guessed what a torment it was not to come into her and spew his seed until he had no more to give.

"Matt, please, I—I want you—to—to love me!" The words were torn from her throat, half plea, half denial. Uttering them was the hardest thing she had ever done. She hated Matt for reducing her to a begging, raving wanton, and hated herself more for falling victim to his seduction.

Lily's words were music to Matt's ears. "I thought you'd never ask, sweetheart."

Then she felt herself stretching and filling with his incredible length and all thought ceased as he thrust inside her again and again. Lily erupted and cried out, bringing Matt's own climax to its culmination. When both lay quiet and sated, Matt rose on his elbows and kissed her. Her mouth had been dry until he filled it with his wet tongue, and then it was moist and flooded with the taste of him. Lily wanted to bite down on it but wisely refrained. She didn't know Matt well enough to gauge his reaction to so bold a measure. Instead she lay like a lump of lead beneath him, neither returning the kiss nor responding in any manner to the pressure of his body. It was enough that she had begged him to make love to her when she swore she would never do such a thing. Tears of frustration and shame flooded her eyes when she thought of how he had cleverly manipulated her body and made her want him.

Matt felt the moisture on her face and raised himself off her, lying down beside her. His forehead wore a puzzled frown as he brushed a glistening drop from her cheek. "Did I hurt you?"

"Yes," Lily said, dragging in a trembling sigh.

"How?"

"By deliberately disregarding my wishes."

Matt's lips grew taut. "I thought you enjoyed what I did to you. You begged me to love you."

"My response only proves you're a master at seduction and I'm too inexperienced to resist. Why can't you understand I'd rather this marriage continue without entanglements? I don't enjoy being used. Sex without love is a cold affair I don't wish to indulge in."

"Is that what this is all about?" His upper lip curled in wry amusement. "Love, if it exists, is merely another word for lust. It's an emotion that's much exaggerated, one that few people ever experience but many use indiscriminately. Would you have me lie to you?"

"I want to be loved," Lily said wistfully.

"I love your body," Matt allowed. "I love the way you look and the way your body responds to my touch. I love how you feel beneath my hands and mouth. I love thrusting into you and feeling you close around me—so tight, so hot. I love—"

"Stop!" Lily cried, clapping her hands over her ears. "I don't want to hear any more. It's not enough." Her next words were so low Matt had to bend to hear them. "You could at least have tried."

"Why can't you be happy with what we have?"

"Because we have nothing."

"You have a home of your own to do with as you please."

"And you have my money. Get out of here, Matt,

I think we understand one another perfectly. I may be young but I'm old enough to know you're a mercenary bastard who wouldn't know love if it was staring you in the face. Just because I was forced into a loveless marriage doesn't mean I'm willing to let you use my body."

Matt rose stiffly to his feet, his body so splendid in its nudity Lily felt compelled to turn her eyes away. Why did he have to be so damn—so damn—male! He stared down at her dispassionately, his eyes cold and hard. Damn exasperating female, he thought with a snort of disgust. Leave it to a woman to lie about something she so obviously wanted and enjoyed. Who needed the contrary critters?

"If that's how you feel then far be it from me to intrude where I'm not wanted," he said with cool deliberation. "Besides, I'll be far too busy in the weeks to come to pander to your childish moods."

Without bothering to dress, he picked up his discarded clothing and strode quickly through the dressing room and into his own chambers. Mesmerized, Lily watched the taut mounds of his buttocks flex and unflex as his long, muscular legs carried him from the room. Good riddance, she thought as she reluctantly tore her eyes away from Matt's splendid backside. How much less complicated her life would be, she reflected, without Matt distracting her with his magnificent lovemaking.

Lily was truly a vision when she joined Matt and Sarah for dinner that night. Her father hadn't stinted on her clothes and the cobalt blue dress she wore enhanced her delicate apricot complexion and flaming hair. Jenny proved a competent, if not inventive, hairdresser and had done wonders with Lily's unruly mass of ringlets. Lily moved with unconscious grace as she entered the room, as if totally unaware of her potent appeal and feminine attributes.

Though not lacking in beauty herself, Sarah thought Lily the loveliest creature she had ever seen and considered Matt lucky to have found such an extraordinary wife. Sarah had been told very little about Lily except that she was high-born and extremely wealthy. Though Matt was politely attentive to his wife, Sarah was astute enough to know all was not as it should be between the newlyweds. As the meal progressed it became increasingly evident that Matt and Lily had been feuding earlier. Sarah felt certain her beloved Jeff, the man she was to marry, would not treat her so coldly after so short a honeymoon. Somewhat of a romantic, Sarah searched Matt's and Lily's faces for the starry-eyed expression, the tender lingering looks, the soft touches that bespoke love.

And found them lacking.

No, not lacking, entirely absent.

True, she did detect a certain gleam in Matt's eyes whenever they happened to stray to his lovely bride. Was there a hint of yearning in their dark depths? she wondered hopefully. It was Lily's behavior that truly puzzled Sarah. Lily ignored Matt completely while chattering incessantly about trivial things. Sarah wondered if the reserve she detected between the newlyweds had anything to do with Clarissa. Everyone in Boston was aware of Matt's long-standing affair with the actress. Had Lily somehow learned about it?

Sarah had hoped Matt's marriage would put an end once and for all to his alliance with Clarissa. She would personally strangle her brother if he hurt or humiliated his young bride by deliberately flaunting his mistress.

The meal ended abruptly when Matt slammed down his napkin and excused himself, inventing some vague appointment in town. "Don't wait up for me," he advised Lily. "I probably will be very late."

"Matt, this is your first night home!" Sarah charged, aghast. Her brother's despicable behavior was unpardonable. "I'm sure Lily would welcome your company tonight."

Matt turned to Lily. "Is that true, Lily? Are you pining for my company tonight?" His voice was low and mocking.

Lily felt heat rush to her pale cheeks. She needed no coaching to interpret Matt's meaning. If she cited a preference for his company it was with the understanding that she was consenting to share his bed. Her wily husband had turned the tables on her. If she said yes she would undoubtedly be used again to slake Matt's lust, and if she said no Sarah would surely draw the conclusion that she was a cold woman who would rather be spared her husband's attentions. Her wayward body leaped in anticipation, recalling the way he'd made her feel this afternoon. Yet her mind totally rejected him. After long moments of warring between pride and desire, pride won a difficult battle.

"If Matt's business is important I wouldn't want to inconvenience him," Lily said slowly. She was careful not to look Sarah in the eye. "I'm rather fatigued from the voyage and—and would prefer being alone tonight."

Sarah's startled glance betrayed her thoughts. That didn't sound like an answer from a woman in love. If Lily didn't love Matt why had she married him? she wondered curiously. Did Lily not enjoy Matt's attentions? Sarah knew many women who would envy her position as wife to Matthew Hawke. It was extremely difficult for Sarah to grasp the fact that Lily didn't relish Matt's company. And even more difficult to believe Matt would desert his new bride on their first evening home. The situation was strange and unsettling to Sarah, whose love for Jeffrey Hunter was steadfast and loyal.

Lily escaped to her room as quickly as possible, unwilling to linger and answer Sarah's probing questions. She could tell Sarah was puzzled by Matt's and her behavior toward one another but felt incapable of offering lengthy explanations at this time. Lily felt certain Matt had hurried off to a rendezvous with his beautiful brunette mistress and wondered if Sarah knew about the woman. Pride forbade her from asking.

Lily spent a sleepless night visualizing Matt and his mistress happily engaged in long hours of erotic sex. She was wide awake when Matt returned to his rooms in the early hours of the morning, listening intently as his footsteps approached the connecting door, paused, then retreated after a few tense moments. She hadn't realized she was holding her breath until she began to grow dizzy.

During the cold dreary weeks of winter Lily acquainted herself with her new home. She loved everything about Hawkeshaven, including the lovely formal gardens, which contained many varieties of evergreen trees and shrubs, and stables stocked with purebred horses. The large kitchen was exceptionally well maintained and the entire household was run with impeccable precision. Lily soon learned that Mrs. Geary was an accomplished housekeeper, leaving little for her to do except go over the menus and handle the few disputes involving the help. Lily spent most of her days with Sarah, visiting, riding and shopping. It was a pleasant life, due mostly to Sarah, who kept boredom at bay. As for Matt, he was as scarce as hen's teeth.

Lily saw him briefly in passing. He rose early in the morning and left before she came down to breakfast. He was absent at lunch and present only occasionally at dinner. True to his word, he had not entered her rooms since the day they arrived at Hawkeshaven. Sarah did her best to excuse her brother's unpardonable behavior, repeating his words that he was consumed day and night with re-fitting and arming his ships as privateers. He wanted all three ready to launch by spring.

Shortly after her arrival in Boston Lily met Sarah's fiancé, Jeff Hunter, a promising young lawyer. He proved to be a friendly young man whose deep love for Sarah was enough to endear him to Lily. Jeff was of medium height with thick, sandy hair, his features pleasant rather than handsome. But his sunny dispo-sition and obvious devotion to Sarah more than made up for his lack of looks. Sarah adored him.

Lily found it difficult to hide the eroding situation between her and Matt from perceptive Sarah. Besides the appalling lack of communication between the newlyweds, the outright hostility between them was palpable. The very air crackled around them when they happened to be in the same place at the same time. The tension, the silent messages, were so nerve-racking Sarah usually found an excuse to leave the room. The situation grew so desperate Sarah decided to broach the subject to Lily one pleasant winter day while they were out riding.

Braving Lily's anger, Sarah asked, "Are you happy here, Lily?" They had both dismounted and were resting beneath a giant oak beside a partially frozen brook. "Is Boston all you hoped it would be?" What she really wanted to ask was if Lily was happy with Matt.

"Matt told me so little about Boston and Hawkeshaven I really didn't know what to expect. We hardly knew one another when we married."

"I hope my brother's behavior hasn't soured you on America."

"Hawkeshaven is beautiful and so is Boston. It's very provincial compared to London but I find I don't miss the hustle and bustle of a large city. I'm most grateful for you, Sarah, for the way you've made me welcome here."

"You know I'll be leaving, Lily. Jeff and I intend to marry within the coming year. Jeff's practice isn't exactly flourishing but neither of us wishes to delay our marriage too long. We love each other too much."

"You're not going far, Sarah. I'll still be able to see you often."

"As often as you like, dear. My home will always be open to you. We've grown close these past weeks."

They sat in companionable silence for several minutes before Sarah cleared her throat and said, "I don't mean to pry, Lily, but I know things aren't what they should be between you and my brother. Is there anything I can do to help? I know Matt is terribly busy these days but perhaps he doesn't realize how shamefully he is neglecting you."

Lily sighed deeply. She wanted to confide in someone but didn't know if Sarah was the right person. Unconsciously she sighed again.

Mistaking Lily's pensive sighs for reluctance to discuss her problems, Sarah was quick to add, "If it's too painful to discuss, I'll understand. I thought perhaps Clarissa—" Abruptly Sarah realized what she had just said and clamped her lips tightly together. Lily picked up on the slip immediately.

"Clarissa!" she cried, instantly putting the name and face together until they meshed into the dark, curvaceous brunette who had sailed aboard the *Proud Lady* and captured Matt's attention so thoroughly. She had suspected from the beginning that Matt knew the woman, and that they were more than mere acquaintances, but this was the first time she had heard her name openly spoken. "So that's her name. Somehow it fits."

Sarah was flabbergasted. "You know about

Clarissa? I'd like to wring Matt's neck. I'm sorry, Lily, my brother can be an insensitive bastard at times."

"I not only know about Clarissa, I've seen her. Once in England and again board ship. I—I'm certain she and Matt shared a bed aboard the *Proud Lady* since it wasn't my bed he sought at night."

"Oh, God, Lily, I didn't know. I thought I knew Matt but now I'm not so certain. How could he treat you so heartlessly? Why did he marry you if he intended to go on seeing Clarissa? He could just as easily have remained single. I had so hoped he had found the great love of his life in you."

Lily laughed bitterly, a sound strangely at odds with her youth. "I'm rich, Sarah. Matt needed my fortune."

"You didn't have to marry him, Lily. Unless ... you love him!" Sarah clapped, brightening. "All is not lost if you love Matt. How could he not help but love you back?"

"I hate Matt," Lily said with such vehemence Sarah was momentarily stunned. "I would never have married him if he and Father hadn't decided for me. Father wanted to be rid of me in order to placate his new wife and Matt was eager to wed an heiress. Matt regards love as a silly emotion that has no place in his life."

Sarah was astounded. "Aren't you being a little harsh, Lily? You're awfully young to be so cynical."

"Is it cynical to want love, Sarah? You have it with Jeff, why shouldn't I have it? If not with Matt then with some other man who could love me for myself."

Sarah gulped silently. "Are you certain Matt married you for your money? Perhaps you're mistaken. The way he looks at you sometimes ..."

Lily bit her tongue to keep from screaming out that Matt was a rutting goat who enjoyed making love for the pleasure it gave him. And further refrained from saying he was so good at it he made it wonderful for her despite the fact neither of them loved the other.

Silently Sarah thanked God for Jeff, who would love her even if she were penniless. It was difficult to think of Matt as the cold, callous creature Lily had just described, and truth to tell Sarah wasn't entirely convinced Matt's marriage was merely one of convenience. She sensed a deep emotion that neither her brother nor Lily seemed aware of. "I think you are protesting too vigorously," she observed. "Hate and love are so closely linked it's often difficult to tell them apart. Especially in people with volatile dispositions."

Lily paused, digesting Sarah's thought-provoking notion. Her next words were so wistful they nearly broke Sarah's heart. "It would be so easy to love Matt." Her voice was soft and breathless. "If he showed by word or deed that he cared for me there might be a chance for this marriage. He may have my fortune to use as he sees fit but he'll not use my body to prove his masculinity. I'm sure you know by now we don't share a bed."

"I'm truly sorry, Lily, I wish I could help."

They fell silent, and shortly afterward returned home. Sarah was painfully aware of this new facet to Matt's character that she had never seen before, and of Lily's unhappiness, but was powerless to help.

Spring brought a resurgence of speculation concerning war between England and America. The only question remaining was when hostilities would begin. More American ships were being stopped on the high seas by the British navy and seamen and goods removed or confiscated. Action along the frontier between Canada and the northwestern United States intensified since the Indians were being supplied with arms and ammunition by the English. President Madison had just revived the nonintercourse act against Great Britain, and the War Hawks, as the newly elected western and southern congressmen were now called, urged for war, citing humiliation and economic injuries by Great Britain as just cause.

Matt, now totally involved with his ships and working at a furious pace, came and went at odd hours and was rarely visible at Hawkeshaven. One evening Jeff Hunter brought his business partner to dinner. Matt's absence was neither noted nor remarked upon.

Clay Winslow was a southern gentleman born in Virginia but more interested in reading law than farming. He was gallant, polite, charming, and extremely handsome, and Lily learned that the young lawyer handled all of Matt's business affairs.

From their first meeting it was abundantly clear that Clay was smitten with Lily. His usually glib tongue was strangely thick and unable to articulate in Lily's presence. He thought her the most beautiful, delicate and wonderful creature he had ever had the pleasure of meeting. To Jeff, he waxed poetic over the glorious color of Lily's long, wavy hair, her distinctive amber eyes, her apricot-tinted skin. Matt's deliberate neglect of his bride both angered and dismayed Clay. Especially because he assumed that Matt was still seeing Clarissa Hartley, his mistress before he married. He would have thought the affair between Matt and Clarissa had ceased with Matt's marriage to Lily. Though Clay had yet to see Matt and Clarissa in public he could think of no other reason for Matt's blatant disregard for his bride.

Clay was livid. How could a man in his right mind prefer Clarissa's coarse charms to Lily's youth and beauty? There was no comparison between the overblown actress and Lily's refreshing charm. Since Lily seemed to enjoy Clay's company, Sarah saw no harm in inviting him often for dinner during the long winter months when Matt seemed too preoccupied to entertain his wife.

Spring arrived with a flourish, bringing an end to those long dreary days of snow, fog and slush. The scent of flowers filled the air and Hawkeshaven awoke from its long winter nap. By late May Clay had virtually become a part of the family, his appearance at dinner three times a week with Jeff a foregone conclusion. Lily realized Jeff was growing abnormally fond of her but since he acted the perfect gentleman in all instances she continued to encourage his visits, never dreaming he was falling deeply in love with her. She considered Clay a good friend and enjoyed his visits too much to consider him a threat to her marriage. Not that she had the kind of marriage that would suffer from Clay's constant companionship. On the contrary, she had no marriage at all. Matt ignored her so completely she could have done something outrageous and he wouldn't have cared. Yet not once did Lily consider being unfaithful to Matt. He could enjoy his mistress every night of the week but she'd not compromise her principles by taking a lover.

When war was declared on June 18, 1812, no one was surprised.

That evening when Clay came to dinner they spoke of nothing else but the war and what it meant to Boston residents. Lily realized Matt would be leaving soon and for reasons unknown to her the thought depressed her. When Clay suggested a walk in the garden Lily agreed with alacrity. A pleasant stroll was just what she needed for she hadn't been sleeping well lately. Her dreams had taken a turn that both frightened and dismayed her.

Matt.

Her dreams were always erotic. And always of Matt. His kisses turned her blood to liquid fire, his large tanned hands caressed her flesh with consummate skill. After he aroused her to heights she never knew existed, he thrust into her with the jolting urgency of a thunderbolt. He rode her fast, furious, rode her to the most perfect climax known to womankind. Then she awoke, drenched with sweat, her body arching, aching, unfilled.

Alone.

Strolling side by side, Lily thought nothing amiss when Clay casually curled one arm around her slim shoulders. They stopped at the crest of a low rise to gaze at the city and harbor spread out below them.

"Beautiful," Lily murmured, delighted by the sight of the full moon reflecting off the water.

"Not nearly as beautiful as you, Lily," Clay ventured, emboldened by the romantic setting. "I love you, Lily."

Suddenly Lily found herself in Clay's arms, being thoroughly kissed. In a brief instant of madness she responded to the young man's declaration of love. It had been far too long since a man had held her and she pretended it was Matt. But Matt would never say he loved her. She regained her sanity instantly, shoving Clay away.

"No, Clay, please don't. I'm a married woman. Find someone who is free to love you as you deserve."

"I don't want another woman. I want you. I fell in love with you the moment I saw you."

"You shouldn't say those things, Clay. I enjoy your company and I care for you as a friend, but that changes nothing. I'm still married to Matt."

"Why do you stay with that bastard, Lily? Everyone knows he has a mistress." Lily winced. "You have other alternatives."

Lily bit her lip to hold back the tears. Inadvertently Clay had confirmed what Lily suspected all along, that Matt was seeing Clarissa. A sob lodged in her throat, causing her to hiccup. Clay immediately looked contrite.

"Forgive me, Lily, I don't mean to be cruel. I wouldn't hurt you for the world but you're too intelligent to love a man who neglects you so shamefully."

His provoking words seemed to demand an answer. How did she really feel about Matt? She hated him, of course. She would have staked her life on it. Yet—if she was completely honest with herself she'd admit *hate* was too strong a word. Maybe it wasn't even an appropriate word. He was arrogant, overbearing, stubborn and exasperating. But she definitely wasn't indifferent to him. He roused too many conflicting emotions within her for her to remain unmoved by him. She shivered, recalling how he'd made her beg to be loved, how he'd brought her body to trembling ecstasy.

Damn him!

"Marriage is forever," Lily said slowly, at a loss to explain her feelings where Matt was concerned.

"It doesn't have to be," Clay contended. "I'm a lawyer, remember? Divorce isn't impossible."

"No, that's not the answer," Lily replied, shaking her head. "Not yet, anyway."

"I'll wait, Lily, no matter how long it takes. I'll admit I know nothing of the circumstances surrounding your marriage but I'll honor your decision even though I want to make love to you so desperately it's like a hunger inside me."

Clay's bold declaration brought a flush to Lily's cheeks. "Please, Clay, you shouldn't say those things to me."

"It's no sin for a man to tell a woman he loves her. I love you, Lily, more than my own life."

With a will of their own his arms tightened around her, drawing her close. Then he shocked her by lowering his head and kissing her a second time. The kiss was so gentle, so fleeting it felt like the soft brushing of butterfly wings. The sweet taste of her mouth was more than Clay could bear. With a groan of surrender he crushed her against the hard wall of his chest. The result was Clay's instant and violent arousal. The moment Lily's softness molded intimately to his hardness he was lost.

Neither participant was aware of the dark, brooding figure watching from the concealing shadows of the house. Abruptly the figure whirled and disappeared inside, his expression forbidding, his dark eyes alive with rage.

Suddenly Clay realized he had committed an unpardonable sin. He was openly lusting for another man's wife. Not only that but he had insulted Lily by deliberately flaunting her wishes. He wouldn't hurt her for the world and reluctantly set her aside.

"I'm sorry, Lily, I don't know what got into me. I know you well enough to realize you're not the kind of woman to betray your husband no matter how badly he mistreats you. Just remember, I'll be here for you if you ever have need of me."

Tears blurred Lily's eyes. Why couldn't she have found a man like Clay to marry when she needed a husband? Intuitively she knew she would have had a good life with him. He might not possess Matt's excitement or his flare for life, but Clay was a good man. Too late, Lily lamented. Somehow Matt had spoiled her for other men. Every other man paled in comparison to Matt's vibrant personality, his blatant sexuality, his zest for life.

God, she hated him!

Or whatever one wanted to call that challenging emotion he instilled in her.

Chapter 8

The first thing Lily noticed when she entered her darkened room was the dancing fire newly lit in the hearth. The nights were still chilly and she welcomed the warmth after the stroll in the brisk air of the garden. She'd have to remember to thank Jenny for her thoughtfulness. Usually the maid was waiting for her when she retired for the night and Lily was puzzled by Jenny's absence.

"I dismissed Jenny for the night," informed a cool voice that floated to her from the darkened corner. Lily started violently when a tall, broad-shouldered form stepped out from the shadows.

"Matt!" she gasped, clutching at her throat. "You frightened me. What are you doing here?"

Matt's lips tightened, giving hint to the devils that drove him. "This is my house and you are my wife. I go where I please."

While he spoke he moved forward on the balls of his feet, his loose-limbed frame stopping mere inches from her. The unyielding, arrogant strength in his face, the repressed violence about him, caused Lily to lurch backward. A shot of raw fear jolted through her.

"Are you frightened of me, sweetheart?" His tone was hard and mocking.

"Should I be?" She gulped past the hard lump of

apprehension forming in her throat, refusing to back down from Matt's implacable anger, though she had no idea what she had done to anger him.

"It depends. Do you have reason to fear me? How far has the affair between you and Clay Winslow progressed? Has he bedded you yet? I didn't realize he was making himself indispensable to you while I was involved with other matters."

His contemptible accusations sparked Lily's temper. Overcoming her initial fear, she flung him a scathing retort. "Clay and I are friends. How dare you suggest there is anything illicit between us! If you had chosen to dine with us once in a while you'd know that Clay and Jeff are frequent visitors to Hawkeshaven. Clay is your lawyer, for God's sake! Don't you trust your own friends?"

"I don't trust anyone where you're concerned, Lily."

There was an edge of violence to his voice that stunned her. She'd had no idea he even cared what she did or with whom. But she should have known he'd jealously guard what he assumed was his whether or not he gave a fig about it. And obviously he considered her his exclusive property. He thought their marriage license gave him the right to dictate to her but she was no longer the naive child she had been when she married him.

"If Sarah has fostered this relationship then I've been remiss in my duty toward her."

"For God's sake, Matt, there is no relationship. Can't you understand an innocent friendship between a woman and a man?" Lily shrilled, choking with fury.

"I saw you and Clay in the garden this evening," Matt said tightly. An underlying threat lent menace to his words. "Don't lie to me. I returned home early for the express purpose of speaking with you in private and was shocked to find you in the arms of another man. Dammit, Lily! My eyes didn't deceive me. I *saw* you in Clay's arms. I *saw* him put his hands on you. I'll be damned if I'll stand by and let you freely give him what you deny your own husband. Has he whispered pretty words of love to you? Would I have seen you couple with him had I decided to linger?"

Lily's beautiful brow furrowed as she experienced a gamut of conflicting emotions. Outrage, fury, bitter regret, and others she couldn't even begin to identify. Fueled by Matt's obsessive jealousy, Lily felt the overwhelming compulsion to hurt him just as he had wounded her.

"Would you care if I took a lover? Why is it any different for a woman than for a man? I'm only following your example."

"What in the hell are you talking about?"

"Clarissa!" There, she'd said it. She was relieved it was out in the open. "Does the name ring a bell?"

Matt's shock was boundless. How in the hell had Lily found out about Clarissa? he wondered curiously. He hadn't seen the woman in weeks, hadn't even thought about her. "What has Sarah told you about Clarissa?"

"Sarah told me nothing," Lily insisted, "except for the name of that black-haired vixen who followed us aboard the *Proud Lady*. I knew she was your mistress before we reached Boston. I learned the hard way."

"I can't believe . . . if Clarrie said anything—"

"I saw you with my own eyes, Matt. I saw Clarissa in your arms. How could you? We were on our honeymoon."

"For your information I didn't bed Clarissa, although you gave me leave to do so. If you recall, you banished me from our cabin and refused me your bed. I had every right to seek solace elsewhere had I wanted to."

"Your sexual stamina is remarkable," Lily said with scathing sarcasm. "Did you go to Clarissa's bed after you spent the night in mine?" She didn't believe him for a minute. He had spent his nights somewhere aboard the *Proud Lady* and it certainly wasn't with her.

"Believe what you want, Lily, but I'm telling the truth. Clarissa was my mistress at one time but I haven't seen her in weeks. Is Clarissa the reason you've turned to Winslow?"

"Clay is a friend," Lily maintained stoutly. "Go to your whore, I don't need a man. In case you haven't noticed, Matt, I've grown up. I'm eighteen now and no longer look at the world through the eyes of an adolescent."

"You've had a birthday?" Matt asked, chagrined that his wife's birthday had come and gone without his knowing it. "Why didn't you tell me?"

"I rarely saw you."

"It was your choice, little one," he chided gently. "I realize I've been busy and preoccupied lately but you had only to ask for my attention."

"You left me little but my pride and I refuse to surrender the only thing remaining of myself."

"Pride is a terrible thing, Lily. It doesn't warm you at night or fill your empty body with contentment."

"It lets me sleep at night and it gives me comfort," Lily said with quiet dignity. Lies. Sleep didn't come easily at night and the only comfort came when she recalled how wonderfully Matt had made her feel when he made love to her. "How could I possibly be a wife to you when Clarissa still warms your bed?"

Matt gnashed his teeth in frustration. What must he do to convince the little vixen he wasn't involved with Clarissa? "I think there's another reason for your reluctance to honor our marriage vows. I'll ask you one more time, have you taken Winslow as a lover?"

Now it was Lily's turn to express rage and contempt. Didn't Matt know she'd never betray her marriage vows? She wanted to lash out at him, hurt him in the same vile way he had hurt her these past weeks.

"I don't owe you an explanation. You can scarcely blame me if I did take a lover. Your neglect of me has been appalling. Not that I wanted your attention," she sniffed disdainfully.

Matt's face grew mottled. The damn little witch had a way of making him lose control faster than anyone he knew. "Dammit, Lily, you go too far!" he shouted, grasping her shoulders and shaking her into gaping silence. "No one has the right to touch you but me! You're mine despite the fact that we don't share a bed. I don't share what's mine, nor do I allow anyone to use my property."

"You have no rights, Matt!" Lily goaded, aware that she was treading on dangerous ground but unable to stop herself. When would she learn to keep her mouth shut? "You forfeited those rights long ago. If you were honest you'd admit you had no intention of abandoning your mistress when we married."

Matt lost control. Never had another person roused him to such uncontrollable anger or driven him to this state of unrestrained violence. The dainty, frail woman he had married had the uncanny ability to unleash in him deep emotions for which he had no explanation. His hands tightened on her shoulders and he shook her roughly.

"Matt! Stop!" Lily's cry of pain and dismay quickly gained him his senses and he stared in horror at the wild disarray of her hair and clothing that his violence had wrought.

"Sweet Jesus, Lily, you raise all kinds of demons in me. What in the hell am I going to do with you? I don't want to hurt you, but when I saw you and Winslow together my control snapped."

Lily merely stared at him, too distraught and frightened to reply. She'd seen Matt angry before but never like this. Never on the verge of violence. Had she done that to him? Why should he be jealous of someone he cared nothing about?

"I came home tonight intending to bid you good-bye."

"Good-bye?" Lily repeated stupidly. She knew he would be leaving but the actual words caused her more pain than she cared to admit.

"My ships are armed and the papers commissioning them as privateers are in order. I must leave before the harbor is swarming with English. Whatever damage I can inflict upon the English will help our cause. I intend to disrupt English shipping and put a stop once and for all to their blatant disregard of American shipping. I—I couldn't leave without telling you—without—" God, why was this so difficult? "Without bidding you good-bye," he finished lamely.

Lily gulped noiselessly, her words lost in a welter of conflicting emotions. Did he expect her to say she'd miss him? She would, but he'd never hear it from her lips. Did he want her to say she cared about him? She did, in a way that mystified her, but she'd never give him the opportunity to laugh at her. "I—I wish you well," she said after a long pause fraught with all the things she wanted to say but didn't dare. "Are you taking your mistress?" The moment she said it she wished she could have bitten the words back. Why did she insist on provoking him? Unless it was to protect her heart with the barrier provided by Matt's anger.

Once again Lily succeeded in scorching the corners of Matt's control. "Clarrie is definitely not going to sea with me. The *Sea Hawke* is no place for a woman and even if it were, Clarrie is the last person I'd take with me. Dammit, Lily, forget Clarissa for a moment. It's you I wish to discuss. And Winslow. I forbid you to see him in my absence."

"What? You forbid me? You *forbid* me! What makes you such an arrogant bastard?"

"I won't have you taking a lover while I'm gone."

"You don't know me at all if you think I would deliberately disregard my marriage vows and take a lover. Just because you choose to ignore them doesn't mean I would do the same."

"I may be an arrogant bastard but I'm also a jealous one."

Lily's eyes flew open, startled by Matt's baffling words. What kind of game was Matt playing? she wondered as she watched all the anger drain out of his face and be replaced by another equally puzzling emotion. Was he deliberately trying to confuse her, to evoke feelings she tried desperately to destroy? Her life had become a bitter battle to defeat those same conflicting emotions she was experiencing at this very moment. The look in Matt's hooded eyes gave hint to where all this was leading. A thrill of anticipation slid down her spine. If she was truthful with herself she'd admit that she wanted it to happen.

And if it did she'd hate herself afterward.

"Why are you tormenting me?"

"Don't you know? It beats the hell out of me but I can't help myself. I want to make love to you. I may be gone a long time, Lily. Forever, if luck deserts me."

"Go to your mistress," Lily said heatedly.

Love me, Matt, love me, her heart cried in silent agony.

"If I wanted Clarissa I'd not be here with you."

He stepped closer. Lily felt the heat of his breath brush her cheek and saw the naked hunger in his eyes. Her heart leaped in her breast. Once again he was seducing her with words, beguiling her with his eyes. *Resist!* she told herself. *Resist while there is still time!*

"I don't want to make love with you," Lily lied.

She had to force the words past the constriction in her throat.

"Liar."

His arm curled around her waist, dragging her close, and Lily felt the bold proof of his desire through the thickness of her skirts. Panic seized her. Matt was her husband but he wasn't her master. She began pounding his chest, her fists beating against the massive wall of sinew and muscle.

"No! Let me go! I don't want this. I don't want you."

Anger brought Matt's arousal into full erection. Just thinking about Lily in Clay Winslow's arms produced a kind of madness he was at a loss to explain. For some strange reason he couldn't be in Lily's company for more than five minutes without wanting to strangle her or love her. The tension that exploded between them was a painful reminder of how easily she provoked him to anger. Or was it something other than anger? He was astute enough to realize something deep and profound existed between him and Lily, but stubbornness prevented him from exploring those feelings.

"I can make you want me, sweetheart." His voice was harsh and grating, making Lily aware of the terrible urgency driving him.

His sudden burst of passion overwhelmed her, devoured her, scorched her. She felt as if she had been swept into the whirling center of a dark, churning storm, tossed and trampled by a force stronger than life. No matter how hard she fought, Matt's implacable determination overwhelmed and subdued her, until her body became his to do with as he pleased. With a shuddering sigh of regret, she surrendered her body up to him. Yet some deep emotion inside her forbade her to surrender all and she managed to cling desperately to a small portion of her soul. But in the end Matt stripped even that from her.

He stripped her bare.

Her clothes were ripped away until she stood naked and vulnerable before him. In a purely protective motion, her hands crossed over her breasts, but Matt didn't even allow her that meager solace as he grasped her wrists, bending her arms behind her and pressing her into the curve of his body. She saw his head lowering and deliberately turned her lips away. But unerringly Matt found them, dragging his mouth along the soft contours until her lips turned of their own volition into his kiss. His mouth was hard, hungry, demanding, not asking, taking yet giving unstintedly of himself.

He released her wrists and immediately Lily's arms rose to curl around his neck. She was shocked to find his neck not where it should be. He had dropped to his knees before her, cupping his hands beneath her buttocks, pressing his face into the searing heat of her woman's flesh.

"Spread your legs, sweetheart." His request brought a murmur of protest to her lips.

"Matt, no."

"Do it." He nudged her legs apart. When she still resisted he brought his hands around to do it for her, exposing the most tender part of her. She was pink and moist and Matt had to pause to catch his breath or explode like a youth taking his first woman.

When Matt's lips found her sweet, succulent flesh, Lily shuddered, arching into the warm wetness of his ravaging mouth.

"Oh . . ." She tried to push him away before it cost her her sanity.

"Relax, sweetheart, let me love you like this."

Then Lily lost the will to resist as his mouth and tongue worked magic on her sensitive inner flesh, dipping inside her and exploring roughly, tenderly, with maddening thoroughness. When his forefinger and thumb found the tiny button hidden in the soft folds of her flesh and rubbed it in a most provocative manner, Lily nearly swooned. She arched into his mouth, crying out in sweet agony, the torment nearly driving her wild.

"Matt! Stop! Please! I can't stand it!"

He lifted his head for a brief moment but continued the provoking manipulation with his fingers. "Not yet, sweetheart, you're nearly there." Suddenly he thrust his fingers into her and Lily screamed.

Matt felt her convulse and spasm around his fingers and wanted to thrust inside her so desperately it was like a physical pain in his gut. By sheer dint of will he clung to his control, his fingers moving inside Lily until she stilled and slumped against him. Then he swept her up and carried her to the bed. In seconds he had stripped off his clothes and flung himself beside her.

Lily refused to open her eyes. Refused to let Matt see the pure joy he had given her. It was shameful. It was disgusting. It was wonderful.

She loved it.

She hated it.

She hated Matt.

Then she felt his tongue licking at the nipple of one breast and his hands sweeping along the length of her body.

"Haven't you done enough?" Lily accused hotly. "I'm tired, please go."

Matt chuckled. The sound was oddly disconcerting, and terribly arousing. "Not nearly enough, sweetheart. I'm going to be gone a long time. Who knows how long this war will last? You may hate me afterward but you sure as hell won't forget me."

Then he was kissing her, his mouth demanding things she was unwilling to give, seeking that part of her she vowed not to relinquish. It was a losing battle. She moaned, once again surrendering to the devil she had married.

"Feel what you do to me," Matt said hoarsely, grasping her hand and guiding it down ... down ... Her fingers curled around the velvet hardness of his manhood, feeling the massive strength of his desire grow even larger within her grasp. It both shocked and intrigued her.

"Feel what I do to you." Suddenly he was raising her hand to the warm, wet moisture gathered on the insides of her own thighs, and Lily shuddered as passion renewed itself. The musky fragrance of sex sent her senses reeling.

Matt must have felt the same urgency for suddenly he spread her thighs and thrust inside her. Lily felt herself stretch and fill with him. Her legs tightened around him and she moved her hips, waiting for him to begin the rhythm of love.

"Stop! Sweet Jesus, don't move!" The words burst from his throat in ragged pants as beads of sweat popped out on his forehead. Slowly, oh, so slowly, he regained his control and rotated his hips experimentally. When he found he could bear the fantastic feeling of Lily's tight flesh squeezing him without exploding, he began a slow thrusting of his hips.

Lily sighed in pleasure as her hands roamed over the thick muscles that stretched down his back. Her caresses inspected the contours of his hips, then upward, counting each rib that lay beneath his bronzed skin. There wasn't an ounce of fat anywhere on his body. When her hands moved over his buttocks, Matt groaned and thrust into her so deeply Lily couldn't stop the moan that escaped her throat.

"Am I hurting you, sweetheart?"

"No. Oh, God, no!" She stared into his eyes, seeing the almost feral expression in their dark depths, stunned that he was experiencing those same fierce emotions that she was.

"Then come with me, sweetheart. I won't leave you behind."

His strokes grew fiercer, more desperate as he neared his peak. With amazing skill he held off until he sensed the moment of Lily's climax before giving in to the terrible urgency driving him. He felt her stiffen, felt the tiny tremors deep inside her, squeezing him. The cry burst from her throat in a shrill crescendo, reverberating through the darkness, releasing Matt's rigid control. He thrust, and thrust again, and yet again, then the violence of his climax drew his body taut as a bowstring as hot seed spilled into her womb.

"I nearly forgot how sweet you are," Matt gasped when his heart stilled to distant thunder. "Whether either one of us likes it or not we are bound by our passion."

Lily was too stunned for speech. She had reached for the stars and found them within her grasp. And she didn't understand how such a thing could happen. Matt was using her and she had allowed it by offering her body for his pleasure. No matter that he had brought her to shuddering ecstasy, no matter that he had given as well as received, the sad truth was that he didn't love her.

"I don't understand what happened," Lily said slowly, wonderingly. "How could such a thing happen when we don't love each other?"

Matt chuckled in wry amusement. "Love has nothing to do with enjoyment of sex. People engage in sex strictly for pleasure. Didn't I tell you love was overrated? We have something better than love."

Lily turned her back on him, mulling over Matt's words. Was he right? Could she be happy in a marriage where love didn't exist but where passion abounded? How long would passion last without love? The answer was simple yet so complex it took her breath away. Not long enough yet perhaps too long. Which led to another question. "Would you promise to be faithful to me, Matt?"

Matt went still. Right now he had no desire for another woman. But whether he would feel the same in days, weeks, or months from now was something he couldn't answer. He had stayed with Clarissa five years but in the end had grown weary of her. Lily was asking for a lifetime. A lifetime was beyond his comprehension. He couldn't recall when a woman had affected him as profoundly as Lily, or had given him so much pleasure, but in all truth he couldn't promise to be faithful. Nor could he offer love when he didn't know what it meant.

"I can truthfully say that right now you're the only woman I want," Matt hedged.

"What about tomorrow?" Lily probed relentlessly.

"The way I feel now I'll want you for a very long time." There, that should satisfy her, he thought with smug satisfaction.

Wrong.

"Why can't you admit that you love me?"

She had gone too far.

"Sweet Jesus, Lily, why must you turn something beautiful between us into a verbal battle? I hoped you'd appreciate truth instead of lies. Lies come back to haunt you. If and when I ever say those words to you you'll know I mean them. And if you can keep your mouth shut long enough I'll make love to you again."

He curled his body around her, spoon fashion, pulling her into the hard curve of his chest and loins. Lily felt him swell against her buttocks and gasped. "Aren't you ever sated?"

"No. Not with you in my arms. Why do you think I deliberately stayed away from the house so much? I couldn't bear the thought of you sleeping so close and not being able to touch you."

His hands slid around to her breasts, playing with her nipples as he nuzzled the warm curve of her neck. Then he grasped her leg, lifting it as he settled himself between her thighs.

"What are you doing?"

"Teaching you another way to love." She started to turn on her back. "No, stay on your side, I'm going to slide into you from behind."

Then he was inside her, thrusting deeply, his hands free to explore her thoroughly, maddeningly. To Lily's utter amazement fingers of raw sensation surged through her body and she arched backward into his thrusts.

"That's it, sweetheart. Ah God . . ."

By now he was so attuned to every nuance of her passion that he paced himself accordingly. When he felt her slide toward climax his fingers located her pleasure spot, massaging it gently in order to increase the intensity of her explosion. She reached that plateau of sublime ecstasy and screamed from the sheer joy of it. Her climax sparked Matt's as he threw back his head and howled, convinced that if there was a heaven he had just attained it.

"You're incredible, sweetheart," Matt murmured as he slid out of her. "You were made for love. I adore every incredible inch of your responsive body."

Lily went still. Though she was half asleep, Matt's words registered on her passion-drugged brain. "I'm glad you enjoy using me," she said quietly.

"Ummmm," Matt replied, too sated and exhausted to really listen to her words. "Go to sleep, sweetheart. In a couple of hours I'll want you again. This time you can ride me."

Matt adored her body. He loved making love to her. He wanted her. Nothing in their relationship had changed. As long as she allowed it he would keep using her without making a commitment. He couldn't even tell her he'd be faithful, for God's sake! What kind of a man was he?

A man who had no room in his life for a wife. A

man who took his pleasure indiscriminately. An arrogant, overbearing, stubborn, wonderful, incredible swine!

She hated him!

Lies.

She could love him so easily, she thought as she slipped into sleep.

When Matt reached for her several hours later she turned naturally into his arms, allowing him to introduce her to yet another facet of loving. It was every bit as wild and uninhibited as he'd predicted. She rode him furiously, fiercely, taking as much pleasure from his magnificent body as he took from hers. When it was over he eased naturally into sleep. To Lily's chagrin, words of love were conspicuous by their absence, making his praise and delight at her passion nothing but empty phrases. It was then that Lily came to a decision. Matt was too experienced for her, too knowledgeable in the ways of love and arousal. It was far too simple for him to beguile and confuse her. Far too easy for him to make her want him, and yes, damn it, even to make her love him!

At dawn Matt parted reluctantly from the warmth of Lily's body still sprawled in exhausted sleep in the tangle of bedclothes. He struggled into his clothing, pausing briefly when he was dressed to stare down at Lily's sleeping form. He wore a puzzled frown, as if thoroughly confused by his conflicting emotions where Lily was concerned. For some strange reason he wanted to awaken her and whisper the words she so desperately wanted to hear. But a perverse demon inside him prevented it.

War was a certainty. His death a possibility. Should he find himself in love one day with his lovely wife he hoped it would come at a time when he was free to voice his feelings. Stepping closer to the bed, he bent down and placed a tender kiss on her soft lips.

"I wish I could love you, little one," he whispered

in a voice so low it was barely audible. "Perhaps fate will be kind and give me time to learn the meaning of love. If not you're better off without my clumsy attempts to express my feelings."

Then he turned and quietly let himself out of the room. But he didn't leave the house immediately. He awoke Sarah from a deep sleep to bid her good-bye and leave her a terse message concerning Lily. Sarah was stunned by her brother's words.

"I'm disappointed in you, Sarah."

Blinking sleepily, she asked, "What in the world did I do now?"

"You allowed Lily and Clay Winslow to become close."

"I—I didn't think you would mind," Sarah said, biting her lip in consternation. "You've neglected her so dreadfully I thought Clay would help ease her loneliness."

Sarah's thinly veiled rebuke brought a scowl to Matt's handsome features. "I won't have you undermining my authority with my wife. To put it bluntly, I don't want Winslow in this house again. This is still my home. Do I make myself clear?"

"Perfectly," Sarah snapped, bristling with indignation.

Matt's features softened. He loved his sister too well to remain angry with her. "I'm sorry, Sarah, dear, but I'm concerned about Lily. Obey me in this and when I return I'll try to make up to Lily for my neglect of her."

"You're leaving?"

"My ships are fully armed and ready to sail, I must leave Boston before the British arrive."

"Does Lily know you're leaving?"

Matt's lips curled in a secretive smile. "She knows."

"You've seen Lily already this morning?"

"This morning, last night, and all the hours in between." His owlish grin told Sarah all she needed to know. Gleefully she wondered if her brother had finally awakened to the fact that he and Lily were made for one another.

Lord, she hoped so.

Chapter 9

L ily stretched luxuriously in the morning sun, her
body tingling pleasantly from some distant memory. Reluctantly she cranked open her eyes and
winced as memories flooded her brain. Instinctively
she reached out across the bed, finding it cold and
empty. As cold and empty as her heart. Matt was
gone. Perhaps never to return. And the words she
longed to hear from him were still trapped somewhere within his soul. If he had a soul.

She flushed with shame as she recalled all the
naughty, wonderful things they had done last night
and how she had responded with wild abandon to
his lovemaking. He had but to murmur a request in
her ear and she had eagerly followed his direction,
stunned to learn loving took on many different positions, assumed various innovations she wasn't even
aware of. Matt was a master at love, she thought
with a hint of reproach. A masterful teacher who had
led her to delirious heights of passion and taught her
that they could do more with their hands and
mouths than she'd ever dreamed possible.

Frowning in concentration, Lily tried to recall each
word he had spoken to her during the long night,
and came to the sad conclusion that nothing he said
remotely resembled a declaration of love. It was clear
to Lily that Matt sought her bed merely to gratify his

physical lust and for no other reason. Yet deep in her heart Lily felt the distinct stirrings of love for Matt. The question remained, how long could she live with a man who described his feelings for her as lust? How many times would he break her heart, or be unfaithful? How often would he use love to his own advantage?

I could not exist on the crumbs of Matt's affection, her conscience replied.

If she remained at Hawkeshaven she would be constantly at his mercy, torn apart by his continual wavering between indifference and passion. Lily was unwilling to share Matt with Clarissa, or any other woman, waiting for those nights he chose to come to her instead of his mistress. Forever at his mercy, she'd be helpless to resist the torment of his neglect or the ecstasy of his loving. Her life would become a living hell.

The longer Lily thought about the arrogant, overbearing, magnificent man she had married, the angrier she became. There was no denying the powerful magnetism that existed between them. He had already demonstrated that power by luring her into surrendering her heart to him. Then suddenly a disconcerting thought startled Lily. What if she was pregnant? What if Matt's seed had already taken root and now grew inside her? That notion brought her to an abrupt decision.

Once she was certain she wasn't going to bear Matt a child she would leave him. It mattered little that she would leave behind her fortune. It was more important that she retain her self-respect. She seriously doubted that Matt would come after her and hoped her father wouldn't turn her away. If he did she would find some other means of supporting herself. To remain with Matt meant a lifetime of heartache, of unrequited love, of nights of passion and days of wondering if this would be the night he would choose her instead of his mistress. Only a fool would consent to being used in such a manner and she certainly was no fool.

When Sarah saw Lily later that morning, she thought her sister-in-law looked exhausted and sadder than she would have imagined after sharing a night of love with her husband. Or perhaps Lily was stricken because Matt was leaving, Sarah reflected.

"Lily, Matt wakened me early this morning to bid me farewell," Sarah said, searching for an opening to probe Lily's innermost thoughts.

"Did—did Matt say anything about me?" Lily asked hopefully. "Or leave a message?"

"He mentioned that he spent the night with you," Sarah confided. "Oh, Lily, I'm sure Matt realizes just how lucky he is to have you. Why, when he returns—"

"Nothing will have changed," Lily said with such a wistful smile Sarah's heart constricted with pity.

"But—after listening to Matt this morning I surmised that you and he—that is . . ."

Lily blushed. Sarah was naive about many things. "What happened last night, Sarah, dear, was that your brother needed a woman and spent the entire night proving it. Matt is a healthy, virile animal who takes immense pride in his sexual prowess. It feeds his masculine vanity to come to me whenever the need for diversity comes upon him. It inflates his ego to make me want him. He succeeded all too well." Lily turned pale as painful memories flooded her senses. Her next words were spoken so low Sarah barely heard them. "He made me want him until I thought I would die from it."

Sarah gasped, shocked by Lily's frank words. "Oh, Lily, you're only eighteen and far too cynical. Has Matt done this to you?"

Lily lowered her long lashes until they lay like golden butterflies upon her cheeks. She should not have spoken so bluntly to Sarah. Especially about a brother she adored. But she could not deceive Sarah into thinking that Matt had fallen in love with his wife. Nor could Lily deceive herself. Matt didn't know the meaning of love.

"Don't judge Matt too harshly," Sarah advised, wishing she could help the two lost souls find each other.

"Obviously Matt prefers Clarissa over me."

"Surely you jest," Sarah jeered derisively. "Matt has had sufficient opportunity to marry Clarissa these past five years. But he chose you, Lily, how do you account for that?"

"Money, Sarah dear, money," Lily returned with a hint of sarcasm. "And of course my excellent bloodlines. Neither of which Clarissa possesses."

"Oh, Lily, I hate to hear you talk like that. I thought that after what Matt said about Clay—"

"What did he say?" Lily asked sharply.

"He sounded jealous, Lily. He left orders forbidding Clay to visit Hawkeshaven during his absence. If that's not an indication of love, what is it?"

"Matt is a possessive man who takes pride in ownership," Lily said without a moment's hesitation. "I belong to him and no one touches what is his. He can neglect me, mistreat me, make love to me, but that choice is his to make. It wounds his pride to think I might find another man attractive."

"I—I think you're wrong, Lily. Don't ask me why but in my heart I feel Matt truly loves you. You should have seen his face this morning, he looked like a cat who had just lapped a bowl of cream."

"Why not?" Lily contended. "Wouldn't you be happy after a night of nonstop lovemaking? After you're married you will know what I mean."

"What about you, Lily?" Sarah asked suddenly, catching her off guard. "Do you love Matt?"

Lily stared into space a full minute before fixing

Sarah with glowing eyes. "At this moment I want to hate Matt with every breath I possess." Sarah's cry of distress caused Lily to amend her answer. "But I can't. Last night proved I have strong feelings for Matt. I wouldn't be able to respond to him as I did if some spark of feeling didn't exist in my heart for him."

"Oh, Lily," Sarah enthused, "I knew—"

"I didn't say I loved Matt." Lily frowned, confused by her inability to describe her emotions.

"Of course you didn't, but it's obvious," Sarah crowed delightedly.

"Perhaps," Lily allowed guardedly, "for all the good it does me. Matt doesn't believe in love. I knew how he felt when I went into this marriage but had little choice in the matter."

"I must be the luckiest girl alive to have someone as uncomplicated as Jeff to love." Sarah sighed, overwhelmed by the problems facing Matt and Lily.

"You *are* lucky, Sarah, and it couldn't happen to a nicer person."

Despite the fact that Clay was banned from Hawkeshaven, Jeff came and went at will. During his frequent visits Lily felt like an intruder and usually excused herself immediately after dinner in order to allow the couple time alone. By now loneliness was such a deeply ingrained emotion that it left a permanent ache in Lily's breast. During the following weeks she learned she couldn't possibly be pregnant and felt relieved of a tremendous burden. A child would bind her to Matt in ways that would make her leaving impossible.

Lily saw little of Clay during the summer of 1812. Sometimes she spoke briefly to him when she and Sarah visited Jeff at their law office. Jeff had informed him of Matt's wishes that he not visit Hawkeshaven and Clay had honored those wishes.

No matter how desperately he loved Lily the sad fact remained that she was another man's wife.

Boston was swarming now with English soldiers and Royal Navy ships blocked the harbor so that no American ships were allowed in or out. Lily realized that Matt would be unable to enter Boston Harbor whether he wanted to or not and she prayed for his safety.

Summer gave way to fall and soon the full on-slaught of winter blasted Boston. Privateers and the vital role they played in the escalating conflict were discussed frequently among the townspeople. Priva-teers were sanctioned by President Madison and the havoc they wreaked on British shipping worked with devastating effect. Whenever Lily was privy to gos-sip concerning battles at sea she wondered what part Matt had played in the numerous and often bloody conflicts. Christmas was a bleak and dreary day at Hawkeshaven. Though Lily refrained from mention-ing him, Matt was sorely missed.

Early in the new year Jeff arrived at Hawkeshaven bursting with excitement. When he calmed down en-ough to speak he informed them that his uncle had written inviting him to join his law firm in New Or-leans. It seemed the influx of Americans to New Or-leans brought more business than the elderly gentle-man could comfortably handle. There was much money to be made and he wanted Jeff, his favorite nephew, to share in the windfall. Jeff was ecstatic. He had long dreamed of such an opportunity. Though his own practice, which he shared with Clay, was sat-isfactory, it was far from earning them a fortune. In fact, one man could easily handle the work load now administered by two.

"They say that New Orleans is as gay as Paris," Jeff crowed, his eyes sparkling. "Nothing at all like staid old Boston. There are parties and balls, the opera, plays, and so much more. It's a chance of a lifetime."

"It sounds wonderful," Sarah enthused, clapping her hands.

"I hoped it would, darling, that's why I wrote my acceptance immediately. There is one catch, though."

Sarah's heart leaped to her throat. "What is it? You still want to marry me, don't you?"

"Of course, silly, that's why we need to plan quickly for our departure. My uncle wants me in New Orleans without delay. We'll have to move our wedding date forward so we can be ready to leave at the first break in the weather. I want you to be my wife when we leave Boston."

Sarah's smile turned into a worried frown.

"What is it, darling, are you having second thoughts about leaving Boston?"

"Oh, no, it's not that, Jeff," Sarah was quick to explain. "It's just that I wanted Matt here for our wedding. He'll expect us to wait until he returns from sea. And what about Lily? She'd be all alone here at Hawkeshaven. Perhaps you should go to New Orleans alone and I'll join you when Matt returns."

"No!" He shook his head stubbornly. "I won't leave Boston without you. I'll just write my uncle and refuse the position."

"Oh, Jeff, you can't do that. I know how much you want to go. What about your practice here?"

"It's not so large that Clay can't handle it alone," Jeff replied. "I've already spoken to him and he's agreeable to taking over my clients. But if you want to wait for Matt, darling, I'll understand." He looked so downhearted Sarah's heart was torn with indecision. In the end it was Lily who made the decision.

"Of course you must go, Sarah," Lily scolded sternly. "You love Jeff and nothing else matters. Matt will get over the disappointment of missing your wedding and . . . though I'll miss you greatly, I'll survive."

"Oh, Lily, I do love you so," Sarah cried, throwing her arms around Lily's neck. "I'm going to miss you so much."

The wedding took place the second week in April. It was a small, informal ceremony attended by a few close friends. Sarah was breathtaking in her wedding gown, which had been finished weeks ago in anticipation of the wedding. Mrs. Geary did her part by whipping up a reception feast fit for a king. The only bad moment came after most of the guests had left and Sarah and Jeff climbed into the carriage that would carry them on the first leg of their overland journey. The long trip to New Orleans was to suffice as a honeymoon. Sarah's words when they embraced one last time brought tears to Lily's eyes.

"Matt loves you, Lily, I know he does." Then they were gone, leaving a terrible void in Lily's lonely life.

Once the excitement of Sarah's wedding was over time passed slowly for Lily. One sunny June day she decided to visit the dressmaker. She was in need of a new petticoat and the glorious weather beckoned her outside. Jenny accompanied her in the carriage and they chatted amiably as they drove along the crowded streets.

One of the streets on their usual route was blocked that morning, forcing the coachman to turn the vehicle onto a side street unfamiliar to Lily. In an obscure shop window halfway down the block Lily spied the exact petticoat she had been looking for. Motioning for the driver to stop, she instructed Jenny to wait for her in the carriage while she made her purchase. The name painted on the window of the establishment proclaimed it to be Mrs. Durand's boutique.

Entering the boutique, Lily made her wishes

known to the proprietress, a tiny, birdlike woman with darting black eyes and an engaging smile.

"Madame has excellent taste," Madame Durand enthused in an accent Lily assumed to be French. "Would madame like to try it on?"

"There is no need," Lily replied, visually measuring the waist and length of the pale yellow taffeta garment. "I can see that it will fit. Would you please wrap it for me?"

"But of course, madame," gushed Madame Durand. "If you don't mind waiting a few moments I'll have it pressed and put in a box. To whom shall I send the bill?" With an appraising eye she took in Lily's trim figure and glorious copper curls. Lily would have been mortified had she known Madame Durand assumed her to be the mistress of a rich man and the inquisitive woman couldn't wait to learn the name of the lucky gentleman.

"Send the bill to Captain Matthew Hawke's solicitor. I will give you the address," Lily said innocently.

Madame Durand's eyes bulged grotesquely as she repeated, "Captain Matthew Hawke?"

"That's correct. Is there a problem?"

"Oh, no, madame, please forgive me if I seem rude."

"As long as there is no problem I will copy the name and address if you would be so kind as to furnish me with pen and ink."

"That won't be necessary, madame, I know the address. If you'll be patient I'll see to your purchase." With quick darting movements she disappeared behind a curtain, leaving Lily to wonder at her strange behavior.

"Mrs. Hawke, I hardly expected to find you in Mrs. Durand's establishment."

Lily whirled, recognition shuddering through her. It was the first time she had come face-to-face with

Matt's mistress. Deliberately Lily lifted her small chin and turned away.

Clarissa ignored the snub as she carefully positioned herself until she couldn't possibly be ignored. "Do you know who I am?" she asked brazenly.

"I know," Lily whispered, clinging to her composure with the tenacity of a drowning swimmer.

"I suppose Sarah told you. Or was it Matt?" Her dark gaze raked Lily with contempt. Goading Matt's young wife was more enjoyable than she would have imagined.

"Does it matter?"

"I suppose not," sniffed Clarissa, shrugging her elegant shoulders. "Matt and I go way back. Five years, to be exact. You didn't expect things to change because he found it necessary to marry, did you? If he's bedded you it's only because it was his duty."

Lily bit her lip until she tasted blood. Tears sprang to her eyes but stubbornly she blinked them away, determined to prevent Clarissa from seeing how deeply she'd been hurt. If Clarissa wanted to spar verbally Lily decided to give as good as she got. "If Matt loves you so much why am I the woman he married? I am the only woman who can give him a legitimate heir."

"Matt married you for your money," Clarissa jeered cruelly. "You have it, I don't." Lily had no response, for Clarissa had hit upon the truth. "You are a fool if you believe Matt will remain faithful to you when he returns. You may bear his children but it is me he will turn to for comfort and love. You aren't woman enough to satisfy a man like Matt, dear."

"Time will tell," Lily responded cryptically.

"Have you heard from Matt since he left?"

"It's no concern of yours whether or not I've heard from my husband," Lily contended stiffly.

"Then it wouldn't interest you to know I've had

several communications from Matt before the English blockaded the harbor," Clarissa lied blandly.

"He's written you?" Lily's eyes widened with disbelief.

"Of course."

"Is—is he well?"

"Well enough," allowed Clarissa, extremely delighted with herself. She was almost certain Lily had heard nothing from her husband and it pleased her to know Matt didn't care enough about his wife to keep in touch.

Madame Durand chose that precise moment to step through the parted curtain at the back of the shop with Lily's neatly wrapped parcel in her hands. The smile died on her lips when she saw Clarissa chatting with the lovely copper-haired woman madame assumed to be Captain Hawke's new mistress. Aware of Clarissa's previous alliance with Matt, Madame Durand prayed there would be no trouble.

"M-miss Hartley, I didn't know you were here," she stammered. Her lively eyes darted furtively between Clarissa and Lily. "I'm sorry to have kept you waiting."

"That's perfectly all right," Clarissa allowed. "Mrs. Hawke and I have been having a nice chat."

"Mrs.—Mrs. Hawke?" That both the wife and mistress of Captain Hawke should meet in her shop was a calamity Madame Durand had never considered. It was more or less an unwritten law that wives and mistresses never shopped the same establishments. Her shop was known to cater specifically to the pampered mistresses of wealthy Bostonians. Madame Durand never expected to see the wife of a prominent citizen enter her establishment and now that she saw Matt's beautiful wife she couldn't imagine why he preferred a woman like Clarissa to his own lovely bride.

"Is my gown ready, Madame Durand?" demanded
Clarissa, ignoring the woman's obvious dismay.

"Yes, yes, of course. Let me see to Mrs. Hawke's
purchase first and I'll get it for you." Her eyes
flashed an apology to Lily as she handed her the parcel. "I'm sorry, my dear."

Bestowing a shaky smile on the little woman, Lily
turned wordlessly toward the door. But Clarissa
wasn't finished with her. She would settle for nothing less than complete humiliation.

"Please send my bill to Captain Hawke's solicitor,"
she instructed, "I believe you have the address."
Even though Matt had long since terminated her various accounts about town, Clarissa found great satisfaction in allowing Lily to believe he still paid for her
clothing. Once Lily was out of hearing she conveniently changed her mind and informed the confused
proprietress she would pay cash for her purchases.

Once outside the shop Lily allowed herself the luxury of tears. They slid down her cheeks in a silent
stream of pain and humiliation. Leaning against the
side of the building clutching the box to her breast,
she breathed deeply, willing her quaking knees to
move. If she had been inclined to believe Matt when
he told her he hadn't seen Clarissa in weeks, that no
longer was the case. Unless Matt was still involved
with Clarissa he would not be paying for her clothing, she reasoned.

"Lily, are you ill?" Startled, Lily looked up to see
Clay bending over her, concern clouding his warm
brown eyes.

"I—no, I'm fine, Clay," she denied, unwilling to
share her shame with another human being.

"You've been crying!" Clay exclaimed, noting the
sparkling tears on her cheeks. "Is it Matt? Has something happened to him?"

"Not that I know of," Lily said dully.

"I know something is wrong. Do you want to tell me?"

"Not here, not now," Lily said quickly, glancing at the door of the boutique. It certainly wouldn't do for Clarissa to come waltzing out and see how badly her crude remarks had hurt. "Come to the house later, Clay, there is something I'd like to discuss with you."

Clay looked puzzled. "Something pertaining to business?"

"No, this is a personal matter. Please, Clay, I can't explain now but it's important to me."

"What about Matt's wishes that I not visit Hawkeshaven in his absence?"

Lily smiled thinly. "Matt's not here and I suddenly have need of a friend."

"I'll be there, Lily," Clay said, sensing Lily's distress. "I'll see you to your carriage now and drop by later."

"Thank you, Clay, I knew I could count on you."

Lily was quiet and thoughtful during her ride home to Hawkeshaven. She had many things to think about, many decisions to make, all of them painful. Boston Harbor had been blockaded several weeks now and she knew Matt wouldn't be able to get through even if he wanted to. But she was still an English citizen and daughter of a nobleman, making it much easier for her to leave Boston than if she was an American citizen. Lily had considered leaving Matt for some time now but hadn't been able to bring herself to that final decision. With a few cutting barbs Clarissa had made the decision for her.

Clay arrived at Hawkeshaven promptly at six o'clock that evening after office hours.

"What's this all about, Lily?" he asked when she led him into the study—a room she had chosen for its privacy.

Dragging in a deep breath, Lily blurted, "I'm leaving Matt. I want you to help me find passage to England."

"What! Why now? There's a war on, for God's sake! Few American ships are allowed to enter the harbor."

"There are plenty of English ships anchored in the harbor," Lily insisted stubbornly. "I'm an Englishwoman and the daughter of a nobleman, obtaining passage shouldn't be difficult. Lord Stuart Montague is a powerful figure in Parliament, anyone will recognize the name."

"What made you come to this decision?" Clay asked curiously.

Lily flushed. "Let's just say I met a 'friend' of Matt's who convinced me that my marriage has little chance of succeeding."

"Clarissa Hartley," Clay said tightly. "That explains your tears today. I'm sorry, Lily, I hate to see you hurt. Perhaps divorce is the answer. There is no need to return to England, I'll take care of everything."

Lily laughed harshly. "You know Matt as well as I do. He considers me his property and would never let me go. I—I want to be gone before he returns."

Before his kisses and promises of sublime pleasure persuade me to remain, she thought but did not say.

"Matt has methods of persuasion that—that—" Blushing, she faltered, her silence speaking more eloquently than words.

Clay's handsome features hardened. Knowing Matt he could well imagine the methods of persuasion Matt used on his innocent, inexperienced bride. "Say no more, Lily. But leaving Boston isn't necessary, you know. I love you. I'll protect you from Matt."

Lily shook her head. "No, Clay, it's better this way. Matt may not want me but he'll allow no other man to have me. He's possessive, ruthless and utterly without principle. You're the best friend I've ever had but that's all it can ever be."

"Don't tell me you love Matt after the way he's neglected you?"

"My feelings are confused where Matt is concerned but suffice it to say he has made his choice. Even if Father and Leonie turn me away I'm determined to return to England. With Father's influence I can obtain a divorce with little trouble." She didn't say that her father would more than likely advise her to return to her husband. It didn't matter, there were always other options.

"If you're so dead set on returning to England I'll do what I can to help," Clay agreed reluctantly. "I'll go down to the harbor and find a ship whose captain is willing to transport you to England, if you're sure that's what you want."

"It's what I want," Lily said with quiet dignity.

Lily stood at the rail of the H.M.S. *Dauntless*, a frigate in the British navy, watching the American shore fading away in the distance. Things had moved fast after she enlisted Clay's help. The British still controlled Boston and its harbor and the *Dauntless* was preparing to sail on a routine voyage to England when Clay spoke with the captain, casually mentioning that Lily was the daughter of Lord Stuart Montague and wanted to return to England immediately. The good captain was only too happy to offer passage. He commiserated with Lily, being stranded far from home in a country at war with her own homeland, and was delighted to offer assistance.

Lily left the care of Hawkeshaven and the servants in Clay's capable hands, explaining to the servants that she was going on a trip. Both Jenny and Mrs. Geary strongly disapproved of Lily's going off alone, especially during a time of war, but were unable to dissuade her or convince her to take along one of them as companion. Lily thought it best not to reveal that she was going to England and stoutly maintained that she needed no traveling companion. Parting from Clay had not been easy for he had adamantly insisted he would come to England for her one day. He had even loaned her money to see her to her father's home once she reached England since she had little ready cash of her own.

"I imagine you'll be happy to reach England safely, Lady Montague."

Lily turned and smiled at Captain Waverly. He was in his late forties, his dark hair was tinged with gray and his tall, portly figure wore his uniform well. He knew Lord Montague personally and felt honored to be transporting his daughter home after an ill-advised visit to America. He felt strongly that Lord Montague should have kept his daughter home at a time when strife between the two nations was imminent. But far be it from him to tell the gentry how to conduct their affairs.

"Yes, very glad," Lily allowed, choking on the words. She hated to lie to the good captain but if he knew she was married to an American privateer he might not have agreed so readily to transport her to England.

"I'll see you safely to your father, my lady, never fear," Waverly boasted. "The *Dauntless* is one of His Majesty's finest ships and quite capable of defeating warships and privateers plying these waters. We've sunk scores of those bastards—er, pardon my language, my lady—pirates already. I hope you enjoy your voyage, Lady Montague, I'm certain it will prove uneventful."

Lily hadn't the slightest inkling that far from being uneventful, the voyage would change her life forever.

Part 2

1813–1814

Love and hate, both potent and live,
But only one would emerge and survive.

Chapter 10

For the first two weeks there was nothing to break the monotony of the voyage but blue skies and endless ocean. The sailors were polite but offered little diversion, forewarned by their captain to treat their guest with the respect due a daughter of a lord of the realm. Though Captain Waverly allotted Lily precious time from his duties and did what he could to stave off boredom, such as sharing the evening meal with her and engaging in a game of chess afterward, Lily felt as if she had far too much time on her hands to think of Matt and pine for what might have been had he been inclined to offer a bit more of himself than his body.

When the storm swept down on them Lily was almost grateful for the distraction, until she realized it was to be more than merely a typical summer storm. The churning, swirling mass swooped down from the north, tossing the *Dauntless* helplessly atop seething waves then trying to capsize her by dashing her down between tunnels of angry, foaming water. Cowering below in her cabin, Lily heard the thunderous roar of one of the masts as it crashed to the deck, instantly snuffing out the lives of two crewmen.

Lily remained in her cabin for the entire three days of the violent storm, alternately suffering bouts of nausea and fright. Meals were cold and unappetizing, when they came at all. Not that it mattered. Lily couldn't have swallowed a bite had a grand feast been laid out before her. On the fourth day she awoke from a fitful sleep to a gentle rocking and was gratified to note that the ship no longer plunged wildly but had settled down to a more sedate motion. Rising gingerly, she groped her way to the porthole and blinked in amazement. As quickly as it had appeared the storm gave way to calm seas and tranquil skies. Dressing hastily, she hurried topside to a scene of utter chaos.

Wreckage littered the deck from stern to bow. Spars and ropes hung precariously from shattered masts while sailors scurried to and fro in an effort to remove these dangers to life and limb. At least two bodies lay beneath a canvas sail spread out on deck while nearby the captain and ship's doctor tended crewmen who had sustained injuries during the storm. Captain Waverly looked up, saw Lily hovering nearby, and frowned.

"Go back to your cabin, my lady, this is no place for a female. Until this mess is cleared away it's much too dangerous for you on deck."

"I can be of more use helping with the injured," Lily insisted. Her face was set with quiet determination as she pushed back her sleeves and refused to budge.

"I hardly think . . ." began the captain. But by that time it was already too late for Lily was on her knees before an injured sailor, staunching the flow of blood with a linen pad the doctor had handed her.

When the fearsome damage to the *Dauntless* was assessed the news was grim. In addition to losing the mainmast, the rudder had snapped and the hold was full of seawater. Divers were sent down only to report that the rudder was beyond repair, making the *Dauntless* and her crew totally dependent on the capricious winds and tides to carry them where they would.

"We are not too far off normal shipping lanes," Captain Waverly said with gruff bravado once he learned the extent of damage to his ship. "I'm certain one of His Majesty's ships will come upon us soon enough." Privately he thought they had a better chance of being intercepted by American privateers than rescued by his own countrymen, but he wisely withheld that bit of information.

For the next few days their aimless drifting in an unending sea of blue seemed no more than an idyllic pleasure cruise to Lily. Except for the boredom and waiting for another English ship to find them, nothing had changed. Until the captain decided food and water should be rationed in the unlikely event rescue did not come soon. Still Lily did not worry too much for Captain Waverly insisted that the tides would eventually carry them to land. Yet for some unexplained reason Lily couldn't shake the premonition of impending disaster that grew more desperate with each passing day.

Then one day her flagging spirits were miraculously restored when she heard the cry from aloft. "Sail ho!"

"Where away?" shouted the captain, raising the spyglass to scan the distant horizon. Lily hurried to his side, excitement tinged with fear churning inside her.

"Starboard, sir!" came the excited response. Bobbing atop the sea at the mercy of fate did not appeal to the crewmen and they welcomed the prospect of imminent rescue.

"Can you make out her colors?" rejoined the captain.

"She's too far away, sir,"

"Is she English?" asked Lily anxiously as she

squinted her eyes at the tiny speck that grew larger with each passing minute.

" 'Tis too soon to tell, my lady," muttered the captain ominously. He had his suspicions but refrained from voicing them until he was certain.

On pins and needles Lily waited for the ship converging on them with a brisk wind at her back to be identified. She prayed the ship was English and nervously wondered what would happen to her should they be captured by an American privateer.

"She's raised her colors, sir!" hollered the sailor clinging to the mast far above them. "She's flying the stars and stripes! By God, she's American, Captain! God help us all!"

Lily knew a moment of raw panic. "Oh, no!"

" 'Tis all right, my lady," soothed the captain, patting her heaving shoulders. "No harm will come to you. Being a great lady you'll soon be ransomed and sent home to your father."

"Do you intend to surrender without a fight?" Lily asked, incredulous.

"We have no choice," came his weary reply. "If we were seaworthy I'd give those devils a battle they would long remember. The *Dauntless* is every bit as good as the finest vessel afloat, whether American or English. My ship is well armed and we would have engaged the American in a rousing battle, but being rudderless and missing our mainmast makes that impossible. Nothing short of a miracle would bring us home the victory."

"What about your cannon?" Lily prodded when she realized the captain meant to surrender without firing a shot.

"Without maneuverability guns are useless," Waverly explained patiently. "No, my lady, 'tis senseless to put up a fight when we cannot possibly win. Besides, your life and the lives of my crew are too valuable to waste in useless combat." Captain

Waverly was a very wise man as well as a cautious one.

The captain left shortly to stand on the bridge and direct his men as they waited for the privateer to fire a shot across their bow. Lily gaped in silent horror as the American ship rapidly closed the gap between them. When they were close enough to make out the figures scurrying about the deck, Waverly shouted down at her, "Go to your cabin, my lady. 'Tis best you're not seen until I can inform the American captain myself of your presence and discuss arrangements for your ransom."

Lily nodded, not wishing to compound Captain Waverly's problems by disobeying his orders. She cast one last look at the menacing ship bearing down on them and quickly went below.

Captain Matthew Hawke balanced his lanky frame on the bridge of the *Sea Hawke*, legs planted wide apart, spyglass trained on the ship that appeared to be helplessly adrift.

"What do you make of her, Dick?" he asked his first mate, who hovered at his elbow watching the frigate's progress.

" 'Tis difficult to say, Captain," replied Dick Marlow, a young man of good birth who had joined Matt's crew to defend his country against the invading English. "She seems to be floundering, with no apparent course or direction. We've had her in our sights for quite some time now and she appears to veer with the wind. I think she is damaged, sir. Her mainmast is missing."

"You'll make a good sailor yet, Dick." Matt smiled, well pleased by his choice of first mate despite the young man's lack of experience. "When we're close enough order the men to fire a round across her bow."

"Aye, sir." Dick saluted smartly, his face alive with

anticipation. "I hope she puts up a fight. The men are itching for another encounter with those pesky English."

Matt watched the young man swagger off then raised his glass once more to scan the deck of the frigate. They were so close now he could easily read the name painted in bold letters across the hull. H.M.S. *Dauntless*. She was a good ship; Matt had heard much about her and her intrepid captain. It would certainly be a feather in his cap if he could bring her in as a prize. Suddenly his arm faltered as he swept the deck with the spyglass. He blinked repeatedly, training the glass on a bit of color moving across the deck. Bright rays of sunshine reflected off a flash of red and a swish of ruffle, then it quickly disappeared down the ladder leading below deck.

"Damn," Matt cursed aloud. Did the English captain have a woman aboard his ship? A wife? Or mistress?

Matt's mind drifted back to the last time he had seen hair exactly that shade of red and a jolt of raw desire engulfed him in a blanket of longing so excruciating it was like a physical pain. Lily. During the months he'd been away from Lily she haunted his dreams, more often than he would have liked. She had responded to him so sweetly their last night together it had been a struggle to leave her the next morning.

He could almost smell the enticing fragrance of her skin, feel her coral nipples rise against his mouth, taste the sweetness of her flesh. Desire scorched a path along his loins as he thought of her opulent lips and extravagantly warm eyes the color of thick honey. Jesus! he thought with a hint of self-derision, no woman had ever affected him like Lily. He had always prided himself on his ability to take his pleasure without commitment or admitting things he did not feel. Now here he was waxing poetic about a woman no more than a green schoolgirl who hadn't one tenth the knowledge of men that Clarissa possessed. When he returned to Boston, he reflected thoughtfully, he fully intended to explore his feelings where his wife was concerned. Even if it meant learning things he didn't want to know.

The roar of cannon blasted Matt from his reverie. He looked across the water as his men sent a volley across the bow of the *Dauntless* and was surprised to see a white flag run up almost immediately.

"There's no fight left in her, Dick," Matt muttered when his first mate appeared at his side.

" 'Tis no wonder." Dick grinned cheekily. " 'Tis easy to see the fearful damage she sustained now. And I'm willing to bet she's rudderless."

"Clearly the *Dauntless* didn't weather the recent storm well. Fortunately we were holed up in Nassau or we might have ended up in a like predicament. Still," he mused thoughtfully, "I don't trust the English. When we're within hailing distance I'll speak with the captain."

A surprisingly short time later the *Sea Hawke* rode easily beside the disabled *Dauntless*. Cupping his hand to his mouth, Matt shouted across the water. "Ahoy, the *Dauntless*! I wish to speak with your captain."

Seconds later a voice boomed back, "Captain Waverly of His Majesty's Navy, here."

"I am Captain Hawke of the *Sea Hawke*, a privateer sanctioned by the United States government. I hereby claim the *Dauntless* as my prize. My men will be coming aboard to relieve you of your cargo and valuables and it will go easier on you if you offer no resistance," Matt coolly informed Captain Waverly.

"We are disabled, Captain Hawke, and at your mercy," called back Waverly. "Otherwise we would have accepted your challenge and engaged in battle. I am no coward, sir!"

"I never assumed you were," replied Matt as he prepared to cross over the boarding planks being run out by his men. The boarding hooks had already been secured while Matt spoke and the ships now rode the gentle waves side by side.

Within minutes Matt stood facing Captain Waverly on the deck of the captured *Dauntless* while his men rounded up the English crew. They were sullen and belligerent while being herded aboard the *Sea Hawke* and locked below but offered no physical resistance. They resented surrendering to the enemy without a fight.

"Are you carrying passengers, Captain?" Matt asked, still curious about the swish of a woman's skirt he had caught a fleeting glimpse of. Or had he been without a woman so long he was imagining things?

"It so happens the *Dauntless* does carry a passenger," Waverly admitted. "A very important passenger. She is the daughter of a member of Parliament. We were returning her to her father and I request that the lady not be molested."

Matt snorted in disgust. "Do you think Americans are savages? You have my word that her ladyship will not be harmed. Indeed, I would be the last person to damage so valuable a piece of property. She will be ransomed along with yourself and your crew. Where is her ladyship? I should like to meet her."

"I ordered the lady below," Waverly answered, unwilling to expose Lily to a ruthless American privateer like Captain Hawke.

"Mr. Marlow!" Matt bellowed. Within seconds the young man appeared beside his captain, brandishing a sword in one hand. "There is a lady below in one of the cabins, be so good as to escort her topside."

"Aye, sir," snapped the first mate crisply as he wheeled about to execute his captain's orders.

"Captain Hawke," cut in a voice at Matt's elbow.

Turning, Matt acknowledged Rob Freemont, the second mate.

"What is it, Mr. Freemont?"

"Several crewmen from the *Dauntless* say they were taken by force from American vessels and impressed by these British bastards, if you pardon the language. What do you want done with them?"

"Separate them from the others until I've had time to speak with them."

"Aye, aye, sir."

Matt turned to address the captain but the words froze in his throat when he saw Dick Marlow escorting his reluctant and resisting captive from below.

"I found the lady, Captain Hawke," Marlow said, obviously flustered by the lovely young woman he had discovered in a cabin below. He held her firmly by the wrist, dragging her forward as she dug in her heels, refusing to budge. But Lily's resistance was pointless for all too soon she stood before Matt's towering form.

She spared him a disparaging glance, but what she saw made her gasp in shock. "Matt! No! It can't be!" She cringed at the look of utter astonishment in his dark eyes. They both froze in stunned tableau. Through the roaring din in her ears she heard him speak her name.

"Lily."

Then came his anger. The crushing, raw rage at finding Lily on an English ship when he thought her safely in Boston.

"What in all that's holy are you doing here?" He threw the words at her like stones, each one finding its mark on her tender hide.

Lily gulped, her mouth working wordlessly while her amber eyes clawed him like talons. Matt looked furious enough to eat her alive, she thought in a rush of terror. His lips thinned, his nostrils flared and she couldn't even begin to describe his eyes. They had taken on the tortured dullness of disbelief.

"Are you acquainted with Lady Montague?" asked Captain Waverly as he watched the tension explode between the privateer and the lady.

"Very well acquainted," Matt said tightly, impaling Lily with the diamond hardness of his brittle gaze. "The lady is my wife. Tell the good captain, sweetheart. Tell him that we are indeed wed. Don't be shy."

Matt's voice was calm and composed but his mock tranquility didn't fool Lily one bit. The underlying edge of steel cleanly cut through her. Captain Waverly looked askance at her, but suddenly Lily's mouth was filled with great wads of cotton. All she could do was stare at him dumbly while shivers raced down her spine.

"Well, Lily, Captain Waverly is waiting for your answer," Matt prodded with quiet menace.

"It's true," Lily whispered shakily. "Captain Hawke is my husband. I didn't mean to deceive you, Captain, but I didn't think you would take me to England if you knew I was married to an American."

"Quite right," Waverly said with a hint of reproach. "Have you also lied about being Stuart Montague's daughter?"

"Oh, that's true enough," Matt said, forestalling Lily's answer, "but I doubt his lordship would be happy to see his daughter on his doorstep."

"I'm sorry," Lily said contritely, not pleased with her deception since the good captain had done his best to make her welcome aboard his ship.

"I had no idea I was contributing to marital problems," Waverly said grumpily, sparing Lily a disgruntled look.

Abruptly Matt turned to his first mate. "Take Mrs. Hawke to the *Sea Hawke* and lock her in my cabin,

Mr. Marlow." A sudden chill hung on the edge of his words. "See that her trunks are stowed aboard."

"Matt." Lily's voice quavered.

"Now, Mr. Marlow!" Matt roared, fearing to trust himself another minute in his wife's vexing presence. She was damn lucky he didn't turn her over his knee. She had humiliated him before his men and made a fool of him, and he wasn't certain he could forgive her. Running away had been a reckless thing to do and what made it even more disturbing was the fact that he didn't know what had provoked her into leaving. He hadn't seen her for weeks, for God's sake!

Seething with impotent rage, Lily held her head high as Dick Marlow guided her across the boarding plank and then into Matt's comfortable cabin. "I'm s-sorry, Mrs. Hawke," the badly shaken young man stammered as he shut the cabin door. "I'm only following captain's orders. I—I have to lock you in."

"It's not your fault, Mr. Marlow," Lily replied, forcing a smile. "You are obliged to obey your captain." The key scraped in the lock and Lily sank dejectedly onto the taut surface of the bunk, well aware that she had gone too far this time by provoking Matt's temper in a way that brought out the worst in him. She fully expected to suffer the full brunt of his anger.

Actually Lily didn't know what to expect. She'd seen Matt's anger before but doubted anything she had viewed thus far remotely resembled what he was feeling now. Of all the privateers plying the ocean why did the *Sea Hawke* have to be the ship to come upon the disabled *Dauntless*? she wondered dismally. Would Matt beat her? She had never suffered physical abuse at his hands and felt reasonably certain he wouldn't hurt her. Physical abuse wasn't his style. But she knew with an ingrained certainty that he would devise some subtle form of punishment. A gamut of conflicting emotions shuddered through her as she contemplated the various methods available to Matt.

The dull scrape of metal brought Lily to her feet. She didn't want to be at a disadvantage when she faced her husband. Tall and menacing, Matt stepped through the door, barely sparing a glance at his wayward wife. Through slitted eyes she watched Matt remove his jacket and fling it carelessly across a chair. His shirt followed, and Lily stirred uneasily at the sight of his powerful chest, lightly furred and bared to the waist. With slow deliberation he removed the belt from the loops of his trousers.

"Wha—what are you going to do?"

He seemed to notice her for the first time. "Nothing . . . yet." His large tan hands flexed as he tested the strength of the leather then slapped it against his thigh. Lily flinched, her eyes never leaving the strip of rawhide. "First things first, sweetheart. Frankly I'm more interested right now in hearing how you came to be aboard the *Dauntless* than in marring that delicate hide of yours."

Lily dragged in a deep, ragged breath, facing Matt's anger squarely. Her tiny pointed chin raised a notch as she spit defiance at him. "I was leaving you, of course. What else would I be doing aboard an English ship?"

"What kind of life would you have in England when your own father doesn't want you?" Matt retaliated spitefully. "You have no money of your own, you'd be totally dependent on him and his new wife for your livelihood."

"What kind of life do I have with you?" Lily shot back. "You've taken my fortune and used it to attack the country of my birth. You flaunt your mistress before the whole world and if that isn't enough you use me when no other woman is available." Her stomach roiled dangerously beneath his withering glance but she stood her ground with amazing fortitude. Matt couldn't help but admire her.

"You're not leaving me, Lily." The deep timber of his voice sent ripples of awareness dancing down her spine. "You're mine and I jealously guard what is mine."

Lily sent him a bewildered glare. Why was Matt so insistent on keeping her? she wondered. "Why do you bother, Matt, when obviously we don't suit each other? Once I am gone from your life you are free to indulge your passion for Clarissa."

"Clarissa be damned!" Matt exploded. "I haven't seen Clarissa in months, and truthfully, I couldn't care less. I told you before I left Boston that Clarissa was part of my past and had no place in my future."

Did she detect a slight softening in his hawklike features? Lily wondered in silent contemplation. She struggled desperately to sort her confused emotions into some semblance of order. She felt as if she were swimming through a haze of contradictions, with no answers available. Why did Matt insist that Clarissa meant nothing to him? Had he finally come to the realization that he cared for his own wife? Surely not! He had never confessed to any feelings for her except perhaps for lust. She knew for a fact that Matt had been in touch with Clarissa, for Clarissa had admitted as much.

Matt's next question completely unnerved her. "Who helped you find passage to England? I don't think you did it alone. Was it Sarah? Or Jeff? I'll have to think twice about allowing their marriage if they betrayed me in this manner."

Lily had no intention of telling Matt that Clay had helped her find passage to England. Instead, she sought to steer the conversation in another direction. "There is nothing you can do. Sarah and Jeff married months ago."

That unexpected piece of information brought a

frown to Matt's face. "They were supposed to wait until I returned."

"Who knows how long this war will last? It might be months, or years even before they'd be able to marry if they waited for you. Jeff's uncle offered him a position in New Orleans and he and Sarah were married before they left."

"Sarah is in New Orleans?" Matt's scowl grew darker. "It seems I have little control over any of my womenfolk."

"Sarah and Jeff were so much in love I advised them not to wait for your return."

A sudden, terrible thought entered Matt's brain and refused to be dislodged. "You've been alone at Hawkeshaven all this time? Has Clay Winslow been around to assuage your loneliness?"

Lily flushed, realizing she had merely postponed the inevitable by changing the subject to Sarah and Jeff's marriage. She faced him squarely. "Leave Clay out of this. I haven't broken my marriage vows, if that's what you're hinting at."

"Tell me, Lily," Matt demanded in such a cold calm voice it raised goose bumps on Lily's flesh. The calmness of his voice belied the turmoil churning inside him and Lily realized this was but a prelude to a more violent side of her husband.

"Clay found passage for me aboard the *Dauntless* but it was at my bidding. I was determined to leave you, Matt, and nothing would have stopped me even if Clay had refused to help me."

"You have deliberately disobeyed my wishes. How long have you been seeing Winslow?"

"You don't own me, Matthew Hawke!" Lily exploded furiously. "What was I supposed to do for friends in Boston? After Sarah left visits from acquaintances stopped. I'm English, there is too much hostility right now with the English occupying Boston for your friends to accept me."

"So you turned to Winslow."

"No! Not even then. I saw Clay once, after your mis—after Clarissa pointed out to me that old habits are hard to break. She'll always come first with you, Matt, why do you keep denying it?"

Matt opened his mouth and flung out a string of curses that singed Lily's ears. His eyes were so cold and unrelenting Lily gave an involuntary shudder. She would have been stunned to learn his fury wasn't directed at her this time. "That little bitch! You're mistaken in believing her, Lily. You could trust me for once."

"Have you ever given me reason to trust you?" Lily shot back defiantly.

Matt's mouth tightened as he drew the belt though his fingers in a menacing manner. Lily eyed the strip of leather with misgiving. Did he still mean to beat her? If he did he'd have a fight on his hands.

"Go ahead and beat me!" she challenged, trying to ignore the storm clouds gathering in his face.

Almost absently Matt glanced down at the belt in his hands, as if unaware of what he was doing. Then he looked at Lily, standing so proud and defiant before him. Beat her? It was certainly a thought worth considering, but hardly his style. Though Lord knows the stubborn little witch needed to learn a lesson. There were too many other things he'd rather do to Lily. All of them more satisfying than marring her lovely flesh.

"Perhaps I shall beat you, since you seem to expect it," Matt proclaimed in a voice as cool and clear as ice water. "Take off your clothes."

Lily blanched. She couldn't believe Matt actually meant to abuse her. Leaving him must have angered him more than she realized. "You can't beat me like a naughty child, Matt."

"Why not? You've behaved like one. Proper wives don't go traipsing off by themselves."

He stepped closer. Lily backed away. He stalked her like one would a trapped deer. Lily resisted, retreating step by step until he had her backed against the bulkhead.

"Your clothes, Lily, take them off."

Unconsciously he caressed the belt he held in his hands. The tip of Lily's tongue darted out to lick her dry lips. That simple motion seemed to fascinate Matt as he stared with interest at the small drops of moisture glazing her lips. He could almost taste the sweetness left behind by her tongue and his loins reacted violently. His eyes slid downward to her chest, noting with satisfaction the rapid rise and fall of her breasts. Good, he thought smugly, he had frightened her. Reluctantly he raised his dark eyes, impaling her with his impiacable gaze.

Lily gulped in silent fear, recognizing defeat but unwilling to admit it. When Matt reached out and fingered the delicate lace at her neckline, she expected her dress to be rent from hem to collar. Instead Matt began unbuttoning the tiny row of buttons marching down her bodice with infinite patience.

"Let me do it for you." His touch sent shivers down her spine.

Lily's fingers flew to replace his, preferring to do it herself rather than suffer Matt's touch. If he learned just how profoundly his touch affected her she'd never live it down. He looked like a pirate standing before her with his chest bared and his dark face wearing a look that a devil would envy. Even now, even when she knew he meant to hurt her, she wanted him. She wanted to run her hands through the crisp black hair covering his chest. She wanted to caress and stroke every inch of his magnificent flesh. And God help her but she wanted to feel him thrust inside her and stroke her to rapturous oblivion.

She hated him.

Chapter 11

Matt knew he was deliberately frightening Lily but was so angry with her he couldn't help himself. He had never abused a woman in his life but she didn't need to know that. Besides, the moment his hands touched the satin softness of her skin he knew beating Lily was the very last thing he wanted to do to her.

His dark eyes were hooded as he watched her unfasten the front of her dress. Her fingers were shaking and he had to stifle the urge to tear them away and finish the job himself. When the edges of her bodice gaped open, exposing the swelling tops of her breasts, she raised her head and stared at Matt. Though badly shaken, she had lost none of her spirit and Matt couldn't help but admire her. But it didn't make him any less angry.

"Now what?" Lily asked, facing him squarely.

"Take off your clothes," Matt repeated tightly. "Don't be bashful on my account, I've seen you without clothes before."

"You're an arrogant swine, Matthew Hawke," Lily said.

He smiled thinly. "And you're a disobedient child who deserves a beating."

"Beating me won't prove a thing except that you're stronger than I am."

Suddenly Matt tossed the belt aside and reached for her. She screamed in dismay as he jerked the dress from her shoulders, sliding it past her hips and lifting her to kick it aside. Then he set her on her feet and calmly released the tapes holding her petticoats. When she stood before him meagerly clad in a thin chemise that came just past her hips and stockings held up by garters, Matt stepped back and raked her with his eyes from head to toe. Lily shivered as a ghost of a smile curved his full lips.

"Who said I was going to beat you?" he mocked caustically.

Suddenly she was in his arms and he was kissing her, his mouth punishing yet oddly tender as she tried to turn her face away from the force of his kiss. There was no escape. Matt twisted one hand into the tangled mass of coppery curls, bending her backward until she thought her neck would snap, forcing his bruising lips against hers. With his free hand he explored her body, pushing her chemise up around her waist. She started violently when he growled deep in his throat and ripped the flimsy garment from her body, leaving her vulnerable to his hands and mouth.

Abruptly breaking off the kiss, Matt whispered in her ear, "Marring your tender flesh will accomplish little except perhaps salve my wounded pride. I know of a far better way to bring you to heel. Open your legs, sweetheart, and welcome your husband as a good wife should."

"Go to hell!" Lily panted breathlessly. Matt's kisses had sent her whirling helplessly into a hot, swirling abyss and she hated being cast in so defenseless a position. Not only was she forced to defend herself against Matt's amorous aggression but against her own wayward body. His touch awakened memories in her she wanted to forget.

Lily's mutinous reply did little to hinder Matt as

he swept her off her feet and tossed her atop the bunk, straddling her so that she was pinned between the bulging muscles of his thighs.

"Have you forgotten how wonderful I make you feel?" Matt asked huskily. He bent his head and licked the nipple of one of her breasts, then took it in his mouth and suckled while his hand gently squeezed the nipple of her other breast.

Lily gasped. She had forgotten nothing.

"Can you truthfully say you don't want me to make love to you?"

No!

"Yes," she lied, closing her eyes against the sudden jolt of pleasure dancing from nerve to nerve. "Loving isn't meant to be punishment."

Matt's mouth was working its way down the delicate curve of her hip toward that warm, wonderful place that gave him so much pleasure when her words finally sank in. His mouth had already found her tiny swelling bud and was gently massaging it with his tongue when he stopped in mid-stoke.

Loving isn't meant to be punishment.

Sweet Jesus! Did Lily consider his loving punishment? Is that what he wanted her to think?

Lily choked back a sob, disgusted with the unnerving ability Matt had to make her body behave in ways totally foreign to her. With his mouth and hands he turned her blood to warm, thick honey, sapping her of the will to move her limbs and reduced her to a quivering mass of muscle and flesh that existed solely for his attention. The will to resist had fled, only to be replaced by the need to feel Matt's flesh against hers, moving inside her, stroking her to places she never knew existed.

The need to be loved.

With a groan of surrender, Lily welcomed the violence of Matt's passion as her arms held him close and her hands moved restlessly along his back to his buttocks, inviting him, urging him, needing him. It took several minutes for her to realize that Matt had gone still. His mouth no longer moved over her flesh and his hands had paused in their restless pursuit. He was still leaning over her, his head bent down and his eyes closed. His breathing was harsh and irregular and Lily felt his muscles flex as he fought for some semblance of control.

He didn't raise his head until he had been victorious in the battle with his raging passion. Beads of sweat dotted his brow and his muscles still quivered, and instinctively Lily knew his victory had been hard won. She only wished she could conquer her own emotions as easily. Her body, long deprived and aching, yearned for fulfillment, fulfillment only Matt could give her. Liquid fire raged through her, making her nipples sensitive and culminating in that tender place between her legs. Lord help her but she wanted him!

She hated the way he stripped her of her pride.

Slowly Matt levered himself off Lily and fell heavily to his side, one arm flung over his eyes. He lay motionless for several agonizing minutes until his breathing had returned to normal, then he sat up, turning to stare at Lily with something akin to amazement. Sex had always been second nature to him, a simple appeasement to a primitive need. He never imagined taking a wife would alter his thinking to such a degree. Lily was a complicated, infuriating creature who constantly confused and confounded him with her wisdom.

Loving is not meant to be punishment.

Those simple words had shriveled his passion more quickly than a dash of cold water. He waited in vain for those profound sentiments to evaporate once he had time to mull them over, but found they had rooted themselves in his brain for all time. Why is it that in all the years he had known Clarissa she had never said anything so thought provoking? Heaving a sigh of regret he hauled himself out of bed.

Beside him, Lily stirred uneasily. What did Matt have in mind now? Had he changed his mind and decided to beat her after all? Couldn't he tell she wanted him? Didn't he know he had left her aching and needy? "Wha—what are you going to do?"

"I'm getting out of here," Matt rasped from between clenched teeth. "I decided you're not worth my time." *Lies!* He wanted her so desperately it was a gnawing ache in his gut. "Fortunately for you, I'm too angry to beat you. Once I start I fear I'll kill you." *More lies.* He couldn't mar her tender flesh if his life depended on it. He wanted to make love to her but after Lily had tossed out her provocative statement he wasn't sure he wanted to love her for the right reason. "I'm locking you in the cabin."

Lily jerked upright, grasping the blanket to cover her nakedness. "What will that prove?" She swung her head around to look at him and was instantly sorry.

He was facing her as he reached for his shirt and Lily's face flamed as her eyes slid down his body to where his arousal bulged against the fabric of his trousers. Her tongue flicked out to moisten her dry lips, recalling how his male member felt thrusting into her, hard as steel yet soft and smooth as velvet. The recollection was so incredibly vivid she couldn't suppress the tiny moan that escaped her throat. The sound caught Matt's attention and he glanced at Lily, noting the direction of her gaze. A devilish grin settled on his roguish features.

"If you beg me prettily I might be persuaded to stay and make love to you."

Suddenly aware of what she had been staring at, Lily raised her eyes. "Go to hell! I don't want you to touch me."

Matt shrugged. "Whatever you want, sweetheart."

She flung him a condescending glare. "I want you to leave me alone."

"As you wish. I'll see that someone brings you food later. Meanwhile I suggest you make the most of your confinement by contemplating your mistakes."

"My mistake was in marrying you. Had I been given a choice I would have selected anyone but you."

"Dammit, Lily, why must we constantly be at each other's throats? Before I left Boston we seemed to have reached an understanding. What happened to make you leave? We could have dealt well with one another in the years to come if you hadn't demanded more than I was willing to give."

"Sharing you with Clarissa shamed me," Lily said in a voice so low Matt had to strain his ears to hear. "Loving you would be so easy, Matt, but forgiving you for keeping Clarissa as your mistress is asking too much."

Matt's featured softened. "Why must you spoil everything by mentioning an emotion I don't believe in? Isn't it enough that our lovemaking is incredibly passionate? Few married couples have even that much."

"No, it's not enough."

"I haven't seen or heard from Clarissa in months. I hadn't the time nor energy to expend on a mistress since we've been married."

"You expect me to believe that?"

"You could trust me."

"Do you trust me?"

"I—" Good Lord, what was she trying to do, confuse him? How could he trust her when she was so damn beautiful it hurt his eyes to look at her? When she was more desirable than any woman he had ever known, Clarissa included? When she left him without a word or explanation? He frowned. "I don't have time for this conversation, Lily. We'll talk later, after I decide what to do with you."

Fully dressed now, he turned and strode purposefully out the door. The distinct sound of scraping metal told Lily that he had locked the door behind him. Damn him, damn him, damn him! she fumed in silent rage. Desolation such as she had never felt before washed over her and she felt the walls closing in on her. Why was it necessary to lock her in the cabin? she wondered dismally. Where could she go on a ship in the middle of the ocean? If he was trying to prove his mastery over her he failed miserably. His high-handedness only made her more determined than ever to find a way to escape a marriage neither of them wanted.

Lily paced the cabin for hours, or what seemed like hours. Matt hadn't returned to the cabin but Dick Marlow brought her a tray of food sometime after dusk. He set it down on a small table, sent her an apologetic smile and left, carefully locking the door behind him. Evidently Matt had warned the young man about becoming overly friendly with his wayward wife.

Lily picked at the food. It was appetizing enough but she felt little hunger. All she could think of were the insults and the verbal lashing she intended to give Matt when he showed up again. To her chagrin he didn't return to the cabin at all that night. Nor the next. Her needs were seen to quite adequately but Matt kept his distance. She couldn't help but wonder what he was plotting and vowed to foil whatever plan he had for her. On the third day Lily became so distraught over being kept prisoner in the cabin and disturbed about her fate that she decided to do something about it. She began pounding on the door with a tin cup, setting up such a terrible racket that Matt came storming through the door, his face dark and threatening.

"What in the hell is going on in here?" Matt thundered. His pointed gaze nailed her to the wall but to Lily's credit she didn't flinch.

"I want to know what you're going to do with me. How long must I stay locked in this cabin?"

"Until I say otherwise."

"What kind of answer is that? Even criminals are allowed exercise and fresh air. It's stifling in this cabin and if you don't let me out I'll raise such a ruckus you'll wish you'd left me with Captain Waverly."

Matt's dark brows lifted a fraction of an inch. "Captain Waverly and his men are chained in the hold. Do you wish to join them?"

Lily blanched. "I— No, but neither do I want to stay in here for days on end. Can't you relent and allow me a little freedom? Where can I go in the middle of the ocean?"

Matt stared at her and she felt as if she were being swallowed by his eyes, by the implacable authority that radiated around him. For three days he had avoided Lily, waiting for his anger to cool, and now all he could think about was tossing her skirts up and thrusting into her like a rutting goat. With an odd sense of detachment he pictured her nude and sprawled beneath him, her glorious red-gold hair spread about her like a flaming blanket. Aware that his musings were taking him on an erotic journey, Matt shook his head to clear it of such dangerous thoughts. The effort was futile.

"Matt, did you hear me? Haven't you punished me enough? If you won't let me go topside at least tell me what you intend to do with me."

Running his long tanned fingers through his hair, Matt sent Lily a quelling look. "Truth to tell I haven't decided what's to be done with you, Lily. I can't take you back to Boston for the English have blockaded the harbor."

"Where are you taking Captain Waverly and his crew?"

"To Nassau in the Bahamas, where arrangements can be made for their ransom."

Lily's face turned thoughtful. "Why not leave me in Nassau?"

"Like hell!" Matt roared.

"Will you keep me aboard the *Sea Hawke*?"

"Too dangerous," Matt muttered distractedly. He had pondered the problem long and hard and realized he couldn't keep Lily with him aboard the *Sea Hawke*. The *Sea Hawke* was a privateer whose mission was to engage the enemy in fierce battle. Any one of those battles could snuff out his life and the lives of his crew. He didn't want that for Lily.

"You could take me to New Orleans," Lily suggested. "I could stay with Sarah until the war ends."

"I'll think on it," Matt replied, wondering why he hadn't thought of it himself.

Perhaps the idea of Sarah being in New Orleans was too new for him to come up with so simple a solution. As far as he knew New Orleans was still accessible to American ships and if not he could always sail to Jean Lafitte's island of Barataria and leave his ship while he took Lily through the swamp to New Orleans. Matt had become acquainted with Lafitte two years ago when he had come to the aid of the pirate who proudly flew an American flag. Lafitte's ship had been engaged in battle with a Spanish galleon and Matt had helped in defeating the galleon. After the battle Matt was issued a standing invitation to visit the pirate stronghold any time he chose.

"Where are we now?" Lily asked curiously. The only view out the single porthole was that of heaving seas and blue skies. They could be anywhere.

"In two or three days you should be able to see some of the more than two hundred islands that make up the Bahamas. Very few of them are inhabited. Nassau is the principal city and a pirate haven."

"Can I go ashore?"

"Absolutely not! You have no idea the stir a beautiful woman like you would cause among the locals. They're all rough, unprincipled men who would sell their own mothers for the right price."

"Are there no women in Nassau?"

"Oh, there are women aplenty, if you call pirates' whores and prostitutes women. No, Lily, you'll stay aboard ship where I know you'll be safe the short time we'll be in Nassau. It shouldn't take long to arrange a place for our prisoners to be kept until the English ransom them. Such arrangements are common in Nassau and I have only to return for my money at a later date. Now if your questions are answered, I have duties to attend to." He turned to leave.

"If I'm not allowed on deck I'll make such a racket down here you'll have to tie me up to stop me."

Matt's eyes glowed darkly. "That can be arranged."

"Matt, please, what harm can it do? I need air and exercise. I'm going crazy in here by myself. What purpose is being served by keeping me imprisoned in this cabin?"

Matt's lips tightened. What purpose indeed. Keeping Lily out of sight made it easier for him to bear having her so near when she was so obviously unattainable. Out of sight, out of mind, the old saying went. Only in this case it wasn't working. He wanted her even when he couldn't see her. The only reason he didn't exercise his marital rights was because he still couldn't figure out if his wanting Lily was the result of anger and the need to punish or if he wanted to love her because he ... Sweet Jesus! Mentally he shook himself, aware of the dangerous ground on which he was treading.

"Very well, Lily," Matt relented. "You may go topside whenever you wish as long as you don't distract my men."

Matt felt himself drowning in the smile she bestowed on him and his precious control slipped another notch. If he wasn't careful she'd have him saying things he didn't mean just so he could do all those wonderful things to her he'd been dreaming about at night. Lord preserve him from women who read more into sex than simple gratification, expected marriage to be made in heaven and believed love meant eternal happiness. Only someone as young and naive as Lily would demand all three. Abruptly he turned and stormed out of the cabin.

During the following days Lily wondered if Matt's blatant neglect of her was meant as punishment. If it was, it was working. When she went topside for air he rarely spoke to her, but her skin tingled as his dark, brooding gaze followed her every move. His eyes were unyielding, his expression implacable, but Lily could sense the deep inner struggle churning within his powerful body. With profound insight she wondered if he wanted her as badly as she wanted him. Wanting Matt, needing him as she did, still wasn't enough to persuade her to accept him on his terms.

How soon before he tired of her and found another to take her place? If not Clarissa, then some other beautiful woman to sate his jaded appetite. He had her fortune, did he have to possess her body and soul? Love was such a fragile emotion, yet Lily knew what she felt for Matt could be nurtured with little effort into love. The passion between them was magnificent but she wanted more than that. He had taught her body to crave love, why did he have to be so damn miserly when it came to her heart? There were times when Lily felt a flicker of something deep and profound in Matt but it disappeared so quickly she might have imagined it.

She stood at the ship's rail now, searching the horizon for some of the islands that made up the Bahamas, knowing they were close but unable to see them yet. When Dick Marlow joined her, she smiled up at him. He was a friendly young man whom Lily had quickly taken a liking to. He was virtually the only man aboard the *Sea Hawke* who dared Matt's displeasure to speak to her.

"You should see them soon," Dick said, pointing vaguely. "They'll appear first as tiny jewels amidst a setting of blue velvet surrounded by white cotton."

Lily strained her eyes but saw nothing. "Matt said we'll be stopping just briefly in Nassau."

"Aye, to set the prisoners ashore and arrange for their ransom."

"I wish—"

"See to your duties, Mr. Marlow, I'll answer Mrs. Hawke's questions."

Matt's face was set in a ferocious scowl and a trill of keen awareness shot through Lily as he dismissed his first mate. Dick hesitated, aware of the tension between Matt and his wife and fearing for Lily's safety. Though he didn't think Matt would hurt his wife, Dick knew, as did the entire crew, that they didn't share a cabin and that Lily had been caught in the act of leaving her husband. Dick had experienced Matt's temper firsthand and felt sorry for Lily.

"That is all, Mr. Marlow," Matt said tightly.

Dick had no recourse but to salute smartly and take to his heels.

"I don't want you bothering my officers or crew," Matt remonstrated.

His insinuation smarted and Lily's temper flared. "Make what you want out of it but Dick and I were merely exchanging pleasantries."

The use of his subordinate's first name sent jealousy raging through Matt. He couldn't recall when Lily had smiled up at *him* in such a beguiling manner. Of course he never considered that he had given her little cause to smile of late.

"Mr. Marlow is going to remain in Nassau to collect the ransom," Matt revealed, watching closely for Lily's reaction. When she merely nodded he seemed satisfied and changed the subject. "When we reach Nassau I want you to remain below. 'Tis best no one knows there's a woman aboard."

Lily digested that statement and though she couldn't discern the logic, gave Matt no argument. Once he left ship she'd do what she pleased anyway. She might even sneak ashore and find passage to England. But Matt must have guessed her thoughts for once they reached Nassau he locked her in her cabin, where she fumed and paced in impotent rage till the wee hours of the morning.

Matt and Dick sat in the crowded inn quaffing ale. The English prisoners were lodged in a hut on the beach and arrangements had been made to send a ransom request to England. Matt imparted instructions to Dick concerning the young man's stay in Nassau and Dick took his leave to look for lodging for himself. Matt's dark eyes roved restlessly about the large common room, the din of voices making coherent thought nearly impossible. Beside him two rough sailors were arguing over a gaudily dressed woman. Two minor fights were in progress across the room and several pirates were engaged in boisterous song.

A few of the pirates he recognized, some he didn't, but all were dangerous, armed to the teeth, and itching for a fight. Matt was itching, but not for a fight. A woman, that's what he needed. A simple lusty woman who could take his mind off his wife who demanded things of him he couldn't offer. He wanted a woman who asked for nothing beyond the pleasure he could bring her; a woman who would settle for sex, not love.

"Be ye needin' a woman, lovey?"

She was an artificial redhead, deep-bosomed, whose eyes promised secret pleasures. Instinctively Matt knew she would be uninhibited and utterly frenzied in bed. She was just what he needed to cleanse his blood of the cold, unyielding vixen he had married.

"That depends," Matt said archly. "If the woman is you I might find myself in desperate need."

"Me room's above stairs. Ye won't be sorry. I'm clean and know how to please a man." She paused, arching her back to give Matt the full benefit of her large breasts. "Me name's Lily. Call me Lil."

Matt started violently. Lily! Sweet Jesus! Was fate playing some vile trick on him? Was there no escaping the tawny-eyed enchantress who disturbed his dreams and turned his life upside down? Suddenly Matt saw this as a golden opportunity to thumb his nose at fate, to dupe the perverse demons who chased him. Grasping Lil's wrist, he dragged her toward the stairs.

"Impatient devil, ain't ye?" Lil giggled, making no protest as she eagerly followed Matt up the stairs. She was the most popular whore at the Gilded Goose but seldom had she seen a man as appealing as Matt. "What's yer name, lovey?"

"Matt," Matt growled tersely. "Which is your room?"

Lil pointed and Matt pulled open the door, shoving her inside. She wore a short red dress that clashed dreadfully with her hair but Matt noticed nothing save for her large breasts straining above the neckline of her bodice. He turned her around and began undoing the laces.

"Be careful," Lil chided, "that's me best dress."

"I'll buy you another."

Matt was driven. Driven by the need to purge the picture of Lily's delicate beauty from his mind. Driven by the urge to throw caution to the wind and race back to his ship and tell Lily exactly what she longed to hear. Driven by devils who whispered that there was no need to change his life merely because he had taken a wife. Driven by habits too ingrained to toss aside. But a force far stronger than any of those just mentioned made itself known in the most basic way.

Lil's clothes lay in a heap on the floor. Matt stepped back to admire her beauty and stared in horror at the sagging curves of the coarse, faded prostitute he was about to bed. Desire died as quickly as it had been born and Matt went cold. Had Lily done this to him? Before he met her he would have bedded Lil without the slightest hesitation, and enjoyed it immensely. It wouldn't have bothered him in the least that her huge breasts drooped or that her stomach protruded. He would have taken his pleasure and forgotten her ten minutes after he left.

Sweet Jesus! Had Lily spoiled him for any other woman?

Growing alarmed by Matt's silence, Lil sidled closer. "What's wrong, lovey? Ye was all hot and eager a minute ago. Do ye want Lil to help ye along?" She reached out, grasping him between the legs, and her brows arched upward in surprise. "I can see Lil's got her work cut out for her. Take off yer clothes, lovey."

Matt drew back in aversion. This had never happened to him before and he knew exactly where to place the blame. "Sorry, Lil, I'm not in the mood." He dug in his pocket, withdrew a coin and tossed it on the bed. "Maybe some other time." Turning on his heel he made a hasty retreat. Lil's gasp of outrage was tempered only by the size of the coin Matt left behind.

Matt paused below just long enough to down another glass of ale before leaving the inn. His brow was furrowed, his face screwed up in a frown. He knew exactly what he wanted and it wasn't a redheaded whore who probably had bedded more men than he had met in his lifetime.

Lily.

What had happened back there at the inn left a lasting impression on him, one that gave him pause for thought. If he was perfectly honest he'd admit that Lily had somehow made herself indispensable to him. Lord knows he had tried to ignore her, fought against making a permanent commitment that would tie him down to one woman forever. He had even admitted he didn't intend to remain faithful. But dark forces inside him were working to disavow all he'd claimed. Whether he liked it or not he had been more faithful to Lily than God intended any man to be. And more incredible was the fact that he couldn't even begin to explain it.

Matt was pensive as he boarded the *Sea Hawke* and climbed below to the cabin he was using since he had given Lily his own quarters. It was well past midnight and all was quiet aboard ship. The watch reported nothing amiss and Matt wondered if Lily was still furious with him for locking her in for the night. He paused before her door, his fingers inches from the key, his body taut with the need to open the door and look upon her. No, dammit, he wanted to do more than simply look at her. He wanted to peel the clothes from her sweet little body and thrust into her again and again until he purged her from his blood.

Even if it took a lifetime.

Chapter 12

When Lily tried the door latch the following morning it opened easily beneath her fingertips. She assumed someone had unlocked her door early this morning and wasted no time in dressing since the hour was already late. When she appeared topside she was met by a blurry-eyed Matt. He looked terrible, as if he hadn't slept a wink the night before. Was he as miserable as she was? Lily wondered distractedly as Matt growled out a greeting.

"Was your trip ashore successful?" Lily ventured coolly.

"Very." His sheepish grin led Lily to believe he had done more last night than arrange for the ransom of his captives. With an indignant huff she whirled to stare at the busy harbor. Only it wasn't there. Sometime during the night they had put out to sea and nothing but calm blue water and the outline of distant islands obstructed her view.

"We've left Nassau!"

"We sailed on the midnight tide since there was no reason to linger."

"Where are we going?"

"I've set a course for New Orleans. It's one of the remaining ports not yet blockaded by the British."

"How long will we stay in New Orleans?"

"*You* are the only one remaining," Matt corrected.

"Once I set you ashore and see you safe with Sarah and Jeff I'll be returning to sea. This war is not yet over. Now if you'll excuse me I've duties to attend to. If you haven't yet had your breakfast go to the galley, Cook has saved you some food."

Lily turned to watch him walk away, wondering who the woman was he had bedded last night. Was she someone he had known previously or just a woman he had chosen at random to assuage his lust? Not that it mattered, she tried to tell herself. As long as Matt didn't bother her he could bed anyone he pleased. She even began to believe her lies, until she recalled how wonderfully he made love, how marvelous he made her feel, and how absolutely earthshaking was her response to him.

Lily's eyes narrowed thoughtfully as they caressed the manly sway of his slim hips, the taut mounds of his buttocks tightening with each step as he climbed the ladder to the bridge. His back was straight and narrow, his shoulders broad. Suddenly he turned— and found her gaze lingering on him in a manner that suggested anything but disinterest. For a breathless moment their eyes clung, then Matt flashed her a impudent grin and continued on his way. Lily flushed and lowered her head, concentrating on anything but Matt's arrogant smirk. Was the man a sorcerer? she wondered, giving an angry toss of her head. How did he know she was staring at him?

That night Matt boldly entered Lily's cabin without announcing himself. She was preparing for bed and had just pulled her prim white nightgown over her head when Matt burst into the cabin. A single lamp swung from the bulkhead and she froze as he paused just inside the door, staring at her so intently she felt certain he could see right through her single garment.

"What do you want?" she asked, finally finding her voice.

"This is my cabin, I can come in here anytime I please."

"Then find me another cabin where I won't be disturbed," Lily shot back defiantly.

"You're still my wife, Lily."

"That didn't stop you from bedding another woman in Nassau!"

Matt paled. His sudden lack of color served only to confirm Lily's suspicion that Matt had spent his spare time in Nassau in the arms of a woman. "You don't know that!"

"I do now." Her voice was so calm it belied the turmoil churning inside her soul.

"Why shouldn't I seek solace elsewhere when my wife refuses to perform her wifely duties?"

"Why, indeed?" Lily repeated with studied indifference. "I told you before I don't enjoy being used for that purpose."

"You enjoyed my lovemaking."

"I suppose I did," Lily allowed grudgingly. "You're very good at it."

Matt smiled thinly. "There is much more I can teach you."

"I don't need your lessons."

The corners of Matt's mouth turned down in grim response. "What exactly does that mean? Has Clay Winslow been teaching you things in my absence?"

"You're disgusting," Lily said, deliberately turning her back. "Please leave, I'm tired."

Matt stood glaring at her back, his fists clenched tightly at his sides. He had no earthly idea why her goading caused him to lose all restraint. Lord knows he had reason enough to beat her into submission, but strangely all he wanted to do was strip the offensive white shroud from her body and love her until she cried for mercy. In his mind he visualized how she felt and tasted beneath his hands and mouth, and those tantalizing images were all that was needed to bring him to her side in two long strides.

Lily gasped as she felt Matt's fingers tighten on the soft flesh of her shoulders and spin her around. "Disgusting? You think I'm disgusting? You have no idea what that word means. I may be disgusting but you like it."

Lily felt herself slam into his chest. Before she could regain her breath, Matt's mouth slanted down on hers. She whimpered in protest as his tongue pried her lips apart and delved without mercy into the heated warmth of her mouth. A great roaring filled her ears and she grew dizzy from lack of oxygen, but still Matt continued his punishing kisses. Until she grew limp in his arms and he felt her sag helplessly against him. Only then did he relent and release her mouth. By then he had the top buttons of her nightgown undone and lowered his mouth unerringly to the rosy tip of one breast.

Lily drew in a shuddering breath as the moist heat of his mouth penetrated the sensitive nipple. She felt it swell and harden against his tongue and silently cursed her wayward body for responding to a man she couldn't stand. When Matt lifted her into his arms and carried her to the bed she suddenly realized she had goaded him beyond human endurance and nothing short of a miracle would stop him now. The sad thing was that at this point she didn't know whether she wanted to stop him or not. Her body was afire, her blood boiling in her veins, and when Matt knelt on the bed beside her and raised her nightgown, little resistance remained. When his hands found that moist place between her legs and he plied his fingers with consummate skill, her willpower scattered into tattered shreds.

He was panting now, and his eyes were hard as glittering diamonds as he released his straining manhood from the confines of his trousers. She felt him full and hard against her thigh and waited breathlessly for him to penetrate her last defenses. But Matt had other ideas. Slowly he lowered his mouth to where his fingers had been only moments before.

"Is this disgusting?" he asked as his tongue slid over her swollen inner flesh.

"Yes! No! Oh, God, I don't know! I can't think when you do that."

Matt didn't answer as he buried his mouth deeper into her groin, seeking, finding, tormenting her with his lips and tongue. His tongue was thrusting deeper now and Lily seized his head, trying to dislodge him, but ended up holding him closer as he found the tiny sensitive bud of her womanhood and began flicking it provocatively with the tip of his tongue. She arched against him and he grasped her buttocks to hold her still. The only sound in the room was Lily's harsh breathing punctuated by Matt's stifled groans.

Matt welcomed the violence of her passion, reveled in it as he skillfully brought her to the edge of sanity. Suddenly a cry rose from her throat, but it was a cry of wanting, of need, a plea for release from the torment of his loving. Taking pity on her, Matt drove her relentlessly toward climax. Lily paused at the edge for an anxious moment then tumbled over into the bottomless pit of ecstasy.

"Now it's my turn," he gasped as he raised himself and poised over her.

Slowly regaining her wits, Lily felt Matt's powerful erection prodding between her legs and she opened wider to accommodate him. He had barely penetrated when someone set up a frantic pounding on the door. Matt froze, his powerful muscles straining to regain control as he loomed over Lily. The terrible expression on his face spelled trouble for whoever dared interrupt him at such a crucial moment.

"Cap'n," the voice on the other side of the door called as he renewed the racket. "The watch has

sighted a ship. The moon is bright tonight and she's
clearly visible through the glass if ye'd care to take a
look."

"Hell and damnation!" Matt spat through clenched
teeth as he struggled to bring his raging passion
under tight rein. "I'm coming, you can stop that in-
fernal racket."

"Aye, aye, sir," came the muffled reply. Immediately the sound of retreating footsteps echoed down
the passageway.

Scowling from frustration, Matt heaved a ragged
sigh and slowly lifted himself off Lily. Still dazed,
Lily lay still, watching dazedly as Matt stared at her
with a mixture of regret and astonishment. "You win
again, love." He spoke in a voice so low she barely
heard his words. "But then you always do." It took
him but a few moments to adjust his clothes and
then he strode jerkily from the cabin. It was a long
time before Lily realized that Matt would not return
this night and finally fell into an uneasy sleep.

Dawn had just given way to brilliant sunlight
when Lily awoke the next morning. She stretched,
feeling strangely content, until she remembered the
reason for her contentment. Matt had done it again.
He had touched her and kissed her and completely
carried her away until she was putty in his hands,
ready and willing to let him do whatever he pleased
with her. Why must she be a spineless ninny where
Matt was concerned? she wondered as anger built
slowly and steadily inside her. Then she recalled that
she had decided to leave Matt for that very same reason. Though he thrilled her with his loving he promised her nothing.

Suddenly Lily's thoughts flew to that moment last
night when Matt had nearly taken possession of her
and was torn away at the last possible moment. A
ship! The watch had sighted a ship. Was it English?
Or another American privateer in search of prey? Or

since they were still so near to the Bahamas perhaps it was pirates. Since speculation would gain her nothing but a headache, Lily rose swiftly, washed and dressed and went topside. She saw Matt on the bridge, a spyglass to his eye as he tracked the swift approach of the unknown ship. She thought he looked tired and drawn and wondered if he had slept at all last night.

Shifting her gaze in the direction in which Matt and most of the crew were looking, Lily saw the vague outline of the ship that obviously was pursuing them. Unfortunately it was still too far away for her to make out the vessel's colors.

"If she's English we'll stand and fight." While Lily strained her eyes to catch a glimpse of the approaching ship, Matt had left the bridge to stand beside her. "She won't be the first enemy ship we've sighted and challenged since we left Boston and she won't be the last." His confidence reassured Lily.

"How soon will she catch us?"

Matt squinted into the distance. "By late afternoon, with that brisk wind at her back. Could be we're in for a blow, but we'll not run. The men are prepared to fight and eagerly look forward to another victory."

"Have there been so many?" Lily asked in a hushed voice.

"Victories?"

Lily nodded.

"Aye, I've taken my share of prizes in the months since I've joined the war. So far I've been lucky, sustaining little damage or loss of life, although there have been injuries to my crew."

He was staring at her so intently she felt impaled by his gaze. "What is it, Matt? Why are you looking at me like that?"

"I don't want to see you hurt, Lily, but neither do I want to disappoint my crew by turning tail and running," he surprised her by saying. "We haven't lost a battle yet but there is always a first time. When the time comes, remain below where you won't be in harm's way. From what little I can tell from this distance she appears to be an English warship. She's fast and well armed, but so is the *Sea Hawke*."

"I have every confidence in your ability," Lily said so seriously Matt couldn't help but smile.

"At least you have confidence in something I do," he intoned dryly. Then he was called back to duty, leaving Lily to stare fretfully at the approaching ship. For some obscure reason she couldn't shake the feeling of impending doom. From the moment she first glimpsed the vague outline of the ship a terrible foreboding stirred restlessly in her breast. It was a feeling that persisted throughout the long day.

Shortly after noon Matt's prediction proved true when it was established that the ship was indeed an English warship. To Lily she looked huge and forbidding as she scudded before the wind. At the rate she was traveling she would reach the *Sea Hawke* about the time Matt estimated. Preparations for battle were already under way; the deck swarmed with men running out cannon and preparing arms with which to defend themselves. Little heed was paid to Lily as she clung to the rail, her amber eyes filled with a fear she couldn't name.

When the English warship came within firing range, Matt suddenly seemed to remember her. "Go below, Lily, and don't come topside no matter what you hear. If you've never been in a sea battle you have no idea how fierce the noise and smoke can be, and knowing your penchant for curiosity you'll be tempted to investigate. I'm warning you now, don't do it. Lock your door and open it for no one but me. Is that clear?"

"But, Matt—"

"No argument, Lily. Just do as I say." His expression was so implacable that Lily didn't have the nerve to defy him, so she agreed.

He ushered her to her cabin immediately. But instead of turning instantly to return topside, he pulled her into his arms and kissed her fiercely. His mouth roamed freely from her lips to her brow, down her cheek to the wildly beating pulse at the base of her throat, then back to her lips. He crushed her tightly against him until she could feel the erratic beat of his heart beneath his clothing.

"You owe me," he whispered against her lips. Then abruptly he released her. She watched in stunned silence as he turned on his heel and retraced his steps. Not until he disappeared up the ladder did Lily find the strength to enter her cabin and lock the door behind her.

Lily clapped her hands over her ears to drown out the terrible sound of booming cannon and cries of agony that drifted down to her. Matt was right, she silently agreed, nothing could have prepared her for the din of battle or the horrible screams of the wounded following the explosion of cannonball and shrapnel. Speculating on the possibility that one of those voices belonged to Matt nearly drove her crazy. Why did he insist she remain below when she could be of some help? And why did she agree to such an insane request when she could be of use helping with the wounded? Suddenly the sound of clashing metal was added to the crashing of cannonballs, and Lily's attention sharpened. Had a new element been added to the battle?

No sooner was the thought out than the answer came in a rush of near panic. The metallic clashes meant that the *Sea Hawke* had been boarded and hand-to-hand combat was being waged topside. Suddenly Matt's warning fled like ashes before the wind as Lily unlocked the cabin door and peered cautiously into the deserted passageway. Thick coils of smoke rolled along the corridor, leading Lily to believe that the ship was afire. Smoke clogged her throat and she coughed and gagged, but finally she reached the ladder, where fresh air wafted down to her. Or as fresh as the air could be considering the acrid odor of battle. Rung by rung she made her way up the ladder, poking her head out the hatch when she reached the top step. The ship lurched crazily and Lily's first thought was that they were sinking. But then she realized that sometime during the battle the wind had risen and light rain was now lashing both ships and their occupants.

Matt knew they were in for the fight of their lives when he first saw the size and firing power of the warship. She was the *H.M.S. Reliant*, whose renown had preceded her. Her captain was reputed to be a man of cunning and courage. Matt rightfully assumed the *Reliant* was carrying troops to fight in the United States and therefore had twice the manpower that was available to him aboard the *Sea Hawke*.

After having emerged victorious from battles with several English merchantmen and frigates, he now had the misfortune to come upon a warship that possessed the ability to beat him. As the *Reliant* swiftly closed the distance between them it became increasingly evident that he couldn't have run from them and escaped even if he had wanted to. And he did consider it, for Lily's sake. But the ship was too fast and there was nowhere to hide in the open sea despite the fact that the Bahama Islands lay just over the horizon.

To Matt's credit, the *Sea Hawke* fired the first shot, quickly returned by the *Reliant*. And then the battle began in earnest. But for all his quick maneuvering he couldn't escape the relentless pursuit of the *Reliant*. She scored a few solid hits on the smaller *Sea Hawke*, causing considerable damage and starting fires. But surrender never entered Matt's mind. Not even when grappling hooks bound the two ships together and men in crisp red uniforms began streaming over the boarding planks brandishing swords and firing weapons.

Two soldiers had Matt backed up against a broken mast now as he skillfully parried their thrusts, but it was a losing battle. He was tiring rapidly and the wound he'd taken in his shoulder earlier was bleeding profusely, making his right arm numb. Besides the deep slash in his shoulder, he was covered with blood from numerous other cuts and he realized that if the tide didn't turn in his favor soon the battle was lost. His one consoling thought was that from what he knew of the captain of the *Reliant*, Lily would be returned to her father without being harmed. Perhaps that was the best thing that could happen to her.

Suddenly Matt became aware that the wind was howling all around them, buffeting both ships and causing them to bounce against one another. He heard them banging together and realized immediately the danger that existed should the storm develop into something more serious. This area of the southern Atlantic was known for the fierce hurricanes that came out of nowhere and struck with devastating effect.

Suddenly the ship lurched and Matt fell to his knees, leaving himself vulnerable for attack. His two opponents realized this at the same time and poised for the kill. Matt scrambled for his sword but it was too late. He closed his eyes for a moment of silent prayer but found his mind filled with thoughts of Lily. He regretted being unable to finish what he'd started the night before but rejoiced that he had given her a moment of bliss even if he had been left wanting. In the next moment he opened his eyes to await death like a man and was shocked when a body came hurtling out of nowhere to knock the two English soldiers from their feet. They went sliding across the slick deck in a tangled mass of arms and legs.

Lily had spied Matt immediately when she peered from the hatch, and her face went white. He was crouched at the feet of two British soldiers who had their swords raised to deliver the killing blow. Without a thought for her own safety, she propelled herself across the deck and smashed into the two men who threatened Matt's life. They went flying across the deck, but in the process she could not check her own momentum and slid helplessly after them. As she went flying past, Matt recognized her instantly and made a wild grab for her dress. But his weakened right arm prevented him from holding on to her. She continued on, gaining speed on the rain-slicked deck as she neared the railing.

Matt held his breath when Lily caught hold of the rail and appeared to succeed in stopping her headlong flight. He rose unsteadily to his feet, intending to go to her aid, when a sudden gust of wind and an unexpected swell tilted the ship, spilling Lily into the sea. Roaring in shock and outrage, Matt scrambled to the rail. Lily was nowhere in sight. Without a second thought, he dove in after her.

He dove deep, deeper still, and opened his eyes. He saw nothing in the murky depths but seaweed and wind-whipped foam. He rose to the surface, gasping for breath and frantically searching the vast emptiness for some sign of Lily. Nothing. Drawing a deep breath, he dove again, this time deeper, until he thought his lungs would burst. Just when all hope fled he felt something brush his face. Instinctively he grabbed for it, realizing immediately that he held on to a hank of Lily's long hair. With a spurt of energy he didn't know he possessed, he hauled her to the surface.

Had anyone seen them go overboard? he wondered desperately as he looked toward the ship. The wind was howling now and heavy rain was pelting the area. He could barely make out the shapes of the two ships. He thought his eyes were deceiving him when he saw the *Reliant* pull away from the *Sea Hawke* and sail away.

Bobbing on the wind-tossed waves, Matt somehow kept Lily afloat, wondering how long he could continue to do so if the storm turned out to be a dreaded hurricane. Already his right arm was numb, and worse yet he didn't know if Lily was dead or alive. She hung in his arms like dead weight, putting more strain on his body than he could bear in his condition. Loss of blood had taken its toll and he fervently wished he and Lily could have reconciled during their last moments together.

Suddenly something butted into Matt, knocking the breath from him. He went under, then came to the surface sputtering. At first he thought it was a shark and despaired of coming to such a horrible end. But then he saw in the eerie half-light of the storm that it wasn't a shark at all but a large section of mast from the *Sea Hawke* that had been blasted away by one of the cannon from the *Reliant*. It still had a good-sized piece of sail attached to it. Shifting Lily to his weak right arm, Matt made a grab for it with his stronger left arm. He managed to seize a piece of the sail and pull the mast toward him until he could grasp it.

Cautiously he shifted Lily until he could slide her atop the mast. He turned her on her stomach and water poured from her mouth. Then he slowly and painfully lifted himself atop the mast until he was straddling it directly behind her. After he rested a while he used the knife attached to his belt to tear strips from the sail and tie Lily onto the mast so she wouldn't slip off in case something happened to him.

Then he did the same for himself, stretching out and binding himself to the mast at the waist. Those tasks had depleted his diminishing strength. All he could do now was hope and pray someone aboard the *Sea Hawke* would see them and that the storm wasn't a fierce hurricane.

Matt's prayers were only half answered. The storm blew itself out toward morning but the only man that had seen them go overboard had been wounded shortly afterward and lay unconscious on the deck.

Chaos reigned aboard the *Sea Hawke*. The captain of the *Reliant* recognized the beginning of a storm, possibly a hurricane, and made a decision that saved the *Sea Hawke* and her crew. He realized that a worsening storm could damage or even destroy both ships, lashed together as they were, and decided to flee to shelter rather than weather the storm on the open sea. They weren't far from the Bahamas, where hundreds of sheltered cays and coves existed. His judgment was sound, one any captain with many lives depending on him would make. Unfortunately for him but fortunately for the *Sea Hawke*, the storm never developed into a full-blown hurricane. By the time that fact became apparent, the disabled *Sea Hawke* was limping toward a safe haven in Nassau.

And by the time the injured seaman aboard the *Sea Hawke* had regained his wits and related his story to the second mate, the ship was in no condition to begin a search of the area. At any rate, if the captain and his wife still lived they would have been blown many miles away by now. When the *Sea Hawke* reached Nassau, Dick Winslow was the first to learn of the disaster. The stricken first mate took charge immediately, ordering repairs made without delay and vowing to begin a search the moment the *Sea Hawke* was seaworthy. Unfortunately the young man had no notion the damage was so extensive that it

would be weeks before the ship was ready to insti-
gate a search of the many islands and cays compris-
ing the Bahamas.

Matt had no idea how long they had been drifting.
His terrible thirst told him it had been at least a day,
and maybe more, for much of the time he had been
floating in and out of consciousness. Lily was still
unconscious but showed signs of waking, giving
Matt meager reason to rejoice. He almost wished she
would remain comatose for when she regained her
wits she was bound to be as thirsty as he was. The
sun was relentless now after the storm and he could
feel his skin burning. He had carefully covered Lily's
tender skin with the remnants of sail but there wasn't
enough to salvage for himself.

Still, there was much to be thankful for. They were
still alive, and from his deductions not far from the
Bahamas. Any time now they could drift to one of
those distant islands and exist forever, if need be, off
the bounty of the lush land. The thought of himself
and Lily alone on a deserted island was mindbog-
gling. Despite his weakness his body stiffened at the
notion of having Lily to himself every hour of every
day, sleeping with her in his arms every night, making love to her whenever the mood struck him.

With no weapon but the knife still safely attached
to his belt, she would have to rely on him for her
livelihood, look to him for shelter and food. She
would come to depend on him for protection and
maybe even learn to love—good Lord, what was he
thinking?

"Matt?"

Her voice was thin and reedy but his name was
clearly discernible. She licked her dry lips but little
moisture was deposited on their cracked surface.

"I'm here, Lily."

"Where—where are we?"

"Floating in the ocean somewhere near the Bahamas."

"Are we alive?"

Though it hurt to smile he did so anyway. "I hope so. I'd hate to be this hot and thirsty in Heaven. Or perhaps I've gone in the other direction," he croaked wryly.

"Don't joke, Matt, this is serious," Lily chided crossly. "Why can't I move?"

"Because I've tied you to the mast. I've done the same to myself. It probably saved us for we've both been unconscious for many hours."

"Oh."

"Why did you do it, Lily?" Matt asked abruptly. "Why didn't you stay below like I told you?"

Lily was silent for a long time before answering. "The thought that you might be hurt or dying drove me topside. I—I wanted to help."

"You did, believe me, but you nearly lost your life in the bargain. Do you remember what happened?"

"I recall nothing after I hit the water." Suddenly she twisted her head around to impale him with her amber gaze. "How did you get tossed overboard? Why didn't I drown?"

Silence.

"Matt, did you hear me? How did you fall in the ocean?"

Matt's voice was low and strident. "I jumped."

"What!"

"I jumped in after you."

Lily fell silent, too stunned to speak. She thought of many things she wanted to say but could only utter two short words. "Thank you."

"You saved my life so it's no more than right that I save yours," Matt said, discounting his selfless act of bravery.

After that they both fell silent, each contemplating

their own thoughts and hopes for a future they might never have. How long could they exist without water? With a sailor's sure knowledge, Matt knew it wasn't nearly long enough.

Chapter 13

The roaring in her ears expanded and receded like the pounding of surf on a windy day and with difficulty Lily cranked open her salt-encrusted eyes. The blazing sun blinded her and she quickly shut them against the relentless glare. Then slowly other things began registering in her hazy brain. She no longer bobbed helplessly atop wind-tossed waves but was suddenly conscious of solid ground beneath her. And water lapped at her at relentless intervals. Sounds also became a part of her new awareness. The raucous cry of birds invaded the dim recesses of her mind. Shaking her head to clear it of cobwebs, Lily managed to open her eyes and raise her head.

The sight that met her eyes was the most magnificent she'd ever had the pleasure of viewing. Land! Miraculously the mast she and Matt were lashed to had drifted to one of the seven hundred islands or numerous cays in the Bahamas. What extraordinary luck, she reflected, having been fully prepared to meet death in the middle of the ocean. Instead, she and Matt were lying on a peaceful sandy beach that looked like a beautiful paradise. Twisting her head around, she saw Matt lying still as death behind her and a jolt of raw panic shot through her.

"Matt!"

No answer.

"Matt, can you hear me?"

Silence.

Frantically Lily fumbled with the strips of sail binding her to the mast, cursing when her numb fingers took far too long to untie the wet canvas. Despairing of ever releasing those tight knots by herself, she suddenly recalled Matt's knife. Reaching behind her, she located it still thrust into his belt and drew it forth. She made short work of her own bonds then turned to work on Matt's. When he was free she rolled him off the mast and onto his back. He looked so pale it frightened her. Gingerly she touched his forehead. He felt hot—so hot. And the skin exposed to the sun had baked to an angry red.

Then she noticed the oozing wound on Matt's shoulder and a strangled cry left her throat. It had nearly stopped bleeding and the salt water had washed it clean, but it still looked swollen and ugly with jagged edges of flesh surrounding the open wound. Lily realized it needed stitching but since she had neither thread nor needle there was nothing she could do to hold it together. She also realized she needed to get Matt out of the surf, for the tide was coming in and he was in danger of floating back out to sea.

Grasping Matt beneath the arms, she dragged him with difficulty up the sandy beach to the line of trees ringing the sparkling crescent of sand and water. After making him comfortable she decided to drag the mast up the beach also, thinking that the stout section of wood and remnants of sail clinging to it might come in handy. By the time she finished, Matt showed signs of waking.

"Water," Matt croaked, licking his dry lips as he attempted to rise. Lily pushed him back down with gentle pressure.

"Lie still, Matt, you've lost a lot of blood and you're feverish."

Matt squinted against the sudden glare of sunlight. "Lily? Where are we?"

"I—I don't know. Some island, I think. I'm thirsty too but I don't know if water is available."

"I'll take a look," Matt said weakly as he attempted once again to rise. He managed to balance himself on his elbows for several seconds before falling back down. "Give me a few minutes to rest."

Astutely Lily knew Matt would need more than a few minutes of rest. "Stay where you are, I'll go." She rose unsteadily to her feet, took two steps then stopped abruptly. "What will I carry water in if I do find it?"

Matt's brow furrowed, trying to solve the dilemma and finding it extremely difficult to concentrate. His unfocused gaze wandered to the beach. "Coconut shells. Make use of those shell halves that washed up on the shore. Fill them with water."

Grateful at having the problem solved so easily, Lily hurried off. She was every bit as thirsty as Matt. "Don't get lost!" Matt shouted as she disappeared into the tangle of trees and dense shrubs lining the shore. What he refrained from revealing was the fact that many of these islands had no source of fresh water. If this was one of them they had little hope of surviving. •

Hindered by heavy, wet skirts, Lily stumbled through the jungle, fearing to go too far and become hopelessly lost. But her terrible thirst drove her deeper and deeper into the lush underbrush. Suddenly she became aware that she had been following a trodden path. The path wound through the jungle as if leading to a specific destination. As the path widened it became obvious to Lily that others had been here before. Was the island inhabited? she wondered as a shiver of dread passed through her. So far she hadn't seen any people. What if the inhabitants were unfriendly? That terrible thought filled her with unmentionable fear.

She came upon the sparkling pool quite suddenly. It was clear and blue and set in an exotic setting surrounded by a profusion of wildflowers of every color and description. Large pink birds with long legs and necks stood poised on one foot, staring back at her. The sight took her breath away and for a few moments she stood and gawked. Then she remembered her thirst and quickly dropped to her knees to drink her fill. The water was cool and refreshing and more delicious than the most precious wine. After she had drunk her fill she dunked her head beneath the surface to rinse the salt from her face and hair. After she'd seen to Matt she fully intended to return to bathe herself and wash her clothes. Matt's, too.

Matt chafed restlessly when Lily failed to return in what he determined was a reasonable length of time. It was so easy to become lost or disoriented in a tropical jungle setting and he knew Lily had no experience in a situation like this. He shouldn't have let her go off on her own but their need for water was so acute he had ignored his better judgment. When he thought too much time had elapsed since Lily wandered off on her own, he staggered to his feet, rested briefly against a palm tree to steady himself, then took several wobbly steps in the direction in which Lily had disappeared. Fortunately he hadn't gone far when Lily suddenly appeared through the dense foliage.

"I found it, Matt, look!" She held out two coconut halves sloshing with water. He accepted one and drank deeply.

"Thank God," he breathed when he had quenched his thirst. "I was so afraid—well, never mind, we're going to be just fine now until rescue arrives."

Lily helped him back to the beach then dropped down beside him. "I found a path, Matt. It led directly to the pool. Do you suppose the island is inhabited?"

Matt's attention sharpened. "A path? Did it look as if it had been traveled recently?"

Lily's brow puckered in thought. "It was somewhat overgrown so it couldn't have seen much traffic. It was so peaceful there by the pool," she said wistfully.

"I doubt the island is inhabited," Matt ventured.

"Then how do you account for the path?"

"Very few of these islands and cays have fresh water. I'd be willing to bet that pirates put in here from time to time for fresh water to fill their casks. Fruit is probably plentiful, too. Luck was surely with us, love, when we drifted to this particular island."

"Pirates! What if they come back? What will they do to us?"

Matt knew exactly what pirates would do to a beautiful woman like Lily but he wisely kept it to himself. If their incredible luck held they'd be off the island long before any pirates returned. At least one crewman from the *Sea Hawke* must have seen them fall into the sea and he expected to see a search party arrive any day now. When Matt saw the *Reliant* back away from the *Sea Hawke* after he dove into the sea after Lily, he felt positive his ship would make it to Nassau and safety.

"Don't even think about that, love. We'll be rescued long before pirates come back to this island."

"How do you feel, Matt? I wish I had needle and thread to stitch that wound. And something to give you for fever. I could gather fruit to feed us but even if I caught a small animal I couldn't cook it without fire."

Matt grinned, reached into his pocket and drew forth a small leather pouch. Inside was flint, needle, thread, hooks and a length of line. Lily squealed in delight. "I don't believe it!"

"A good sailor always carries the bare essentials with him. He never knows when he'll be shipwrecked. And I still have my knife. We won't starve, that's for sure. How good are you with a needle?" he asked, handing her the implement.

"I've never sewn on human skin before but I don't imagine it's any different from stitching on material," she said slowly. Despite her brave words she eyed Matt's wound with misgiving. "There's nothing to dull the pain."

"Just do it," Matt said from between clenched teeth.

Lily nodded and carefully threaded the needle. Matt groaned when the first stitch punctured his flesh. Fortunately he passed out before the next.

Lily kept checking Matt's head from time to time but found that his temperature was still far too high. When he began shivering she cut the remaining sail from the mast and covered him with it. When that didn't seem to help she removed his clothes and then her own and cuddled up next to him, pulling the meager piece of sail over them in the unlikely event that someone on this godforsaken island would happen upon them. Her body heat soon warmed him and he fell into a fitful sleep. Moments later Lily joined him.

When she awoke much later it was dark, but the moon was so bright it blanketed the island in a silver shroud. She became aware of the sizzling heat of Matt's body and fear such as she had never known before seized her. What if Matt died? What if she was left alone on this deserted island?

"Are you awake, Lily?" The sound of his voice reassured her, but not much. "Is there any water left?"

She located the coconut shell and helped him drink. "How do you feel?"

"Like hell. But if this is what it takes to get you in

bed with me without any clothes, I'll gladly endure it."

Lily flushed. "How could you jest at a time like this?"

"Who's jesting?" His hand slid up the naked length of her hip to rest on her breast. He started to rise over her but weakness quickly laid his intentions to rest. "Damn!" He reached out again but Lily scooted away.

"Behave," she rebuked gently. "You'll open up your wound. I've stitched it and it's stopped bleeding but you'll do yourself harm if you tear it open."

With a sigh of regret Matt sank down again onto his soft bed of sand. "Lie down beside me."

"Only if you promise to be good."

"It seems as if I can do nothing else."

Gingerly she snuggled down beside him again. "Go to sleep, tomorrow I'll find us something to eat."

Lily reached up and plucked a plump hand of bananas hanging just within her reach. Hunger had awakened her early, and donning only her shift and shoes, she walked toward the pool in search of ripe fruit for their breakfast. She returned with the bananas, ate two of them immediately and left the rest beside Matt, who was still sleeping soundly. Then gathering up her remaining clothing as well as Matt's, she started back toward the pool. The clothes were stiff with salt and needed a thorough washing before they could be comfortably worn again.

Lily lingered a long time at the pool, first bathing then dunking the clothes and wringing them out. She laid them out on bushes to dry and sat at the pool's edge drying her hair in the hot morning sun. She had no idea how enchanting she looked, nude, her red-gold hair reflecting the sun and curling about her face in wild disarray. Oblivious to all but the peacefulness of her surroundings, she stretched luxuriously, suddenly glad to be alive, and lifted her face to the welcoming warmth of the healing rays.

Leaning on a stout walking stick, Matt paused several feet behind Lily. It was obvious to him that she hadn't heard him approach and he didn't want to frighten her. But most of all he wanted to fill his eyes and his senses with the enthralling sight of her. She was absolutely breathtaking. Matt made a strangled sound deep in his throat and pain from his wound wasn't the only agony he was suffering at the moment. He wanted to make love to Lily with every fiber of his being—and it nearly killed him to think he wasn't strong enough to do either of them any good.

"You're so lovely looking at you hurts my eyes," he said softly.

"Oh." Lily whirled, surprised to see Matt standing behind her yet relieved it was him and not some strange man. Instinctively her hands flew to shield her breasts and she drew her legs up in a purely reflexive motion. "What are you doing here?" Like her, he was completely nude, but unlike her he seemed at ease with his nudity.

"I need a bath," he said, wrinkling his nose.

"You should have waited until I returned. What if you had gotten lost? Or fallen?"

"The path was easy to follow." Matt shrugged. "But you can help me now if you'd like. How is the water?"

"Wonderful," Lily said, jumping to her feet. She reached for her shift.

"Don't," Matt said softly. "It will just get wet. Besides, I enjoy looking at you. You've nothing to worry about, I can't do anything about it."

Biting her lip in indecision, Lily couldn't keep her eyes from wandering over the bold contours of Matt's body. Despite his wound and weakness he looked strong and virile. He was so stubborn, so powerful and so damn tenacious. When he wanted something he didn't rest until it was his. "Did you eat your bananas?" she asked, tearing her eyes away from his nakedness and abruptly changing the subject.

"Yes, thank you. Later I'll show you how to fish."

"Are you still in pain?"

"More than you know," he said cryptically. His manhood jumped in response and Lily blushed and turned her eyes away.

"You—you wanted a bath," she stammered, suddenly flustered.

He reached out his hand and she hesitated but a moment before taking it. He was still somewhat unsteady and felt hot to her touch, but obviously he was well on the road to recovery. Together they entered the pool.

"Wash my back," he said, impaling her with his gaze.

"There's no soap."

"Use sand."

She did, scooping up a handful from the bottom and gently scrubbing his back and shoulders. When she finished she moved away from him, but he was still so weak he began to sway unsteadily. She helped him to the bank and sat beside him while he rested for the trip back to the beach.

"I never thanked you properly for saving my life," Matt began slowly.

"Yes you did, you saved mine in return."

"Lily."

He reached out, threading his fingers in her hair and pulling her close. His lips touched hers gently, reverently, with more tenderness than he'd ever shown her before. One long finger traced a line along her cheek, down the delicate length of her throat to the puckered tip of her breast. His tongue parted her lips, savoring her special essence as he sucked on her lips and explored the soft inner surfaces of her mouth.

Heaving a ragged sigh, Lily pulled away. "No, Matt, you're not ready for this. And—and I'm not sure I am either—unless . . ."

"Unless what?"

"What's going to happen after we get off this island?"

"What does it matter? You're my wife."

"We'll talk about it later," she said, rising to her feet. She lent Matt a helping hand and he rose with difficulty. Then she gathered up their damp clothes and they dressed in silence.

During the following days Matt rapidly regained his strength. Little fever remained now and his wound seemed to be healing with no ill effects, except for the scar, which would always be there to remind him of his narrow escape. They existed on fruit and the occasional fish Matt was able to catch. Once they captured a green turtle that had wandered along the beach and after Matt cleaned it he used the shell to cook a savory stew out of turtle meat and edible roots he dug up with his knife. There seemed to be little animal life on their island but they certainly wouldn't starve living off the bounty of their catch.

The days were pleasantly hot and the nights sultry. Most of the time Matt wore nothing but the remnants of his trousers. He convinced Lily to discard her petticoats but she resisted his suggestion that she wear only her thin shift. One night while they dined on fish, bananas, mangoes and papaya, Matt kept staring at her so intently it made Lily uncomfortable. She began to fidget and then to chatter nervously.

"How long do you think it will be before we're rescued?"

"Shouldn't be too long," Matt replied, his eyes never leaving Lily's face. "Don't you like being alone with me?"

Lily ignored his last sentence. "We've been here over a week. What if—"

"Don't speculate, love. You worry too much, help will arrive." He fell silent, then suddenly said, "Let's take a dip in the pool."

"Now?" Lily asked, surprised. They had lingered over their meal so long the moon was already a huge silver ball high in the sky.

"Why not? Are you afraid? If someone is on the island besides us we would have seen them by now. We're quite alone, love."

His last sentence did little to reassure her. He was fully recuperated now and the way he had been looking at her the past couple of days left little to the imagination. He wanted her, that much was clear. But the question was: Did he want her because he needed a woman and she was the only woman handy or did he want her because he loved her? Men like Matt took whatever was available to them and she never wanted to be used like that again. Why couldn't he love her?

"Lily, did you hear me?"

"I heard," she said dully. "I don't think—"

"That's the problem, you think too much. Come along," he said, grasping her hand and pulling her to her feet. "A dip in the pool will feel wonderful after today's heat." She stumbled along beside him, unable to think of a reason to refuse and too weak physically to resist. His strength had returned along with his health.

The sight of the pool bathed in brilliant moonlight nearly took her breath away. She stood at the edge of the woods, drinking in the intoxicating view. How romantic it would be, she reflected wistfully, if she was with a man who loved her. She glanced at Matt, who now stood poised at the edge of the pool, and was stunned to see that he had already stripped off his pants. His body, gilded by the play of shadows against moonlight, had the rugged look of an unfinished sculpture. She had seen many not as grand as Matt in museums in Paris. There was an air of isolation about him as he stood there in an attitude of self-command and studied relaxation, as if he hadn't a care in the world. She recognized in him a firm strength she had come to depend on. The mesmerizing picture of his virile, nude body gilded by moonlight would remain imprinted on her brain forever.

"Are you coming?"

His voice jolted her abruptly from her silent ruminations. She hesitated but a moment before answering. "Yes."

She removed her dress and shoes and sidled up beside him. Matt looked at her and frowned. "Take off your shift."

"I—why?"

"Because I asked you to."

"I'd feel more comfortable with it on," she resisted stubbornly.

"I'd feel more comfortable with it off. You owe me, love, remember? I'm all well now and I want you."

"Do you think that's wise, Matt? I'd rather we didn't . . . further complicate our lives right now. Once we're back to civilization you'll continue privateering and I—I'll—probably go back to England one day." She wanted to share his love, not just satisfy his lust.

"I think not," Matt contradicted. "You're mine, Lily, and what's mine, I keep."

Lily was stunned. "Why should it matter to you what I do? You have Cl—"

"No, don't say it!" Matt warned, frowning darkly. "No one exists for me right now but you. Shall I take off that shift for you?" He lifted his hands to the neckline, fully prepared to rip it from neck to hem.

"No! I'll do it," Lily intervened, shoving his hands

aside. "Lord only knows how long we'll be here and these are the only clothes I own."

"I'd rather have you without them." His eyes gleamed with feral delight as the offending shift drifted down her body and settled at her feet. He reached out with one hand to touch her breast and Lily shivered with repressed passion as she felt his dark hand caressing her naked flesh. His rough palm was painfully exciting against the tender mound. She had resisted him so long her body ached with the need to feel Matt's special brand of love again. "You have perfect breasts." His touch turned into an erotic caress that thrilled her to her toes.

"I love your nipples. They're like ripe little fruits begging to be tasted." He lowered his head and sucked a dusky tip into his mouth.

Lily gasped in raw pleasure when he flipped the swollen bud with his tongue then bit down gently with his teeth. He felt her stiffen and a chuckle rumbled through his chest. He knew exactly how he was affecting her. Abruptly he released her and drew her forward into the water. When they were waist deep he stopped and pulled Lily into his arms, then ducked down beneath the calm surface of the water with her still clasped against him.

"Ma—Matt!" He laughed when she came up sputtering. "Are you trying to drown me?"

Instead of answering he bent his head and licked the sparkling drops of water sliding off the tips of her breasts. "You taste delicious."

"Matt, I—"

"Don't talk, just feel. Let your body speak for you. I want you, Lily. I want your response, your passion. I want your soul."

Made breathless by his words, Lily dared to ask, "What will you give me in return?"

Matt went still. His mind searched furiously for an answer and when it came it shocked him so thoroughly it rendered him speechless. When had the attraction he felt for Lily grown into this powerful obsession? He had never wanted her more. Never needed her with such compelling urgency. He nearly burst with the need to thrust his love deep inside this beautiful, unpredictable, headstrong and independent woman. Not just now, but forever. The emotion he had resisted for so long slowly and completely destroyed the wall he had built around his heart.

Matt's silence continued so long tears sprang to Lily's eyes and her keen disappointment brought a sob spilling from her throat. What did she expect, words of love? She knew Matt better than to expect flowery phrases when he didn't know the meaning of love. But oh how she hoped ... After all, he had jumped into the sea to save her, hadn't he? Even if he didn't want her in love he still wanted her in lust. Wasn't that enough to satisfy her?

No.

"Lily."

"It's all right, Matt," Lily said softly, dully. "I've known were I stood with you from the beginning. I shouldn't have asked you to give what you don't feel."

"Ask me again."

"What?"

"Ask me again," he repeated.

She gazed into his eyes, hope and despair warring with one another. In the moonlight his eyes were nearly opaque silver but there was no mistaking the hot spark of desire that leaped out to consume her. The breath slammed from her chest but her words were clear if somewhat shaky. "If I render you my soul, what will you give me in return?"

"My love, Lily, I give you my love."

"Oh, God, Matt, don't say it if you don't mean it. If you want me badly enough to lie, I'll not resist. I don't think I could even if I wanted to."

"I'm not lying, love. I've not come to this decision easily but it's time I admitted what I feel in my heart for you."

Lily felt as if she were melting. Hearing Matt tell her he loved her was the last thing she had expected. "Oh, Matt, you don't know how long I've waited to hear those words."

Suddenly she was floating as he lifted her high in his arms and carried her from the water. With great tenderness he laid her on her back on the fragrant grass beside the pool. "Let me show you how much I love you."

She inhaled with sharp pleasure as his mouth settled over hers. The kiss was as soft and sweet as a slow summer rain. The passion between them had always been magnificent but it was magnified now that he had told her he loved her. Something unique and compelling bound them and Lily was happy now to give it a name.

Love.

With slow relish he dragged his lips over hers, feeling every part of her mouth with every part of his. Desire scorched a path along her body as she surged against him, and still his kiss went on and on. She absorbed all of him, his strength, his intensity, his passion. When he moved over her she accepted his weight gladly. His limbs were hard and warm, the heat of his body scalded hers. He used his lips and hands with studied expertise, forging a breathless, exquisite torment until wave after wave of raw molten pleasure buffeted her.

"Touch me," Matt pleaded raggedly as he found her hand and placed it on that part of him that begged for her touch.

Her hand closed around him, surprised at how smooth the skin felt beneath her fingertips. Like steel encased in the softest velvet. He thrust against her and moaned.

"Let me touch you in the same way."

His hand slid down her stomach, past the silky forest at the juncture of her thighs to the slick crevice between her legs, where he began a gentle, teasing massage. Lily sucked her breath in sharply when a long tan finger penetrated her moistness. When he added a second finger, moving them in and out in a provocative manner, Lily jerked convulsively. In a purely reflexive motion her hand tightened around his swollen member, and Matt made an inarticulate sound deep in his throat. Thinking she had hurt him, Lily withdrew her hand.

"Oh, God, no, don't stop!" Timidly she replaced her hand and Matt released a shuddering sigh. "I love it when you touch me like that. Do you like me to touch you?"

His hand was doing such marvelous things to her she could not speak, merely nodding in response to his question. She loved everything about him, the way he smelled, masculine, clean, invigorating. She savored the way he made her feel, the way he worked so lovingly, so leisurely on her body. But she was quickly reaching the point when she wanted to feel him inside her, needed him so desperately she was reduced to begging.

"Matt, please, I can't stand much more of this! It's been so long and I need you so desperately. I want you now." She locked her legs over his and arched toward him in blatant invitation.

"I know what you want, love, I want it too," Matt panted as he nudged her legs apart and positioned himself between them.

He rained flurries of wild kisses along her forehead and temples, down her jawline to her throat, to her breasts. Taking a nipple into his mouth he sucked vigorously as he pushed himself deep, deeper within her tight flesh. Lily felt herself go hot and liquid at the feel of his swollen manhood taking full possession of her. Once he was deeply seated he began a new assault of slow rise and fall against her quickening flesh.

Suddenly she cried out in blissful agony as her world splintered into a million pieces. Seconds later Matt joined her.

Before his soul left his body he whispered urgently against her lips, "Say it, Lily."

"I love you, Matt."

Chapter 14

They slept as naked as God made them beside the pool that night, afraid to break the magic spell that enclosed them in a little world all their own. It was a world where only love existed, where ugly realities weren't allowed to intrude and tender feelings were freely expressed.

Lily was awakened once in the wee hours of the morning when Matt whispered in her ear, "Wake up, love, I can't seem to get enough of you."

She was lying on her side with Matt curled around her. She felt his erection nudge her from behind and he parted her legs as he slid between them. Cupping his hand against the hot nest of downy hair at the juncture of her thighs, he guided himself into her, a slow glorious slide into ecstasy. Lily gasped and thrust against him. As he began the gentle rocking motion inside her, his warm, dark hands filled themselves with her breasts, teasing their tips until she was whimpering with pleasure. He took her to the highest mountain then flung her over the brink. He was waiting for her when she drifted back to earth.

When Lily awoke next the sun warmed her skin and the song of hundreds of birds disturbed the stillness. And Matt no longer slept beside her. She was trying to decide whether or not to go in search of him when he suddenly appeared from out of the dense scrub carrying a banana leaf filled with fruit.

"I thought you'd be hungry when you awoke," he said, staring at the provocative display of nudity spread out before him. Carefully he set down the fruit and took Lily's hand. "Shall we bathe before breakfast?" The glint in his eye warned Lily that bathing was the last thing on his mind.

"Aren't you ever satisfied?"

"Not where you're concerned. When you're denied something you want badly and you finally get it, you want to gorge yourself on it. That's what I'm doing."

For fifteen minutes they played like carefree children in the pool, and when the games turned amorous they returned to the bank and made love. After they bathed again they sat down to enjoy the fruit Matt had gathered earlier.

"I've been thinking," Matt said once their meal was over. "We still have a piece of sail left. We should build some kind of shelter."

"On the beach?" Lily asked.

"No, but not too far from the water. Perhaps amidst the trees lining the beach, where no one can see us unless we choose to be seen."

Lily mulled his words over for several minutes before realizing what he was hinting at. "You think someone unfriendly might land on this island?"

"It's possible," he admitted lightly. "I'd prefer we were rescued by my own men or an American ship rather than the English or ... pirates. I'll make a signal flag from a piece of sail and when I'm certain our visitors are friendly, I'll wave it."

"Assuming someone will come to the island," Lily said dryly.

"Someone is bound to. We just don't know when."

"It's difficult to believe it is winter at home," Lily said wistfully. "It's so warm and pleasant here. I wish—" Flushing, she bit back the words.

"What do you wish, love?"

"Nothing "

"Say it."

"It's just that you're so different here, Matt. I'm afraid when we go back to civilization everything will change. You seem younger, more carefree. I would never have believed you could be like this."

"Are you afraid I'll change when we return?"

"I—yes. It isn't easy to forget the moody, silent man I married. Nor your high-handed, overbearing manner. I lost count of the many times you told me you didn't intend to remain faithful. I'm afraid to believe you've changed overnight. It—it's almost too good to be true."

"I reckon I was an arrogant bastard," Matt mused in rueful reflection. "But I had no reason to believe love existed."

"Now you do?" Lily asked skeptically. "What changed your mind?"

"You did," he conceded with a dazzling smile. "But Lord knows I didn't come to it easily. I fought my feelings every inch of the way."

"I want to believe you, Matt, truly I do, but ..." Lily's words trailed off.

She barely knew the Matt of the past few weeks; he was someone she had dreamed about from the time she was a child. Was it being stranded on this deserted island that changed him? she wondered curiously. Would it last? Somewhere in the back of her mind logic produced an answer that wasn't to her liking. Once the real world intruded upon their paradise Matt would revert back to his old self. Love came easily when only two people existed on a deserted island. But once they returned to civilization she feared that worldly distractions would rob her of his love. One of the distractions she feared most was Clarissa Hartley. The simple truth was that one woman wasn't enough for a man like Matthew Hawke.

"What are you thinking, love?"

"I'm thinking," she began slowly, "that what you say and do now has no bearing on what you do or say once we leave here."

"Don't you believe I love you?"

"I believe you love me—now."

"Forever."

Lily closed her eyes, desperately wanting to believe Matt yet fearing the terrible hurt of his rejection later. When she opened them Matt was handing her her shift. "Let's go back to the beach and work on that shelter."

The spot Matt selected for their lean-to was several yards from the beach, well hidden by tall palms and scrub. He stretched the length of canvas between two sturdy trees and used banana leaves and palm fronds to fill in the sides. The front was left open as an entrance. It was roomy enough to stretch out under and protect them from rain yet too low to stand upright beneath.

Once it was completed the happiest and most idyllic time in Lily's life began. She and Matt played in the surf, bathed in the pool, scoured the area between the pool and the beach for food and spent countless hours making love—beneath the moon, in the middle of the day, on the sand, beside the pool, in the water, whenever and wherever the mood struck them. Needless to say the mood struck them quite often. They were like children in the Garden of Eden, where nothing disturbed their joy or diminished the pleasure they found in one another.

Yet Lily's nagging fear that her bubble would burst once they were rescued came back time after time to haunt her. It returned at the oddest moments, even while they were making love and her body sang with unrestrained ecstasy.

Days passed, and then weeks, until Lily lost all track of time. If Matt hadn't cut notches in a tree representing their days on the island neither of them would have known how long they had been stranded. So far they had little use for the signal flag Matt made, having sighted no ships in the vicinity. It was as if the world had passed them by and their little island was the center of their universe.

Most of the time they ran around as naked as God made them, saving their clothing for the day they were rescued. Lily no longer felt embarrassment at appearing nude before Matt and Matt often teased her at how quickly she discarded her inhibitions. They would be engaged in tasks necessary to their survival when that special look came into his eyes, and Lily would know that he wanted her. By mutual consent they would sink to the ground and indulge their passion.

"My god, we've been here months!" Matt gasped one day after he had added another notch to the tree.

Time had passed so quickly he hadn't realized they had been stranded so long. Where was his crew? Had his ship been damaged too badly to make it to port safely? Hadn't anyone seen him and Lily go overboard? Speculation ran rampant through his brain. He had expected someone to come upon them long before now. Not that he begrudged this time spent with Lily. It was just that he had no idea how the war was progressing or if the British had succeeded in subduing his beloved America.

"Why, we must already be well into 1814," Lily said, amazed.

"Perhaps today I'll make a trip to the other side of the island," Matt suggested. He had wanted to do it for quite some time but somehow never got around to it. "It's likely that ships are more apt to arrive there than here. If one has visited recently I'm bound to see signs of it. Do you want to come along?"

"I think not," Lily said slowly. "My shoes are in no condition for a trek through the jungle and I wouldn't think of going barefoot. How long will you be gone?"

"I have no idea, depends on how large this island is. It might even be a cay, but with the plentiful water supply I'm more inclined to think it is an island. I probably won't return until tomorrow. Or even the day after that. Will you be all right?"

"There is nothing or no one here to harm me." Lily smiled. "There aren't even any wild animals to speak of. There is still thread left in your kit, I'll use it to mend our clothes while you're gone."

"I'd leave the knife but I may need it to cut through vines."

"Don't worry, Matt, I probably will spend most of the time sleeping anyway. We have few responsibilities here but we seem to get little rest." Her eyes sparkled with mild rebuke as she thought of how often they made love when they should have been sleeping. Matt merely grinned.

"I love to make love to you. In fact . . ." He reached out, grasping her around the middle and pulling her into his arms. "Since I won't be around for a couple of days we ought to make love right now." Hand in hand they had walked to the beach and were now standing in the warm sand, looking for edible conch, crab and any other delicacies that washed ashore.

Lily giggled, loving the way her nipples felt against the rough hair covering his chest. As was their normal habit they were both naked as they waded in the surf looking for food. "You'll have to catch me," she said, twisting from his grasp and scampering off down the beach.

She turned once to look over her shoulder but Matt hadn't moved, he was merely watching her with wry amusement. But he was so full of tricks she didn't trust him so she simply slowed down but didn't stop. Suddenly his feet grew wings and his long legs churned as he took off after her. She didn't have a chance.

"I wanted to give you a running start," he said when he caught up with her a few moments later. "Are you in the mood for games?"

"It depends," she said archly. "What kind of game do you have in mind?"

"The kind of game where we both win even if we lose." Lily looked puzzled when Matt dropped to his knees before her. She started to follow but he held her firmly in place. She glanced down to see that he was already erect, but he seemed in no particular hurry.

He cupped her breasts and lifted them, teasing the hard little nipples with his thumbs. Her mouth opened on a soft gurgling sigh. With slow relish he tongued her navel, his hands drifting down to her buttocks to press her against his devouring mouth. She put her fingers in his hair, threw back her head and hung on for dear life.

"Open your legs," he whispered urgently. A sea gull swooped down from the sky and dove into the water not two feet from them, but nothing short of a tidal wave could have stopped Lily from obeying Matt's hoarse command.

Then he was kissing her there, sucking, nipping, using his tongue to part her and slide maddeningly into her tender, moist flesh. Lily would have fallen if Matt hadn't paused to lay her back against the hot sand. He looked at her and smiled and Lily noted that his mouth was wet. Then her thoughts skidded out of control as he parted her legs, pushed her knees up and bent his head to her again. Lily jerked, and jerked again. She had become so sensitive there she was certain she could tolerate little more of his torture without breaking apart. But these months alone with Lily had taught Matt just how much she could tolerate.

He had brought her to climax many ways since they had been married and this was but one of them. "Matt! I don't think I can stand this!"

His throaty laugh told her she wouldn't escape so easily as he continued his relentless assault, this time bringing his fingers into play as well as his mouth. Her stomach clenched, her knees flexed and her toes curled as the universe spun around her crazily. Nothing existed but her body and his mouth. Her head thrashed from side to side as the explosion came, spinning her to the stars, where she fragmented into a million pieces. It was not a soft, sweet release that came from gentle loving, but a wild, furious end to the tempestuous agony Matt had built inside her.

Then he was over her, in her, filling her with himself, driving her once again to that peak of ecstasy. She groaned as she felt him thrusting deep, so deep he touched her soul. Immediately Matt stilled.

"Am I hurting you?"

"Oh, God, no, it's just that it's so deep—so good."

Her erotic words almost put an end to his loving. He could have climaxed then and there, but he forced himself to hold still inside her until he felt her quicken around him. Then he began again that sweet drive toward release. He grasped her hips and lifted her higher, and her pleasure grew so acute it bordered on pain. Thrusting to the hilt, using his powerful hips to piston her, he felt himself losing control.

"I can't wait, love," he groaned as if in agony. Grinding his teeth, he unleashed himself, unaware of the raw cry that tore from his throat. He despaired of leaving Lily behind and was rewarded when he felt her convulse around him and heard her scream as she joined him.

Afterward they lolled on the hot sand in mutual contentment until Matt decided it was time he left to explore the other side of the island. His last words sent a chill coursing through her.

"Don't show yourself if we have visitors, love." He said it half in jest, considering the fact that they had seen no one since they landed on the island, but Lily took his warning to heart.

The rest of the day passed in monotonous pursuits, making Lily wish she had accompanied Matt on his trek across the island. She mended, napped, collected crabs and small sea animals and even tried her hand at fishing. She spent a sleepless night missing Matt's arms around her and awoke early the next morning. She didn't even venture down to the shore until later that day, spending hours at the pool bathing and then gathering fruit to replenish the dwindling supply kept on hand in their lean-to.

Humming to herself, Lily stepped out from the concealment of the trees onto the sandy strip of beach. For some unexplained reason since Matt was gone she felt more comfortable being reasonably clothed, so that morning she had donned her shift. It wasn't much but at least it offered a semblance of protection. From whom she sought protection she couldn't even begin to guess. Until she reached the beach. It was swarming with men.

Men of every size and description dressed in an odd assortment of clothing were splashing ashore from longboats and pulling them up upon the beach. Lily could see barrels and baskets inside the longboats and guessed the men had come to the island for water and fresh fruit. Their ship was anchored a few hundred yards offshore in deep water beyond the shoals. Shocked by the sight of so many men after so lengthy an isolation, Lily froze. Suddenly she realized her perilous position and the danger that existed should she be seen. She whirled and took to her heels.

The men weren't wearing red uniforms so Lily

knew they couldn't be English and from their fierce looks and the ragged clothes they wore she seriously doubted they were American privateers. That left pirates and she certainly didn't want to be found by that repulsive breed of men. She almost made it to the protection of the trees lining the beach when one of the men spied her. At first he couldn't believe his eyes but when he realized he wasn't hallucinating he alerted his companions to his startling discovery and took off after her. The others were hard on his heels.

Sobbing in fear, Lily dodged through the jungle, pushing aside vines that tore at her hair and face and tangled her legs. She could hear dozens of pairs of feet pounding after her and voices calling out to her in many languages. Dear God, she thought frantically, why hadn't she been more careful? Why hadn't she thought to conceal herself until she was certain the beach was free of intruders? She had grown so accustomed to seeing no one but Matt on this island that even though she knew the possibility existed for visitors she hadn't given it a moment's thought today or taken precautions. Now it was too late.

On and on she ran, until the breath was pounding in her breast and her sides were bursting with pain. If her pursuers weren't so close she might have found concealment in the dense scrub but she was given no opportunity to look as the pirates closed in on her. Her bare feet were bleeding now and when she tripped on an exposed root, she yelped in pain and fell flat on her face. Behind her, one of the pirates chortled gleefully and flung himself atop her. The others formed a ring around them, gawking.

"What ya got there, Dooley? Damn me if it don't look like a gel."

"Sure as hell feels like a gel," Dooley chuckled, crudely exploring Lily's soft buttocks. "She's soft in all the right places."

"Flip 'er over," demanded another pirate. "Let's see if she's got a face to match 'er body."

Lily sputtered indignantly when the pirate named Dooley flung her over on her back. The ugly faces leering down on her filled her with unspeakable fear.

"Goddamn," Dooley said irreverently as he studied Lily's perfect features. "Ain't ye a beauty. Where in the hell did ye come from, little gel?"

Lily's mouth worked but nothing came out. What would these men do to her? Where was Matt? Would they kill Matt when he returned from his trek to the other side of the island?

"Answer me, gel, where did ye come from?" Dooley demanded, placing his face so close to hers she gagged at his fetid breath. "Can't ye talk English? If ye babble in French or Italian or Spanish, we got men aplenty that speak them fancy languages."

"I—I speak English," Lily found the courage to answer.

"What are ye doing on this island?"

"Shipwreck," Lily said, hoping her lie appeased him.

Dooley mulled over her answer but didn't seem satisfied. "Who's with ye? How many others survived the shipwreck?"

"Me!" Lily cried. "Only me. There's no one on the island but me." She wouldn't mention Matt even if they tortured her. "Let me up."

Dooley stood aside while Lily rose unsteadily to her feet. She knew the shift she wore exposed more than it concealed and folded her arms self-consciously across her breasts. The dozen or so men crowded around her were all but salivating as they raked her thinly clad body from head to toe. The shift barely covered her hips and was so worn in places her skin could be seen right through it.

"Let's take 'er now, Dooley, afore Frenchy comes

ashore and spoils our fun. Ye know the capt'n's gonna want 'er once he sees 'er."

The majority of the men nodded agreement as they eyed Lily greedily.

"Suits me fine, Garp." Dooley shrugged. "But I get 'er first since I'm the one what found 'er. The rest of you can draw lots."

Stark, raw panic sent a shiver down Lily's frail body. She had counted fifteen men. If every one of them raped her she'd be dead before they finished. But perhaps it was best that way, she considered with icy logic. Then her thoughts scattered when Dooley shoved her hard and she fell to the ground. She lay on her back, dazed, staring up at him as he fumbled with his pants. She could see the men behind him drawing twigs that one of the men had gathered and held in his palm and comparing them one against the other.

When Dooley dropped to his knees beside her, Lily suddenly came alive, kicking and screaming and fighting for her life. Grasping her arms and pinning them over her head, Dooley slapped her repeatedly across the face. Stars exploded in her head, and certain that he had put an end to her struggles, he slid atop her.

"*Mon Dieu*, what is going on here? Who is this woman?"

Lily had no idea who the speaker was but she was eternally grateful to him. She had no inkling that Frenchy Ballieu was one of the most feared pirates still terrorizing the Caribbean. He was cruel, ruthless and utterly devoid of decency. He never gave quarter nor did he spare lives. But he spoke and looked like a gentleman and dressed with a certain flare that belied his true nature. If Lily looked on him as her savior she was destined for a big disappointment.

"Help me, please."

Frenchy's glittering dark gaze settled disconcertingly on Lily, noting her beauty, her youth, the ravishing curves barely concealed by her short garment.

"Aw, Frenchy, ye ain't gonna spoil our fun, are ye?" Dooley appealed. "I was the one what found the gel."

Cold black eyes swung to Dooley, then back to Lily. "Just where did he find you, *ma chèrie?*"

Lily gulped past the lump in her throat. "I—was shipwrecked and drifted to this island."

"She says she's alone," Dooley added importantly. He was still sprawled across Lily but when Frenchy continued to glare at him in a menacing manner, he reluctantly rose to his feet.

"Are you alone, *ma petite?*" Frenchy asked as he offered a hand to Lily. Gratefully she accepted it. His voice was so mild and courteous that some of Lily's fears dropped away.

"As you can see there is no one here but me," she offered as she tried to shield herself from his penetrating gaze. It was as if he could see right through her and it frightened her. Still, he had saved her from being raped by his crew and she was indebted to him for that much.

"Search the island," Frenchy growled in a voice that brooked no argument. Dooley and some of the men grumbled but moved smartly to obey his order. "And don't dawdle. I sent you ashore to gather fruit and fill the casks with water, not spend the afternoon pleasuring yourselves."

"What about the gel?" Dooley dared to ask.

"What about her?" Frenchy challenged.

"Will ye share her? Me and the men ain't had a woman since Barbados and we're all hankering fer a piece of 'er."

"*Mais oui*, don't we always share and share alike? You will get your turn—when I tire of her. *If* I tire of her," he added once Dooley and the others were out of hearing. Then he turned to Lily, his smile reminding her of a cat who had just discovered a whole saucer of cream. "Now, *chèrie*, shall we go?"

"Wh—where are we going?"

"To my ship, of course. You will be a welcome addition in my bed. And after that my men can have you until you no longer please them. Then, before you're worn out completely, I'll sell you to a brothel in Algeria."

"My God, you're despicable. I didn't know men like you existed." She had looked upon the pirate captain as her salvation but now realized she had merely jumped from bad to worse.

Frenchy threw back his head and laughed raucously. "You are quite refreshing, *chèrie*. I predict it will be a long time before I give you over to my crew."

Then he grasped her arm and dragged her behind him through the jungle to the beach where some of his crew who had just come ashore were rolling casks up the beach toward the freshwater pool. They seemed quite shocked to see their captain striding from the woods with a beautiful woman in tow and some of them stopped to gawk.

"Back to work, *mon ami*," he called, continuing on without breaking stride. "As you can see I have found a companion to ease our lonely hours." He laughed and waved his hand as the men cheered wildly then resumed their tasks.

"Sit down, *ma chèrie*," Frenchy invited, pointing to a spot on the sand beside one of the longboats. "It will be many hours before the men return with water and fruit and have made a thorough search of the island. While we're waiting you may tell me about yourself." His tone seemed friendly but beneath his mild facade Lily sensed an underlying threat that dared her to disobey.

"There's not much to tell," Lily said, choosing her words carefully. She didn't want to let on that she wasn't alone on the island. "I was aboard an English ship returning to England when the storm struck. The ship broke up and sank and I grabbed onto a broken mast and floated here with the tide."

Frenchy looked at her skeptically. "How long were you afloat?"

"I'm not sure. Two or three days. That time was confusing because I passed in and out of consciousness."

"What happened to the other survivors?"

"As far as I know there were none," Lily insisted.

"How long have you been here?"

"A long time. Months."

"Am I to believe you existed solely on your own for all that time? What did you eat? How did you survive?"

"There's water aplenty, as you well know. And fruit and shellfish that wash ashore with the tide."

"Now for the important question," Frenchy said. "*Who* are you?"

"My name is Lily Montague," Lily said, refusing to use Matt's name. He was too well known in circles that might include Frenchy and those like him. "There is nothing else to know."

"I know you are a lovely woman, *chèrie*," Frenchy said, raising her chin with a thick forefinger. "Are you a virgin?"

Flushing, Lily shook her head.

"A pity," Frenchy sighed regretfully, "but there is much to be said for experienced women. Soon I will discover for myself just how experienced you are."

Lily stiffened when he touched her lips lightly with his own. Frenchy laughed but did not persist, knowing full well he would have her soon. He was a patient man and could wait for his pleasure, after duties were dispensed with.

"If you return me to civilization unharmed, I'll see that you're amply rewarded," Lily offered hopefully.

If her father wouldn't pay ransom perhaps Sarah and Jeff would.

"Are you rich? Do you perchance have a rich husband?" Frenchy asked, his attention sharpening.

"I have no husband," Lily denied, silently asking Matt to forgive her for lying about something so precious to her. "And I'm not rich, but I have . . . friends who might be willing to pay ransom. Providing I'm returned unharmed," she stressed pointedly.

"Ransom doesn't interest me," Frenchy said, smiling salaciously. "But you do, *chèrie*. I have decided that I want you, and Frenchy Ballieu is a man with large appetites. You, my little pigeon, will satisfy one of them. Rest now," he advised, rising to his feet. "We may have to pass the night on the island and I want you well rested when I'm ready for you. And just so you don't try to escape I'm going to bind your hands and feet."

As it turned out, the crew of the *Black Bird*, Frenchy's ship, did spend the night on the beach. They built a huge fire, made of savory turtle-and-shellfish stew and drank enormous quantities of rum carried off their ship for the night's revelry. Left bound a short distance away, Lily shivered and prayed they had forgotten all about her.

Chapter 15

Matt had spent the night huddled beneath a banana tree missing Lily's warmth beside him, wishing she weren't so far away. He'd been surprised to find the island so large. Judging from the length of time it was taking him to reach the opposite shore, he estimated it was more than eight miles wide at that point. But he was nearly to the other side of the island now for he could smell the sea and hear the raucous cry of gulls and pounding surf. Other distant sounds penetrated through the jungle but Matt was still too far away to identify them. They sounded like human voices but he realized cries of birds often mimicked human sounds.

What had surprised him most about the island was the fact that it was so hilly. The flat crescent of beach gave way to forest which covered low hillocks which eventually led down to the opposite shore. The going was extremely difficult due entirely to the thick vegetation, jungle and scrub forests. He hoped Lily wouldn't be overly concerned when he failed to return in the time he had allotted himself, but if all went well he wouldn't be more than several hours later than he'd predicted.

Crashing through the trees, Matt caught glimpses of the sea now and couldn't wait to plunge headlong into the surf. He was hot and tired and dirty from his hike over rough terrain. Thank God his boots were still in good shape, he thought, even though his clothes hung like rags from his tall frame.

The sounds Matt heard earlier became more distinct now and he paused, his ears attuned to the familiar cadence of human speech. Either his ears were deceiving him or there were people on the beach beyond the trees. Instinctively he quickened his pace, then suddenly thought better of it as he realized visitors to the island didn't necessarily mean they would be friendly. They could be English—or pirates. Either way, caution was definitely advised.

Matt was so close to the shore now the sparkling blue water reflected through the trees, nearly blinding him. He paused where the crescent of white sand met the forest and stared in disbelief at the ship anchored a few hundred yards offshore in deep water. The beach held traces of recent activity but was now deserted. A longboat was being lifted out of the water onto the ship and Matt could see men scurrying about making ready to raise sail and depart. His heart was beating so furiously it sounded like thunder in his ears. The ship was as familiar to him as his own name.

The *Sea Hawke*.

Damnation! Matt thought frantically. His ship was about to depart without knowing he and Lily were on the island. Rushing down to the water's edge, Matt cupped his hands to his mouth and hailed the ship in a loud voice. Evidently the activity aboard the *Sea Hawke* all but drowned out the sound of his voice. Yanking off his shirt, he waved it in the air and jumped up and down. If the ship left now it might never return.

Aboard the *Sea Hawke*, Dick Marlow stewed in gloomy silence as the crew prepared to unfurl the sails. How many of the seven hundred islands and

cays must he visit before he was ready to admit that
Matt and Lily were dead? All of them, his conscience
replied. He knew Matt was a resourceful man and
felt confident that he and Lily had reached one of the
islands or cays alive. But after visiting countless barren islands and cays that couldn't possibly support
life his confidence wavered. Now he had one more
island to add to his growing list of places where no
sign of life existed.

Frowning darkly, he mounted the ladder to the
bridge and took the wheel. The wind hadn't caught
the sails yet but he waited patiently, preparing to
guide the *Sea Hawke* to yet another island in his endless search for Captain Hawke and his wife. In desperation his eyes swept the beach one last time,
looking for something he knew wasn't there. Suddenly a figure emerged from the forest, rushing
down to the water's edge and waved frantically.

"Lower the sails!" Dick shouted. Perplexed but
obeying instantly, the men snapped to.

"What's amiss, Mr. Marlow?" asked the second
mate as he watched the crew scurrying to obey
Dick's command.

"Look." Dick pointed toward shore. "What do you
see?"

The second mate swung his gaze toward shore.
"Damnation, 'tis a man! Do you reckon it's the captain?"

"I'm willing to bet all I own that we have found
our missing captain," Dick crowed gleefully.

"Lower the longboat!" Dick commanded as he
leaped from the bridge.

By now several others had seen the figure standing
on the beach and they scrambled for a place in the
longboat, each wanting to be among those to rescue
their captain. They saved room for Dick and once he
was seated the boat was lowered. When the boat hit

the water the men bent their backs to the oars and rowed with all their strength.

Once Matt was certain he had been seen he stopped waving and lowered his head to thank God for sending the *Sea Hawke* to his rescue. It wasn't as if he couldn't spend his life with Lily on this island but he was desperate to rejoin the war, if it wasn't already over by this time. If it was over, he fervently prayed the United States had emerged victorious, with its freedom intact.

The longboat scraped the sand and Dick jumped out, splashing through the water to reach Matt. The young man was so obviously glad to see him Matt couldn't help but grin.

"It's about time," Matt said as Dick began pumping his hand and slapping his back.

"Do you know how many islands there are in this blasted chain?" Dick complained.

"Seven hundred, at last count. Plus numerous cays I couldn't even begin to count."

"So you know what we were up against. The worst part was not being able to begin the search immediately. The *Sea Hawke* was severely damaged by the *Reliant* and required extensive repairs before she was seaworthy. We were delayed several weeks while repairs were being made. Why didn't you show yourself when we first came ashore? We very nearly didn't see you."

"Lily and I drifted to the opposite side of the island," Matt explained. "We've been camped there ever since. It wasn't until yesterday that I decided to explore. Thank God I did."

When Matt mentioned Lily, a great relief swept over Dick. "When I didn't see Mrs. Hawke I was afraid ..." His sentence drifted off. "Where is she?"

"Her shoes were nearly worn through so I left her behind," Matt said. "She'll be as happy to see you as I am."

"Then you're both well? I can see *you* haven't suffered from your ordeal but Mrs. Hawke doesn't have your stamina."

"Lily is fine." Matt grinned. "I daresay we could exist here forever if need be. What's happening with the war?"

"British forces hold the Mississippi as far south as Illinois and enemy ships ravaged the shores of Chesapeake Bay and burned public buildings in Washington. Rumor has it that a full-scale invasion by the British of a major port is in the making. No one seems to know which port it will be but guesses are New Orleans will be the target. Most scoff at the notion but General Andrew Jackson and his troop of Kaintucks have already been dispatched to New Orleans to fortify the city against possible invasion."

"My God, Sarah is in New Orleans and that's where I intend to leave Lily," Matt said. "If Boston Harbor is still blockaded I have no recourse but to take Lily to New Orleans."

"It's impossible to get in or out of Boston Harbor," Dick revealed, "so New Orleans is still your best bet. Chances are talk of invasion is just that—talk. Shall we get Lily now? I imagine you'll both be glad to leave. The watch spied the *Black Bird* yesterday and we think Frenchy might be looking to anchor off one of these islands to replenish his store of water and fruit."

"Frenchy Ballieu? Jesus, why didn't you tell me sooner?" Matt exploded. "I don't want that sadistic bastard within a hundred miles of Lily."

"I'm sorry, Matt, I just didn't think. Besides, when I saw no other ships anchored offshore I forgot all about him."

"You can't second-guess a man like Frenchy or predict what he'll do," Matt said quietly. "He may be anchored at the opposite side of the island right now." His face contorted with pain as he mulled over that terrifying thought. Why hadn't he insisted that Lily come with him? Hackles raised on the back of his neck as an appalling premonition assailed him.

His fears were silently conveyed to Dick, who said, "Get in the longboat and we'll row out to the *Sea Hawke*. The sooner we reach Mrs. Hawke the better. I'm sure everything is all right but we'll all feel better once she's aboard the *Sea Hawke*.

Matt made no move to comply as he paused in thoughtful contemplation. "I have this strange feeling that I should return the way I came. If the *Black Bird* is anchored on the opposite side of the island I'd prefer they don't know we're here. If they are there and they've discovered Lily it would make better sense to launch a sneak attack. Leave half the men aboard the *Sea Hawke* and the rest will come with me. Since I've already cut a path through the jungle the going will be much easier. If we're lucky we'll reach there by nightfall."

It was a good hour before the party going with Matt assembled on shore. They numbered twenty men, including Dick Marlow, all armed and eager to do battle.

It was growing dark and Lily's stomach rumbled with hunger. No one had thought to bring her a portion of the turtle stew, which was fine with her since being ignored was what she desired above all. She prayed they would forget her entirely and leave the island. Unfortunately that wasn't likely to happen. Frenchy was beginning to pay more attention to her now, openly leering at her as he swilled rum straight from the bottle. Lily knew they were talking about her for she caught snippets of conversation regarding her obvious assets, followed by raucous laughter.

Lily closed her eyes and thought about Matt. She wondered where he was and what would happen to him if he stumbled upon the pirates. Her one consolation was that Matt was far too astute to walk un-consciously into a den of sea scavengers. She hoped he wouldn't try to take on the entire crew of the *Black Bird* single-handedly and prayed he'd remain concealed no matter what happened to her. Sadly, Lily knew Matt better than to think he would leave her to the mercy of pirates if he was aware of what was happening. When Matt saw she was in peril he'd disregard all danger to himself in order to rescue her. And seal his own death.

Finally, the thing Lily had dreaded the most came to pass. Frenchy walked to the water, fastidiously washed his hands and face and swaggered in her direction.

"Give it to 'er good!" Dooley shouted, making an obscene gesture with his fingers. Loud guffaws and lewd comments spurred Frenchy on as one after another of his men offered advice.

Lily held her breath as Frenchy stopped just inches from her, his long sturdy legs planted wide apart, arms crossed over his wide chest. "Did you think I had forgotten you, *ma chèrie*?"

"I hoped you had," Lily bit out from beneath clenched teeth.

"Never let it be said that Frenchy Ballieu ignores a beautiful woman."

Lily sucked in a shaky breath as he whipped out his knife and neatly severed her bonds. A moment of intense pain followed but she quickly recovered. She couldn't afford to be caught off guard for she knew exactly what Frenchy had in mind for her.

"I briefly considered waiting until I had you in the comfort of my bed aboard the *Black Bird*," Frenchy said smoothly, "but I find my need is too great."

He grasped her wrists and pulled her to her feet.

"Where are you taking me?"

"Unless you want my men to watch, *ma chèrie*, I thought we'd go a short distance into the woods."

"I'm not going anywhere with you," Lily said, digging in her heels.

A nasty chuckle rumbled from Frenchy's chest. "You have no choice."

Scooping her up in his arms, he upended her over his shoulder like a sack of potatoes. When she pounded his back with her fists and kicked her feet, he delivered several stinging swats to her bottom. Ribald laughter followed in his wake as he strode swiftly toward the trees. He had no idea his progress was noted by hostile eyes as well as those of his envious crew.

"Let me at that bastard," Matt ground from between clenched teeth. "If he's hurt Lily I'll make him suffer in ways that make his sadistic games seem tame." He lunged forward, only to find himself forcibly restrained by Dick Marlow.

"We'll get him, Captain, but wait until he's out of sight of his men. Then you and I can go after him while the others attack those left on the beach. There's nearly forty men to our twenty. You've always advised that the element of surprise works wonders when you lack numbers."

Matt and his crewmen had reached their destination several minutes before and crouched behind the dense scrub watching the proceedings on the beach. It took them a while to locate Lily and when they did it was too late to approach her unseen for Frenchy had already risen and ambled over to her. His intention was quite clear when he flung her over his shoulder and made off toward the woods.

"We have damn little time to waste," Matt whispered urgently as Frenchy disappeared into the woods with Lily. "Obviously Frenchy's men have been drinking heavily and they don't expect company. I'm going after Frenchy while the rest of you sneak up from behind and subdue his crew."

"I'll go with you," Dick insisted.

"No, I can handle that bastard alone. You'll be needed to lead the others. Just give me ten minutes to reach Frenchy before you attack. I don't want him alerted too soon."

Dick looked disappointed but offered no protest. "Aye, aye, sir. Good luck."

"The same to you, Mr. Marlow." Crouching low, Matt slipped noiselessly into the darkness. His steps were so silent not a leaf rustled to announce his passage.

Lily realized it would do no good to scream so she saved her energy to fight off Frenchy's attack. His shoulder dug painfully into her stomach as she bounced against him and her bottom still stung from his heavy-handed blows, but that was the least of her worries. They were entering the woods now and any minute Frenchy would fling her to the ground and ravish her. The pirate captain was a big, powerful man who could easily subdue her, but Lily intended to fight to her last breath. How could she endure ravishment after knowing the tenderness of Matt's loving?

Where was Matt? she wondered desperately. He should have returned by now. Thank God he hadn't. She could just picture him barging into this den of pirates and getting himself killed. Suddenly her thoughts fragmented into a million pieces as Frenchy flung her to the ground and loomed over her. In the moonlit darkness she could see his leering grin, and his salacious intent struck her like a physical blow as he slowly peeled off his elegant jacket.

"Now, *ma petite*, we shall see just how experienced you are. We can do this without fuss or you can fight. Either way I will win. Hurting women never bothered me so if you choose to fight I promise you'll live to regret it."

He reached down and ripped her thin shift from

neck to hem. Lily screamed, aware that her cries were no doubt giving his men much enjoyment but unable to stop herself. When Frenchy dropped down beside her, she rolled adroitly out of his way. But her victory was short-lived when he grasped her hurtfully and shoved her beneath him.

"The time has come, *ma chèrie*. Open your legs."

"*Your* time has come, Frenchy, get away from my wife."

Startled, Frenchy's head snapped up, his black eyes glinting with malice. "Who dares interrupt!" he roared.

"Matthew Hawke," Matt spat out. "And you have committed the unpardonable sin of putting your hands on my wife." He held a knife in his right palm, his body poised and waiting for Frenchy to make the first move.

Frenchy dropped back to sit on his heels, staring at Matt in thoughtful contemplation. He looked relaxed but Matt was astute enough to know the man was wound as taut as a spring, just waiting for the right moment to uncoil and strike.

"Matthew Hawke," Frenchy repeated with mock amusement. "I have heard the name. Rumor has it that the British have placed a price on your head. You have taken too many of their ships to be allowed to continue disrupting their shipping."

"Get up, Lily," Matt said quietly, "and move away from that Frenchified bastard." Lily scrambled to her feet and stood beside Matt. She couldn't believe Matt was here. Didn't he know that interfering now was tantamount to a death sentence? Even if he fought Frenchy and won there was his entire crew to deal with.

"You are a brave man, Matthew Hawke," Frenchy drawled lazily, "albeit a foolish one. My entire crew is gathered on the beach waiting for my return. How far can you get on this small island? You can't escape them. Eventually you and your wife will be killed. If she really is your wife." His nasty sneer intimated that he didn't believe Matt's claim that Lily was his wife.

"Matt, it's true," Lily concurred frantically. "There are nearly forty men on the beach. Oh, why didn't you stay hidden when you saw what was happening?"

His smile was delivered with such maddening calm Lily felt like strangling him. Didn't he realize he was in danger of losing his life? "I didn't like this bastard putting his hands on you, Lily. Has he hurt you? If he has I'll cut off his fingers first, then his hands, after that each part of his body until he dies a slow death."

Lily shuddered. "No, he hasn't hurt me."

"You're as good as dead, Hawke," Frenchy snarled, slowly rising to his feet. "You are foolishly brave, *mon ami*, but sadly outnumbered."

Suddenly a terrible racket came from the direction of the beach and a puzzled frown darkened Frenchy's brow.

"Not as outnumbered as you think," Matt said with slow relish. "And I am definitely not your friend. What you hear is my men attacking yours. Surprise is on our side, by now I would imagine your crew has been disarmed and subdued."

Lily sucked in a shuddering breath.

Frenchy spun around to face Matt, his eyes dark with menace, his complexion mottled with anger. He started to reach for the dagger attached to his belt.

"Go ahead, Frenchy, I'd love to slit you from stem to stern. If you don't think I can do it, try me."

Cocking an ear to the beach, Frenchy listened to the cries of the wounded, realizing that his men were too full of food and rum to put up much of a fight. He was also astute enough to know that challenging Matt now was pointless. His hands dropped to his sides. When Dick Marlow's voice sounded through the trees calling Matt's name, he knew he had made a wise choice.

"Where are you, Captain? Are you all right?" Dick called as he stomped through the underbrush.

"Over here, Mr. Marlow," Matt returned. He kept his eyes glued on Frenchy, not trusting him for a moment. "Have you and the men taken care of the *Black Bird*'s crew?"

"Aye, Captain, all is well," Dick crowed gleefully. "The men are rounding up the survivors now. What about him?" He pointed to Frenchy, keeping his eyes carefully averted from Lily, who stood slightly behind Matt trying unsuccessfully to hold together the tattered remains of her shift.

"Frenchy will join his crew on the beach. When the *Sea Hawke* arrives, the surviving pirates will be left on the island until another ship arrives to rescue them. If it's the English who come they will all face a hangman's noose. I lay claim to his ship and half our crew will be transferred to the *Black Bird*."

"You're taking my ship?" Frenchy thundered.

"It will be put to good use," Matt replied smoothly. "One more ship with which to battle the British. Take Frenchy to the beach, Mr. Marlow, but first might I ask you for the loan of your coat? My shirt is as tattered as Lily's shift and I wouldn't have her embarrassed before my men."

"Aye, Captain," Dick said with alacrity as he peeled off his jacket and held it out to Lily. "May I say, Mrs. Hawke, that I'm pleased you're unharmed? When I saw the *Black Bird* in the vicinity I had no idea she would pick this island to land on." Then he disarmed Frenchy and prodded him toward the beach with the point of his own dagger.

Lily looked to Matt for an explanation. But Matt had no patience at the moment for lengthy explanations as he pulled her into his arms and held her close. "I nearly went crazy when Dick told me they had spotted the *Black Bird*. I had this terrible premonition that he'd choose this island to supply his ship with fresh water and fruit."

Then he was kissing her, her mouth, her chin, her nose, telling her by his actions just how frightened he had been for her. It felt so good to be safe in his arms again that she melted against him, returning his kiss with a fervor that spoke eloquently of her love. Reluctantly Matt broke off the kiss, realizing that this was neither the time nor the place to indulge their passions. Plenty of time for that later when they were alone.

"As much as I regret putting an end to this, love," Matt said, "I must. The men are awaiting my orders on the beach." He took her hand and led her from the trees to the beach where his crew had subdued the pirates with an expediency that said much for their training at Matt's capable hands. The pirates were bound together with their captain and had been left huddled on the sand.

"What are your orders, Captain?" Dick asked as Matt and Lily approached.

"Have you sent men out to the *Black Bird*?" Matt asked.

"Aye, sir, and they've signaled that the ship is secure. Only three men were left aboard as guards."

"When do you expect the *Sea Hawke*?"

"She'll be coming around the bend at daybreak to pick us up."

"Tell the men to bed down on the beach tonight. Tomorrow we'll decide who will sail with the *Black Bird* and who will stay with the *Sea Hawke*. Lily and I will spend the night in the lean-to I built close to the pool."

Hand in hand Matt and Lily walked through the moonlit darkness to the lean-to that had been their home for so long she had lost track of the days and weeks. She would always have fond memories of this little piece of paradise where Matt had first told her he loved her. She had been happy here and yet feared the future that lay ahead of them. It was so easy to love and be loved on this deserted island where nothing and no one existed but her and Matt. Would things change once they reached civilization? It was bound to, Lily supposed, wondering if she'd ever be this happy again.

"You're so quiet, love," Matt said as they paused beside the lean-to. "One would think you're unhappy about leaving the island."

Lily bit her bottom lip to keep it from trembling. Truth to tell, she was terrified about leaving. "I've been so content here, Matt."

The rugged lines of Matt's face softened into a smile. "So have I, but all good things must come to an end."

"That's what I'm afraid of." The words came on a tremulous sigh.

"I love you, Lily, you have nothing to fear. I'll be rejoining the war but I'll come back to you. I swear it."

"Do you also swear to be faithful?" Lily dared to ask.

"Even that," Matt replied solemnly. "Now if you'll be quiet long enough I'll show you how much I love you."

Lily didn't protest as he slid Dick Marlow's coat from her shoulders and drew off her tattered shift. "You're so beautiful," he said reverently. "Your body glows like gilded silver in the moonlight. I want to remember you like this always."

Then he was kissing her, winding his fingers in her hair and holding her in place while he ravished her mouth. Lily's arms slid around his neck, giving freely, almost desperately as she realized she would no longer have Matt solely to herself. And if he returned to the war she might lose him forever. Both were aware of that fact, adding a poignancy to their loving that was heretofore missing.

Matt's heart was thumping wildly in his chest as he broke off and stepped away in order to remove his clothes. Lily watched him as he removed his tattered shirt then stripped off his boots and pants. He was hard and lean and wonderfully virile. In Lily's estimation there wasn't another man to compare with Matt's superbly fashioned body. Existing solely on fruit and fish had further honed and hardened his already fit physique.

Her eyes slid down his massive chest, lingering for a breathless moment on the narrow curve of his hips before lowering to that hard male part of him that gave her so much pleasure. He was already erect and Lily sucked in a shaky breath as he moved against her, letting her feel the strength of his love. Lily had the sudden urge to touch him and reached between them, enclosing the stiff length of him in her hand. A tormented groan slipped past Matt's lips and Lily drew her hand away.

"No, oh God, no, don't stop!" He placed her hand on him again, holding it in place with his own. Then he showed her the motion that gave him the most pleasure. A quick learner, she stroked him until his breath rasped through his chest in short, harsh pants. Then he stopped her. "Enough, love. I want to give you pleasure, too."

With mutual consent they entered the lean-to, lying down on the soft grass and leaves Matt had fashioned for their bed. They lay side by side, facing one another, when Matt began caressing Lily with slow, teasing strokes. Her breasts, her legs, her belly, that soft place between her legs. Until the air was redundant with her small cries and harsh breathing. When he took one of her nipples into his mouth and teased it with the tip of his tongue, then nipped and sucked,

Lily nearly lost control. When his fingers slid inside her, she screamed.

"Matt!"

"Not yet, love, it's too soon. I want to worship every inch of you."

And he did. Lily was sobbing and convulsing in agony when Matt finally took pity and thrust into her. His passion and control was magnificent to behold as he stroked them both to the most perfect climax they had ever attained.

"Wake up, love, the *Sea Hawke* arrived hours ago but you were sleeping so soundly I didn't want to awaken you until the absolute last minute."

Lily muttered something unintelligible and rolled over on her stomach. When Matt swatted her sharply on the bottom, she yelped indignantly and glared at him. "Go away, Matt."

A chuckle rumbled from Matt's chest. "It's time to leave, love."

Leave.

The very word produced a chill of apprehension. But Lily quickly tossed it aside as she scrambled for the dress she had so carefully preserved. It was in terrible shape but her trunk of clothes was stowed aboard the *Sea Hawke* and she'd soon be presentable again.

A short time later she accompanied Matt to the beach where the crew was assembled. Dick Marlow had been appointed captain of the *Black Bird*, renamed *Lady Hawke* in honor of Lily, and his chest was nearly bursting with pride. A skeleton crew was selected to sail under him and both ships were to rendezvous in Nassau, where Matt hoped to enlist sufficient men to crew both ships. Then he intended to take Lily to New Orleans, where she could sit out the war with Sarah and Jeff. Providing that port was still open to American ships.

Lily was stunned when Matt told her that he had boarded the *Black Bird* while she still slept and discovered a treasure trove in Frenchy's cabin. Gold coins, precious gems, silver and artifacts were stored there in locked caskets. After he shared with his crew he would still be a very wealthy man. Provided he could get it to safekeeping before something unforetold happened to him or his ship.

"We'll never have to worry about money again, love," Matt said as he settled her in the longboat that would carry them to the *Sea Hawke*.

No, not money, Lily stewed in silent contemplation. Money was the least of her worries.

Chapter 16

Sharing Matt's cabin aboard the *Sea Hawke* brought bittersweet memories to Lily. They were of both sad times and happy times, but could not compare with the ecstatic months spent on their island paradise. Matt had little time to spare for her now as they sailed to Nassau with the newly named *Lady Hawke* following close behind. Lily spared a brief moment wondering if Frenchy and his crew would be rescued, then promptly forgot about him. He wasn't worth worrying over, she decided.

The time Lily and Matt spent together was not wasted by words, enough had already been said on the island. Both realized that their time together was necessarily limited by the war and they would soon be parted. Unable to bear the thought of separation, perhaps permanently, they made love with a desperation they had never known before.

They reached Nassau in four days and once again Matt refused to allow Lily ashore, only this time Lily did not worry about Matt visiting the local whores for she knew he had little energy left to expend on other women. While ashore Matt was lucky enough to sign on sufficient men to crew his two ships. He also received a bit of bad news. Another of his ships, *Sky Hawke*, had been sunk by a British frigate. He mourned its loss, especially the loss of life, but war did not discriminate.

They lingered in Nassau over a week. Before they left they learned that on September 11, 1814, an American naval victory on Lake Champlain saved New York from invasion via the Hudson Valley. Talk was still circulating concerning a full-scale invasion of a major port by the British and New Orleans was still being discussed as a possible target.

Both the *Sea Hawke* and the *Lady Hawke* departed Nassau early in October with a full crew. Matt's destination was New Orleans while the *Lady Hawke* sailed forth under Captain Dick Marlow to disrupt British shipping. Plans were made to rendezvous on one of the Florida Keys in December if the war wasn't ended by then.

To Matt's relief the British navy was nowhere in evidence as they sailed into the mouth of the Mississippi River and made their way to New Orleans. Lily stood at the rail as they docked at one of the long quays. A wild profusion of sights and sounds drew her rapt attention to the teeming streets below. Gaily dressed Negroes of varying shades ranging from black to pale cream roamed the docks freely. The women wore colorful turbans wound around their kinky hair and swished their petticoats playfully at the dock workers, causing Lily to laugh aloud at their spirited antics.

"It's quite a sight, isn't it?" Matt said as he stepped up beside her.

"Have you been here before?"

"Many times. I love New Orleans. Nothing can repress the high spirits of the inhabitants. Even now, with the city overflowing with Andrew Jackson's soldiers, everything is gay and lively."

Lily turned her attention to the blue-clad soldiers lounging against walls or striding along the quay in aimless pursuit. "I think rumors of a British invasion are unfounded," she scoffed. "We saw no sign of British ships in the Gulf."

"Let's hope you're right," Matt said skeptically. He didn't put anything past the persistent British. They could be gathering even now on some nearby island, preparing for an attack. He had no idea how close to the truth his thoughts had taken him.

"Sarah will be surprised to see us," Lily said gleefully. "I can hardly wait to greet her."

"My little sister is in for quite a shock," Matt concurred. "We've no cargo to unload so I see no reason to linger aboard the *Sea Hawke*. We'll leave as soon as docking is completed. I've given the crew their share of Frenchy's treasure and two weeks shore leave, they've earned it."

"Two weeks," Lily protested. "Must you leave so soon?"

"I've been out of the war many months, love, surely you can understand my need for haste. It will take nearly that long to bring aboard fresh food, water and ammunition else I'd leave sooner."

"Sarah will be disappointed."

"Sarah will understand. Do you have her address?"

"Yes, I received one letter from her before I left Boston. She and Jeff live at thirty-one Rue Dumaine."

A short time later they debarked and Matt hired a hack to take them and Lily's trunks to Rue Dumaine. During the ride through the city Lily hung out the window gawking at the kaleidoscope of sights, sounds and scents. Everywhere she looked large stores of food and arms were stockpiled on the levee. That—as well as the large numbers of militia—was reminiscent of a city under or about to be placed under siege. It was obvious not everyone considered the rumor of attack a big joke.

As they drove through the main part of the old city, Lily was charmed by the lacy wrought-iron surrounding balconies and windows. She caught tantalizing glimpses of jewellike gardens enclosed by high walls and gasped in delight. It was almost like being in Paris again. Matt smiled indulgently at her obvious enjoyment of the quaint surroundings and wondered anew why he had resisted love for so long.

Lily absorbed the special flavor of New Orleans like a sponge. At first it was a shocking conglomeration of colorful people and crowded streets, especially after the isolation of their island. She was careful to miss nothing as she hung out the window of the hack, but it still stunned her when she saw a handbill attached to a pole announcing a performance at the opera house featuring Clarissa Hartley. Evidently Clarissa's theater troupe was in town performing before the public and with a jolt of apprehension Lily wondered what it would mean in regards to her marriage.

Abruptly she drew back from the window in silence, wondering if Matt had seen the handbill. She knew he had when she caught him staring at her, as if waiting for her to broach the subject. She decided to ignore it. She had been too happy with Matt these past few months to dredge up old memories of Clarissa Hartley. Besides, she knew Matt loved her, he'd never hurt her by taking up with Clarissa again, would he?

Matt had seen the handbill but didn't know if Lily had. He wanted desperately to reassure her, to tell her Clarissa meant nothing to him, but her silence placed him in an awkward position. He didn't want to reopen old wounds nor did he want to call Lily's attention to the fact that Clarissa was in town if she hadn't seen the handbill. In the end he remained silent.

The hack turned the corner into Rue Dumaine and Clarissa was forgotten as it pulled to a stop before number thirty-one. Matt jumped to the street to help

Lily alight while the driver hauled out Lily's luggage. The driver had no sooner been paid off and left them standing amidst their trunks when Sarah came sailing out the door straight into Matt's arms.

"Oh, oh, I can't believe it," she gushed, laughing and crying at the same time. "To visit New Orleans at a time like this . . ." She shook her head in disbelief. "Don't you know we're a city under siege? Or at least that's what the authorities want us to think. Oh, forgive me, come in, come in. I'm dying to hear how you got out of Boston. Since Matt is here too I imagine you sailed on the *Sea Hawke*." Sarah was so excited she couldn't stop babbling. When she embraced Lily, there were tears in her eyes.

"You haven't changed, Sarah." Matt laughed, hugging her close as they walked the short distance to the house. "How is my new brother-in-law?"

"Busy." Sarah laughed. "This has been a good move for us, Matt. Unlike Boston, Jeff has more clients than he can handle. I hope you weren't too disappointed over missing our wedding."

"I'll survive," Matt said. "As long as you're happy."

"Ecstatically," Sarah assured him, blushing.

Sarah took them directly to the small but elegant parlor, ordering tea immediately. A creamy-skinned quadroon of exceptional beauty left immediately to do her bidding.

"Fleta is a free woman of color," Sarah informed them while they waited for their tea. "Jeff and I refuse to own slaves. But of course you'll learn all that later. Right now I'm dying to know what brings you to New Orleans and how it happens that you and Lily are together at a time I'd expect Matt to be at sea bedeviling the British."

Lily and Matt exchanged meaningful looks. Did they really want Sarah to know that Lily had left him and Matt found her aboard a British warship he had boarded?

"It's a very long story, Sarah. Suffice it to say that Lily and I both left Boston months ago and have been stranded nearly as long on a deserted Bahamian island."

"How romantic," Sarah said, sending Lily a special look that said, I told you so.

"I'm leaving Lily in your care when I rejoin the war," Matt said. "I've been absent far too long and my services are desperately needed. Perhaps I'll offer my assistance to General Jackson. He can tell me where I'm needed most."

"How—how long can you stay?"

"I planned on two weeks. It should take that long to supply my ship and see to small repairs."

"So soon?" Sarah wailed. "I haven't seen you for so long, Matt. Everyone has heard about your fearless exploits and I've been so worried. Can't you persuade him to remain, Lily?"

"I wish I could." Lily sighed wistfully.

"Does it still bother you that I'm fighting against your countrymen?" Matt probed with gentle insistence.

Lily assumed a thoughtful pose. "No, not anymore. America is my country now and I want freedom and justice as much as you do."

"I can't believe I'm hearing this," Sarah gloated with secret glee. "I always knew you two were right for one another but were too stubborn to admit it. Being stranded must have brought you both to your senses."

Matt leered wolfishly at Lily. "I don't know about Lily but it sure opened my eyes. Those months were the happiest of my life."

"And mine." Lily blushed becomingly.

While Matt and Lily gazed rapturously at one another, Sarah's heartfelt relief was more than mere happiness at Lily's and Matt's newfound love. She knew Clarissa Hartley was in town and she dreaded the thought of Matt abandoning his wife for his mistress again. But now that she knew Matt was too much in love with Lily to be distracted by an old flame, she could relax.

As the days sped by Lily grew distraught at the swift passage of time. In a matter of days Matt would be gone. She fervently prayed fate would be kind and bring him back safely to her. Unfortunately she had seen little of him these past days. He had called on General Jackson and was now involved with whipping some of the civilian volunteers into a fighting force to be pitted against the British should they attack New Orleans as expected. As it was his stay in the city stretched to three weeks, which suited Lily just fine.

A puzzling thing occurred one day when Lily left the house alone to go shopping. Either she was mistaken or she had seen Clarissa Hartley lingering outside the house. It bothered her for a while, though she mentioned it to no one. Matt had given her no indication that he was being unfaithful to her and she had no reason to suspect him or question him about his former mistress. In the end she let the subject die a natural death.

One day Matt told her how Jean Lafitte, a notorious pirate and local hero to the citizens of New Orleans, had placed his entire fleet of ships at Governor Claiborne's disposal.

"Claiborne promptly turned down Lafitte's offer," Matt said, shaking his head. "Lafitte considers himself an American citizen but Claiborne doesn't trust him. Especially after he learned the British offered Lafitte thirty thousand pounds to allow British ships into Barataria, his island stronghold south of New Orleans."

"Perhaps Claiborne is wise," Lily suggested.

"I think Lafitte's offer is genuine," Matt replied after a thoughtful pause. "He wants to aid in the war, and has vowed to petition Jackson himself in order to fight on the side of the Americans."

In late November, Matt informed Lily that the *Sea Hawke* was ready to sail and General Jackson had given him leave to depart.

"I've seen so little of you, Matt," Lily wailed when she was told the news. "Some nights you didn't even return home. Perhaps you should stay in New Orleans and wait for the promised attack. I'm sure your help would prove invaluable to General Jackson."

"I must go, Lily," Matt said quietly. "I'm to rendezvous with *Lady Hawke* in a few days. Dick will be expecting me. I'm anxious to see how he fared."

Their loving that night was fierce, their passion for one another insatiable.

Clasping Matt's narrow hips between her knees, Lily took his incredible length into her body, breathing deeply as she felt herself stretch to accommodate him. Matt raised his head slightly and sucked an engorged nipple into his mouth, running his tongue maddeningly over the tender bud before suckling gently. Lily moaned, arching her back, forcing his manhood deep—so deep inside her. Matt shuddered, his tempo quickening into a wild, driving fury as he continued suckling and teasing the nipples of both breasts. Suddenly he reversed positions, rolling Lily beneath him as he thrust into her again and again.

Lily lowered her head and tasted the warmth of his throat, nuzzled the soft curls on his chest as she teetered on the edge of sanity. When Matt inserted one hand between them and found that sensitive bud nestled in the red curls at her apex, Lily cried out, pressing upward against his tender torment.

"Now, love, now," Matt gasped raggedly. "Come to

me now. I want to savor this moment for all those long lonely nights to come."

His words, so wonderfully erotic, so magnificently coaxing, pushed her over the brink, falling, falling into the abyss, only to climb once more to the peak as he took her on one ecstatic journey after another.

Afterward, Matt slept contentedly while Lily lay wide awake, unable to bear the thought of another separation. What if Matt never returned? She loved him too much, too desperately to allow him to slip out of her life again. If something happened to Matt she wanted to be with him. Yet she knew he'd never agree to take her along. But decisions didn't necessarily have to be the man's prerogative, Lily concluded in her usual reckless manner. She was always plunging headlong into potentially dangerous situations and somehow managed to survive.

During the long night in which she held Matt close to her heart, she made secret plans that could possibly result in death. But nothing was more important than being with Matt at a time when his need for her was the greatest. A sly smile curved her lips when she finally drifted into a light sleep. Matt was up and dressed when next she opened her eyes.

"Is it morning already?" she asked as she stretched and sat up in bed.

"It's early yet, go back to sleep, love."

"Weren't you going to wake me and tell me good-bye?"

"We said our farewells last night in a way I'll always remember."

"Do you sail with the morning tide?"

"No, we sail at dusk on the evening tide, but there is still much to be done before we're ready to depart so I won't be back. I've always hated lengthy good-byes, so kiss me, love, and wish me good fortune."

"Take me with you!"

"Are you mad?" Matt laughed, bending down to

enfold her in his arms. "You're too precious to me to risk your life."

"Some captains bring their women with them," Lily observed.

"Doxies. They only bring their doxies," Matt pointed out, flashing a roguish grin. "Cheer up, love, I'll be back before you know it."

"Promise me, Matt, promise me you'll come back," Lily begged with almost frantic urgency.

"I've already promised you forever, isn't that enough?"

"Forever," Lily said softly. "It's enough, Matt." But only if I'm along to see that nothing happens to you, she thought but did not add.

Twilight shrouded the levee in ever lengthening purple shadows as people hurried home to their suppers. Darkness fell early in late November and the evening chill settled uncomfortably in Lily's bones as she crouched behind a stack of barrels directly opposite the quay where the *Sea Hawke* was docked. Activity around the ship was at a maximum now as Matt issued orders prior to sailing. Men of all sizes, shapes and descriptions were trudging back and forth across the gangplank from the ship to the dock, toting aboard the last of the supplies and ammunition needed for a lengthy stay at sea.

Keeping her eyes on Matt where he watched from the bridge, Lily pulled her cap lower over her ears and waited anxiously for the right moment. It arrived when Matt's new first mate, Paul Dickens, requested his advice about a situation developing starboard and took his attention away from the men loading supplies. The moment Matt disappeared from the bridge, Lily acted. Wearing a heavy padded jacket over Matt's cast-off clothes, her fiery hair concealed beneath a woolen cap, she appeared no different from many of the young lads whose scrawny frames and smooth faces marked them as first-time seamen.

Scooting behind one of the sailors, Lily shouldered a sack that didn't look heavy enough to weigh her down and began the long trek up the gangplank, praying fervently that she wouldn't be challenged by the watch. She didn't expect to remain disguised forever, just until they were too far at sea for Matt to turn back to New Orleans. She didn't doubt for a minute that he'd be angry, angry enough to wring her neck. But somehow she'd convince him that she belonged aboard the *Sea Hawke* with him, not waiting at home wondering if he was dead or alive.

Bending under the weight of the sack, Lily sucked in a sigh of relief when no one called out a warning. So far so good, she thought gleefully. All things considered, it hadn't been difficult to carry out her plan. Composing a letter of explanation to Sarah had been an almost painful task. She hoped Sarah understood why she had to leave, but loving Jeff like she did Lily felt certain Sarah would realize that this was something Lily had to do.

"Yer laggin' behind, lad, get a move on."

Lily hadn't realized she'd been dawdling until the sailor behind her gave her a nudge. She had reached the hold now and was ready to descend the ladder with her sack of supplies. Her intention was to conceal herself in the hold until the ship was under way. Once she set the sack in place beside the others, she deliberately dallied, hoping everyone would leave without paying her any heed. She and the sailor behind her had carried aboard the last of the supplies and she counted heavily on being able to conceal herself in the hold. It was not to be.

"Quit yer dawdlin', lad, there's work to be done on deck. This yer first trip out?" The sailor behind her felt more or less obligated to show the ropes to the sprout who looked as if he was barely out of the schoolroom.

"Aye," Lily muttered in as deep a voice as she could muster.

"Yer a mite young but you'll get use to the routine. Come along, now, I'll show ya what needs doin'." He gripped her collar and pushed her none too gently up the ladder. Lily had no choice but to do his bidding.

The shadows had deepened now and activity increased as the men awaited orders to unfurl the sails. Matt paced the deck, his keen eyes missing nothing, impatient now to rejoin the war. Every ship he sank or captured would be one less available to attack New Orleans or any other important port city. He noted nothing amiss on the deck and was about to order the gangplank run in when he saw a woman alight from a hack and approach the ship. It was still light enough to make out her features and Matt recognized her immediately. Clarissa! What in the hell was she doing here? She was calling and gesturing wildly and against his better judgment Matt motioned her aboard. He had no idea he was being watched by a youthful crewman whose mouth gaped open in shock and whose amber eyes turned dull with the pain of betrayal.

To Lily it looked as if Clarissa had been expected aboard the *Sea Hawke*, that Matt had summoned her for a final tryst before sailing. Had he been seeing Clarissa all those days and nights when he had professed to be too busy to come home? Matt seemed to have no qualms about taking his doxy aboard the *Sea Hawke*, for obviously he preferred Clarissa to his own wife. It hurt. It hurt like hell. She was just about to sneak back down the gangplank and go back home when she was cornered by the same seaman who thought he was being helpful.

"Yer needed below in the hold, lad. The cargo

needs rearrangin' and yer the only one small enough to crawl into the spaces that need fillin'.'"

"But—" She glanced back at Matt and saw that his arms were around Clarissa now and they were speaking in urgent tones. His face wore a curious look but Lily couldn't tell from his expression exactly what he was thinking.

"No arguin', lad. I'll show ya what needs doin'. What's yer name? They call me Baldy."

Baldy was apparently a misnomer, for every inch of the man's exposed skin was covered with thick black fur, including his face and head. "My name is ... Luke," Lily said, thinking swiftly.

Just as Matt was leading Clarissa to his cabin, Lily turned reluctantly toward the hold. Perhaps if she pretended to follow orders now she'd still be able to sneak away before the ship sailed. There was no way she was going to remain aboard with Matt's mistress. Vaguely she wondered if Matt intended to keep Clarissa with him or if she'd leave once he'd bedded her. Lily couldn't envision the woman remaining at sea for any length of time for she was the type who craved the limelight and enjoyed constant attention. She also wasn't the kind who relished placing her life in danger. No, Lily decided, Matt would probably bed her but not take her with him. She cast a glance of pure malice at Matt, and saw him leading Clarissa down the ladder to his cabin, before descending into the hold.

Matt scowled fiercely as Clarissa picked her way daintily up the gangplank. He couldn't imagine what she wanted but she had seemed so desperate that he injudiciously motioned her aboard. Of course he had known she was in New Orleans. He had read the handbills and even seen her at a distance on an occasion or two. When she tried to seek a private moment with him he had studiously avoided her. He didn't want anything to disturb the trust that had developed between him and Lily over the past months. Yet his association with Clarissa had been one of long duration and he felt he owed it to her to listen to her now, especially since he was leaving and she was desperate enough to come down to the docks to see him.

He should have been prepared for Clarissa's exuberant greeting, but he wasn't. When she literally threw herself at him he had no choice but to open his arms to receive her or be bowled over by her. But to his credit, he quickly set her aside.

"What is it, Clarrie? Why are you here?"

"You could say you're glad to see me, Matt," Clarissa said, screwing her mouth up into a naughty pout.

"That would be lying," Matt countered before she got ideas that he was in need of a mistress. "If you've something important to say, you'd best say it for as you can see I'm preparing to sail."

"This is important, Matt, else I wouldn't be here. I know you've been avoiding me but I need help."

"Help? What kind of help?"

"Can we talk in private? Your men are staring at us."

Matt cursed beneath his breath. Why wouldn't his crew stare at them? They knew he was married and most of them held Lily in high regard. Lord, wouldn't Lily be livid if she knew Clarissa was here now? he thought with a pang of relief. Thank God she was home where this innocent encounter couldn't be misunderstood.

"Very well, Clarrie, come to my cabin. But I can only give you a few minutes."

"That's all I need," Clarissa said cryptically. The hungry way in which her dark eyes devoured Matt belied her words. After all this time she still hadn't found anyone to replace him and harbored the hope that he would return to her one day.

Once inside Matt's cabin, Clarissa settled herself in a chair while Matt stood over her, waiting for her explanation. "What is it you wanted to say?" he prodded.

Clarissa licked her dry lips. Now that she was here she didn't know where to begin, or how Matt would react. She really was desperate and Matt was her last hope. "I need money, Matt, lots of it."

"For Christ's sake, Clarrie, are you still unable to curb your spending?" He recalled that when she was his mistress he chided her often about her extravagance.

"An actress needs clothes, and pretty jewels, and lacy underthings. I didn't realize how much I was spending until the bills arrived."

"Isn't there a man in your life who'll accept responsibility for your expenses? It's not like you to be without a protector for any length of time."

"Of course there's been men, lots of them," Clarrie shot back defiantly, "only the last one completely fooled me. I thought he was rich and let him gull me into thinking his money was merely tied up for a short period of time. He 'borrowed' most of what I'd saved up and when the bills started arriving he conveniently disappeared. The hotel confiscated all my beautiful wardrobe and my theater troupe is leaving New Orleans for Natchez and I haven't the cost of the fare out of town. To make matters worse my manager refused to advance me any more salary."

Matt's scowl grew even darker. Truth to tell he felt somewhat obligated to give Clarissa the money she asked for. They had been lovers for five years despite the fact that he had never harbored deep feelings for her and she probably took other men to her bed when he was absent for longer than she could abide. On his part the relationship was a comfortable one since he had found no one he could love or wanted to make his wife. Until Lily came along.

"You're my last hope, Matt," Clarissa pleaded. "I desperately need to get to Natchez and without my wardrobe I have no way to earn a living."

"You're fortunate to have found me with sufficient cash on hand," Matt said slowly as he removed a small casket from his desk drawer. He had brought a small portion of Frenchy's treasure with him in case it was needed to purchase supplies in distant ports. "How much do you need?"

Clarissa's eyes widened when she saw the sparkle of gold. She licked her lips and mentioned an amount so ridiculously outrageous Matt bent her an austere glance and counted out half of what she asked for. He dropped it into her open palm. Clarissa carefully placed it in her reticule, knowing full well Matt had been generous but miffed that he hadn't given her the entire amount she had requested. Still, it was enough to pay her debts, buy a ticket to Natchez on a riverboat and keep her for several months. At least until she found another man to be responsible for her bills.

When Clarissa made no move to leave, Matt gripped her elbow and lifted her from the chair. "Good-bye, Clarrie, I'd advise you to hang on to that money as long as possible."

"Matt, I'd like to repay you." She sidled closer, leaving no doubt in his mind as to the kind of payment she was offering.

"I need no repayment, Clarrie. This relieves me of any responsibility to you once and for all."

"For old time's sake, Matt, let me show you how much I appreciate your help."

"You can show your appreciation by leaving and allowing me to sail on schedule. I have a wife, now Clarrie. I love Lily. Not even you can convince me to do something I'll regret later. Good-bye, Clarrie, I doubt that we'll meet again."

"Don't be too sure of that, darling," Clarissa said

in a throaty purr that hinted at future dealings. "One day I'll pop up when you least expect it and thank you properly."

Then she sailed out the door, leaving Matt shaking his head and wondering what he had ever seen in Clarissa Hartley.

Part 3

1814–1815

—— ⌒◯◯⌒ ——

When one finds true love 'tis often too late
Unless one believes in good fortune and fate.

Chapter 17

E xhausted from work she wasn't accustomed to, Lily finished the task Baldy set for her and sat down on a sack of grain to rest before sneaking off the ship prior to sailing. Well aware of Matt's voracious sexual appetite, she didn't think the *Sea Hawke* would sail yet for several hours. At least not until he had his fill of Clarissa. Leaning her head back against a barrel, her face contorted with pain as she relived in her mind the way in which Matt had welcomed his mistress aboard his ship.

That was the moment when the love that had blossomed in her heart for Matt had shriveled and died. If she came face-to-face with him right now she would spit at him. The last few months had been nothing but a lie conceived by Matt to make her a willing participant in the game of love. No, she silently amended, not love, sex. Love had nothing to do with what he felt for her. He wanted her body because no one else was available. Lust. Pure and simple, Matt's sexual appetites demanded more than one woman in his bed. She should have realized a woman like her with no previous experience couldn't possibly satisfy him like Clarissa did.

All the love that Lily harbored in her heart for Matt rearranged itself into raw hate.

Feeling rested, Lily rose and moved stealthily toward the ladder, wanting to be off the ship before Baldy returned, making escape impossible. Lily had no intention now of remaining aboard with Matt. If Clarissa hadn't remained aboard to take care of Matt's sexual needs he'd only use Lily to appease his lust while at sea. He'd promise her things he didn't mean, promises he had no intention of keeping. He didn't know what the word *faithful* meant. And love was an emotion foreign to his nature.

Suddenly the ship lurched under Lily's feet and a terrible fear came over her. They were under way! The *Sea Hawke* was sailing before she got a chance to leave. Dear God, what was she to do now? How long could she hide her sex and her identity? What would Matt do once he found out she had sneaked aboard without his permission?

Cautiously she poked her head out of the hatch, immediately aware of the increased activity on deck now that the ship was moving. A quick glance told her that they were too far down the river for her to jump overboard and make her way ashore. She had no choice now but to blend in with the other sailors and keep her identity hidden as long as possible.

"Get yer butt on deck, Luke!" Lily looked up to see Baldy hovering over her, shaking his head in exasperation. "Did ya fall asleep in the hold?"

"N-no," Lily stammered, pulling her cap down over her ears as far as it would go. "I just finished."

"Lend a hand to Gramps in the galley. As scrawny as ye are 'tis about all yer good for."

"Gramps?" Lily said, hauling herself out of the hatch.

Baldy grinned. "We call him that 'cause he's the oldest man aboard. Ye'll see what I mean when ye meet him. Don't let him scare ya, he's as gentle as a lamb." Then he turned and went back to his work, his ribald laughter booming across the deck.

Lily hurried to the galley, keeping an eye out for

Matt. He was still on the bridge, handling the wheel as he guided the ship downriver into the Gulf. When he happened to glance her way she bowed her head and scooted across the deck. Vaguely she wondered what had happened to the sailor who used to cook aboard the *Sea Hawke*. His name was Pate and the meals he produced were surprisingly good, if somewhat bland. Perhaps, she surmised, he transferred to *Lady Hawke* when Dick Marlow took charge of the captured ship.

" 'Bout time Baldy sent me some help, but from the looks of ye, ye ain't got the strength to hold up your pizzle to take a leak."

The speaker was thin, wiry, and at an age when most men took to their rocking chairs. Sagging wrinkles and leathery skin lent his face a permanent scowl, attesting to his great age. Bushy eyebrows and sparse whiskers matched the tufts of white hair sticking out at odd angles from his nearly bald head. He looked grouchy and mean and tough enough to chew nails.

Lily blushed furiously at the crusty old man's words. No one had ever spoken to her like that. "I—I'm stronger than I look," she stammered, staring at Gramps with something akin to horror.

Gramps scowled, shook his head and muttered, "The cap'n must be hard up to sign on a scrawny lad like you. Well, don't stand around, boy, hop to it. Peel them taters. When ye finish with that ye can scrub out the iron pot so's I can start 'em cookin'."

And so the evening went.

After supper was eaten and the pots were scrubbed clean, Lily was so tired she barely had the energy to drag herself to a secluded corner on deck and bed down. Few ships provided quarters for crewmen, forcing them to find a comfortable spot for themselves on deck in which to sleep. And since no one knew Lily was a woman she had to make do like

the men. She had no idea how long she could survive the hard work assigned to her but thanked God
she hadn't been ordered to climb the rigging like
she'd seen the others do.

Several days passed, days in which Lily's soft muscles hardened and her body grew taut and supple
from the labor she'd been required to perform. She
had formed an uneasy truce with Gramps and he appeared even to like her. His gruffness, she suspected,
concealed a kind nature that he allowed few people
to glimpse, and so long as she performed her duties
without complaint he treated her with bluff disdain.
Doing galley duty, Lily decided, was better than letting Matt take advantage of her. And that's exactly
what he would do if he found out she was aboard
his ship.

She had seen blessed little of Matt since they left
New Orleans and she was convinced now that she
could pull off this charade as long as she liked. Most
of the crewmen accepted her as one of them and
most treated her kindly because she was the smallest
and weakest "man" aboard. And since Gramps
seemed satisfied with her performance she was assigned permanently to galley duty. Everything
seemed to be going well until the day she left the
galley for a breath of air and was told to climb the
rigging to the crow's nest.

Baldy, whose name Lily learned was really Baldwin, was third mate, and he had decided that "Luke"
should learn more about ships than what sailors ate
at mealtimes.

"Go on, lad," he encouraged. "If ye want to be a
sailor ye have to learn to do somethin' 'sides
cookin'."

Lily blanched. Heights frightened her, especially
when she'd be atop something as tall as a mast. "I—I
can't."

"Sure ye can. I'll give ye a boost." Hoisting her up

by the waist, Baldy placed Lily on the first rung of the crude ladder and nudged her upward.

Unspeakable fear gnawed at her when she glanced down and saw Baldy standing several feet below her, his face set in implacable lines. There was no way he was going to let her back down. Dragging in a steadying breath, Lily climbed up one rung, then another, and another, swaying in the breeze as she clung tenaciously to the wooden rungs.

"Don't stop now, lad!" Baldy called from below. "Yer doing just fine."

Lily glanced down and froze. The water looked like it was a mile below her and she wasn't even halfway to the top yet. She couldn't go on, she just couldn't! She swiveled her head to tell Baldy that she couldn't do it, that she was coming down, and saw Matt standing beside the third mate. He was looking up at her strangely, his face wearing a puzzled frown. He was speaking to Baldy but Lily couldn't hear what they were saying. She only knew that to retreat now was cowardly. She'd be damned if she'd give away her identity and be forced by Matt to share his bed. She had made love with him for the last time in New Orleans. Sucking in a trembling breath, she slowly inched her way upward.

"What's amiss, Mr. Baldwin?"

Matt had been watching Baldy and the young lad for some time and noted the youngster's reluctance to climb into the rigging. He had no idea why Baldy was insisting the lad perform so daring a task for it was ship's policy not to force men new to the sea to climb the rigging until they grew accustomed to the ship. Matt had to give the lad credit, he was reluctant but game. But when he saw the lad sway in the wind and nearly lose his grip, a terrible fear seized him. Something in the way the lad moved, in the shape of his legs partially revealed beneath the baggy trousers, stirred his memory.

"I thought 'twas time for the lad to learn what sailin' is all about," Baldy said, keeping his eyes glued to the slight form now hanging precariously from one of the rungs.

"He looks terrified," Matt observed.

"He's a game little devil, I'll give him that," Baldy said with a hint of pride. "I've seen men older than him refuse to climb the riggin'."

"What's the lad's name?" Matt asked curiously.

"Luke. Didn't give a last name. I was a mite surprised, though, that ye'd hire on a tender sprout like that. He don't weigh enough to stay upright in a good breeze. He's been helpin' Gramps in the galley. Ain't heard no complaint."

"I didn't sign him on," Matt said thoughtfully.

"Must have been Dickens."

As if on cue, Dickens approached Baldy and the captain. Curiosity had gotten the best of him when he saw them talking and gazing up into the rigging. "Are you talking about me, Captain?"

"Aye." Matt nodded. "Did you sign on that lad?" He pointed skyward to where Lily had paused to catch her breath.

Dickens squinted up at her, shielding his eyes against the glare of the sun. "Strange, I don't recall the lad. I would remember someone as puny as him and most likely have sent him packing."

"Do you reckon he's a stowaway?" Baldy offered.

Matt glanced up again to check on the lad's progress and his heart thudded wildly against the wall of his chest when he saw the lad's feet slide off a rung and dangle in the air. His body swayed helplessly in the breeze and Matt sensed the boy's fear, heard his mindless cry of terror. A curse ripped from Matt's throat. Why hadn't he noticed the lad before now? he wondered curiously. The lad's youth, his obvious lack of experience, his inability to function as a seaman, should have been noted before he was signed on to serve aboard a privateer. He started up the ladder.

"I'll go, Cap'n," volunteered Baldy.

"No, I'll get the lad," Matt bit out, trusting no one but himself to rescue the youngster. If he was a stowaway he'd soon get to the bottom of it and put the boy ashore at the first port. He damn sure wasn't going to spend the rest of his time at sea coddling a green lad barely out of the schoolroom.

Lily's eyes squeezed shut and she hung on with a tenacity she didn't know she possessed. Her fingers were frozen around the small strip of wood supporting her weight and her arms felt as if they had pulled from their sockets. She knew with a certainty that she was going to fall and land at Matt's feet. It would serve him right, she thought spitefully. Perhaps when he saw her sprawled on the deck he'd feel remorse over his infidelity.

"I'm coming, lad, don't panic!"

Lily's eyes snapped open. Daring to glance down, she saw Matt slowly climbing the mast toward her. She was so shocked one hand lost its grip and she made a desperate lunge to reestablish her hold.

"Hang on!"

"Hurry!"

Matt's breath caught painfully in his throat and he cursed whoever had signed on such a green lad. And if he was a stowaway he'd beat him to within an inch of his life for putting him through such anguish. He certainly didn't relish seeing the boy's broken body lying on the deck.

Then he was behind Lily, steading her with his strong, tan hands, guiding her feet to the rung below. "Easy now, don't look down. I've got you, I won't let you fall."

The moment Matt put his hands on her Lily knew she was safe. Forcing a calmness she didn't feel, she willed her frozen fingers to release their grip so he could guide her down the ladder. When they reached the bottom her shaky legs refused to function and she would have fallen if Matt hadn't kept a tight hold on her. She had no idea he was regarding her with somber curiosity, or that his dark eyes had grown pensive and thoughtful.

"You little fool," Matt rapped out curtly. "You had no business signing aboard a ship when you know nothing about sailing. If you did indeed sign on. No one seems to recall hiring you." His eyes narrowed dangerously. "Are you a stowaway, lad?"

Keeping her head down and her eyes trained on her feet, Lily muttered an unintelligible reply. Clearly in shock, she was beyond putting two sentences together that made sense. Lily felt the heat of Matt's dark gaze pierce her and swayed drunkenly. Had he discovered her secret?

"What should we do with the lad, Cap'n?" Baldy asked, feeling remorse over sending a green lad into the rigging when he was so obviously unfit. "He was doin' right well in the galley."

Lily held her breath as Matt assumed a thoughtful pose. At length he said, "I have a need of a cabin boy. That task shouldn't be beyond the lad. I'll find out soon enough if he was signed on or came aboard illegally. Is that all right with you, Luke?"

Lily nodded, wondering which was worse, climbing the rigging or being forced into intimate contact with Matt for endless days and nights. Close on the heels of that thought came the question of how long it would be before he saw through her disguise.

"Get along with you, then. For the time being you can straighten up my cabin and see to my needs. And fix a pallet for yourself, you can bed down with me." It was a good thing Lily's eyes were lowered or she would have seen the unholy gleam in Matt's dark eyes.

* * *

Lily was sprawled in a chair nearly asleep when Matt returned to his cabin later that evening. She had done as instructed, putting his clothing in order and dispensing with some of the clutter in the cramped cabin. Although truth to tell, there was little enough to do for Matt was not a messy person. His person and belongings were normally kept neat, clean and carefully organized. Once she had completed her meager tasks she took advantage of Matt's absence to quickly strip and bathe all over, something she hadn't been able to do for several days. After she had slipped back into her bulky clothes she had nothing to do but think about Matt and how he had fooled her into believing he would be faithful to her. Every time she pictured Clarissa in Matt's arms her anger intensified, until the love she had felt for him was buried beneath a ton of hate.

How long could she fool him into thinking she was a young lad? she wondered bleakly. She couldn't remain here in the same cabin with him during the entire time at sea, that much was certain. Living in such close quarters was bound to make him suspicious, although she welcomed the privacy away from the crew. It had become increasingly difficult to find the place and time to perform her more personal tasks. At least in Matt's cabin she'd be alone much of the time. Suddenly the door swung open and Matt strode into the room. A single lamp swung from the rafters, cloaking the cabin in purple shadows and nearly obscuring Lily where she sat. She crouched down in the chair, hoping to remain invisible for as long as possible.

Matt did not have to look at Lily to know she was there. "Have you eaten?" His words were clipped, as if bordering on the edge of anger as he busied himself with something on his desk.

Lily started violently. He hadn't forgotten her!

"Aye," she said gruffly, striving to keep conversation at a minimum. "Gramps brought me something."

Matt merely nodded and Lily could tell from the tenseness of his body and the lines on his brow that he was displeased at something or someone. Probably her, she suspected. By now he'd probably learned that "Luke" was a stowaway and was about to unleash his terrible temper on her. She shuddered, waiting for the ax to fall.

Matt turned slowly, looking directly at Lily for the first time since he entered the cabin. His expression told her little, except that he intended to deal harshly with the young stowaway.

"Where are you from, Luke?" His dark eyes nailed her to the wall.

Startled, Lily cleared her throat and croaked, "New Orleans."

"How old are you?" Matt shot back, giving her little time to think.

"Uh—fifteen, sir."

"Who signed you on?"

"I—" Lying was difficult with Matt staring at her. "No one. I wanted to fight the British."

"So you picked my ship to stow aboard."

Lily said nothing, keeping her head carefully averted from his probing gaze.

"I'm too tired tonight to decide what's to be done with you. But I'm certain I'll be able to come to a decision after a good night's sleep."

He sat down on the edge of the bunk and began removing his boots. Next he peeled his shirt off and tossed it aside. When his hands moved to the fastenings on his trousers, Lily averted her eyes. The rustle of material told Lily that he was now nude. It wasn't until she heard the creak of the bunk as he lowered himself onto it that she darted a glance at him. Matt lay on his back, the sheet pulled up only as far as his hips. As desperately as Lily wished it, she couldn't take her eyes off the sight of dark curly hair matting his bare chest. He glanced in Lily's direction, an inscrutable look on his face.

"There's an extra blanket and pillow in the chest against the wall, I suggest you get some sleep."

He watched as Lily slid from the chair and moved swiftly toward the chest.

"On second thought, there's plenty of room in the bunk, you can share it with me." He slid over, making room for Lily's slight form.

Lily gulped past the lump forming in her throat and shook her head. "The floor will do just fine."

"Suit yourself—Luke." He watched her carefully as Lily fixed a pallet and lay down.

"Aren't you going to get undressed?"

"I prefer sleeping with my clothes on," Lily said, pitching her voice low.

Matt grunted but did not protest, merely turning on his side away from her. Dragging in a ragged sigh, Lily slanted a leery glance in Matt's direction then fell promptly asleep. It had been an eventful day and she was exhausted. Tomorrow would be time enough to think about finding methods of staying out of Matt's way so he wouldn't discover her identity.

She awoke sometime during the night to find herself in Matt's bunk, lying fully clothed beside him. She felt the heat of his body though her layers of clothes and warning bells went off in her head. She started to ease herself off the bunk, fearing to awaken Matt, only to discover he was already awake.

"Where are you going?"

She didn't answer his question, but posed one of her own. "How did I get here?"

"I carried you. You looked uncomfortable and this bed is big enough for two. I've shared it many times and found it quite accommodating."

"I'll bet." Her wry sarcasm did not escape Matt. "It

ain't right, sir," she contended, reverting to the kind of speech one might expect from an uneducated lad, "you being the cap'n and all. The floor will do for the likes of me."

"On the contrary, Luke, I quite like you here beside me." His arm eased around her waist, pulling her close.

Lily gasped and stiffened, unwilling to believe what Matt's words implied. Not once in all the time she had known him and shared his bed would she have suspected that he liked young boys. What kind of depraved man was he? Weren't women enough for him? Obviously not for he was pressing his body against her now, letting her feel the heat raging through him.

"Don't!" The desperation of her cry finally caught Matt's attention and he loosened his hold, allowing Lily to scoot away. "I—I'm not like—*that*. Please, let me go topside with the crew. I'd feel more comfortable there." Now she had one more reason to hate him. Did Clarissa know he liked boys?

Matt's chest was rumbling suspiciously but Lily paid it little heed as his arms wrapped around her again and held her firmly in place. When he could no longer hold back his laughter it erupted from his lips in loud bursts.

Lily froze, his sudden mirth confusing her. Why was Matt laughing? What had she done to provoke joviality? "Let me go!" she insisted, becoming angrier by the minute.

"You little fool, I just wanted to see how long you could keep up this pretense."

"You know?" Her face turned as white as the sheet. She stared at Matt incredulously, going absolutely still.

"Do you think I wouldn't know my own wife? I am familiar with every luscious inch of your beautiful body. The moment I touched you I knew who you were. Why do you think I sent you to my cabin? I had to get you out of my sight until my temper cooled. You don't know how close to a beating you came. I'm still not sure you're safe. What in the hell are you doing aboard the *Sea Hawke*?"

"I—I—" She'd be damned if she'd tell him her original purpose was to be with him, that she couldn't bear the thought of a long separation.

"Was the thought of parting from me so unbearable?" Matt asked. His voice held a tenderness Lily sought desperately to ignore.

"No! It wasn't that at all. I—I wanted to help with the war."

"Liar. Dammit, Lily, didn't you know you wouldn't get away with it? Or the danger you placed yourself in? Not just from the British but from my crew. Few of them are gentlemen and some, particularly when they've been deprived of women for long periods of time, make do with young boys in the same way you thought I was doing. Why do you think I've signed on no cabin boy? I feared what the crew would do to him. I can assure you it wasn't unintentional."

"What are you going to do with me?" Lily asked, risking his anger.

"First I'm going to make love to you, then I'm going to take you back to New Orleans."

"No."

"No, what? No I can't make love to you or no you don't want to go back to New Orleans?"

"I want to go back to New Orleans," Lily said, tilting her chin defiantly, "but I'm definitely not going to let you make love to me."

Matt frowned. "Where did that come from? Mere days ago you were quite happy to make love with me."

"That was . . . before."

"Before what?"

"You deceiving bastard!" Lily spat out, disgusted with Matt's pretense. "I saw you bring Clarissa Hartley aboard the *Sea Hawke* the night we sailed. I saw you embrace her and take her into your cabin. Do you think I'm too stupid to know what went on in there?"

Matt let out a frustrated groan. "What do you think happened?"

"Why are you tormenting me like this? I trusted you. You promised you'd be faithful but Lord only knows how often you saw Clarissa in New Orleans while pretending to be involved in various activities concerning the war."

"Your trust was quick to die, Lily," Matt said earnestly. "What must I say to convince you that I didn't break any of my promises to you?"

"It's too late," Lily said dismissively.

"Christ! Tell me why you disguised yourself and came aboard and I'll tell you why Clarissa was here."

"Let me up, I'm going topside."

"Lily, you're not leaving this bed. Why did you sneak aboard the *Sea Hawke*?"

"Because I was a fool!" Lily shouted. Her voice ended on a note sounding suspiciously like a sob. "I loved you! I wanted to be with you if there was danger. I mistakenly thought you loved me."

"You weren't mistaken, I do love you. If you'll be quiet long enough I'll tell you what Clarissa was doing here."

"I don't want to hear it," Lily insisted stubbornly. Could her heart bear another lie? Matt had ripped it to shreds so often it was no longer repairable. She struggled against the confinement of his arms.

"Dammit, Lily, you're going to listen even if I have to tie you to the bed until you believe me. I didn't invite Clarissa aboard the *Sea Hawke* that night."

"You could have fooled me."

Matt ground his teeth in frustration. "She needed a favor and I was the only one who could help her."

"I can well imagine the kind of favor she needed. Is she more passionate than I am, Matt? Did you both laugh at my awkward attempts at lovemaking?"

"Nothing happened, love. Clarissa wasn't in my cabin over fifteen minutes."

"Many things are accomplished in fifteen minutes."

"Making love isn't one of them, you should know that by now. Clarrie needed money. She was desperate. She had been trying to see me for days but I never made myself available to her. In desperation she came down to the levee."

Lily didn't believe him for a minute. A woman like Clarissa could get money from any number of "protectors." She told him so, plus exactly what she thought of a man who'd lie about something as important as love and fidelity.

Matt was at his wit's end. Nothing he said was getting through to Lily. He felt like shaking her until her senses returned but knew he could never lay a hand on the woman he loved more than his own life. There was only one thing left to do and that was show her how much he cared for her. He knew it was going to be a battle to convince Lily to let him love her but he was desperate.

His face set in determined lines, Matt threw himself across Lily, pinning her body to the bed. Lily squealed. "What are you doing?"

"I'm going to get these damn clothes off you so I can make love to you."

"Like hell you are!" Lily protested, flinging herself from his grasp. It did her little good for Matt simply scooted her back beneath him and leaned on her a little harder. Then he began peeling away the layers of her clothing.

First came the heavy padded coat, which he flung

to the floor with a grunt of satisfaction. He was dismayed at the layers of clothing she had wrapped herself in but determination lent him the necessary skill to strip away her protective coatings.

"Damn you! I hate you!" Lily panted as she found herself slowly and methodically divested of all her protective layers.

"No you don't," Matt grit out tightly. "You're just too damn stubborn to listen to reason."

"And you're too damn hedonistic to realize that not every woman is yours for the taking. I don't want you, Matt. The only man worthy of my love is one who means it when he promises me forever."

"I know how to persuade you," he said silkily, sure of himself and Lily's response.

"I'm aware of your kind of persuasion, I've experienced it many times."

He had succeeded in removing everything but Lily's shift, which she clung to with a tenacity that said much about her need to resist Matt's seduction. He had used it one time too many for her to succumb again without offering vigorous protest.

"You're not strong enough to resist," Matt reminded her as he pried her hands from her shift. With an efficiency of motion he stripped it from her and tossed it aside.

"If you do this against my will I swear I'll never forgive you," Lily said tightly. "I—I'll hate you!"

"I'll risk your hate, love," Matt whispered as he caught her lips in a kiss that seared her soul. "I've risked it before."

Chapter 18

"Don't touch me, Matt, I'll scream," Lily threatened. "Your crewmen think I'm a boy, consider how bad it will look if they believe you're abusing a young lad."

Matt merely smiled, planting kisses over Lily's eyes, cheeks and throat. It didn't bother him what the crew thought, they'd learn soon enough exactly who Lily was. Besides, nothing mattered now but loving his wife, showing her by action, since she refused to believe his words, that he loved only her. Cupping her breast, he slid his lips over a distended nipple, loving the way it puckered and filled his mouth. He knew she was having a difficult time keeping her passion from soaring out of control and loved her all the more for it.

Lily squeezed her eyes tightly shut and tried to think of anything but what Matt was doing to her and how wonderful her body felt beneath his skillful caresses. He was kissing her now, outlining her lips with the hard tip of his tongue then probing them apart to sample their special sweetness while his hands stroked her breasts. He still lay atop her and she could feel his erection thicken and grow as it prodded her stomach. He nudged her legs apart with his knees and settled between them before Lily had time to clamp her thighs tightly together.

285

"I don't want this, Matt," Lily protested when she felt him probing her with his hardened length. "Why didn't you keep your mistress aboard if you needed a woman so badly?"

"I have no mistress." Matt panted as he struggled for control. "You're the only woman I need. Open your legs wider, love, it will take more than your meager strength to keep me out."

"You're damn sure of yourself, aren't you?" Lily ground out as she tried to block from her mind all the marvelous sensations Matt was creating inside her.

Disdaining an answer, Matt shifted slightly and inserted his hand between them, moving unerringly to the curly red hair at her apex. In just a few breathless seconds he found what he was searching for, the tiny button where pleasure began. Rubbing it gently with one fingertip, Matt waited for Lily's gasp before saying, "It's not me I'm sure of, love, it's you. I know all your sensitive places and what gives you the most pleasure."

As if to prove his words he slid down her body and replaced his finger with his mouth. No matter how much she wished it Lily couldn't control the shudder that shook her body. "God I hate you!" she cried as she arched her back to give him better access.

Matt raised his head and smiled. "I know you do, love. I'm not sure if I could stand it if you loved me." Then he lowered his head and continued his tender torment. Beyond the bounds of human endurance, Lily grasped his dark head and held him closer, pushing herself against him as he lashed her with the hot roughness of his tongue.

When he felt her teeter on the brink of climax, he raised his head and asked, "Do you want me to stop, love?"

Confusion dulled Lily's mind. Stop? Did she want

him to stop when her body vibrated with need and her blood boiled in her veins? She opened her mouth to tell him that's exactly what she wanted, but the words stuck in her throat.

Damn him, damn him, damn him! "Yes! No! Oh God, don't stop, not now, I couldn't bear it."

"I couldn't bear it either, love," Matt admitted as he raised her legs over his shoulders and thrust into her.

A strangled cry slipped past Lily's throat. "I'll never forgive you for this," she gasped before reason left her. Then she gave herself up to his masterful strokes, matching him thrust for thrust as her hands discovered anew the firm smooth flesh of his back and buttocks. It was heaven and hell. It was pure torture. It was magnificent. She loved it, she hated it. She wanted it to go on forever.

The end came in a blinding flash of raw sensation that rocked the universe.

Matt didn't move until he softened and slipped out of her. Then he rolled to his back, waiting for his heart to stop pounding and his breath to resume its natural cadence. He was startled when Lily jumped to her feet and began pulling on the clothes Matt had just recently discarded.

"What in hell are you doing?"

"What does it look like?" Once she was fully clothed she moved her pallet as far from the bed as she could get and lay down.

"Dammit, Lily, it's foolish to make yourself uncomfortable when this bed is large enough for the two of us."

"This room isn't large enough for the two of us," Lily shot back sullenly. "I don't want you touching me, Matt. I can't trust my body. You're too experienced; you know exactly how and where to touch me to make me want you. But it won't happen again."

"You're the most exasperating female I've ever

known," Matt charged angrily. "This whole matter has gone too far."

"I agree. I just want to go back to New Orleans where you can't make me say things I don't mean."

"You loved me once."

"That was before I knew you were bedding Clarissa again."

"Damnation! I'm not bedding Clarissa. What will it take to make you believe me? Could I have made love to you like I just did if I had a mistress?"

"You're a vigorous, virile man, Matt, you're quite capable of pleasing more than one woman."

Matt spat out an oath. "Are you coming back to bed?"

"No." She turned her back on him, attempting to ignore him.

Suddenly he was towering over her, feet planted wide apart, arms akimbo, his face dark with rage. "I've had just about all the foolishness I can put up with for one day. First I find you've been living amongst my crew for several days, placing yourself in unspeakable danger, then I had to rescue you from the rigging. When I found out you weren't a green lad but my own wife, I wanted to beat you. It took hours for my temper to cool. You've gone too far this time. Get those filthy clothes off and get in bed."

It was a command, not a request.

Lily had seen Matt angry before but never this furious. Many times in the past she had provoked him to anger; this was the first time she felt threatened by him. She didn't think he was the type to abuse a woman, and although there was always a first time, she was wise enough to know when to hold her tongue—and that time had arrived. Unwilling to stretch his control to impossible limits, Lily rose from the pallet, sent Matt a scathing glare and began stripping off her clothes. His nude body reacted violently as he watched Lily undress but he didn't budge an inch until she was completely bare.

"Will you promise not to touch me?" Lily dared to ask. She looked so adorably defiant standing there cloaked in the mantle of her nudity that if Matt hadn't been so damn annoyed he would have pulled her into his arms and made love to her again.

"If that's what it takes. Why should I force you when there are plenty of willing women available? I suddenly find myself bored with your games. Get in bed."

Lily bristled angrily but nevertheless scooted in bed, pulling the covers up to her neck. Matt climbed in behind her, turned his back and prayed for sleep. Unfortunately his body was too aware of Lily's warmth pressing against him in the narrow bunk to relax. Sleep became a luxury that eluded him the rest of the night. Lily was too exhausted to resist the lure of much needed rest and she fell almost immediately into a deep slumber. Sometime during the night when Matt pulled her into his arms, she sighed and snuggled deeper into the warmth of his body.

Matt was already awake and gone when Lily opened her eyes the next morning. The sun was shining brightly through the porthole and she could see the dim outline of land in the distance. She was washed and dressed when Matt returned to the cabin later that morning. He carried a tray of food, which he sat down on his desk with an impatient thump. Risking a glance at him, Lily noted that his face still wore an angry scowl and he appeared no less angry with her than he had last night. When he finally turned his attention on her, his scowl deepened.

"Your being aboard has disrupted my schedule and my crew. I've already told the men about your little charade and they are none too happy about being tricked into thinking you were a young boy signing on for his first voyage. Baldy is most vocal about sending a woman up the rigging. He thought he was doing his duty by teaching a lad about sailing."

"I—I'm sorry," Lily said truthfully. "I didn't mean to keep up the pretense so long. I wouldn't have if you hadn't—"

"Don't say it, Lily," Matt warned sternly. "You have no idea what really happened in this cabin with Clarrie and as long as you don't take my word on what occurred I refuse to discuss it further with you."

Lily swallowed convulsively then adroitly changed the subject. "Is that New Orleans I see in the distance?"

"No, it's one of the Florida Keys, where I'm supposed to rendezvous with Dick Marlow and the *Lady Hawke*. I didn't want to worry him by not showing up on time and since we were so close I decided to meet him first and take you back to New Orleans afterward."

"Oh." She turned to stare out the porthole. She could feel the heat of his glare singe her back and wondered if he was angry because she had stowed aboard his ship or because she didn't want him touching her again. Probably a combination of both, she suspected.

Matt wanted to shake Lily until her teeth rattled and her good sense returned. Didn't she know he loved only her? Why wouldn't she believe he wanted nothing to do with Clarissa? Women, he thought, grunting with contempt. They were stubborn and contrary and in constant need of reassuring. He had thought Lily was different. Most women lacked courage, but Lily seemed to have an abundance. Many women would have meekly accepted his mistress and been happy to be spared the physical side of marriage. Lily's passion had been a welcome surprise. He bitterly regretted having told her he didn't intend being faithful but old habits are difficult to lose. As it turned out, he had never been unfaithful to Lily, not once. Convincing her of it was another matter. Right now he was too angry with her to try.

"You may come topside whenever you wish," Matt said when Lily continued to stare out the window. "But be prepared to face the crew's disapproval. They don't appreciate being made fools of. And since I have no women's clothing aboard, you'll have to make do with what you're wearing."

"These will suffice," Lily replied, slicing a mutinous glance over her shoulder.

Matt nodded and turned on his heel, his angry strides carrying him from the cabin. Lily nearly collapsed with relief. It was pure torture being in the same room with him. He had a way of scrambling her thoughts and making her body react independent of her mind. She had to be on her guard every minute, she predicted, or he'd take advantage of her again. The thought frightened her. She had no will where Matt was concerned.

Lady Hawke had arrived at the meeting place a whole day before the *Sea Hawke* made its appearance. Dick Marlow was full of news and he and Matt spent several hours in Dick's cabin catching up. When Dick came aboard the *Sea Hawke* later, Matt's crew greeted him exuberantly. Especially when they heard the *Lady Hawke* had sunk an English merchantman and her hold was bursting with loot.

Suddenly Dick spied Lily sitting forlornly on a coil of rope, only he had no idea it was Lily. He turned to Matt and said, "I didn't know you were signing on youngsters."

Matt laughed, motioning for Lily to join them. Reluctantly she rose, dusted off her hopelessly soiled breeches and walked with slow deliberation to where Matt and Dick stood conversing on the bridge. When she finally faced them, Dick's eyes bulged and his face assumed an incredulous look.

"Lily—Mrs. Hawke! What in all that's holy are you doing aboard the *Sea Hawke*?" I thought Matt left you in New Orleans with his sister."

"I did," Matt said. His voice shook with quiet anger. "Only Lily had other ideas. She stowed aboard posing as a seaman and I didn't discover her identity until several days later." He gave no other details, such as having to rescue her from the rigging or the fact that Lily had seen Clarissa Hartley come aboard just prior to the sailing.

"I'm happy to see you, Mrs. Hawke, but hardly under these circumstances," Dick said earnestly.

Obviously he was not thrilled at having Lily exposed to danger. He had spied a large convoy of English ships converging on a small island in the Caribbean and had discussed it thoroughly with Matt. It seemed highly likely that the British navy was indeed preparing for a strike at an American port City. And New Orleans still seemed the most likely target.

"Nice to see you again, Dick," Lily said, smiling at the young man.

Dick returned the smile but sensed immediately something was wrong, something Matt wasn't telling him. Matt's face wore a permanent scowl and when the captain looked at Lily, Dick was startled by the anger simmering in the depths of Matt's dark eyes. Adding further to the mystery were the sullen looks Lily flung in Matt's direction. Even the crew seemed less disposed toward Lily than they previously had been.

"Excuse us now, Lily, Dick and I have serious business to discuss," Matt said curtly, promptly turning his back on his recalcitrant wife.

Fuming inwardly, Lily stalked away. She was furious that Matt didn't trust her enough to reveal his plans to her, or allow her to remain to listen to their discussion. Her mind was just as good as theirs and in some instances better.

"What do you suggest we do, Matt?" Dick asked once Lily was out of hearing. "Governor Claiborne and General Jackson should be informed about the British fleet gathering so close on their doorstep."

"My thoughts exactly, Dick. I'm returning to New Orleans in any event to deliver Lily back to Sarah and Jeff. And you need to offload the loot from the merchantman into safekeeping. I suggest we both return to New Orleans, report to General Jackson and offer our services in the battle that promises to be the turning point of the war. Since we're only a few days out of New Orleans we should arrive before the British."

Lily watched listlessly as the *Sea Hawke* entered the mouth of the Mississippi. In four days Matt had barely spoken to her, except to issue crisp orders he expected to be obeyed without question. He hadn't even had the decency to explain to her why both ships were returning to New Orleans with undue haste. Not only that, but extra lookouts had been sent into the rigging and ordered to keep their eyes peeled. Who was Matt looking for?

Lily had gotten little sleep during the past few nights. Matt had insisted she sleep in his bunk each night and it had been nerve-racking to lie beside him and feel his naked warmth penetrating her flesh like shards of jagged lightning. Each morning she woke up more exhausted than the night before. Fortunately Matt never tried to make love to her, nor did he touch her. But she could tell he was waiting—waiting for her to make the first move, waiting for her to be worn down by his indifference. Well, it wasn't going to happen, Lily resolved. Never again would she beg Matt to love her or be hurt in ways that ripped out her heart.

On December 2, 1814, both the *Sea Hawke* and the *Lady Hawke* docked at long piers jutting out into the harbor. Nothing had changed in the week and a half Matt and Lily had been gone. Supplies were still stockpiled on the dock and General Jackson's Kaintucks were in evidence, still giving the impression of a city under siege. Then, curiously, Lily did note a subtle but marked difference. The citizens seemed in turmoil. They gathered on corners and spoke in hushed tones, often gesturing wildly, their faces set in grim lines. An expectant hush had settled over the city, as if a British attack was no longer a possibility but a certainty.

Matt hustled Lily into a hired hack and they departed immediately for thirty-one Rue Dumaine. But suddenly Matt changed his mind and ordered the hack to drop him off at Place d'Arms, General Jackson's headquarters.

"What is it, Matt?" Lily asked, growing alarmed. "Why is the city in turmoil? Why is it so important that you see General Jackson immediately?"

Matt hadn't wanted to frighten Lily but realized she had a right to know what was going on. "General Jackson must have it on good authority that the British will attack New Orleans soon."

"You know something, don't you?" Lily demanded to know.

"Dick Marlow saw a large fleet of British ships gathering on a nearby island. It most likely indicates that attack is imminent. I'm on my way now to inform General Jackson and offer my ships and men in defense of the city."

Lily drew in a shaky breath. "Why didn't you tell me before now?"

"I didn't want to cause you needless worry." Matt shrugged carelessly. "I knew we'd beat the British fleet to New Orleans and you'd learn soon enough about the attack. We're here," Matt suddenly announced as he glanced out the window. "I'm sending you on to Sarah's house, stay put until I return." The hack slid to a halt and Matt jumped to the ground. He spoke briefly to the driver then hurried off without a backward glance.

After a short wait Matt was shown into General Jackson's office. The battle-scarred soldier appeared weary as he greeted Matt. Defending a city whose citizens took a possible attack lightly had left him harried and did little to help his cause. Matt was certain the lines in the general's careworn face had deepened considerably since they had last met barely two weeks ago.

"What brings you back to New Orleans so soon, Captain Hawke?" Jackson asked curiously.

"It's a long story, General," Matt said dryly, "but suffice it to say I couldn't have arrived at a more propitious time. I thought you'd want to know that the British fleet was sighted within striking distance of New Orleans."

Jackson shook his head wearily. "It's as I suspected. I have few men and resources available but we'll fight them with everything we have."

"Both the *Sea Hawke* and the *Lady Hawke* are at your disposal, General. They are well armed and ready to do battle in defense of the city."

"Your ships will be a welcome addition to our cause," Jackson replied. "I've also received an offer from Jean Lafitte expressing his desire to lend both ships and men should an attack be waged against the city."

"I'm aware of Governor Claiborne's unwillingness to trust Lafitte. Are you of the same mind?"

"I think Lafitte's offer is genuine," Jackson said thoughtfully. "I spoke with the man several times and have already accepted his generous offer. I'll send word to him immediately. Thank you, Captain, for bringing me this valuable information and for volunteering your ships. They are much appreciated."

If Lily had known how worried Sarah had been about her she would never have stowed away aboard Matt's ship. Matt's distraught sister had been beside herself waiting for Matt to return Lily to New Orleans. She knew it was only a matter of time before Matt discovered Lily aboard the *Sea Hawke* and returned her and she could well imagine his anger.

Several days had passed since their return, and the situation concerning the attack grew bleaker. Not only within the beleaguered city but also between Lily and Matt. They shared a bed because there was no spare room available in Sarah's small house. But they were like intimate strangers growing further apart daily. Lily hated the distance between them but feared trusting Matt again. Sleeping with him was a torment she endured each night for the sake of keeping peace in Sarah's household. How could she still want Matt after the way he had lied to her? How could she need him so desperately knowing that he would never remain faithful to her? How could she still love him when she hated him?

Though Matt had volunteered his services to General Jackson in any capacity, he still found time to desire his wife. He wanted her to respond to him in the same extraordinary way she had on their island, passionately and willingly. He needed her to realize she loved him and understand he hadn't been unfaithful. Each night lying beside her had been an agony of longing; waiting for her to come to her senses was pure torture. But to his regret, Lily gave no indication that she felt anything for him but loathing. If this blasted war wasn't demanding his time and attention he'd find a way to make her love him again. There were days he was so angry at her continued aloofness that he came close to forcing her to make love with him. Just before that happened her words of long ago came back to haunt him.

Love isn't meant to be punishment.

Lord knows he was frustrated enough to punish his reluctant wife, but loving her was what he really wanted to do. Until this war was resolved he would have neither the time nor the energy to expend convincing Lily that he loved only her.

War news filtering into the city was not good. It soon became evident to the fun-loving Creoles that their beloved city was soon to be turned into a battle-ground. The arrival of the British fleet at the mouth of the Mississippi was reported very early in December and by December 12 the British fleet was anchored off Lake Borgne, prompting the male population of New Orleans to turn up in droves at General Jackson's headquarters to volunteer their services.

While awaiting the British attack, Jackson tackled the almost impossible task of whipping those zealots into a viable fighting force. The general pressed Matt into service and again gave him the responsibility of training those happy-go-lucky citizens who were unaccustomed to discipline. During those days Matt rarely came home.

On December 23 word was received that the British, against all odds, were ferrying men and guns ashore across Lake Borgne in scrounged flatboats to Pea Island. From there a cooperative Spanish fisherman showed them the Bayou Bienvenue, the only waterway into New Orleans that hadn't been blocked by Jackson. It led directly to the west bank of the Mississippi, only eight miles from the city. Matt and Dick Marlow made immediate plans to join Jean Lafitte's privateers, who had come out of hiding from Barataria to challenge the British navy.

Matt made one last attempt to settle things between him and Lily before he left, perhaps never to return. He found her alone in their room, where she spent many lonely hours during these hectic days trying to make sense out of her marriage. When Sarah attempted to question Lily about her behavior toward Matt, Lily only drew deeper into her shell, refusing to divulge the reason for her coldness. Sarah had hoped things had changed between the pair, especially since she saw no signs that Matt was reverting back to his old habits, and he was truly puzzled by Lily's aloofness.

Lily was putting away freshly pressed laundry when Matt burst into the room. Startled, she looked up at him, mildly surprised to see him home in the middle of the day. An unpleasant premonition tingled along her spine when she tried to interpret the look on his face. "Matt, what are you doing home at this time of day?"

Matt scowled, wishing Lily would drop her defenses where he was concerned and just once trust him. None of this unpleasantness would have resulted if she believed him when he denied being involved with Clarissa again. Clarissa was his past, Lily was his future. If he had a future after today. When he returned—if he returned—he'd devote all the time necessary to make things right between him and Lily. He only hoped he'd be able to control his temper. She had a way of infuriating him that made them both say things they later regretted.

"Is it so strange that I'd want to see my wife before leaving to engage in battle?"

Lily gulped past the lump in her throat. "You're leaving?"

"The English are ferrying men and arms to the left bank of the Mississippi, only eight miles from the city. General Jackson is raising defenses along Rodriguez Canal."

"Are you going to Rodriguez Canal?"

"No, the *Sea Hawke* and the *Lady Hawke* will join Jean Lafitte's fleet to engage the enemy."

"I—good luck, Matt." A wayward tear slid down her cheek and deliberately she turned her back. She wouldn't give Matt the satisfaction of knowing how much she really cared for him, despite all her protests to the contrary. He might take his marriage vows lightly but she didn't.

"Dammit, Lily, is that all you've got to say?" Matt choked out. "I could be killed and you don't seem to give a damn! Have you forgotten how close we became on our island?"

Forgotten? Dear God, she recalled every hour of every day. Remembered it every night when she lay beside Matt struggling to keep from trembling whenever he brushed against her.

"I've forgotten nothing, Matt, but apparently you have. It didn't take long for the happy glow to wear off and for you to start looking for another woman. Truth to tell, it's no more than I expected."

Lily felt the heat of his anger singe her as he grasped her shoulders and forced her to face him. "You're the most exasperating female I've ever known! You make me so angry I can't even think straight. I came here today hoping you had learned something about trust. I wanted to love you before I left, Lily, but your misplaced jealousy and false accusations make me wish I'd left you back in England in that intolerable situation you created. Even then you were too headstrong and impetuous for your own good."

"I would have been fine if you hadn't interfered!" Lily shot back. Her anger escalated, matching Matt's in volume and intensity. "Take your hands off me, you're hurting me."

Only then did Matt realize he was still gripping Lily's shoulders. His fingers were digging into her flesh so brutally they had turned white. Abruptly he released her, stepping back. His temper was not a pleasant thing and unleashing it fully, against a helpless female, was not in his nature.

"This will have to wait until I return—if I return," he said ominously. "Even then I'm not sure we have anything on which to build a marriage. I never lied to you on that island. I promised you forever and I meant it. I was wrong to believe you loved me. Obviously you'd rather be with another man. Clay Winslow, perhaps?"

Lily's mouth flew open, ready to deny such an outrageous accusation. Then abruptly she changed her mind. If that's what he thinks, then let him, she fumed in silent indignation. He had been too sure of her, she had foolishly fallen in love with him too soon. Let him stew and fret like she had these past weeks. Loving him had been easy, forgiving him would take longer. She could forgive him almost anything but his indiscretions with Clarissa Hartley. And in time she supposed she would even forgive him that. But not yet, not today; the wound was too raw, too deep.

"Perhaps you're right," she observed coolly. "I'm sure Clay would never be unfaithful."

"Damn you, woman!" There was a slumbering threat of destructive violence in him as his fists clenched and unclenched at his sides. "You're more of a bitch than Clarrie ever was. If I'm not fortunate enough to survive this battle I wish you and Clay joy of one another. But so help me God, Lily, I'll come back to haunt every intimate moment you spend with your new lover."

Whirling on his heel he stormed from the room.

A tremor passed over Lily, as if someone had just walked over her grave. Shocked at his words as well as her own unreasonable behavior, she couldn't believe she was sending Matt off to fight—and perhaps die—with angry words and recriminations. What if he had been telling the truth? What if he hadn't been unfaithful? What if he truly did love her?

Those disturbing thoughts galvanized her into action. Racing from the room and down the stairs, she tore open the front door and ran into the street.

"Matt!"

She had waited too long. He was gone.

Chapter 19

Despite Sarah's best efforts, Christmas was a dismal affair. The one uplifting piece of news was that Jean Lafitte's ship *Carolina* was pounding the English on the left while American troops were attacking on the right, blunting the English spearhead. Lily could not help but wonder if Matt was out there in the middle of it, aiding Lafitte's fleet. Despair and regret stabbed at her conscience when she recalled how angry Matt had been when he left her and the appalling things she had said to him. If only she could take them back, relive that brief space of time when she tried to deny her love for Matt.

On January 1, 1815, Jeff left to join the fighting at Rodriguez Canal, where the English were reported to be gathering for an attack. It was rumored that General Jackson would make his stand at the wide ditch and it seemed as if the entire city had amassed at the battle site. For days the ominous thunder of big guns could be heard throughout the city and gossip ran rife as to what was actually taking place.

Sarah came rushing home from the marketplace one day bursting with good news. "Jean Lafitte's ship *Louisiana* pinned down and engaged the enemy, preventing an attack on the city," she enthused excitedly. "Isn't it wonderful? Big guns are being taken from Lafitte's ships and deployed along Rodriguez

Canal, manned by Dominique You and his cannon-eers."

Lily thought the news indeed wonderful but more important things were on her mind. "What about *Sea Hawke* and *Lady Hawke*? Have you heard anything of them? Or of Matt?"

Sarah's eyes turned bleak. "No, nothing, just that they are in the Gulf protecting the city from enemy attack. Nor do I have news of Jeff. I'd die if anything happened to him, Lily. I—I haven't told anyone except Jeff yet that we're going to have a baby."

Lily's face lit up. "Oh, Sarah, how wonderful! I wish ..." Her words trailed off as she stared into space. How she'd love to have Matt's baby. They hadn't mentioned children but instinctively Lily knew Matt would be a wonderful father. Since it hadn't happened thus far she began to doubt it would happen at all. She hated the thought of going through life barren, with no one to call her own or lavish her love upon.

"It will happen for you one day, just you wait and see," Sarah predicted, sensing Lily's longing.

Lily didn't have the heart to contradict Sarah, but in her soul she knew a child wouldn't keep Matt from straying. Being faithful wasn't in his character.

On January 8 the noise from the battleground was deafening. Throughout the day word of the battle being waged filtered in slowly with the wounded. Sarah and Lily were among the first to volunteer their services to the hospital. Both worked tirelessly, staunching blood, cleansing hideous wounds and giving solace to the dying. At the end of each day they returned home exhausted and sick at heart over the senseless loss of lives.

The roar of cannon grew louder and more threatening as the women on Rue Dumaine awaited word of their men. They were sitting at the dinner table now, picking listlessly at their food when the thunder of cannon abruptly and without warning ceased. The silence was ominous.

"The guns!" exclaimed Lily, tensing. "They've stopped!"

"What does it mean?" Sarah wondered in a hushed voice.

"It must mean that the battle is over," Lily said hopefully. "Dear Lord, let the Americans be victorious." The sentiment was repeated by Sarah.

It was well after midnight before the women learned the outcome of the decisive battle for New Orleans. Neither had gone to bed; worry over the fate of their men made sleep impossible. Suddenly the door was flung open and Jeff burst through, dirty, exhausted, but otherwise unharmed. After taking Sarah in his arms and tenderly kissing her, he began describing the battle to the impatient women.

"If it hadn't been for Jean Lafitte and his brave men we might not have been victorious," Jeff explained with enthusiasm. His admiration for the pirate was boundless. "His cannoneers set up their big guns along the battle line on the Rodriguez Canal and pounded the enemy relentlessly while his ships attacked the English from the water. You should have seen it, Sarah, Lily, it was truly awesome. No one will ever have cause to doubt Lafitte's loyalty again."

Only one thought was uppermost in Lily's mind. "Did any of Matt's ships engage the enemy?"

"*Lady Hawke* and *Sea Hawke* were right in the thick of it," Jeff replied, sliding his eyes away in a gesture that Lily found disturbing.

"Then the battle is over and the British have been repulsed." Sarah sighed thankfully. "Does this mean the war is over and we can get on with our lives?"

"The British have been soundly beaten this day," Jeff assured them. "A great victory for the Americans. They won't be back. What's left of the fleet have already hightailed it back to England to lick their wounds."

"When do you suppose Matt will return?"

Once again Jeff's eyes refused to meet Lily's probing gaze. Sighing regretfully, he knew what his dreadful news would do to both Sarah and Lily. But he realized it would be far better coming from him than a stranger.

Lily felt a knot tighten around her chest as alarm bells went off in her head. Jeff's curious behavior frightened her. Deep in her heart she felt he was deliberately withholding something from her, something devastating. Was Matt hurt? Was Jeff searching for a way to tell her he was wounded? Fear rose like a dark specter to haunt her with terrifying thoughts.

"Jeff, please, if something has happened to Matt I want to know. Is he wounded?" I'll go to him immediately."

"Oh, no," Sarah gasped, suddenly made aware of Jeff's deliberate omission where Matt was concerned. "What happened, Jeff?" She looked expectantly at her husband and he steeled himself for the terrible anguish he was about to unleash in both Lily and Sarah.

"Lily, I'd give anything to be able to tell you that Matt is fine, but the truth is . . . I don't know. The *Sea Hawke* took a direct hit to the magazine and sank during the height of the battle."

Lily's face drained of all color as she sagged limply against Jeff. He reached out to support her. Oh God, oh no, how could such a thing happen? Had she sent Matt to his death believing she didn't love him? If he was truly dead she had nothing, not even a reminder of the love they'd shared on the island. Oh why couldn't she be pregnant like Sarah?

"I'm sorry, Lily," Jeff said quietly as he placed his other arm around Sarah, who was sobbing softly.

"What about survivors?" Lily asked shrilly, unwilling to accept the reality of Matt's death.

"Less than a dozen men have been accounted for," Jeff said grimly, "most picked up by *Lady Hawke*. They have all been conveyed back to the city. None of them are Matt. When Dick Marlow arrives he'll tell you more. I'm only relating what he told me when I spoke to him briefly after *Lady Hawke* returned to port."

Sarah was sobbing openly now and Jeff placed both his arms around his grieving wife, lending comfort. Jeff knew how dearly Sarah loved Matt. He had been all she'd had after their parents died and the bond between them was strong.

Once the initial shock wore off, Jeff informed Lily that General Jackson had ordered an immediate search for Matt and others who might have survived the sea battle.

"There is always the possibility that survivors made it ashore on their own," he contended, trying to lend hope where none existed. In truth, he held little hope that Matt survived.

During the following days Lily existed in a void, living in a nightmare from which escape was impossible. When Dick Marlow finally arrived he sadly related all he recalled of the *Sea Hawke*'s last moments. Lily hung on to his every word.

"*Lady Hawke* had tacked to engage an English frigate and was some distance away when the cannonball hit *Sea Hawke*'s store of powder and arms. I wasn't even aware of what had happened until the explosion sent repercussions over the water. When I looked back bodies were flying every which way and the ship was on fire. She sank within minutes. I immediately began picking up survivors. There weren't many . . ."

"Did you see Matt?" Lily probed. Though Dick's

description of the holocaust nearly tore her apart she had to know every tiny detail.

Dick's eyes reflected his misery. "I—no, Lily, I'm sorry. We even picked up the dead, but Matt wasn't among them."

Dick left shortly afterward to see his ship, which had sustained minimal damage and needed certain repairs. It was too early to query Lily about her intention concerning Matt's surviving ships. Besides *Lady Hawke*, there was also *Hawke's Pride*, still somewhere in the Atlantic. An old friend of Matt's, Andrew Calder, was captain of the privateer. Little had been heard from *Hawke's Pride* since the beginning of the war and Dick wasn't certain she was still afloat.

Alone in her room, Lily gave vent to her terrible anguish. The weight of her agony bore down on her with a heavy hand as she recalled every bitter word she had flung at Matt on the day he left to engage the English. Now he would never know she meant none of them, that no matter what he had done or with whom, she still loved him. With a heavy heart she realized she had been unreasonable, unrelenting and vindictive. What made the pain of Matt's death even more unbearable was the knowledge that he might have been telling the truth.

The emptiness of life without Matt stretched out endlessly before her, giving her a brutal glimpse of all those barren weeks, months and years without him. Finally spent, Lily lay like one dead, wishing life could go on without her.

In the days that followed Lily haunted the hospitals, the docks and General Jackson's office, hoping, praying for a miracle that would restore Matt to her. Unfortunately her hopes and prayers were denied her. Not a single word of Matt or his fate was forthcoming from any quarter.

When the sea search for survivors was suspended by General Jackson, Lily was inconsolable. She steadfastly refused to believe Matt was dead despite the overwhelming evidence suggesting otherwise. Surely she would know if Matt was dead, wouldn't she? she asked herself irrationally. She'd feel it in her heart, her bones, in every fiber of her being. She'd know it with every breath she drew. All she felt now was a dull emptiness. Deep inside her existed the conviction that Matt would be restored to her through some miracle.

The day that Matt's name appeared on the list of those men officially assumed dead, Lily was grief-stricken. That's the day she summoned Dick Marlow and expressed her desire to sail aboard the *Lady Hawke*. She wanted to return to Boston and Hawkeshaven. Hawkeshaven was Matt's home and she'd feel closer to him there than anywhere. Despite the terrible anguish in her heart, she felt certain that Matt would want her to return to his home, expect her to take up the reins of leadership and conduct his business as he would have done.

"You can't go, Lily," Sarah wailed, now noticeably pregnant. "Not until my baby is born. I want you with me."

"Jeff will be with you," Lily reminded her gently. It's not that she begrudged Sarah her happiness but rather that she couldn't bear to live in daily contact with the kind of happiness she had always wanted with Matt.

Every time she looked at Sarah, so like Matt in many ways, she was swamped by guilt. Even unto death she would remember that she had sent Matt into battle with angry words and recriminations instead of with kisses and expressions of love. Being unable to forgive herself was just another cross in life she'd have to bear.

It was a sad little group that gathered on the quay the day Lily left New Orleans. Sarah sobbed quietly into her husband's shirt front while Lily fought bravely to hold back her tears.

"Promise you'll come to visit as soon as the baby is old enough to travel," Lily said, her distress as poignant as Sarah's. "And don't forget to send word the moment the baby arrives. I'll be on pins and needles until I know you and the little one are all right."

"You can always stay here with us," Jeff reminded her when Sarah's grief placed her beyond words. "Why must you leave so soon?"

"Oh, yes," echoed Sarah hopefully. "It's not too late to change your mind."

Sadly, Lily shook her head. "Hawkeshaven is my home, I want to be where I can feel Matt's presence. When he returns I want him to find me at home tending to his business."

Sarah gasped, her shock evident. "Lily! Why are you doing this to yourself? The sooner you accept the fact that Matt is never coming home the easier it will be to carry on with your life."

Lily worried her lower lip. She hadn't meant to startle Sarah like that, but she couldn't shake her belief that miracles did exist. Despite her best efforts, the words came tumbling out unbidden.

"I'm sorry, Sarah dear, I know I have no proof or any hope that miracles do exist, but I don't *feel* like Matt is dead. In my heart he's alive."

"Keep him in your heart, Lily," Sarah said, choking on a sob, "for he'll always be in mine."

They parted with kisses and promises of future visits, and within minutes Lily was standing forlornly at the rail of *Lady Hawke* watching Jeff and Sarah grow smaller as the ship slipped down the Mississippi River.

By the time Lily reached Boston she had persuaded a somewhat reluctant Dick Marlow to manage Matt's shipping interests until she could make other arrangements. Though he was still young, Lily had every confidence in his ability. Hadn't Matt given him command of *Lady Hawke*?

When Lily stood before the massive doors of Hawkeshaven, she felt as if her life had come full circle. Not long ago she had looked forward to spending the rest of her days here with Matt and their children. Now it looked as if there would be no children and her life would be an empty shell of longing and dreaming of what might have been.

It was a saddened staff who met Lily at the door. Joseph, the butler, was solemn but subdued, while Mrs. Geary, the housekeeper, sobbed openly when she saw Lily. Jenny's huge blue eyes brimmed with tears but it was Joseph who spoke for all of them.

"Losing Captain Hawke has been a great tragedy to all of us, Mrs. Hawke. Nothing will be the same without him."

"How—how did you know?" Lily asked, swallowing the lump in her throat. She couldn't break down now, not in front of the staff.

"Captain Hawke's lawyer, Mr. Winslow, informed us of the . . . death. We all want you to know we're here to serve you in any capacity."

"Thank you, Joseph. Now if you'll excuse me, I'd like to rest. The trip has exhausted me. If you have any questions, Mr. Marlow will answer them."

Thank God for Dick, Lily thought as she heard him speaking to the staff. All except Jenny, who had dutifully followed Lily up the stairs, were hanging on to Dick's every word. Lily had no stomach to relive Matt's death. In fact, it seemed she had stomach for little these days. She had been seasick during the entire voyage between New Orleans and Boston. Surprising, in view of the fact that she had never suffered seasickness before. She had assumed her general malaise was the result of all that had happened these past weeks and gave it little thought. Now she wondered if something else wasn't wrong with her. Some strange illness that she wasn't aware of.

In a surprisingly short time Lily settled into Hawkeshaven and a routine that filled her empty hours but did little to restore her empty heart. The comfortable mansion and its staff settled around her like old friends. She was distracted for a time by the growing friendship between Jenny, her maid, and Dick Marlow, who was a constant visitor in the house due to the position he had accepted in Matt's business. And it was inevitable that Lily meet Clay again.

He arrived one day shortly after Lily's arrival at Hawkeshaven. Lily had been waiting on word about Matt's holdings and when Clay arrived she knew she would have to face the enormous task of grappling with the reins of leadership, at least until Matt returned. She owed it to him to keep his property intact.

"I hope it isn't too soon to call on you," Clay said, devouring Lily with his eyes. Obviously he still held tender feelings for her and was struggling to control his emotions. When she left Boston two years before he thought he'd never see her again. "There are matters concerning Matt's holdings that need your immediate attention. There is the will. It's quite simple and straightforward, leaving everything to you but for a bequeath to Sarah."

Clay held out the document for Lily's perusal and she spent several agonizing minutes reading it. When she finished, she handed it back to Clay. "I had no idea Matt was so wealthy."

"Until recently the bulk of his resources were in real estate and ships. He had little ready cash. But the war has changed all that. He made regular deposits in the bank when he began privateering, all of them quite substantial. Privateering earned Matt considerable wealth, which has been invested wisely. You're extremely wealthy, Lily, and I can truthfully say you deserve every penny Matt left you."

"You've done a wonderful job, Clay, and I know Matt will be pleased with what you've accomplished when he returns."

Clay started violently. "What! What are you saying, Lily? The first ship that arrived in Boston after the battle for New Orleans reported Matt's death. Dick Marlow confirmed it when he called on me. When did you learn he was alive?"

"There has been no official word of it, Clay, but I know Matt is alive. It's only a matter of time before he returns."

Pity dulled Clay's eyes as he stared at Lily. "Lily, Lily, be realistic. Matt is dead. He's never coming back."

"No, Clay, you're wrong," Lily insisted stubbornly. "I thought you of all people would believe me."

"I've never stopped loving you, Lily," Clay admitted, "and I'll be here for you whenever I'm needed. Hopefully, in time you'll come to care for me just a little. I've always wanted you but not at the cost of Matt's death. I'm sorry he's dead but not sorry that there is a chance for me now.

"Matt and I were friends long before he brought you home to Boston. But I never approved of the way he treated you. He couldn't have loved you like I do."

Lily's gaze turned inward as she recalled the love she and Matt had shared on their island. "Matt did love me, Clay, I'm certain of it now. I'll never forgive myself for rejecting him at the end. I sent him off to war without telling him . . ." Her voice faltered, then grew silent.

"I have no idea what you're referring to but nothing that happened is your fault. Matt didn't deserve your love, and I know you loved him. It was obvious to me from the beginning."

Lily scowled and Clay realized he was disturbing her by resisting her farfetched notion that Matt was still alive. She adroitly changed the subject. "Let's talk about Matt's ships, Lily. Do you wish to keep them? If not I'll have no problem finding a buyer."

"Those ships were Matt's life," Lily mused thoughtfully. "He loved the sea. I couldn't bring myself to sell them. If Dick Marlow agrees to stay on I'd like to engage them in commerce. With your help, of course," she added.

"Your idea is sound, Lily, and Dick seems an intelligent fellow, for all his youth. I'd be happy to work with him in disbursing your affairs."

Lily rose, thereby ending the visit. Of late her energy lagged and though she often felt in need of an afternoon nap she seldom allowed herself the luxury. Today the luxury became a necessity and she couldn't wait to slide between the cool sheets. She still hadn't seen a doctor but knew she couldn't delay much longer.

Lily walked from the doctor's office in a daze. Pregnant. The last time she and Matt loved had resulted in a child. Suddenly the day was brighter, the future not so bleak. In the likely possibility that Matt never returned she'd have a part of him to love and cherish. She hugged herself, savoring the picture of a son or daughter in Matt's image. She wished she had known before she left New Orleans. How thrilled Sarah would have been to know she'd always have something of Matt to love. Lily resolved to write to Sarah immediately. When Lily arrived home, Clay was waiting for her.

'You look much better than you did the last time I saw you," Clay observed, entranced by the sparkle in Lily's amber eyes. She had a special glow about her that Clay found difficult to understand, especially in view of Matt's tragic death.

Lily was bursting with impatience to tell someone her good news. She was over two months into her pregnancy and she wanted to share her intense joy with someone. "I just learned I'm carrying Matt's child," Lily revealed happily.

Clay was stunned. "I—I . . . How wonderful," he said halfheartedly.

"I think Matt will be happy, don't you?"

"Lily, you frighten me when you talk like that. You simply have to come to grips with Matt's death. At least you'll always have a living part of him now but the sooner you stop thinking he's going to pop up unexpectedly the better off you'll be. Think of your child."

Clay's blunt words seemed to unleash something in Lily, something dark and forbidding and unspeakable. It was the terrifying knowledge that Matt was truly dead and she was living in a dream world where realities didn't exist. Her face crumbled and she sagged against Clay as tears trickled from the corners of her eyes.

"No . . ." Her voice was low and harsh, her eyes empty. "My baby needs a father."

"Let me be the baby's father, Lily," Clay said quietly. "I'll raise him—or her—with all the love in my heart. I promise not to let him forget his father and I'll cherish both of you equally."

"Please, Clay, I don't want to talk about it," Lily said, swallowing past the lump in her throat. "Why must happiness be so fleeting? Just go now, I need to be alone."

"I don't want to leave you like this. You were so happy when I arrived. I didn't mean to upset you but you must face reality."

"I—I'll be all right, I just need to be alone."

"Remember what I said. I meant every word."

He drew her from the parlor to the front door. She opened it for him but instead of leaving immediately,

Clay embraced her and planted a gentle kiss on her forehead. They had no idea they were being observed by a woman driving past in a carriage.

Sarah watched curiously from the window as a tall, gaunt man emerged from a carriage and limped up the front walk. It was dusk and she couldn't make out his features, but something familiar and dear tugged at her memory. When the carriage stopped Sarah had naturally assumed it was Jeff, who was due home from the office. But she could see immediately that this man was much taller than her husband. The limp also puzzled her. The man appeared to be in pain, his left foot dragging slightly behind him. Stepping back from the window, she allowed the curtain to drop in place while she waited for her unexpected caller to announce himself.

The knock on the door came almost simultaneously with her thoughts. Since Fleta was busy helping Cook in the kitchen, Sarah answered the summons herself. The waning light of evening shadowed his face and a thick stubble of black covering his chin and jaws lent his features a sinister look, preventing Sarah from recognizing him immediately. In fact, Sarah had the urge to slam the door in his face. He must have recognized her intent for he stepped closer, speaking her name softly.

"Sarah."

A tremor shook Sarah's body and her face turned as white as death. She managed a shaky step backward, fearing that she was either hallucinating or haunted. The ghostly apparition followed.

"No, please, what do you want?"

"Sarah, it's me, Matt. I didn't mean to frighten you."

"Matt? Matt is dead. Who are you?"

"I'm not dead, Sarah, I'm very much alive, though

Lord knows I don't blame you for not recognizing me."

Suddenly Fleta appeared from the kitchen with a lamp in her hands. One of her duties was placing lamps about the house as evening approached. The light from the lamp fully illuminated the deeply concerned face peering at Sarah. Only then did Sarah recognize the dearly beloved features and distinctive eyes belonging to her brother.

"Matt! Oh God, it's really you." She took a step forward then began a slow spiral downward. Matt scooped her into his arms long before she hit the floor.

Sarah floated out of a haze of thick white clouds to find herself lying on the sofa in the parlor. She had no idea how long she had been out but while she was senseless Jeff had returned home and was engaged in earnest conversation with another man. When her eyes began to focus properly and her mind cleared, everything came back to her in a rush of joy so profound she wanted to inform the world of her happiness.

"Matt. You're not dead."

Both men turned in unison at the sound of Sarah's voice.

"And you're pregnant, little sister," Matt said with a smile in his voice.

"How do you feel, darling?" Jeff asked solicitously. He helped Sarah into a sitting position, hovering over her like a mother hen.

"I'm fine, Jeff, really. In fact, I've never felt better." She was grinning from ear to ear, grasping Matt's hand as he sat beside her and pulled her into his embrace.

"I must admit I'm not too pretty to look at," Matt observed wryly.

"You look wonderful but why are you limping?"

Sarah asked worriedly as she quickly inspected Matt for injuries.

"I suppose you were told about the explosion." Sarah nodded. "I was on the bridge when it happened and was blown into the water. I lost consciousness almost immediately and when I awoke I was on a British naval vessel. I was told I passed in and out of consciousness for days after the battle and was unable to communicate. My leg was severely damaged in the explosion and I had sustained head injuries as well. Once I gained my senses I learned I was near death when I was plucked out of the water."

"How did it happen that you were picked up by the British?" Jeff asked curiously.

"An English frigate was sunk by Lafitte about the same time as the *Sea Hawke* was blown to bits. Evidently I was blown some distance from where the *Sea Hawke* went down and the British thought I was one of their seamen. Since I was in no condition to tell them who I was they treated my wounds and kept me aboard. I had no idea that by then I was well on my way to England."

"Thank God you were found. It matters little whether you were rescued by the English or Americans as long as you're alive," Sarah said in a choked voice. "We were devastated when we were told you had gone down with your ship. At first Lily refused to believe you were dead. But you look so thin and gaunt. How did you get back to New Orleans?"

"The moment I arrived in England I signed on as crewman aboard a merchantman. I didn't want to waste time going to London and obtaining funds for passage from Chris so I took the only course available to me. I knew everyone here thought me dead and I wanted to reach home as quickly as possible. I wasn't fully recuperated yet and the voyage wasn't easy, but at least I'm here." Suddenly his face grew hard. "Jeff told me Lily is in Boston. Whatever possessed her to leave New Orleans?"

"I tried to convince her to stay, especially since I wanted her here for the birth of my child. But she was adamant," Sarah said.

"Did she give no reason for her hasty departure?"

"Perhaps she needed to put your affairs in order," Jeff suggested.

"Perhaps," Matt said stonily. *And perhaps she wanted to be consoled by Clay Winslow, the man who handles my affairs*, Matt thought but did not say.

Chapter 20

L ily should have known that seeing Clay, even in an innocent business capacity, would cause gossip in staid Boston, but she hadn't given it a thought. She learned of it when she visited Dick at Matt's office near the waterfront one day. It was shortly after she had agreed to a business lunch with Clay at one of Boston's best hotels. There were countless decisions for Lily to make concerning Matt's holdings and when Clay suggested lunch she readily agreed, especially since she had to go out that day anyway and thought to save him a trip to Hawkeshaven.

Dick welcomed Lily warmly as he launched into a detailed explanation of where the three remaining ships of the Hawke line were being used to carry goods and merchandise.

"*Hawke's Pride* finally arrived back in home port, having heard about the end of the war. If you're agreeable I'll order repairs made and find her a cargo. Andrew Calder has agreed to stay on as captain."

"Do what you think best, Dick," Lily replied, "I trust your judgment."

Dick flushed with pleasure. He knew Matt would want him to do what was right for Lily and the responsibility sat heavily upon his shoulders. Which led him to another subject. In the course of business he had heard disturbing gossip and though he wanted to mention it to Lily he hated to cause her undue distress. His lips turned downward into a frown, immediately alerting Lily.

"Is something wrong, Dick? Is there a problem I should know about?"

"Am I so transparent?" Deception didn't suit Dick; his feelings were clearly revealed in his guileless eyes. He sighed wearily, wishing life wasn't so damn complicated.

An uncomfortable stirring set Lily's nerves on edge. "If there is something I should know then you must tell me."

"Dammit, Lily, I'm no good at this."

"At what?" Lily was truly bewildered.

"Deception. I don't want to hurt you."

"Hurt me?" Now she was truly alarmed. "If you don't tell me what this is all about I'm going to be angry," Lily threatened.

"Gossip concerning you and Clay Winslow is being spread around Boston. Malicious gossip, Lily. I've heard it from several different sources. The latest is that you and Clay are lovers and he's flaunting you in public."

"My God! How can people turn an innocent lunch and business meeting into something vile? Who would spread such terrible untruths about me? Why?"

Dick flushed. He had his own theory but could prove nothing.

He did not fool Lily. "If you know something, Dick, please tell me."

"I don't want to hurt you, Lily, and this is only conjecture, but I'd be willing to bet Clarissa Hartley is behind the gossip."

"Clarissa! I had no idea she was in Boston."

Dick had been too close to Matt not to know about Clarissa Hartley and her connection to Matt. Or the trouble she'd caused Matt and Lily. "Her theater troupe has been in town for several months. She's appearing at the opera house."

"My relationship with Clay is completely innocent," Lily protested. "Our association is strictly business. I don't know what I'd do without you and Clay. I really know nothing about business matters and I want everything in order when Matt ..." Her words trailed off. When would she realize Matt wasn't coming back?

Never!

Dick cocked her a quizzical glance. "What were you going to say?"

Lily bit her bottom lip. "It's not important." No one understood how she felt. If she wasn't careful her friends would accuse her of losing her mind. How much time must pass before she accepted Matt's death? The answer was simple. More time than she had years left on earth.

The outcome of Lily's talk with Dick was that she was careful to avoid occasions that might fuel gossip. Since there were still times she needed to confer with Clay she made certain it was in the privacy of her home with servants in attendance. Though it was expected that a young widow would remarry, a year's mourning was considered a proper interval before seeing other men.

"I don't care what people think," Clay muttered when Lily told him of her decision the next time he stopped by with papers for her to sign. "We've done nothing wrong. I'd never dishonor you or Matt's memory like that. I've always known Clarissa Hartley was a vindictive witch. I don't know how Matt could have—" Lily looked so stricken, Clay wanted to bite his tongue.

"I care what people think, Clay," Lily said with quiet dignity. "I expect to raise my child in Boston, I can't afford to have my name associated with gossip.

I'm sorry, Clay, I know you mean well but our business must necessarily be conducted in my home from now on. And only if it warrants a visit."

"I'm sorry, too, Lily," Clay said sadly. "And it so happens I do have important business to discuss with you. It concerns *Hawke's Pride*. I have an offer for her that you might want to consider. If you do sell you'd still have *Lady Hawke* and *Sky Hawke*. Then there is a matter of a trust fund for your unborn child. I know Matt would want it taken care of."

"Since this promises to be a long session, let's get on with it," Lily suggested.

Before the last batch of papers was signed, Lily grew so weary Clay felt obligated to call a halt to their meeting.

"Tell you what, Lily," he offered. "Why don't I leave these unsigned papers here for the time being. Take a nap, you look like you could use one. I'll drive by tonight after business hours and pick them up."

Lily's relief was evident. "I am tired," she admitted. "Pregnancy is more draining than I would have imagined."

"You look wonderful," Clay said, his eyes shining with admiration. "You're still so slim if you hadn't told me I'd never suspect you're carrying a child."

Lily laughed. "Tell me that in a few months."

Clay's eyes glowed. "I'll tell you as often as you'll let me."

Matt sniffed appreciatively of the tangy air so distinctive to Boston and other seaports. The air was still cool for March and Matt hastened his footsteps. Since he had no trunks to bother with he left the dock immediately, anxious to reach home and Lily.

Lily.

He savored the sweet taste of her name on his tongue. He had no idea what to expect when he reached home. Sarah told him Lily had been inconsolable when told of his "death." But considering the way they parted before he left that day before the fateful battle he doubted Lily was as devastated as she let on. She was probably more relieved than anything. Lord, she was a handful! there seemed to be no way to get through to her. Stubborn to a fault, headstrong, independent, courageous. Yet he'd have her no other way. Except more trusting, perhaps.

He had departed New Orleans immediately after learning Lily was in Boston, and spent the entire journey wondering how Lily would greet him. He tried not to be too optimistic, considering their explosive parting. And he certainly didn't want to frighten her by showing up from the grave, so to speak.

No matter how hard Matt tried he could not dispel the gnawing fear that Lily had already welcomed Clay Winslow back into her life. He worried that she had left New Orleans for the express purpose of seeking comfort from the man who admittedly loved her. Were they already lovers? Had she gone willingly into Clay's arms and bed immediately after receiving word of Matt's untimely demise?

It didn't matter, Matt thought with grim determination. Lily was his. If need be he'd stake his claim over and over in the most basic way until both Lily and Clay realized he'd never let her go. His thoughts took him along such outrageous paths that he grew angrier and angrier, picturing Lily in Clay's arms, responding to him with wild abandon. The vivid image etched itself forever in his brain and hardened his resolve to master his wife, even if it took the rest of his life. He almost smiled at that pleasant thought. A lifetime with a woman like Lily boggled the mind.

Lost in the misery of his rampant imagination, Matt failed to notice the dark-haired woman who stared incredulously at him from across the road, her eyes wide with disbelief.

"Matt!" Her cry was a wild crescendo of joy. "I knew you couldn't be dead!"

With a frantic lurch she hurled herself across the road, disregarding dark puddles of water left from a recent rain that spattered her peach gown with ugly brown stains.

Matt looked up just in time to catch Clarissa's voluptuous form as he unconsciously opened his arms to halt her headlong flight. She collided against him with a soft thud. Gurgling happily, she melted into his embrace. If they weren't on a public street she felt certain Matt would have kissed her and a resurgence of love and passion swelled her heart. She had conveniently forgotten that Matt had more or less washed his hands of her in New Orleans.

"Where have you been, Matt?" she asked breathlessly. "We were told you were dead."

Firmly removing Clarissa's arms from around his neck, Matt took a step backward. At one time he had thought nothing of being seen openly cavorting with his mistress, but all that changed when he married Lily. Lily was the only woman he wanted now; all he had to do was convince her of it.

"It's a long story, Clarrie, and I haven't time now for lengthy explanations. I'm on my way home. I don't want Lily thinking me dead a moment longer than necessary."

"Do you think she cares?" Clarissa sneered derisively. "Your wife was so devastated she took a lover almost immediately after her return to Boston."

Her biting sarcasm wasn't lost on Matt and his face paled beneath his tan. Had his worst fears been realized? "You're lying!" he accused hotly. Clarissa flinched beneath Matt's unrelenting fury but stubbornly refused to recant. "By God, admit you're lying!"

"I'm not lying, Matt, ask anyone. It's common knowledge that Lily has taken a lover."

"Clarrie, if you weren't a woman I'd—"

"If you don't believe me go see for yourself. I'd be willing to bet Clay Winslow's horse is hitched outside your front door. Sometimes he doesn't leave until morning." She rolled her eyes, adding emphasis to her lie.

Matt was astute enough to know Clarissa often bent the truth to her own benefit, but in truth her accusation was no more than he expected. Still, it was like a punch to the gut hearing Lily's infidelity discussed so candidly. No, not infidelity, he corrected, for Lily thought him dead.

"Matt, did you hear me?"

"I heard," Matt said distractedly. Suddenly the day wasn't quite so bright.

"My carriage is nearby, I'll take you home."

Numbly Matt allowed Clarissa to guide him toward her carriage. He climbed inside and sat in stony silence during the ride up Cobb's Hill. Sensing his mood, Clarissa wisely held her tongue. She wasn't really certain they'd find Clay's horse hitched outside Hawkeshaven but she was desperate and had grasped at straws. It was after six o'clock, the time when most offices closed, and she prayed her instincts were right. Everyone knew Clay Winslow was in love with Lily Hawke and it wasn't so farfetched to think they had become lovers.

They were approaching the house now and Clarissa held her breath. She stifled a squeal of delight when she spied a horse hitched to the hitching post. She wanted to shout, "I told you so!"

Matt stared at the horse, as if unwilling to believe what he was seeing. Just because there was a horse didn't necessarily indicate the animal belonged to Clay Winslow. He said as much to Clarissa.

"You'll know soon enough, won't you?" Clarissa said with sly innuendo.

Matt shot her a quelling look then stepped down from the carriage. "Thanks for the ride, Clarrie."

"Matt, wait. I'm staying at the Hampton Hotel, room twenty-one. If—if you feel the need to talk or ... anything, I'll be there waiting for you. I have nightly performances and a daily matinee during the next few weeks but I'm always through by midnight. Matt, I'd do anything for you, you know that."

"That's what I'm afraid of," he said cryptically. Would she tell cruel lies? He'd learn soon enough.

Matt waited until Clarissa drove off then turned slowly toward the house. His steps were slow and hesitant as he approached the door, afraid of what he would find. He was nearly there when at the last minute something prompted him to turn and walk around to the side and peer into the long parlor windows. He didn't know what prodded him to do such a thing, but he had to know where Clay fit into Lily's life before making his presence known. Of course they could be in the bedroom, he supposed, but he preferred to think Lily would be more circumspect than that.

It wasn't dark yet but shadows were lengthening across the lawn when Matt sidled up to one of the windows, giving him an unobstructed view of the parlor. Clay must have just arrived for Lily was inviting him to sit down. She looked wonderful, Matt thought wistfully, not at all like a grieving widow. The painful ache in his loins reminded him that it had been longer than he cared to remember since he'd tasted Lily's sweetness, experienced the thrill of her response, loved her until they were both limp with sexual contentment.

She was wearing black but it served only to enhance her alabaster paleness and bring out the gold highlights in her vibrant hair. It appeared as if she had gained a little weight, but it suited her. Her breasts seemed fuller and her hips womanly round and supple. Just looking at her hurt Matt's eyes. It's no wonder Clay Winslow wanted her.

Matt's reluctant gaze shifted to Clay, who was speaking earnestly to Lily. Lily appeared to be listening raptly, which served only to fuel Matt's anger. He could talk to Lily until he was blue in the face but she paid him little heed. He had dreamed of their reunion, prayed Lily would be thrilled to learn he was alive, but now he wasn't sure. She certainly appeared content with her life and with Clay Winslow paying her court. Unable to hear their words, Matt gazed through the window with rapt attention, trying to imagine what was being said. He would have been surprised had he been able to hear their conversation.

"I'm sorry I'm late, Lily," Clay apologized. "A client arrived at the last minute requesting advice."

"It's all right, Clay, I have nothing to do tonight." Or any other night, she thought sadly. Even fighting with Matt was better than the useless emptiness of her life. Perhaps it would be better once the baby was born, she hoped.

"Have you signed the papers?"

"Yes. I left them on my desk in the bedroom. I'll go get them." She rose, left the room and started up the stairs. For lack of something better to do, Clay followed, watching the graceful sway of her skirts from the bottom of the stairs.

Matt could see into the hallway from where he stood but not beyond. He was livid when he saw Lily leave the room and Clay follow. Raging jealousy made him jump to conclusions, assuming Lily had invited Clay to her bedroom.

Unaware that Matt was moments away from bursting into the house, Clay leaned against the banister, waiting for Lily to reappear. Suddenly he heard her cry out and without a thought for propriety, he bounded up the stairs. Lily was sitting on the floor when he arrived in her room, looking stunned but otherwise unhurt.

"What is it, Lily? What happened?" His face wore a concerned frown.

Lily smothered an embarrassed laugh. "How clumsy of me. Jenny hadn't lit a lamp yet and I foolishly neglected to bring one up with me. I tripped over the stool." She started to rise.

"No," Clay admonished, "don't move. Let me. You could have harmed the baby."

"I feel fine, Clay, honestly," Lily scoffed.

Ignoring her feeble protest, Clay bent and scooped her into his arms. He moved slowly toward the bed where he intended to leave her while he summoned her maid to see to her. Matt chose that moment to charge into the room, his face mottled with rage and disbelief. Lily and Clay hadn't heard the pounding on the door or Joseph's stunned gasp when he opened the panel and saw Matt standing on the threshold.

"Have you no shame, woman! Couldn't you wait at least until I was gone a year to take a lover?"

"Dear God!" Clay went white, dropping Lily abruptly on the bed. "Where in all that's holy did you come from?"

"From Hell."

"Matt . . ." His name slipped past Lily's bloodless lips in a long drawn-out sigh. "I knew you weren't dead."

"You could have fooled me." His voice was dangerously quiet. He hadn't meant to let Lily know he was alive in so abrupt a manner but desperate times called for desperate measures. No man was going to make love to *his* wife as long as he was alive to prevent it.

"My God, man, where have you been? Do you

know your death has been widely published? You've put Lily through unspeakable anguish."

"It's a long story, Winslow, one I prefer to tell my wife when we're alone. Suffice it to say you'll not get the opportunity to make love to her again."

Clay started violently. "What! You think— You can't think so little of Lily that you'd accuse her of such vile things."

"What should I think when I find my wife being carried to bed by another man?" Matt's words hissed loudly through tightly clenched teeth.

Still in shock, Lily merely stared at Matt, unable to concentrate on his words. All she could think of was that he was alive and her baby would have a father. After several agonizing minutes she realized what he was saying and found the strength to protest. "It's not what you think, Matt. Oh God, it shouldn't be like this. Don't you know how desperately I clung to the belief that you were still alive?"

"It's true," Clay concurred. "Lily refused to accept your death. She alone held to the belief that you would return."

"I imagine you did your best to convince her otherwise," Matt ground out venomously. "I might have believed it if I hadn't seen with my own eyes how you were cavorting with Clay in *my* bedroom."

"Obviously there's no placating you," Clay said, his voice ripe with disgust.

"Obviously. The best thing you can do now is leave. I'll deal with my wife in my own way."

Clay tasted a spurt of raw fear. "If you hurt Lily you'll regret it."

Matt laughed harshly. "I don't make a habit of abusing women but there is always a first time."

"Matt," Clay said in a cajoling tone, "there is something you should know. Lily is—"

"Clay, no! Just go, I'll be fine. Matt won't harm me." She wasn't certain she spoke the truth but she didn't want Matt to know she carried his child. Not yet, anyway, not until he cooled down and accepted her explanation of what he was assuming he had interrupted tonight.

Openly skeptical, Clay refused to budge. "No, Lily, I don't trust him. I don't condone violence in any form and right now Matt looks angry enough to do you harm."

"Please, Clay, once I explain to Matt what happened he'll understand."

Matt smiled a bitter smile but said nothing to contradict Clay or lead him to believe he would accept his wife's explanation.

"Are you sure, Lily?"

"Very sure." With an agony of effort she dragged her eyes away from Matt to smile reassuringly at Clay.

Her senses were alive with Matt, from the impossible breadth of his shoulders to his dark eyes. She could feel the tingle of awareness as his piercing gaze raked over her. She knew he was angry but it didn't matter—Matt was *alive*! Nothing mattered but knowing that her world was no longer empty. Her consciousness was stimulated once more with the taste, feel and scent of him. Even his anger was wonderful for it proved miracles do happen.

Clay leveled an austere glance at Matt then reluctantly bowed to Lily's wishes. "I'll leave but I don't like it. If the big bully tries to hurt you, you know you have options." Then he turned and left the room. It wasn't until Matt heard the reverberation of a slammed door echo through the hallway that some of the tenseness left his body.

Lily still half reclined on the bed where Clay had dropped her. Now she gazed up at Matt through lowered lids, devouring the glowering length of him, and silently thanked God for sparing him. "Are—are you all right?"

Matt laughed harshly. "I've got all my parts, if that's what you're asking. Except for a slight limp I've recovered from my injuries."

"You're so thin," Lily said, ignoring his scathing sarcasm. "What happened? Everyone assumed you had drowned when the *Sea Hawke* sank. Except for me," she added quietly.

He lowered himself to the bed, looking at her strangely as he related to Lily the same story he had told Sarah. "I returned as soon as I was able. It surprised me to learn you had left New Orleans. Were you so anxious to return to Clay Winslow that you couldn't stay with Sarah until her child was born?"

A trembling sigh left Lily's lips. "It's not like that, Matt. Clay has helped me tremendously these past weeks. I don't know what I would have done without him."

"I'll bet," Matt intoned dryly. "Take off your clothes."

Lily grit her teeth in frustration. Somehow she had to get past the hard core of Matt's rage and into his heart. She reached out to him, her small white hand a symbol of her vulnerability where he was concerned. Matt stiffened, then seemed to collapse from within as he grasped her hand and pulled her into his arms.

"I'm sorry, Matt, so sorry I sent you away with angry words before the battle for New Orleans."

A groan of incredible agony slipped past his lips. "You're lying, Lily, but God help me for I can't help myself."

"Matt, no—" Her words ended in a gurgle as Matt's mouth claimed hers with a fierceness that left her breathless.

"I've thought of nothing but this since the day I awoke aboard an English ship." With an efficiency of motion he began stripping off her clothes. When she tried to protest he flung her hands away and ruthlessly undressed her, ripping buttons and seams, until she lay bare and shivering on the bed.

Lily tasted the fierceness of his need in his rough kiss as his mouth plundered hers and his tongue explored her roughly. She braced herself for his hard angry kisses when abruptly his mouth left hers, traveled slowly down her cheek, stopped to test the pulse beating erratically in her throat, then continued over the gentle rise of her breast. Then he found her nipple. Her flesh warming beneath his hands and mouth, the erect tip rose unrestrained against his lips as he nibbled and sucked greedily. His hands, those splendid, strong hands, teased and fondled, firing her blood and bringing a moan to her lips.

"Does Clay make you feel like this?" he asked almost hostilely. His hand slid across her silken belly and seared a fiery path into the warm mound at the joining of her thighs. His gentle message sent shivers of ecstasy racing through her and she arched against him. He was torturing her but not in the way Clay had feared.

"Matt!"

A bitter laugh exploded from his throat. "I know what you like, Lily, I've always known. I'm home now, no other man will touch you like this again."

"I want no other man," Lily panted, very close to losing all control. "Can you truthfully say you want no other woman?"

Suddenly Matt went still. He thought he could make love to Lily without emotional involvement. He thought he could vent his raging lust—it was lust, wasn't it?—on his wife and give it no more importance than satisfying his body's needs. He had been without a woman for a long time. But Lily's words gave him pause. Desperately he forced his mind to recall the angry words she had flung at him in New Orleans and the way she had sent him away, with little hope for reconciliation, after he had bared his soul to her. Then he deliberately dwelled on how he had found Lily and Clay together in this very bedroom. And his anger renewed itself.

"Damn you, Lily, how can I believe you want only me after the way I found you just minutes ago? What good would it do now to tell you I want no other woman when you refused to believe me the first time? You're my wife and I'm damn well going to make love to you, but don't attach more to it than mutual satisfaction we gain from the fires we seem to ignite in one another. I freely admit I want you, I've always wanted you."

Suddenly he was tearing off his clothes, flinging them aside with heated abandon. He was beyond words now, beyond everything but his terrible need for Lily. He bent his head once more to kiss and lick her hardened nipples, ignoring her sob of wounded outrage. Then he raised her knees and slid between them. His manhood was erect, larger than Lily had ever seen it before, and she dragged in a shuddering breath. Matt's expression was so furious, so incredibly fierce, she truly feared he might hurt her. Her face must have mirrored her feelings for a bitter chuckle rumbled from Matt's chest.

"Don't worry, I won't hurt you. Sometimes you drive me to violence but physical abuse isn't my way."

As if to prove his words he slid down her body and buried his head between her legs. His tongue flicked out, and Lily screamed as he touched that sensitive place where ecstasy began. He probed relentlessly, his tongue a blade that severed all reserve and sent Lily careening wildly. She clung to his shoulders, thrashing and moaning, calling his name and begging him to stop. He showed no mercy, until her body began to vibrate and her veins thickened with liquid fire, then he surged up and thrust into her.

She screamed again.

Her climax continued in crashing waves of uncontrollable raw passion. When it began to ebb, Matt expertly stroked her to greater heights, savoring the magic of her as she tightly enfolded and enclosed him. He could never duplicate that feeling if he lived to be one hundred. When he sensed Lily could give no more, he allowed himself the luxury of glorious release. Hot waves of searing flame raged through him and exploded in a torrent of fiery sensation.

When he came back to his senses Lily was sobbing quietly.

"Didn't you enjoy that?" His voice was unnecessarily harsh, belying the passion they had just shared. He didn't want her to know how deeply their lovemaking had affected him. Not yet, anyway. Not until he knew where he stood. "Did I hurt you?"

"I think I would have welcomed physical hurt," Lily said quietly. "You treated me like your—your whore, or a possession you want around merely to satisfy your sexual appetite. If I mean no more than that to you, Matt, let me go. It would be far kinder to allow me to disappear from your life."

Matt flung himself from the bed and stood over her, hands on hips, feet spread wide apart in a threatening manner. "If Winslow expects me to conveniently walk out of your life and leave you to him he's sadly mistaken. You belong to me."

His eyes raked over her in an insulting manner. They lingered a moment on the ripe mounds of her breasts with their tantalizing coral tips before sliding downward over the softly rounded curve of her stomach to the fiery triangle between her legs. Abruptly his gaze returned to her stomach. His brow wore a puzzled frown and his silver eyes narrowed as he stared intently at the slight but distinct bulge he had previously neglected to note. It wouldn't even have been noticeable if he didn't know her body so intimately. His mouth went dry and his throat worked convulsively—but no words came.

Lily sucked in her breath, held captive by the intensity of Matt's stare. She'd be damned if she'd tell him about the baby, not now, not until he came to terms with his anger and realized Clay meant nothing to her. Besides, he had said nothing to indicate that his meeting in New Orleans with Clarissa had been accidental like he claimed. When he raised his eyes to her face, she glared back at him, her expression mutinous.

"Do you have something to tell me, Lily? Am I to be a father or does that honor belong to Clay?"

"Go to hell!"

Chapter 21

Matt grit his teeth in frustration. "What's that supposed to mean? I demand you tell me whose baby you're carrying."

"You'll have to figure that out for yourself," Lily shot back. "If I am indeed pregnant as you seem to think."

"Damn you! This is serious, Lily."

Lily tried not to cower beneath his towering rage, tried to match his anger, but it was difficult. He looked so fiercely menacing standing over her, hands clenched at his sides, his face a mask of fury. So wonderfully male. And much too arrogant.

Lily's rebellious expression made Matt realize his anger was getting him nowhere. And that if he didn't leave immediately he was in danger of doing something he'd regret for the rest of his life. Lily looked so—so—adorably belligerent, so damn outrageously beautiful and helpless that he wanted to shake her until her senses returned in one minute and in the next kiss her until she admitted she loved him. Turning abruptly, he flung on his clothes.

"Where—where are you going?"

"I don't know," Matt said, flinging her a scathing glance. "Someplace where I'm appreciated. "But I'll return, Lily, and when I do I want the truth from you. If you're carrying my child there will be no more meetings between you and Winslow."

"You're going to Clarissa," Lily charged hotly. Suddenly her voice turned soft and trembling. "Matt, it shouldn't be like this. You've just returned from a harrowing experience and I—we all—thought you were dead. Why can't you believe that nothing exists between me and Clay except friendship?"

Fully dressed now, Matt stood looking down at her. "For both our sakes I need to cool off, Lily. This isn't exactly the homecoming I dreamed of. But I'll return, and when I do I'll demand some more answers. By then I should be better prepared to accept your explanation of why Clay was in your bedroom."

Lily reached out to him. "Matt, please don't go"—he was already out the door—"to Clarissa." It was too late. Her plea fell like a thud in the empty room.

Lily cursed herself for not telling Matt the truth about the baby. Why did she insist upon tormenting him with the false notion that he wasn't the father? she wondered despondently. Because you wanted him to trust you before informing him about the baby, a little voice whispered in her ear. Just like you trusted him? another little voice questioned. Lily shuddered, recalling how Matt had denied taking up with Clarissa again and how she had refused to believe him.

Why couldn't things be like they were on their island? Lily wondered, distraught over the way they seemed always to be at odds with one another. Loving Matt had come despite their disastrous meeting and marriage, despite fateful events that worked continually to tear them apart, and that love had produced a child inside her. Nothing or no one was going to destroy what she had worked so diligently to nurture. And that included Clarissa Hartley. Somehow, some way, Lily vowed, she'd see that Clarissa was no longer a threat to the happiness she and Matt so richly deserved. Even if she had to call on Clarissa herself and order her to stay out of their lives.

Matt walked for hours, his anger slowly draining, leaving him shaken and exhausted. No matter where his thoughts took him they all arrived at the same gut-wrenching conclusion. Lily had refused to admit she was pregnant or name the father. Of course Matt wasn't certain his suspicion was correct but all the signs were there. Lily's stubborn resistance served only to reinforce his belief that she was involved with Winslow. Damn, damn, damn, he muttered darkly, why had he allowed his temper to race out of control? If jealousy hadn't reared its ugly head he would have insisted upon the truth then and there and remained to listen to Lily's explanation.

Matt's aimless steps continued, and he was hardly aware of where he was going until he happened to glance up and see that he stood before the Hampton Hotel, where Clarissa had mentioned she was lodging. And a glance at his timepiece told him it was just after midnight. Matt frowned. Surely he hadn't planned it this way, had he? That thought brought him up short. Even though Matt knew Clarissa would be more sympathetic and receptive than Lily he felt no compelling force to seek out his ex-mistress. He had finished with her years ago. Abruptly he turned to leave.

"Matt, you came!"

Matt groaned. The last thing he wanted was for Clarissa to find him lingering outside her hotel.

"Oh, darling, you can't imagine how I hoped you'd come to me. I was right about Lily, wasn't I? That's why you're here, isn't it? Thanks to me you knew what to expect when you arrived home."

She took him firmly by the arm and led him inside. The clerk dozing behind the desk paid them little heed, by now quite familiar with Clarissa's comings and goings with various men. For some unexplained reason Matt didn't resist. Clarissa's fawning fed his ego when he needed it the most. What harm would it do to talk to someone who knew him so well? His argument with Lily had shaken him more than he cared to admit and he desperately needed someone to confide in. Someone who knew the situation and could discuss it intelligently.

How little Matt knew women!

Clarissa's room was dark. She quickly lit a lamp and led him to the bed. "Sit here," she urged silkily. Matt glanced around curiously, noting that there was only one chair in the small room. The Hampton Hotel was considered one of the more run-down hotels in a seedy section of Boston and Matt wondered if Clarissa had fallen upon hard times. Were her acting skills slipping or had she run out of "protectors"?

"You look exhausted, darling," Clarissa cooed as she sat opposite him in the chair.

"I am, Clarrie. I've been walking for hours and this damn wound on my leg is giving me fits."

"Why did you leave home?" she asked curiously. Matt frowned, clamping his mouth tightly shut. "You don't have to tell me but it might help if you talked about it. Did you find Clay Winslow with your wife?"

"I—" His voice creaked. "Dammit, Clarrie, the bastard was with Lily, just like you said."

"I'm sorry," Clarissa said, struggling to suppress a triumphant smile. Feeling more sure of herself now, she rose and sat beside Matt on the bed. "I told you I'd always be here for you. I'd never treat you so shabbily if you were married to me."

"Lily thought I was dead, Clarrie, it's not like

340

she was committing adul—well, what I mean is she wasn't aware of doing any wrong."

"Why are you making excuses for her when she hadn't the decency to wait a respectable interval before taking a lover? She was bound to know it would cause gossip."

That was exactly the same question Matt asked himself while he prowled the deserted streets of Boston, but he wasn't about to admit it to Clarrie. It hurt too deeply. Nor was he going to tell her that he suspected Lily was breeding. "I'm too weary to think straight, Clarrie."

"Of course you are," Clarissa sympathized. "Why don't you just lie back and rest for a few hours?"

Matt was sorely tempted. His leg was throbbing painfully and he had a dreadful headache, lingering effects, he was certain, from his ordeal at sea that came and went at will.

"Go on, Matt," Clarissa urged, "we've been friends a long time. No one will have to know where you spent the night, if that's what's bothering you." Matt offered little resistance when she pushed him back against the pillows. "The bed is large enough for two, if it won't disturb you I'll just lie down beside you."

Matt watched warily as Clarissa lay down fully clothed. Since he was fully clothed also, he opined it could harm nothing if he slept a few hours and left before daybreak. To his credit he was asleep within minutes, never giving a thought to Clarissa's warm body curled up beside him.

Matt wasn't certain how long he slept but when he awoke it was still dark outside. A languid sensation crept through his body, setting his loins afire and sending the blood singing through his veins. He stirred restlessly, suddenly finding his arms filled with warm female flesh. The body in his arms stirred, hooking a bare leg around his hips as busy fingers worked deftly at the fastenings holding his clothes together. His shirt was undone now and those same groping fingers slipped inside the gaping edges to tease and tantalize. Matt gasped as his body automatically responded to Clarissa's expert caresses.

Clarissa crowed delightedly as she felt Matt harden against her. "Oh God, Matt, it's been so long since we've been together like this. Love me, please love me."

Making love came as naturally as breathing to Matt, but instinctively he knew he didn't want this. Not with Clarissa. Not with anyone but Lily. Even if Lily had taken Clay as a lover Matt couldn't find it in his heart to cast her aside. He knew he'd return home and listen to her explanation, and in all likelihood realize that he had jumped to conclusions, just as Lily had when she accused him of bedding Clarissa in New Orleans. And if Lily was expecting a child, that child was his. He felt it in his bones, tasted it with every breath he took. Willing his body to behave, he shook Clarissa free.

"Dammit, Clarrie, this isn't what I intended, though obviously it's what you expected."

"Where are you going?" Matt was already on his feet.

"Home."

"Lily doesn't want you. You saw for yourself what she and Clay are up to. Don't leave me like this!"

"It was over between us a long time ago. Don't try to revive something that no longer exists."

"It's still Lily, isn't it?" Clarissa ground out spitefully. "How can you still want her after what she's done?"

"That's just it, I'm not sure she's done anything wrong. She thought I was dead. It hurts like hell to think she's taken up with another man so soon but she belongs to me. Dammit, I love her!"

Clarissa went still, anger over his words of love for

his wife making her incautious. "I've done everything in my power to discredit Lily and still you cling to her. What will it take to make you love me again?"

"I never did love you, Clarrie," Matt said dismissively as he turned to leave. He was so anxious to get away he failed to grasp what her words implied.

"Damn you, Matt, you'll be back," Clarissa called after his departing back. His answer was the resounding thud of the door being slammed shut.

Pale dawn greeted Matt when he left the hotel. He breathed deeply of the fresh tangy air redolent with odors of the sea he loved so well. He knew what he had to do now and he turned his steps firmly in the direction he should have taken in the beginning. If he wanted the unbiased truth he had to go directly to the source.

Matt returned home, ordered water from a still shaken Joseph and commenced to bathe, shave and dress. He was still exhausted but looking better than he had the previous day. After eating a hearty breakfast, he was ready to leave the house. He didn't disturb Lily, unwilling to start another argument that would lead to hasty, angry words that neither of them meant. But fate intervened. Lily arrived in the dining room just as Matt was finishing his tea. She glared at him but said nothing. She already hurt enough without being further damaged by his biting accusations.

Distractedly Matt noted that Lily was favoring her right leg and wondered if he could have unintentionally hurt her last night while making love to her. "Lily." She cocked an eyebrow but remained silent. "Are you hurt? Why are you limping?"

"I—I twisted my ankle," she said, telling him half-truths.

He accepted her answer without question. "I'm

sorry I don't have time for our conversation now, there is something I have to do first."

"Does it have to do with Clarissa?" Lily asked with studied indifference. "I would have thought you had your fill of her last night. You did go to her last night, didn't you? I assumed you had when you didn't return home."

"It's not what you think, Lily. I did see Clarissa but—"

"I don't think anything," Lily interrupted, "and I don't really care. I wanted to explain to you about Clay but you refused to stay and listen. What should have been a beautiful reunion was made cheap by what happened afterward."

"I can't explain now, Lily, but I want you to know that I'm ready to listen to you. It's just that I have something to do first. Will you wait for me, love? I promise that when I return we'll clear up any misunderstanding between us."

More than anything in the world Lily wanted to believe him. But she had been hurt by Matt so many times in the past she was leery. Knowing that Matt had spent the night with Clarissa was nearly too much for her to forgive.

"You're not going to see Clarissa again, are you?"

Matt flushed and his eyelids slid down over his eyes, concealing his expression. "I—I can't promise that, but if I do see her it won't be with the intention you think."

"Oh God, Matt, what's the use of all this if you're going back to your mistress?"

"Never!" Matt said it with such vehemence Lily was momentarily stunned. "You'll just have to trust me." He rose from his chair, walked to where Lily was seated, bent and kissed the top of her head. "There are things we haven't talked about yet. Important things." His gaze turned downward to stare deliberately at her stomach. Then he grinned and strode from the room, leaving a confused Lily in his wake.

Clay Winslow had just arrived at his office when Matt burst through the door. "I tried to stop him," Clay's harassed clerk said as he followed close on Matt's heels.

"It's all right, Pierce, I'll handle this," Clay said, dismissing the poor distraught man. He waited until the clerk closed the door softly behind him before addressing Matt. "What's this all about? Where is Lily?"

"Lily is home where she belongs," Matt said, annoyed. He had known Clay Winslow for a long time and trusted him with his affairs, but that was before Lily. Before the handsome attorney fell in love with another man's wife. But now he had come to learn the truth, even if he had to beat it out of Clay.

"You haven't harmed her, have you?" Clay asked anxiously. "Dammit, Matt, your wife is expecting your child and I know how ruthless you can be at times."

"Is she, Clay? Is Lily carrying my child?"

Clay blustered angrily. "What kind of bastard are you?"

"The kind who wants the truth."

"Don't you believe your own wife?"

"Lily refused to tell me anything about the baby. She hasn't even admitted she is pregnant."

Clay looked troubled. "I suppose she has her reasons."

"If she does I have no idea what they can be except that the child doesn't belong to me."

"You're a damn fool, Matthew Hawke, if you believe that. And I'm going to ask you one more time. You didn't hurt Lily, did you? Or threaten her?"

"I'd never harm Lily," Matt said with quiet dignity. "I love her more than my own life."

Matt's sudden confession stunned Clay. "You have a funny way of showing it."

"I'll admit my temper got out of control when I found you in Lily's bedroom but in all truth you can't blame me. For months I've dreamed of our reunion, of how happy Lily would be to learn I was alive. Walking in on the two of you like that was a shock I hadn't anticipated."

"It was all perfectly innocent. Didn't Lily tell you how it happened?"

Guilt and remorse brought a flush of red creeping up Matt's neck. "I didn't give her a chance."

"My God, man, what did you do to her?"

"Nothing," Matt said slowly, refusing to divulge the intimate details of the incredible passion he and Lily shared. "Nothing that concerns you. I've come for the truth, Clay, and I expect nothing less."

"Sit down, Matt," Clay invited, resisting the urge to shake the stubborn man senseless. Once Matt was seated, he said, "Listen carefully for what I'm about to tell you is the unvarnished truth. I won't lie to you about my feelings for Lily. They are genuine, but Lily has never returned them. There is only one man Lily loves and you know who that is."

"She has a damn funny way of showing it," Matt muttered.

"I don't know what happened between you two and I don't want to know, but Lily has never stopped loving you. Not even while you were carrying on with your mistress."

"I finished with Clarissa the day I married Lily," Matt confided. "I'll have to admit I didn't plan it that way but somehow Lily worked her way into my heart. I didn't think love existed, never intended to remain faithful, until a feisty redhead taught me the meaning of love. We were stranded on a deserted island when I first realized how much Lily meant to me and I expected our life to be wonderful after that."

"What happened?"

"Lily mistakenly thought I was seeing Clarissa again," Matt said bitterly. "She saw something that made her believe I was being unfaithful."

"She jumped to conclusions just like you did," Clay charged. "Things aren't always what they seem. Lily went upstairs to get some papers she signed while I waited for her at the bottom of the stairs. I heard her cry out and rushed upstairs. She had tripped over a stool and twisted her ankle. Thinking she might have hurt her baby I picked her up, intending to carry her to the bed and call her maid. That's when you burst into the room, ready to believe the worst."

"So that's why Lily was limping this morning," Matt said with sudden insight. "She said nothing to me about it."

"Did you give her a chance?"

"Probably not," Matt admitted sheepishly. "Then you deny that you and Lily are lovers?"

"Jesus, Matt, what will it take for you to believe Lily and I are merely friends? I'm her financial advisor, for God's sake! She needed me after you were declared dead."

"What about the rumors?"

"How can you have heard rumors when you just returned last night?" Clay asked curiously.

"I ran into Clarissa Hartley."

Clay slanted Matt a sharp glance. It turned quickly to reproach and a hint of something stronger when Clay thought of all it implied.

"You're wrong, Clay," Matt said, reading Clay's thoughts. "I did see Clarrie last night but that's as far as it went."

"I've been tracking down those rumors and wasn't too surprised to learn they lead directly back to

Clarissa," Clay revealed. "Even Dick Marlow agrees with me that Clarissa is behind them. By the way," he said at the mention of Dick's name, "Dick is doing a fine job with your shipping interests. You'll be pleased with his efforts."

Matt smiled, the first since he entered Clay's office. "I always knew Dick was a good man. But are you certain Clarissa is the one spreading the rumors? I can think of no reason for her to do so since she and everyone else thought I was dead."

"As sure as I can be," Clay said with unflappable conviction. "As for her reason, just the knowledge that you cast her aside for Lily would be enough for a vindictive woman like Clarissa. She always assumed you'd go back to her and when you fell in love with Lily she couldn't abide the rejection. She couldn't get even with you since you were already 'dead' so she did the next best thing by damaging Lily's reputation."

Suddenly something Clarissa said before he slammed out of her room came back to haunt Matt. *I've done everything in my power to discredit Lily.*

Clay's words now made perfect sense. "There is no enemy like a woman scorned," Matt said slowly. "If that's what happened Clarissa will live to regret it."

"Don't do anything you'll regret," Clay advised.

"Are any of my ships in port?" Matt asked.

Clay's brow furrowed in puzzlement. "*Hawke's Pride* has been in port for some time undergoing repairs. I had word from Captain Calder just this morning that she is taking on cargo and has orders to sail to the West Coast with the midnight tide."

Matt's devious grin startled Clay. "What are you planning, Matt?"

"It's best you don't know," Matt said, his grin growing wider. "Suffice it to say if my plan works Clarissa will no longer be a threat to Lily, our child or our future happiness."

"Matt, don't do anything hasty," Clay warned, worried that Matt might take the law into his own hands.

"I don't plan on harming Clarissa, if that's what you mean. I have to go now, Clay, there is much I must do before *Hawke's Pride* sails. But first a call on Captain Calder is in order. I'll leave it to you to tell Dick that I'm alive and well and will be talking with him in a day or two."

"Matt, what—"

It was too late. Matt was already out the door.

Lily prowled the parlor in restless strides, wondering where Matt was and what he was doing. She wanted him to return so they could talk like reasonable people and come to grips with their feelings. There was no doubt in her mind that she loved Matt but she feared she might have killed Matt's love for her after her hasty accusations in New Orleans. Then too there was the deceptive scene Matt had inadvertently walked into the previous night. Now that she had recovered from the shock of the miracle of Matt's return, her thoughts returned time and again to Matt and Clarissa.

It stung when Matt had admitted he had gone to Clarissa last night after making love to her. Her entire body felt like it was being ripped apart. Yet Matt had as good as said that she was jumping to conclusions, that things weren't always what they seemed. Lord how she wanted to believe him. She now knew from experience that innocent events were often mistaken for something entirely different. After finding Clay in her bedroom hadn't Matt assumed she and Clay were lovers? She realized somewhat belatedly that she probably had jumped to the wrong conclusions about Matt and Clarissa in New Orleans.

As Lily paced and fumed, she realized that as long as Clarissa lived she would try to insinuate herself into Matt's life and that true happiness with Matt would be as illusive as a mist. Therefore, Lily reasoned, it was up to her to persuade Clarissa to butt out of their lives once and for all. Lily's mind worked furiously as she framed words in her brain that might sway Clarissa. If need be she'd mention her child and the fact that Matt would have no time for a mistress once their child was born.

Lily knew that Clarissa was appearing in a play being performed at the opera house and that the matinee performance would be over soon. Fueled by grim determination and the conviction that she and Matt belonged together, Lily summoned Joseph and ordered the carriage brought around. She wasn't too proud to fight for what she wanted and she knew convincing Clarissa to leave her and Matt in peace was going to be a fierce battle.

Feeling ill at ease, Lily entered the stage door of the theater. The matinee crowd was gone and most of the actors and actresses had already retired to their dressing rooms or left the theater until their presence was required later that evening. Briefly she questioned whether or not she was doing the right thing by confronting Clarissa and if Matt would be angry at her interference. But her love for Matt and the future happiness of their child drove her to acts she never before considered.

At first the darkened area looked deserted, until she noticed an elderly man sitting behind a desk perusing a tabloid of sorts. He didn't glance up until Lily stopped directly before the desk.

"Can I help you, miss?"

"I'm looking for Clarissa Hartley. I hope she hasn't already left the theater."

"You're in luck, miss, she's in her dressing room, but"—he grinned knowingly—"I don't rightly think she'd welcome your interruption right now."

"I don't understand."

He cleared his throat, leveled a piercing glance at Lily, shrugged his shoulders and said, "Miss Hartley is ... entertaining a gentleman caller in her room, if you catch my drift. I know for a fact she wouldn't be happy about having her ... conversation interrupted."

Lily's shoulders slumped dejectedly, causing the man to add kindly. "If it's important, you're welcome to wait. Miss Hartley's dressing room is down that hallway, first door on the left." He pointed vaguely into the dim recesses of the cavernous area and Lily peered indecisively down the deserted corridor before deciding to follow his suggestion.

"Thank you," she said. "My visit is important, I believe I will wait."

"Just set yourself anywhere," he invited as he focused his attention once more on the tabloid spread out before him.

Lily cautiously felt her way down the hallway until she stood before Clarissa's door. She could hear the murmur of voices through the panel and had no difficulty imagining what was going on inside. Glancing around cautiously, Lily spied several crates pushed against the wall not too far down the hallway from Clarissa's dressing room and decided to wait there since the position afforded her a good view of the room without being too conspicuous. She seated herself somewhat gingerly and hoped the wait wouldn't prove too lengthy. She had left her carriage outside and knew the driver would worry should she fail to appear within a reasonable length of time.

Lily's gray walking dress seemed to blend into the shadows and the casual observer would have difficulty telling that anyone sat perched at the edge of one of the crates.

Behind the closed doors of Clarissa's dressing room, Matt faced the lovely actress. He had arrived several minutes earlier and was greeted exuberantly by Clarissa, who had despaired of ever seeing Matt again. But she should have known her influence with Matt was too deeply ingrained and long-standing for him to walk out on her forever.

"Matt, darling," she crowed delightedly, throwing herself into his arms. "I knew you didn't mean what you said yesterday. I'm thrilled that you've finally come to your senses and realized I mean more to you than any other woman. You'll not regret your decision, darling, I promise."

Matt stiffened, struggling to control the anger he felt over Clarissa's deliberate lies. Clarissa mistook his rigid body for growing passion as she felt a tremor go through him.

"We have plenty of time, darling," she whispered huskily. Her nimble fingers moved purposely toward the buttons on his shirt. "My performance isn't for hours yet."

Only a twitch at the corner of his mouth betrayed Matt's true feelings as he carefully removed her busy hands and placed them at her sides. "No, Clarrie, we haven't time right now. I came to talk."

"Oh, Matt, you're far too serious." Clarissa pouted. "I know a cure for that." With deft fingers she loosened the belt to her robe, hoping to induce Matt into making love to her. It wouldn't be the first time her dressing room had been used for that purpose.

"Cover up, Clarrie," Matt ordered harshly, "what I've come to say is very important."

"Oh, very well," Clarissa replied sullenly, "you win this time." Clearly her curiosity was piqued. "Talk away. Just what is so damn important to keep us from making love?"

"How would you like to go to California, Clarrie?"

"California? Oh, Matt, I'd like nothing better than to go away with you. California or wherever."

"Many opportunities exist for you in California,

Clarrie," Matt continued blandly. "They say women are at a premium there."

For a moment Clarissa looked confused. "Why would I need another man when I have you?"

Matt chose to ignore her question. "Could you be ready to leave tonight after your performance?"

"Tonight? Do you mean it? Of course I can be ready. Tonight is our last show anyway. But what about you? Do you intend to move your business to California? What happened today to make you so anxious to leave your wife? Did she finally tell you she preferred Clay Winslow? That they were lovers?"

Matt grit his teeth to keep from striking Clarissa. "I'll tell you everything when you arrive aboard *Hawke's Pride*. She's taken on cargo and is preparing to sail on the midnight tide. Don't be late," he warned, flashing her a disarming smile.

"I'll be there, Matt, don't worry. You won't regret this, I promise."

Chapter 22

Anxious now to leave, Matt stood poised in the open doorway. "There is much to be done before midnight, Clarrie, it's best I leave now."

Clarissa couldn't resist the urge to fling herself into Matt's brawny arms and plant a lingering kiss on his lips. "Oh, Matt, I'll make you happy," she promised breathlessly. "Until tonight, lover."

Matt closed the door and grinned with wicked delight, unaware that a pair of shocked amber eyes watched from a short distance away. A startled gasp followed by a choked sob caught his attention and he peered down the dim corridor, astonished when a small figure detached itself from the shadows and fled down the hallway. He caught a glimpse of bright hair floating in disarray about narrow shoulders and an anguished groan slipped past his throat.

"Lily."

Matt cursed his rotten luck, wondering what in the hell brought Lily to this place at this particular time. He didn't want Lily learning what he was up to until it was accomplished. Willing his legs into motion, Matt gave chase, both rushing past the startled watchman one after another. Matt caught up with her just as she reached the carriage waiting at the curb for her.

She turned on him, her eyes blazing with unspeakable fury.

"Let me go, Matt! You're despicable!"

Matt grasped her arm, bringing her to an abrupt halt beside the carriage. "Get in, Lily," he ordered brusquely as he lifted her bodily into the conveyance and followed her inside. "What in the hell are you doing here?"

"I could ask you the same question but I already know the answer."

"It's not what you think."

"Ha! I heard Clarissa. You two have an assignation later tonight. I wish you joy of her, Matt."

"You'll understand once I explain."

Lily cocked an eyebrow and rewarded him with a sarcastic grunt.

The ride to Hawkeshaven commenced in silence, Matt preferring to wait until they were in the privacy of their own home to begin a lengthy explanation and Lily too angry and hurt to continue the argument. The moment the carriage pulled up before the front entrance Lily jumped down, bunched her dress in her fists and raced for the house. The door opened at her touch and she bounding past an astonished Joseph, fleeing up the stairs and into her room. Matt was hard on her heels. When she turned to slam and lock the door Matt was already inside. She dragged in a ragged breath when she saw him braced in the doorway, a deep scowl plowing his brow.

"Do you think doors and locks will keep me out, little one?" he asked lazily. "Are you so anxious to escape me?"

"Yes!" shot back Lily, involuntarily stepping back as he stepped into the room and closed the door firmly behind him.

"Without allowing me the courtesy of an explanation?"

"Did you allow me that same courtesy last night when you accused me of taking Clay as a lover?"

Matt flushed guiltily. "I'm sorry, love," he said softly, completely disarming her. "I apologize for hurting you, for allowing my jealousy to fan the flames of my anger. I love you, Lily, I always have and I always will."

"Are you apologizing for accusing me of all those vile things?" Lily asked, her amber eyes wide and uncomprehending. "What made you change your mind?"

"I recalled how you jumped to conclusions when you saw me with Clarissa in New Orleans and realized I was doing the same thing. I had already decided before I learned the truth about you and Clay that it didn't matter what you did or didn't do, that you're my wife and I love you no matter what. I know you thought me dead and if Clay helped comfort you it was with the knowledge that I no longer existed. At first I felt betrayed. Later I realized how ridiculously I acted, how insane my accusations."

Lily found it difficult to believe she was hearing right. This sounded nothing like the arrogant man who had accused her of bedding another. When she finally found her voice her words spoke eloquently of her own guilt. "I realize now that I misjudged you in New Orleans. I'm sorry, for so many things. But no matter what, I never stopped loving you."

Matt groaned as if in pain. "Oh God, love, how I longed to hear you say those words. But there are others I would hear you say. I think you know what I mean."

Lily licked her dry lips. She had dreamed many times of telling Matt about the baby, even when she thought she'd never get the chance to do so. "I'm having your baby, Matt. I hope you're as happy about it as I am. I couldn't understand why it never happened before and when it did I was heartbroken that our child might never know its father."

"I'm ecstatic, love." Matt grinned, pulling her into his arms. "I've never given much thought to children until I married you and then the notion of your body nurturing a child of my loins thrilled me."

Though Lily's heart was bursting with love, she hesitated, suddenly consumed with the picture of Matt emerging from Clarissa's dressing room and their parting words. "What were you doing with Clarissa this afternoon, Matt?"

He drew her toward the bed, sat down and pulled her onto his lap. "After tonight Clarissa will never again cause us trouble. I know now that she started those nasty rumors about you and Clay and she's also the one who instilled me with suspicion in the beginning."

"I have to know, Matt," Lily persisted. "Did you make love to Clarissa?" Though it would hurt her dreadfully, she had to know the truth.

"No, Lily," Matt said softly. "I would be untruthful if I didn't admit it entered my mind, but I couldn't do it. I didn't want Clarissa. You're the only woman I wanted. The only woman I'll ever want."

Lily searched Matt's face, looking for telltale signs that indicated he was lying. She saw nothing in their glowing depths but honesty and trust—and love.

"I want you to know everything, love, because I never want this to come between us again."

Lily grew still, her eyes wide with a terror she couldn't name. She wasn't sure she wanted to know the truth about Matt and Clarissa. "Very well, Matt." Pain speared through her like a well-honed blade but if Matt wanted to tell her all that had transpired between him and Clarissa then the least she could do was listen.

"I did go with Clarissa to her room last night. But not with the intention to bed her. Actually, I can't explain what dark forces drove me to her. After I left you I walked for hours and suddenly realized I was standing outside her hotel. That's where she found me after she left the theater. I offered no objection when she invited me inside. I was hurt and confused and thought she could shed some light on the situation."

"And did she?" Lily asked breathlessly.

Matt laughed harshly. "Hardly. It was my own common sense that finally brought reason to my muddled brain. I left Clarissa at dawn and came home."

"Why didn't you tell me this immediately?" Lily questioned.

"Because there were things I needed to do, people I wanted to see first. I called on Clay."

Lily's eyes grew wide with alarm. "What—what did you do to Clay?"

"Am I so transparent? Nothing, I swear it. I merely listened to his explanation of what took place here last night in your bedroom."

"Did you believe him?"

"Fortunately by then my temper had cooled and I was able to listen without exploding in jealous rage. Actually, by that time I had already realized how gullible I had been to believe Clarissa."

Lily opened her soft lips to speak and Matt felt compelled to take them gently with his own, lavishing all his love and caring in that single tender kiss. He tasted the salt of her tears and felt remorse that he had caused her such anguish. She was going to be the mother of his child and he loved her beyond reason.

"Will you forgive me, love? For our child's sake, for the future we have together and for the love we share? Forgive me."

"Only if you forgive me," Lily replied. "You can't begin to know the guilt I felt over sending you into battle with angry words and accusations when I knew deep in my heart that they couldn't possibly be true."

"We were both wrong, love. This will be a new beginning for us. Our meeting and marriage was somewhat unorthodox and I freely admit I wanted you for all the wrong reasons, but you entered my heart and I was lost forever. Now I'll battle anyone who suggests love doesn't exist."

His fingertips brushed her cheeks, banishing the tears as his eyes made love to her. Retreating beneath closed lids, Lily made no move to escape as he began to caress and stroke her body through the barrier of her clothes. The same strange enigmatic hunger assailed her whenever she found herself in Matt's arms and she willingly gave herself over to the magic of his exciting caresses. He seemed to know exactly where and how to touch her to make her wild with wanting.

His voice was a husky purr, softly pleading and eloquently tender. "I want to make love to you, Lily."

"If you don't I think I shall die."

Matt groaned and buried his face in the tantalizing fragrance of her hair. "I don't want to hurt you or our child."

"Loving doesn't hurt when it's freely given and freely received."

Her words unleashed something profoundly moving in him. Last night when they made love anger stood between them, but now there was only deep abiding love and a passion so powerful he felt consumed by it. His lips covered hers as he kissed her again and again, until he was drunk with the sweetness of her response. He couldn't seem to get enough of those soft pliant lips as he outlined them with the tip of his tongue then nudged them apart to drink deeply of her sweet essence. Lily felt herself growing dizzy from the intensity of his kisses. Suddenly she became aware of a new sensation contributing to her giddiness. While she had grown nearly senseless from his kisses, Matt had slipped one hand beneath her skirts, sliding up the inside of one satin-fleshed leg, coming to rest on the warm moist place between her legs. His mouth absorbed her shuddering gasp as one long tanned finger pierced deeply inside her. He added another then began a slow rhythm that sent Lily arching against his probing fingers.

"Matt!"

"Do you like that, love?"

"Yes, oh God, yes."

"I'll never do anything to hurt you." Lily moaned and moved in concert to his probing fingers. "That's it, love, don't hold back, look at me, I want to see your face when you come to me."

His fingers were doing such wonderful things to her Lily couldn't have held back even if she wanted to. When his thumb found the very center of her pleasure and massaged gently, she nearly leaped off his lap. Then she exploded, wildly, with a devouring fury that seemed to go on and on. When she regained her senses Matt had placed her across the bed and was removing her clothes.

She helped him as best she could and with a kind of erotic detachment watched while he tossed aside his own clothing. Then he stood over her, his virility huge and pointing boldly upward from its dark nest. His body was tense with need, his face taut with desire. Lily's eyes slid over him like warm honey, admiring the width and breadth of his massive shoulders, the shattering strength of his needy manhood, the magnificent expression of love on his handsome features, and she reached out for him.

A groan slipped past Matt's throat. "If you don't stop looking at me like that this will be all over before it begins."

"I want to touch you, Matt. I want to give you the

same kind of pleasure you give me." Her hand found him and she drew him forward. "I want to kiss you in the same way you kiss me." She opened her lips and took him inside.

"Jesus!"

Matt allowed her her way for several heart-stopping moments before abruptly pulling away. She had shattered his control beyond all redemption. Then he was lying across her, tasting a passion-hardened nipple, caressing it with his tongue as his hands boldly fondled the tender flesh between her legs, rekindling her desire to a fever pitch. Lily moaned deliriously, her ardor whipping around him like a whirlwind. His touch was tender and oh so sweet. Then she felt the magnificent length of him prod forcefully against the throbbing center of her and thrust toward his probing strength. He pierced her deeply, swiftly sheathing himself within the warmth of her soft receptive flesh.

He moved forcefully inside her as his hands tangled in the glowing mass of her hair; he felt her sweet surrender and gloried in it. His body, taut and inflamed, moved in a symphony of unleashed passion that rose in devouring fury to encompass them both. The unquenchable flame that licked to life each time they touched renewed itself as completion exploded upon them with a violence that shook the room. It was Heaven at its sweetest and Hell at its hottest. It was a passion born of love.

Later, as they rested in each other's arms, bodies pressed close, legs intimately entwined, Matt asked, "Do you trust me, Lily? Do you love me enough to place complete faith in me and in what I do?"

Lily hesitated but a moment. "I do trust you, Matt, but I'm afraid. What are you going to do?"

"I must leave you tonight for a time but when I return I promise to tell you everything; why I was with

Clarissa this afternoon and the reason for the words you heard us exchange."

Lily flinched. Was it happening again? What did Matt mean? Was he going to see Clarissa tonight? She wanted desperately to trust him but Matt was making it extremely difficult. "Can't you tell me what this is all about?"

"No, love, I can't. I don't want to disappoint you should my plans go awry."

"Do your plans include Clarissa?"

"I don't want to lie to you, Lily, not ever again. I am going to see Clarissa tonight but you have nothing to fear. I'll always be true to you. I ask only that you trust me until I can explain fully."

He sounded so sincere Lily felt inclined to believe him. "Very well, Matt, you have my trust."

"And you have mine," Matt returned. "Let's not waste a moment, I must leave very soon."

"Are you hungry?" Lily asked, suddenly realizing she was famished. Of late her appetite was amazing.

"Starved." Matt grinned, reaching for her.

"Behave, Matt." Lily giggled, brushing aside his hands. "Aren't you ever sated? I'm talking about food. I'm eating for two now."

Matt eyed the slight bulge of her stomach with a jaundiced eye. "Our son doesn't look very big. You must feed him well if he's to grow strong."

"Like his father," Lily said. "I hope all his appetites, if he's a boy, don't match those of his father." Her eyes rolled playfully.

"Have you any complaints, woman?" Matt growled, grabbing for her.

"Not if you allow me time to sustain myself with food and drink between bouts of lovemaking."

"If you're hinting that I'm starving you then I suggest we dress and see what Cook has prepared for supper." His voice smacked of sorely tried patience but his eyes glowed happily. Did a man ever love a woman as much as he loved Lily? And to think he once believed love didn't exist.

"I hope Cook has prepared a feast," Lily said wistfully, rolling easily to her feet.

"I could feast upon your sweet flesh all night," Matt said mischievously, "but if you insist I'll happily watch while you gorge yourself."

Later, after their meal, Matt took his leave. "I may be very late, love, but I *will* return," he promised, taking her in his arms and kissing her with gentle insistence. "Trust me, little one."

"Hurry back," Lily whispered, her mind overwhelmed by the thought of Matt and Clarissa together again. Then he was gone, leaving Lily standing alone and forlorn. She did trust Matt. She did! It was Clarissa she didn't trust.

Matt paced the deck of *Hawke's Pride,* one eye cocked worriedly at the sliver of moon and the other toward the fog-shrouded quay. Captain Andrew Calder stood beside him, alert despite the late hour. All around them men were scurrying about, readying the ship for departure. The ship was well lit by countless lanterns strung about the deck. The lights were ordered purposefully so there would be no mistaking it for anything other than *Hawke's Pride.*

"Are you sure this will work, Matt?" Captain Calder asked nervously. When Matt first outlined the plan to him he was openly skeptical, due mainly to the fact that though not exactly illegal it was risky and unethical.

"Trust me, Andy." Matt grinned. Actually, he wasn't quite as calm and assured as he appeared. What if Clarrie changed her mind? Or missed the sailing?

Suddenly Matt tensed, peering through the mist toward the quay. Both men snapped to attention as the sound of creaking wheels and the *clip clop* of horses' hooves on the stone pier drew their attention. Seconds later a closed coach materialized in the darkness and rumbled to a stop at the end of the quay. A small cloaked figure stepped out and looked toward the ship.

A huge smile creased Clarissa's face as she instantly recognized the man waiting for her at the end of the gangplank. Turning to direct the coachman, Clarissa waited impatiently while he wrestled her trunk from the rear of the coach and lugged it up the gangplank where Matt stood to greet her. The coachman was directed to a large cabin in the stern of the ship while Clarissa moved unerringly into Matt's arms.

"I'm here, darling," she murmured, oblivious to the covert glances she was given by the men engaged in various duties aboard the illuminated deck. "I hope I haven't kept you waiting."

"Thank God," Matt said fervently. Not even her slight tardiness could spoil this moment. "You're here, that's all that matters."

While Matt and Clarissa embraced, the coachman approached and loudly cleared his throat. Matt tossed him a coin and the man tipped his hat and departed, slowly disappearing into the swirling mist surrounding his hack.

Captain Calder chose that moment to make his presence known as he approached the embracing couple. Matt flashed him a grateful smile and abruptly moved away from Clarissa. "Captain Calder," he said, his relief evident. "Allow me to introduce my ... friend, Clarissa Hartley. "Clarrie, this is Captain Andy Calder. Since this will likely be a very long voyage"—he stressed the last words meaningfully—"I hope you two become ... close friends." He watched their reaction to one another carefully; he had too much riding on this meeting for Clarissa and the handsome captain not to like one another.

Matt knew Clarissa well. Andy Calder was an attractive, virile man and his rapt attention fed her ego. And attention is exactly what Andy Calder bestowed upon Clarissa. He liked what he saw and smiled beguilingly, immediately charming Clarissa with his roguish grin and concentrated admiration. Their mutual attraction was clearly evident.

The tip of Clarissa's tongue darted out to lick her red lips and she smiled engagingly, recognizing the captain's keen regard as she preened and postured for him. How wonderful it would be to have two handsome men dancing attendance upon her during the long dull voyage to California, she thought. It was just what was needed to keep Matt's interest in her from lagging. It had been a long time since she was the center of attention. She fluttered her long lashes in a flirtatious manner as she acknowledged Matt's introduction. She failed to notice Matt's devilish grin or hear the sigh of satisfaction rumble through his chest.

"This voyage should prove most enjoyable with both you and Matt aboard," Clarissa said coyly. "Any friend of Matt's is a friend of mine," she added with a look that Andy had little difficulty interpreting. "It's a pleasure to meet you, Captain."

"The pleasure is all mine," Andy returned smoothly.

Actually, Andy Calder was more than a little taken with Clarissa's dark beauty and curvaceous body that even her cloak failed to conceal. Fascinated, his gaze lingered hungrily on her full red lips before sliding downward to settle on the tantalizing curve of her breasts.

"Allow me to show Miss Hartley to her cabin," Andy Calder offered gallantly, taking Clarissa's arm before she had time to protest.

She slid a curious glance at Matt. "Aren't you coming, Matt?" she asked, frowning as a dark threat of something indefinable prickled her spine.

"Later," Matt promised vaguely. Recognizing the confusion furrowing her brow, Matt felt compelled to add in a voice meant for her ears alone, "Get ready for bed, Clarrie, you're in for a pleasant surprise tonight." Eyes shining with delight, Clarissa's brow cleared immediately as she happily accompanied Andy Calder, favoring him with a seductive smile.

Some minutes later the captain reappeared, admiration and a hint of something else—anticipation?—clearly visible in his blue eyes. "Clarissa Hartley is everything you said and more," he observed with keen appreciation. "Are you certain you know what you're doing?"

Matt grinned cockily. "You don't know Lily. I was never more certain of anything in my life. Clarissa Hartley is all yours, Andy. You've a long voyage ahead of you but if I know Clarrie I suspect it will be far from dull. Once she recovers from her rage I'm sure she'll realize her rare good luck in having you to console her."

"I'll do my damnedest to please her." Andy grinned. He tilted his head at a rakish angle and rolled his eyes in a manner suggesting he knew exactly what Clarissa needed to make her happy.

Matt laughed delightedly. "That's what I figured. Your reputation with women is legend, that's why I chose you. You and Clarrie should deal well together." He turned and walked down the gangplank. Andy followed.

"Good-bye, Matt, I'll see that your 'cargo' has a safe and pleasant journey."

"Good luck, Andy, the 'cargo' is all yours. When you reach California see that Clarissa gets this." Matt handed him a bag weighted with coins. "She doesn't deserve it but I wouldn't want to see her stranded."

"Don't worry, Matt, I have a suspicion that by the time we reach our destination Clarissa Hartley won't even recall your name." They shook hands.

"Oh, by the way, did I mention Clarrie is in bed right now awaiting her 'lover'? If I were you I'd leave the ship to the first mate and go to her immediately. She tends to become impatient if left waiting too long."

Matt's laughter lingered long after he disappeared into the heavy gray mists rolling in from the sea.

Thirty minutes later *Hawke's Pride* was but a shadow on the distant horizon as Captain Calder quietly entered Clarissa's darkened cabin, shed his clothes and slipped nude between the cool sheets. No words were spoken as fragrant, heated flesh surrounded and welcomed him. Losing himself in the sensual delight of her body, Andy thanked Matt Hawke for making this possible and fate for placing California thousands of miles away. In the cozy dimness of the bed, Clarissa gave herself up completely to the heated caresses and ardent kisses of the man she assumed to be Matthew Hawke. Never had she known Matt to be so passionate, so incredibly responsive and demanding in his need. Within a very short time it would have made little difference to Clarissa had she realized that the man making wild, passionate love to her was not Matthew Hawke, for Andy Calder was an experienced lover, wise in the ways of women and knowledgeable on how to please them.

It was a strange beginning, but then stranger things have happened. Matt chose well. Clarissa Hartley was a fortunate woman.

Matt tiptoed through the darkened house and into the bedroom where Lily lay sleeping in a chair. By now he assumed *Hawke's Pride* was well on her way to the West Coast and Andy Calder pleasantly engaged in making love to Clarissa. She was out of his hair and that's all that mattered to Matt. He had the rest of his life to devote to Lily and their child—or children, should there be more than one in their future—and he couldn't be more pleased.

A gown and robe of a soft pastel color barely concealed the sweet curves of Lily's body and her flaming red curls tumbled over the arm of the chair in charming disarray. With great tenderness he gathered her in his arms, placed her in the center of the bed and removed her robe. He quickly undressed and joined her. Untangling herself from the web of sleep, Lily opened her eyes and sighed when she felt Matt's hard frame settle down beside her.

"I prayed so hard that you'd return."

"Didn't you trust me?" Matt asked, surprised that she would doubt him.

"I—yes I did trust you. I'll never doubt you again. Oh, Matt, I love you so much!"

"I promised you forever, love, and I've since come to the conclusion that I'll probably love you beyond forever."

"Will you tell me now where you went? And what took place between you and Clarissa?"

"I'll tell you everything, love," Matt assured her, momentarily distracted by the tantalizing sight of a firm white breast visible through the opening on the front of her nightgown. While he spoke he stroked her gently, from her narrow shoulders to the silken length of her thigh. "Nothing happened between me and Clarrie. All I did this afternoon was arrange a voyage for her aboard *Hawke's Pride*. She's going to California."

Lily was astounded. "I can't believe she'd agree to leave. Knowing Clarissa it doesn't seem likely that she'd pick up at a moment's notice and go so far away when we both know she'd do anything to get you back." Suddenly comprehension dawned and

Lily's eyes grew round. "My God, Matt, you tricked her! You tricked her into believing you were going with her!" Shock turned abruptly into hilarity and Lily began to giggle with unrestrained delight.

Her mirth sparked Matt's sense of humor as he thought of the devious fait accompli he'd pulled off, and he joined her in laughter. "I've placed Clarissa in good hands," he said, still chuckling. "By the time she reaches California she will have forgotten Matthew Hawke ever existed."

"Somehow I doubt that," Lily said, certain that nothing or no one could ever make her forget a man like Matt. "What you did was quite outrageous, you know."

"I know," Matt agreed. His smile suggested that he'd do it again if he had the chance. "But enough of Clarissa. What about our child? When will you make me a father?"

"In six months. I didn't realize I was breeding until I arrived back in Boston. I was sick during the entire voyage from New Orleans but didn't think a thing about it until the condition continued and I consulted a doctor."

Matt rested his hand lightly on her stomach. "You're still so slim. If I didn't know your body so well I would never have known."

"That is all likely to change soon," Lily predicted. "I'll get fat and ungainly and—"

"No! You will only grow more beautiful as my child grows inside you. Each day I love you more. Lily, Lily." Matt groaned, hugging her fiercely. "Was there ever a woman like you? Courageous, loving, passionate, fiercely independent—I could go on forever."

"Forget the words, my love." Lily smiled impishly. "Show me how much I mean to you. Make love to me."

"Gladly, little one." Never had Matt been so deliriously happy. As their bodies meshed and entwined in the rhapsody of love, Matt paused for a breathless moment to count his blessings.

Epilogue

"Don't leave me, Matt," Lily begged. Her eyes
were dulled, her body taut with pain.
"Please stay with me."

Matt slid a glance at the doctor, who pursed his
lips disapprovingly and shook his head. Ignoring the
doctor's unspoken warning, Matt staunchly refused
to budge from Lily's bedside.

"This is no place for a man, Captain Hawke," the
doctor chided sternly when he saw that Matt intended to remain firmly entrenched during the entire
birthing process. He found that husbands tended to
complicate matters. "Leave this to me and Mrs.
Geary."

"My wife wishes me to remain and so I shall,"
Matt insisted with quiet determination. "I put Lily in
this predicament and I will not allow her to face this
alone." Matt's expression was so implacable that the
good doctor threw up his arms in surrender and allowed Matt his way with as much good grace as he
could muster.

From the onset it was obvious Lily's labor was not
going as well as it should. It was mid-morning when
Lily felt the gush of water followed some minutes
later by the first contraction. And now, hours later,
Lily lay exhausted and wracked with unbearable
pain. The child's delay in coming into the world sty-

mied even the doctor and he began to ready the instruments necessary for an assisted birth.

"Matt, are you still here?" Lily called out weakly.

"Right beside you, love," Matt assured her as he knelt at the head of the bed and grasped her slim hand. Immediately Lily quieted and a kind of peace settled over her. With Matt beside her she could face anything.

When the doctor moved to the foot of the bed and began another painful examination that left Lily moaning and tossing in agony, Matt ground out angrily, "Is that necessary? My wife is suffering enough already."

"I'm only doing my job, Captain," the doctor answered testily, then went on to mutter something about husbands who interfered where they were neither wanted nor needed. "Your wife's labor is a bit prolonged but I can assure you she is in no danger and will survive. As long as you allow me to do my job unhindered," he added with a hint of reproach.

Duly chastised, Matt devoted his full attention to Lily, who lay white and limp beneath the sheet. The huge mound of her stomach quivered with each successive contraction and it was all Matt could do to remain calm while his wife struggled to bring forth the fruit of his enjoyment. If he had known it was going to be like this he would have ... The thought died a sudden death as he recalled the pleasure of making love to Lily. But if it meant her life he'd take a vow of chastity, even if it killed him.

"Am I going to die, Matt?" Lily asked, her eyes huge in her pale face.

"You're going to be just fine, love," Matt assured her with a confidence he didn't feel. "The doctor said you are progressing well but that our son or daughter is somewhat reluctant to make his or her appearance. Hang on, it can't be much longer."

But as the hours dragged by Matt began to doubt

his own brave words. Mrs. Geary tried to persuade him to seek a few minutes' rest but he steadfastly refused to leave Lily's side. Even the doctor left the room periodically to refresh and fortify himself with coffee liberally laced with Matt's best brandy, but Matt remained to bolster Lily's flagging strength.

What if he should lose her? he asked himself fearfully during those long hours in which he berated himself for causing her suffering. Why did he have to be such a greedy lover, making love to Lily endlessly until his seed took hold in her fertile womb? Lily meant everything to him. She was his whole life. No, Matt denied vehemently, Lily would not die. He would not let her die. She was strong, young and in good health. Hadn't the doctor said she was in no danger? Then why didn't this child enter the world? What made him cling so tenaciously to his warm nest inside Lily?

Mrs. Geary's concerned glance swept over Matt, amazed that he seemed to be suffering as much as his wife. Who would have ever thought a man like Captain Hawke would be so undone by childbirth? His clothing was soiled and wrinkled and a blue stubble darkened his strong chin. His eyes were red-rimmed and deeply shadowed with violet, attesting to his genuine concern.

When the doctor examined Lily again his dour expression turned to one of satisfaction. "Ah, at last," he announced with guarded optimism. "Your child is about to make his appearance, Captain Hawke."

He had no sooner uttered the words when Lily gave a shriek and bolted nearly upright. Only Matt's restraining arms saved her from lurching off the sweat-soaked bed. Matt's soft words of encouragement and comfort quieted her sufficiently to allow her to follow the doctor's urgent instructions as she strained to push her baby into the world. With the final exertion Lily felt herself slipping slowly into a land of shadow and darkness. The last sound she heard was a slap and a lusty, wonderfully welcome wail of indignation. It was the sweetest sound Lily had ever heard. Matt's delighted laughter followed and then Lily knew no more.

Sunlight stabbed repeatedly in Lily's eyes and she sawed her head back and forth in an effort to escape the bright beams. She shifted cautiously, and her body screamed in vigorous protest. Though sore and stiff in every muscle, she felt strangely content. She smiled a secret smile then jerked her eyes open when she heard a low rumbling chuckle near her ear.

"Matt." She sighed, reaching for his hand.

"You look like a cat who just lapped a dish of cream," Matt said tenderly. "How do you feel, love?"

"Probably better than you look," Lily said, wrinkling her nose. He looked and smelled as if he hadn't changed his clothes or bathed in days.

Just then a lusty wail rent the air and Lily gazed raptly toward the cradle at the foot of the bed. "Do you have a name for our son, love?" Matt asked, barely able to contain his pride.

"A boy?" Lily asked, frowning. "I had hoped for a girl."

"I hope you're not too disappointed."

"Perhaps a little," Lily admitted slowly. "But there is plenty of time for a daughter."

"No!" Matt said, aghast, shaking his head in vigorous protest. "I won't put you through that again."

Lily smiled lovingly at her strong, virile husband, who had faced death many times but was nearly undone witnessing childbirth. "We shall see, love, we shall see," she said cryptically. "At the moment I just want to hold our son, after our son's father kisses our son's mother. If it's not too much trouble."

"Nothing concerning you is too much trouble, Lily." His eyes had grown suspiciously moist and though he knew it wasn't considered manly, he made no effort to stem the flow. "Thank you, love, thank you for my son. If it's all right with you I'd like to call him Christopher after my cousin. If not for him we would never have met."

His kiss was as gentle as the summer rain and as rewarding as the flowers that followed.

ICE & Rapture

CONNIE MASON

**Winner of the *Romantic Times*
Storyteller of the Year Award!**

Cool as a cucumber, and totally dedicated to her career as a newspaper woman, Maggie Afton is just the kind of challenge brash Chase McGarrett enjoys. But he is exactly the kind of man she despises. Cold and hot, reserved and brazen, Maggie and Chase are a study in opposites. But when they join forces during the Klondike gold rush, the fiery sparks of their searing desire burn brighter than the northern lights.

___4193-6 $5.99 US/$6.99 CAN

Dorchester Publishing Co., Inc.
P.O. Box 6640
Wayne, PA 19087-8640

Please add $1.75 for shipping and handling for the first book and $.50 for each book thereafter. NY, NYC, and PA residents, please add appropriate sales tax. No cash, stamps, or C.O.D.s. All orders shipped within 6 weeks via postal service book rate. Canadian orders require $2.00 extra postage and must be paid in U.S. dollars through a U.S. banking facility.

Name _ _ _ _ _ _ _ _ _ _ _ _ _ _ _ _ _ _
Address _ _ _ _ _ _ _ _ _ _ _ _ _ _ _ _ _
City _ _ _ _ _ _ _ State _ _ Zip _ _ _ _ _
I have enclosed $_____ in payment for the checked book(s).
Payment <u>must</u> accompany all orders. ❑ Please send a free catalog.

CONNIE MASON

"Each new Connie Mason book is a prize!"
—Heather Graham, bestselling author of
A Magical Christmas

Love Me With Fury. When her stagecoach is ambushed on
the Texas frontier, Ariel Leland fears for her life. But even
more frightening is Jess Wilder, a virile bounty hunter who
has devoted his life to finding the hellcat responsible for his
brother's murder—and now he has her. But Ariel's proud
spirit and naive beauty erupt a firestorm of need in him—
transforming his lust for vengeance into a love that must be
fulfilled at any cost.

___52215-2 $5.50 US/$6.50 CAN

Pure Temptation. Fresh off the boat from Ireland, Moira
O'Toole isn't fool enough to believe in legends or naive
enough to trust a rake. Yet after an accident lands her in
Graystoke Manor, she finds herself haunted, harried, and
hopelessly charmed by Black Jack Graystoke and his
exquisite promise of pure temptation.

___4041-7 $5.99 US/$6.99 CAN

Dorchester Publishing Co., Inc.
P.O. Box 6640
Wayne, PA 19087-8640

Please add $1.75 for shipping and handling for the first book and
$.50 for each book thereafter. NY, NYC, and PA residents,
please add appropriate sales tax. No cash, stamps, or C.O.D.s. All
orders shipped within 6 weeks via postal service book rate.
Canadian orders require $2.00 extra postage and must be paid in
U.S. dollars through a U.S. banking facility.

Name _____
Address _____
City _____State_____Zip_____
I have enclosed $_____ in payment for the checked book(s).
Payment <u>must</u> accompany all orders. ☐ Please send a free catalog.

SHADOW WALKER
CONNIE MASON

Bestselling Author of *Flame*!

"Why did you do that?"

"Kiss you?" Cole shrugged. "Because you wanted me to, I suppose. Why else would a man kiss a woman?"

But Dawn knows lots of other reasons, especially if the woman is nothing but half-breed whose father has sold her to the first interested male. Defenseless and exquisitely lovely, Dawn is overjoyed when Cole Webster kills the ruthless outlaw who is her husband in name only. But now she has a very different sort of man to contend with. A man of unquestionable virility, a man who prizes justice and honors the Native American traditions that have been lost to her. Most intriguing of all, he is obviously a man who knows exactly how to bring a woman to soaring heights of pleasure. And yes, she does want his kiss...and maybe a whole lot more

_4260-6 $5.99 US/$6.99 CAN